TREVAYNE

"Trevayne, listen to me. You may never forgive me for what I am about to say to you. If you feel strong enough, I'll accept the consequences and expect your roughest condemnation tomorrow. I won't rebut you. But you must think now. The country knows you've been chosen. The hearing is only a formality now. If you tell them to shove it, how are you going to do it without paining your wife further? . . . Don't you see? This is exactly what they want!"

Trevayne took a deep breath and replied evenly. "I have no intention of paining my wife further or of allowing any part of you to touch us. I don't need you, Mr. President. Do I make myself clear?"

TREVAYNE

Robert Ludlum

BANTAM BOOKS
NEW YORK • TORONTO • LONDON • SYDNEY • AUCKLAND

FOR GAIL & HENRY

To the Savoy! To Hampton!
To Pont Royale and Bernini!
And everything else
My thanks

TREVAYNE

*A Bantam Book / published by arrangement with
the author*

PRINTING HISTORY
TREVAYNE *was first published in January 1973*
Bantam edition / September 1989

ISBN 0-553-28179-8

Published simultaneously in the United States and Canada

PRINTED IN THE UNITED STATES OF AMERICA

20 19 18 17 16

Introduction

Every now and then throughout the human odyssey, forces seem to almost accidentally come together, producing men and women of startling wisdom, talent, and insight, and the results are wondrous, indeed. The arts and the sciences speak for themselves, for they are all around us, embellishing our lives with beauty, longevity, knowledge, and convenience. But there is another area of human endeavor that is both an art *and* a science, and it, too, is all around us—either enriching our lives or destroying them.

It is the guardianship of a given society under the common laws of governance. I'm not a scholar, but the courses in government and political science that I was exposed to in college indelibly left their marks on me. I was hooked, fascinated, smitten, and were it not for stronger proclivities, I might have become the worst politician in the Western world. My "cool" levels off at around 300 degrees Fahrenheit.

For me, one of the truly great achievements of man is open, representative democracy, and the greatest of all the attempts throughout history to create such a system was the magnificent American experiment as expressed in our Constitution. It's not perfect, but to paraphrase Winston Churchill, it's the best damn thing on the block. But wait.

Someone's always trying to louse it up.

That's why I wrote *Trevayne* nearly two decades ago. It was the time of Watergate, and my pencil flew across the pages in outrage. Younger—not youthful—intemperance made my head explode with such words and phrases as *Mendacity! Abuse of Power! Corruption! Police State!*

Here was the government, the highest of our elected and appointed officials entrusted with the guardianship of our system, not only lying to the people but collecting millions upon millions of dollars to perpetuate their lies and thus the controls they believed were theirs alone to exercise. One of the most frightening statements to come out of the Watergate hearings was the following, delivered, in essence, by the nation's chief law enforcement officer.

"There's nothing I would not do to keep the presidency . . ." I don't have to complete the exact sentence; the meaning was clear—to keep it *ours*. The presidency and the country was *theirs*. Not yours, or mine, or even the neighbors across the street with whom we frequently disagreed in things political. Only *theirs*. The rest of us were somehow neither relevant nor competent. *They* knew better, therefore the lies had to continue and the coffers of ideological purity kept full so that the impure could be *blitzkrieged* by money and buried at the starting gates of political contests.

I also had to publish *Trevayne* under another name. I chose Jonathan Ryder—the first the name of one son, the second a contraction of my wife's maiden name—not because of potential retribution, but because the conventional wisdom of the time was that a novelist did not author more than a book a year. Why? Damned if I could figure it out—something to do with "marketing psychology," whatever the hell that is. But wait. All that was nearly twenty years ago.

Plus ça change, plus c'est la même chose, say the French. The more things change, the more they stay the same. Or perhaps history repeats its follies ad nauseam because man is a creature of helter-skelter appetites and keeps returning to the troughs of poison that make him ill. Or perhaps the sins of the generational parent are borne by the offspring because the kids are too stupid to learn from their parent's glaring mistakes. Who knows? All that's been truly documented from time immemorial is that man continues to kill without needing the meat of his quarry; he lies in order to avoid accountability or, conversely, to seize the reins of accountability to such extent that the social contract between the government and the governed is his alone to write; he endlessly seeks to enrich himself at the expense of the public weal and, while he's at it, tries all too frequently to turn his personal morality or religion into everyone else's legality or religiosity, no quarter given to the unbelievers of pariahdom. Good heavens, we could go on and on. But wait.

Last year our country witnessed two of the most disgraceful, debasing, inept, disingenuous, and insulting presidential campaigns that living admirers of our system can recall. The candidates were "packaged" by cynical manipulators of the public's basest fears; "sound-bite zingers" were preferable to intelligent statements of position; image took precedence over issues. The presidential debates were neither presidential nor debates but canned Pavlovian "responses" more often than not having little or nothing to do with the questions. The ground rules for these robotic pavanes were drawn up by glib intellectual misfits who thought so ill of their clients that they refused to allow them to speak beyond *two minutes!* The orators of the cradle of democracy that was ancient Athens, wherever they are, can be heard vomiting. Perhaps one bright day in the future we'll return to legitimate, civilized campaigns, where an open exchange of ideas can be heard, but this will not happen, I'm afraid, until those who convince us to buy deodorants hie back to the armpits. They've worn out their welcome in the election process, for they have committed the two cardinal sins of their profession—at the same time. They've made their "products" appear simultaneously both offensive and boring. Of course, there's a solution. If I were either candidate, I'd refuse to pay them on the grounds of their moral turpitude—hell, it's as good a reason as any. Which of those imagemakers would go into court expounding one way or the other on that one? Enough. The campaigns turned off the country.

This numbing fiasco followed barely twenty-four months after we citizens of the Republic had been exposed to a series of events so ludicrous they would have been a barrel of laughs but for their obscenity. Unelected (?) officials fueled the fires of terrorism by selling arms to a terrorist state while demanding that our allies do no such thing. Guilt became innocence; malfeasance brought honor-to-office; zealous, obsequious poseurs were heroes; to be present was to be absent; and to have creatures soiling the basement was a sign of efficient house management. By comparison, Alice's looking-glass world was a place of incontestable logic. But *wait*—all right, you're ahead of me.

Someone's always trying to louse it up. That great experiment, that wonderful system of ours based on open checks and balances. *Mendacity? Abuse of Power? Corruption? Police State?*

Well, certainly not with lasting effect as long as citizens can voice such speculations and shout their accusations, however extreme. We can be heard. That's our strength and it's indomitable.

So, in a modest way, I'll try to be heard again in that voice from another time, another era, always remembering that I'm fundamentally and merely a storyteller who hopes you enjoy the entertainment, but perhaps will permit me an idea or two.

I have not attempted to "update" the novel or adjust the licenses I took with actual events or geography, for they served the story I was writing. As anyone who has built or remodeled a home will tell you, once you start tinkering, you may as well throw away the schematics. It becomes a different house.

Thanks for your attention.

ROBERT LUDLUM
a.k.a. (briefly) Jonathan Ryder
November 1988

PART 1

1

The smoothly tarred surface of the road abruptly stopped and became dirt. At this point on the small peninsula the township's responsibility ended and the area of private property began. According to the United States Post Office, South Greenwich, Connecticut, the delivery route was listed on the map as Shore Road, Northwest, but to the carriers who drove out in the mail trucks it was known simply as High Barnegat, or just Barnegat.

And the carriers drove out frequently, three or four times a week, with special-delivery letters and certified-receipt-requested manila envelopes. They never minded the trip, because they received a dollar each time they made a delivery.

High Barnegat.

Eight acres of ocean property with nearly a half-mile bordering directly on the sound. Most of the acreage was wild, allowed to grow unhampered, untamed. What seemed contradictory in spirit was the compound—the house and grounds seventy yards up from the central beach. The long rambling house was contemporary in design, great expanses of glass encased in wood looking out over the water. The lawns were deep green and thick, manicured and broken up by flagstone paths and a large terrace directly above the boathouse.

It was late August, the best part of the summer at High Barnegat. The water was as warm as it would ever be; the winds came off the sound in gusts which made the sailing more exciting—or hazardous—depending on one's point of view; the foliage was at its fullest green. In late August a sense of calm replaced the hectic weeks of summer fun. The season was nearly over. Men thought once again of normal weekends and five full days of business; women began the agonizing process of selection and purchase that signaled the start of the new school year.

Minds and motives were slowly changing gears. Fri-

3

volity was ebbing; there were more serious things to consider.

And the steady flow of house guests diminished at High Barnegat.

It was four-thirty in the afternoon, and Phyllis Trevayne reclined in a lounge chair on the terrace, letting the warm sun wash over her body. She thought, with a degree of satisfaction, that her daughter's bathing suit fitted her rather comfortably. Since she was forty-two and her daughter seventeen, satisfaction could have turned into minor triumph if she allowed herself to dwell on it. But she couldn't because her thoughts kept returning to the telephone, to the call from New York for Andrew. She had answered on the terrace phone, because the cook was still in town with the children and her husband was still a small white sail far out on the water. She'd nearly let the phone ring unanswered, but only very good friends and very important—her husband preferred the word "necessary" —business associates had the High Barnegat number.

"Hello, Mrs. Trevayne?" had asked the deep voice on the other end of the line.

"Yes?"

"Frank Baldwin here. How are you, Phyllis?"

"Fine, just fine, Mr. Baldwin. And you?" Phyllis Trevayne had known Franklyn Baldwin for several years, but she still couldn't bring herself to call the old gentleman by his first name. Baldwin was the last of a dying breed, one of the original giants of New York banking.

"I'd be a lot better if I knew why your husband hasn't returned my calls. Is he all right? Not that I'm so important, God knows, but he's not ill, is he?"

"Oh, no. Not at all. He's been away from the office over a week now. He hasn't taken any messages. I'm really to blame; I wanted him to rest."

"My wife used to cover for me that way, too, young lady. Instinctively. Jumped right into the breach, and always with the right words."

Phyllis Trevayne laughed pleasantly, aware of the compliment. "Really, it's true, Mr. Baldwin. Right now the only reason I know he's not working is that I can see the sail of the catamaran a mile or so off-shore."

"A cat! God! I forget how young you are! In my day no one your age ever got so damned rich. Not by themselves."

"We're lucky. We never forget it." Phyllis Trevayne's voice spoke the truth.

"That's a very nice thing to say, young lady." Franklyn Baldwin also spoke the truth, and he wanted her to know that. "Well, when Captain Ahab bounds ashore, do ask him to call me, will you, please? It's really most urgent."

"I certainly shall."

"Good-bye, my dear."

"Good-bye, Mr. Baldwin."

But her husband *had* been in touch with his office daily. He'd returned dozens of calls to far less important people than Franklyn Baldwin. Besides which, Andrew liked Baldwin: he'd said so a number of times. He'd gone to Baldwin on many occasions for guidance in the tangled webs of international finance.

Her husband owed a great deal to the banker, and now the old gentleman needed him. Why hadn't Andrew returned the calls? It simply wasn't like him.

The restaurant was small, seating no more than forty people, and situated on Thirty-eighth Street between Park and Madison avenues. Its clientele was generally from the ranks of the approaching-middleage executives with suddenly more money than they'd ever made before and a desire, a need, perhaps, to hold on to their younger outlooks. The food was only fair, its prices high, and the drinks were expensive. However, the bar area was wide, and the rich paneling reflected the soft, indirect lighting. The effect was a throwback to all those collegiate spots from the fifties that these drinkers remembered with such comfort.

It was designed precisely with that in mind.

Considering this, and he always considered it, the manager was slightly surprised to see a short, well-dressed man in his early sixties walk hesitantly through the door. The man looked around, adjusting his eyes to the dim light. The manager approached him.

"A table, sir?"

"No. . . . Yes, I'm meeting someone. . . . Never mind, thank you. We have one."

The well-dressed man spotted the person he was looking for at a table in the rear. He walked abruptly away from the manager and sidled awkwardly past the crowded chairs.

The manager recalled the man at the rear table. He'd insisted on that particular table.

The elderly man sat down. "It might have been better to meet someplace other than a restaurant."

"Don't worry, Mr. Allen. No one you know comes here."

"I certainly hope you're right."

A waiter approached, and the order was given for drinks.

"I'm not so sure *you* should be concerned," said the younger man. "It strikes me that I'm the one taking the risk, not you."

"You'll be taken care of; you know that. Let's not waste time. Where do things stand?"

"The commission has unanimously approved Andrew Trevayne."

"He won't take it."

"The feeling is that he will. Baldwin's to make the offer; he may have done so already."

"If he has, then you're *late*." The old man creased the flesh around his eyes and stared at the tablecloth. "We heard the rumors; we assumed they were a smokescreen. We relied on you." He looked up at Webster. "It was our understanding that you would confirm the identity before any final action was taken."

"I couldn't control it; no one at the White House could. That commission's off-limits. I was lucky to zero in on the name at all."

"We'll come back to that. Why do they think Trevayne will accept? Why should he? His Danforth Foundation is damn near as big as Ford or Rockefeller. Why would he give it up?" Allen asked.

"He probably won't. Just take a leave of absence."

"No foundation the size of Danforth would accept a

leave for that length of time. Especially not for a job like this. They're *all* in trouble."

"I don't follow you. . . ."

"You think they're immune?" asked Allen, interrupting. "They need friends in your town. Not enemies. . . . What's the procedure? If Baldwin *has* made the offer. If Trevayne accepts?"

The waiter returned with the drinks and both men fell silent. He left, and Webster answered.

"The conditions are that whoever the commission selects receives the President's approval and is subject to a closed hearing with a bipartisan committee in the Senate."

"All right, all right." Allen raised his glass and swallowed a large portion of his drink. "Let's work from there; we can do something there. We'll disqualify him at the hearing."

The younger man looked puzzled. "Why? What's the point? *Someone's* going to chair that subcommittee. I gather this Trevayne's at least a reasonable man."

"You gather!" Allen finished his drink rapidly. "Just what *have* you gathered? What do you know about Trevayne?"

"What I've read. I did my research. He and his brother-in-law—the brother's an electronics engineer—started a small company dealing in aerospace research and manufacturing in New Haven in the middle fifties. They hit the motherlode seven or eight years later; they were both millionaires by the time they were thirty-five. The brother-in-law designed, while Trevayne sold the hell out of the products. He cornered half the early NASA contracts and set up subsidiaries all over the Atlantic seaboard. Trevayne pulled out when he was thirty-seven and took on a job with the State Department. Incidentally, he did a whale of a job for State." Webster raised his glass, looking over the rim at Allen. The young man expected to be complimented on his knowledge.

Instead, Allen dismissed his companion's words. "Shit. *Time*-magazine material. What's important is that Trevayne's an original. . . . He doesn't cooperate. We know; we tried reaching him years ago."

"Oh?" Webster put his glass down. "I didn't realize . . . Oh, Christ. Then he knows?"

"Not a great deal; perhaps enough. We're not sure. But you still miss the point, Mr. *Webster*. It seems to me that you've missed the point from the beginning. . . . We don't *want* him chairing that goddamned subcommittee. We don't want him or anyone *like* him! That kind of choice is unthinkable."

"What can you do about that?"

"Force him out . . . if he's actually accepted. The backup will be the Senate hearing. We'll make damn sure he's rejected."

"Say you succeed, then what?"

"We'll nominate our own man. What should have been done in the first place." Allen signaled the waiter, gesturing at both glasses.

"Mr. Allen, why didn't you stop him? If you were in a position to do that, why didn't you? You said you heard the rumors about Trevayne; that was the time to step in."

Allen avoided Webster's look. He drained the ice water in his glass, and when he spoke, his voice had the sound of a man trying very hard to maintain his authority; with lessening success. "Frank Baldwin, that's why. Frank Baldwin and that senile son-of-a-bitch Hill."

"The Ambassador?"

"The goddamned Ambassador-at-large with his god-damned embassy in the White House. . . . Big Billy Hill! Baldwin and Hill; they're the relics behind this bullshit. Hill has been circling like a hawk for the last two or three years. He talked Baldwin into the Defense Commission. Between them they picked Trevayne. . . . Baldwin put up his name; who the hell could argue? . . . But *you* should have told us it was final. If we'd been certain, we could have prevented it."

Webster watched Allen closely. When he replied, there was a hardness he hadn't displayed before. "And I think you're lying. Somebody else blew it; you or one of the other so-called specialists. First, you thought this investigation would burn itself out in the forming, be killed in committee. . . . You were wrong. And then it was too late. Trevayne surfaced, and you couldn't stop it. You're not even sure you can stop him now. That's why you wanted to see me. . . . So let's dispense with this crap about my being late and missing the point, shall we?"

"You watch your tongue, young man. Just remember who I represent." The statement was made without commensurate strength.

"And you remember that you're talking to a man personally appointed by the President of the United States. You may not like it, but that's why you came to me. Now, what is it? What do you want?"

Allen exhaled slowly, as if to rid himself of anger. "Some of us are more alarmed than others . . ."

"You're one of them," interjected Webster quietly.

"Yes. . . . Trevayne's a complicated man. One-part boy genius of industry—which means he knows his way around the board rooms; one-part skeptic—he doesn't subscribe to certain realities."

"Seems to me those assets go together."

"Only when a man's dealing from strength."

"Get to the point. What's Trevayne's strength?"

"Let's say he never needed assistance."

"Let's say he refused it."

"All right, all right. That's valid."

"You said you tried reaching him."

"Yes. When I was with . . . Never mind. It was the early sixties; we were consolidating then and thought he might be a valuable addition to our . . . community. We even offered to guarantee the NASA contracts."

"Sweet Jesus! And he turned you down." Webster made a pronouncement, not an inquiry.

"He strung us along for a while, then realized he could get the contracts without us. As soon as he knew that, he told us to go to hell. Actually, he went a lot further. He told me to tell my people to get out of the space program, get out of the government money. He threatened to go to the Attorney General."

Bobby Webster absently picked up his fork and slowly made indentations on the tablecloth. "Suppose it had been the other way around? Suppose he *had* needed you? Would he have joined your 'community'?"

"That's what we don't know. Some of the others think so. But they didn't talk to him; I did. I was the intermediary. I was the only one he really had. . . . I never used names, never said who my people were."

"But you believe the fact that they *were* was enough? For him."

"The unanswerable question. He threatened us after he got *his*; he was sure he didn't need anyone but himself, his brother-in-law, and his goddamned company in New Haven. We simply can't afford to take the chance now. We can't allow him to chair that subcommittee. . . . He's unpredictable."

"What am I supposed to do?"

"Take every reasonable risk to get close to Trevayne. The optimum would be for you to be his White House connection. Is that possible?"

Bobby Webster paused, then answered firmly. "Yes. The President brought me into the session on the subcommittee. It was a classified meeting; no notes, no transcripts. There was only one other aide; no competition. I'll work it out."

"You understand, it may not be necessary. Certain preventive measures will be taken. If they're effective, Trevayne will be out of the picture."

"I can help you there."

"How?"

"Mario de Spadante."

"No! Absolutely no! We've told you before, we don't want any part of him."

"He's been helpful to you people. In more ways than you realize. Or want to acknowledge."

"He's *out*."

"It wouldn't hurt to establish a minor friendship. If you're offended, think of the Senate."

Allen's wrinkled frown dissolved. He looked almost appreciatively at the presidential aide. "I see what you mean."

"Of course, it will raise my price considerably."

"I thought you believed in what you're doing."

"I believe in protecting my flanks. The best protection is to make you pay."

"You're an obnoxious man."

"I'm also very talented."

2

Andrew Trevayne ran the twin hulls of the catamaran before the wind, catching the fast current into the shore. He stretched his long legs against a connecting spar and reached over the tiller to make an additional wake in the stern flow. No reason, just a movement, a meaningless gesture. The water was warm; his hand felt as though it was being propelled through a tepid, viscous film.

Just as he was being propelled—inexorably propelled—into an enigma that was not of his choosing. Yet the final decision would be his, and he knew what his choice would be.

That was the most irritating aspect; he understood the furies that propelled him, and he disliked himself for even contemplating submission to them. He had put them behind him.

Long ago.

The cat was within a hundred yards of the Connecticut shoreline when the wind abruptly shifted—as winds do when buffeted against solid ground from open water. Trevayne swung his legs over the starboard hull and pulled the mainsheet taut as the small craft swerved and lurched to the right toward the dock.

Trevayne was a large man. Not immense, just larger than most men, with the kind of supple coordination that bespoke of a far more active youth than he ever bothered to reminisce about. He remembered reading an article in *Newsweek*, surprised at the descriptions of his former playing-field prowess. They'd been greatly exaggerated, as all such descriptions were in such articles. He'd been good, but not that good. He always had the feeling that he *looked* better than he was, or his efforts camouflaged his shortcomings.

But he knew he was a good sailor. Maybe more than good.

The rest was meaningless to him. It always had been, except for the instant of competition.

There would be intolerable competition facing him now. If he made the decision. The kind of competition that allowed no quarter, that involved strategies not listed in any rulebook. He was good at those strategies, too. But not from participation; that was important, immeasurably important to him.

Understand them, be capable of maneuver, even skirt the edges, but never participate. Instead, use the knowledge to gain the advantage. Use it without mercy, without quarter.

Andrew kept a small pad fastened to a steel plate on the deck next to the tiller. Attached to the plate was a thin rust-proof chain that housed a waterproof casing with a ball-point pen. He said these were for recording times, markers, wind velocities—whatever. Actually, the pad and pen were for jotting down stray thoughts, ideas, memoranda for himself.

Sometimes things . . . just "things" that seemed clearer to him while on the water.

Which was why he was upset when he looked down at the pad now. He had written one word. Written it unconsciously, without realizing it.

Boston.

He ripped off the page, crumpled it with far more intensity than the action called for, and threw it into the sound.

Goddamn! Goddamn it! he thought. No!

The catamaran pulled into the slip, and Trevayne reached over the side and held the edge of the dock with his right hand. With his left he pulled the release sheet, and the sail fluttered as it buckled. He secured the boat and stood up, pulling down the rest of the canvas, rolling it around the horizontal mast as he did so. In less than four minutes he had dismantled the tiller, stowed the jacket, lashed the sail, and tied off the boat at four corners.

He looked up beyond the stone wall of the terrace to the wood and glass structure that jutted from the edge of the hill. It never ceased to excite him. Not the material possession; that wasn't important any longer. But that it had all come out the way he and Phyl planned it.

They had done it together; that fact was very important. It might never make up for other things, perhaps. Sadder things. But it helped.

He walked to the stone path by the boathouse and started up the steep incline to the terrace. He could always tell what kind of shape he was in by the time he reached midpoint of the climb. If he was out of breath, or his legs ached, he would silently vow to eat less or exercise more. He was pleased to find that there was little discomfort now. Or perhaps his mind was too preoccupied to relate the stress.

No, he was feeling pretty good, he thought. The week away from the office, the continuous salt air, the pleasantly energetic end of the summer months; he was feeling fine.

And then he remembered the pad and the unconsciously—subconsciously—written word. *Boston*.

He didn't really feel fine at all.

He rounded the last steps to the flagstone terrace and saw that his wife was lying back in a deck chair, her eyes open, staring out at the water, seeing nothing he would see. He always felt a slight ache when he watched her like that. The ache of sad, painful memories.

Because of *Boston*, goddamn it.

He realized that his sneakers had covered the sound of his steps; he didn't want to startle her.

"Hi," he said softly.

"Oh?" Phyllis blinked. "Have a good sail, darling?"

"Fine. Good sleep?" Trevayne crossed over to her and kissed her lightly on her forehead.

"Great while it lasted. It was interrupted."

"Oh? I thought the kids drove Lillian into town."

"It wasn't the kids. Or Lillian."

"You sound ominous." Trevayne reached into a large rectangular cooler on the patio table and withdrew a can of beer.

"Not ominous. But I am curious."

"What are you talking about?" He ripped off the flip-top on the can and drank.

"Franklyn Baldwin telephoned. . . . Why haven't you returned his calls?"

Trevayne held the beer next to his lips and looked at

his wife. "Haven't I seen that bathing suit on someone else?"

"Yes, and I thank you for the compliment—intended or not—and I'd still like to know why you haven't called him."

"I'm trying to avoid him."

"I thought you liked him."

"I do. Immensely. All the more reason to avoid him. He's going to ask me for something, and I'm going to refuse him. At least, I think he'll ask me, and I want to refuse him."

"What?"

Trevayne walked absently to the stone wall bordering the terrace and rested the beer can on the edge. "Baldwin wants to recruit me. That's the rumor; I think it's called a 'trial balloon.' He heads up that commission on defense spending. They're forming a subcommittee to make what they politely phrase an 'in-depth study' of Pentagon relationships."

"What does that mean?"

"Four or five companies—conglomerates, really—are responsible for seventy-odd percent of the defense budget. In one way or another. There's no effective control any longer. This subcommittee's supposed to be an investigative arm of the Defense Commission. They're looking for a chairman."

"And you're it?"

"I don't want to be *it*. I'm happy where I am. What I'm doing now is positive; chairing that committee would be the most negative thing I can think of. Whoever takes the job will be a national pariah . . . if he only half works at it."

"Why?"

"Because the Pentagon's a mess. It's no secret; read the papers. Any day. It's not even subtle."

"Then why would anyone be a pariah for trying to fix it? I understand making enemies, not a national pariah."

Trevayne laughed gently as he carried the beer over to a chair next to his wife and sat down. "I love you for your New England simplicity. Along with the bathing suit."

"You're pacing too much. Your thinking-feet are working overtime, darling."

"No, they're not; I'm not interested."

"Then answer the question. Why a national pariah?"

"Because the mess is too ingrained. And widespread. To be at all effective, that subcommittee's going to have to call a lot of people a lot of names. Fundamentally act on a large premise of fear. When you start talking about monopolies, you're not just talking about influential men shuffling around stock issues. You're threatening thousands and thousands of jobs. Ultimately, that's any monopoly's hold, from top to bottom. You exchange one liability for another. It may be necessary, but you cause a lot of pain."

"My God," said Phyllis, sitting up. "You've done a lot of thinking."

"Thinking, yes. Not doing." Andrew bounced out of the chair and walked to the table, extinguishing his cigarette in an ashtray. "Frankly, I was surprised the whole idea got this far. These things—in-depth studies, investigations, call them whatever you want—are usually proposed loudly and disposed of quietly. In the Senate cloakroom or the House dining room. This time it's different. I wonder why."

"Ask Frank Baldwin."

"I'd rather not."

"You should. You owe him that, Andy. Why do you think he chose you?"

Trevayne crossed back to the terrace wall and looked out over the Long Island Sound. "I'm qualified; Frank knows that. I've dealt with those government-contract boys; I've been critical in print about the overruns, the open-end agreements. He knows that, too. I've even been angry, but that goes back a long time ago. . . . Mainly, I think, because he knows how much I despise the manipulators. They've ruined a lot of good men, one especially. Remember?" Trevayne turned and looked at his wife. "They can't touch me now. I haven't a thing to lose but time."

"I think you've just about convinced yourself."

Trevayne lit a second cigarette and leaned against the

ledge, his arms folded in front of him. He continued to stare at Phyllis. "I know. That's why I'm avoiding Frank Baldwin."

Trevayne pushed the omelet around the plate, not really interested in it. Franklyn Baldwin sat opposite him in the bank's executive dining .room. The old gentleman was speaking intensely.

"The job's going to get done, Andrew; you know that. Nothing's going to prevent it. I just want the best man to do it. And I think you're the best man. I might add, the commission's voice was unanimous."

"What makes you so sure the job'll get done? I'm not. The Senate's always yelling about economies; it's a hell of an issue, and always will be. That is, until a highway project or an aircraft plant is closed down in some district. Then suddenly the shouting stops."

"Not this time. It's beyond cynicism now. I wouldn't have become involved if I thought otherwise."

"You're expressing an opinion. There has to be something else, Frank."

Baldwin removed his steel-rimmed glasses and laid them beside his plate. He blinked several times and gracefully massaged the bridge of his patrician nose. He smiled a half-smile, half-sadly. "There is. You're very perceptive. . . . Call it the legacy of two old men whose lives—and the lives of their families for a number of generations— have been made most pleasantly productive in this country of ours. I daresay we've contributed, but the rewards have been more than ample. That's the best way I can put it."

"I'm afraid I don't understand."

"Of course not. I'll clarify. William Hill and I have known each other since childhood."

"Ambassador Hill?"

"Yes. . . . I won't bore you with the eccentricities of our relationship—not today. Suffice it to say, we can't possibly stay around too many more years; not sure that I'd want to. . . . This Defense Commission, the subcommittee—they're our ideas. We intend to see them become working realities. That much we can guarantee; in our different ways we're powerful enough to do that. And to use that dreadful term, sufficiently 'respectable.' "

"What do you think you'll gain?"

"The truth. The extent of the truth as we believe it to be. This country has the right to know that, no matter how much it may hurt. To cure any disease, a correct diagnosis has to be made. Not indiscriminate labels hung by self-righteous zealots, nor vindictive charges hurled by malcontents. . . . The truth, Andrew. Merely the truth. That gift will be ours, Billy's and mine. Perhaps our last."

Trevayne had the desire to move, to be physically in motion. The old gentleman opposite him was succeeding in doing exactly what he thought he'd do. The walls were closing in, the corridor defined.

"Why can this subcommittee do what you say? Others have tried; they failed."

"Because, through you, it will be both apolitical and in no way self-seeking." Baldwin replaced his glasses; the magnification of his old eyes hypnotized Trevayne. "Those are the necessary factors. You're neither Republican nor Democrat, liberal nor conservative. Both parties have tried to recruit you, and you've refused both. You're a contradiction in this age of nomenclature. You have nothing to gain or lose. You'll be believed. That's the important thing. . . . We've become a polarized people, slotted into intransigent, conflicting positions. We desperately need to believe once again in objective truth."

"If I accept, the Pentagon and everyone connected with it will run to the hills—or their public relations' mimeographs. That's what they usually do. How are you going to prevent this?"

"The President. He has assured us; he's a good man, Andrew."

"And I'm responsible to no one?"

"Not even me. Only yourself."

"I hire my own staff; no outside personnel decisions?"

"Give me a list of those you want. I'll have it cleared."

"I call it as I find it. I get the cooperation I deem necessary." Trevayne didn't ask these last questions, he made statements which, nevertheless, anticipated answers.

"Total. That I'll guarantee. That I can promise you."

"I don't want the job."

"But you'll take it." Another statement, this time from Franklyn Baldwin.

"I told Phyllis. You're persuasive, Frank. That's why I was avoiding you."

"No man can avoid what he's meant to do. At the moment he's meant to do it. Do you know where I got that?"

"Sounds Hebraic."

"No. . . . But close. Mediterranean. Marcus Aurelius. Have you met many bankers who've read Aurelius?"

"Hundreds. They think he's a mutual fund."

3

Steven Trevayne looked at the expressionless mannequins clad in tweed jackets and varying shades of gray flannel slacks. The subdued lighting of the College Shoppe was appropriate for the quietly wealthy image sought after by the residents of Greenwich, Connecticut. Steven looked down at his own Levi's, soiled sneakers, and then noticed that one of the buttons on his old corduroy jacket was about to fall off.

He consulted his watch and was annoyed. It was nearly time. He'd told his sister that he'd drive her and her friends back to Barnegat, but he'd stipulated that they were to meet him by eight-thirty. He had to pick up his date over on Cos Cob by nine-fifteen. He was going to be late.

He wished to hell his sister hadn't picked this particular night to have an all-girl gathering at home, or at least not to have promised rides for everyone. His sister wasn't allowed to drive at night—an edict Steven Trevayne thought was ridiculous; she was seventeen—so when these occasions arose, he was elected.

If he refused, his father might just find that all their cars were in use and he'd be without wheels.

He was almost nineteen. He'd be off to college in

three weeks. Without a car. His father said no car while he was a freshman.

Young Trevayne laughed to himself. His father was right. There was no earthly reason why he should have a car. He didn't want to travel first class; not that way.

He was about to cross the street to the drugstore and telephone his date when a police car pulled up to the curb in front of him.

"You Steven Trevayne?" asked the patrolman at the near window.

"Yes, sir." The young man was apprehensive; the policeman spoke curtly.

"Get in."

"Why? What's the matter? I'm just standing here . . ."

"You got a sister named Pamela?"

"Yes. Yes, I do. I'm waiting for her."

"She won't make it down here. Take my word for it. Get in."

"What's the matter?"

"Look, fella, we can't reach your folks; they're in New York. Your sister said you'd be down here, so we came after you. We're doing you both a favor. Now, get in!"

The young man pulled open the back door of the car and got in quickly. "Was there an accident? Is she all right?"

"It's always an accident, isn't it?" said the policeman who was driving.

Steven Trevayne gripped the back of the front seat. He was frightened now. "Please, tell me what happened!"

"Your sister and a couple of girl friends started out with a pot party," answered the other patrolman. "At the Swansons' guest house. The Swansons are in Maine . . . naturally. We got a tip about an hour ago. When we got there, we found it was a little more complicated."

"What do you mean?"

"That was the accident, young fellow," interjected the driver. "Hard stuff. The accident was that we found it."

Steven Trevayne was stunned. His sister may have had a stick now and then—who hadn't?—but nothing hard. That was out.

"I don't believe you," he said emphatically.

"You'll see for yourself."

The patrol car turned left at the next corner. It was not the way to Police Headquarters.

"Aren't they at the station?"

"They're not booked. Not yet."

"I don't understand."

"We don't want any story out. If they're booked, we can't control it. They're still at the Swansons'."

"Are the parents there?"

"We told you, we haven't been able to reach them," answered the driver. "The Swansons are in Maine; your folks are in town."

"You said there were others. Girl friends."

"Out-of-staters. Friends from boarding school. We want the local parents first on this one. We've got to be careful. For everyone's sake. You see, we found two packages of uncut heroin. An educated guess would put the price around a quarter of a million dollars."

Andrew Trevayne took his wife's elbow as they walked up the short flight of concrete steps to the rear door of the Greenwich Police Station. It had been agreed that they would use this entrance.

The introductions were polite, abrupt, and the Trevaynes were ushered into a Detective Fowler's office. Their son was standing by a window and walked rapidly to his parents the moment they entered the door.

"Mom! Dad! . . . This is a bunch of crap!"

"Just calm down, Steve," said the father sternly.

"Is Pam all right?"

"Yes, Mother. She's fine. They're still at the Swansons'. She's just confused. They're all confused, and I don't blame them one goddamned bit!"

"I said cool it!"

"I'm perfectly calm, Dad. I'm just angry. Those kids don't know what uncut horse is, much less how or where to sell it!"

"Do you?" asked Detective Fowler impersonally.

"I'm not the issue, cop!"

"I'll tell you once more, Steve, get hold of yourself or shut up!"

"No, I won't! . . . I'm sorry, Dad, but I won't! These jokers got a phone tip to check out the Swansons'. No name, no reason. They . . ."

"Just a second, young man!" broke in the police officer. "We're not 'jokers' and I would advise you not to use that kind of language!"

"He's right," added Trevayne. "I'm sure Mr. Fowler can explain what happened. What was this phone call, Mr. Fowler? You didn't mention it when we spoke."

"Dad! He won't *tell* you!"

"I don't *know!* . . . That's the truth, Mr. Trevayne. At seven-ten this evening the desk got a phone call that there was some grass at the Swansons'; that we should look into it because there was a lot more involved. The caller was male, spoke with kind of a . . . well, high-toned speech. Your daughter was the only one mentioned by name. We followed it up. . . . Four kids. They admitted sharing a single cigarette between them during the last hour or so. It was no party. Frankly, the patrolman suggested we forget it. But by the time they radioed in their report, we'd gotten another call. Same voice. Same person. This time we were told to look in the milk box on the Swansons' guest-house porch. We found the two packages of heroin. Uncut; we figure two hundred, two hundred and fifty thousand. That's a lot of involvement."

"It's also the most transparent, trumped-up incrimination I've ever heard of. It's completely unbelievable." Trevayne looked at his watch. "My attorney should be here within a half-hour; I'm sure he'll tell you the same thing. Now, I'll stay and wait, but I know my wife would like to go out to the Swansons'. Is that all right with you?"

The detective sighed audibly. "It's fine."

"Do you need my son any longer? May he drive her?"

"Sure."

"Can we take her home?" asked Phyllis Trevayne anxiously. "Take all of them back to our house?"

"Well, there are certain formalities . . ."

"Never mind, Phyl. Go on out to the Swansons'. We'll call you as soon as Walter gets here. Don't worry. Please."

"Dad, shouldn't I stay? I can tell Walter . . ."

"I want you to go with your mother. The keys are in the car. Now, go on."

Trevayne and Detective Fowler watched the two of them leave. When the door was shut, Trevayne reached into his pocket for a pack of cigarettes. He offered one to the police officer, who refused.

"No, thanks. I eat pistachio nuts instead these days."

"Good for you. Now, do you want to tell me what this is all about? You don't believe there's any connection between that heroin and those girls any more than I do."

"Why don't I? It's a very expensive connection."

"Because if you did, you'd have them down here and booked. Precisely because it *is* expensive. You're handling the entire situation in a very unorthodox manner."

"Yes, I am." Fowler walked around his desk and sat down. "And you're right, I don't believe there's a connection. On the other hand, I can't dismiss it. Circumstantially, it's explosive; I don't have to tell you that."

"What are you going to do?"

"This'll surprise you, but I may be guided by your attorney."

"Which reinforces my statement."

"Yes, it does. I don't think we're on opposite sides, but I've got problems. We've got the evidence; I certainly can't ignore it. On the other hand, the manner of our getting it raises questions. I can't legally hang it on the kids—not considering everything . . ."

"I'd have you in court on false arrest. *That* could be expensive."

"Oh, come on, Mr. Trevayne. Don't threaten. Legally, those girls, including your daughter, admitted using marijuana. That's against the law. But it's minor, and we wouldn't press it. The other is something else. Greenwich doesn't want that kind of publicity; and a quarter of a million dollars' worth of uncut heroin is a lot of publicity. We don't want a Darien here."

Trevayne saw that Fowler was sincere. It *was* a problem. It was also insane. Why would anyone want to incriminate four young girls to the extent of throwing away such an enormous sum of money? It was an extraordinary gesture.

* * *

Phyllis Trevayne came down the stairs and walked into the living room. Her husband stood in front of the huge glass wall looking out over the sound. It was long after midnight, and the moon was an August moon, shining brightly on the water.

"The girls are in the adjoining guest rooms. They'll be talking till dawn; they're scared out of their wits. Can I get you a drink?"

"That'd be nice. We both could use one."

Phyllis crossed to the small built-in bar to the left of the window. "What's going to happen?"

"Fowler and Walter worked it out. Fowler will release the finding of the packages and the fact that they were uncovered as a result of telephone tips. He's forced to do that. But he won't mention any names or locations on the grounds that an investigation is under way. If he's pressed, he'll say that he has no right incriminating innocent people. The girls can't tell him anything."

"Did you talk to the Swansons?"

"Yes. They panicked; Walter calmed them down. I told them Jean would stay with us and join them tomorrow or the day after. The others are heading home in the morning."

Phyllis handed her husband a drink. "Does it make any sense to you? At all?"

"No, it doesn't. We can't figure it out. The voice on the phone was moneyed, according to Fowler and the desk sergeant. That could mean any of thousands; narrowed somewhat because he knew the Swansons' guest house. That is, he didn't hesitate calling it 'the guest house'; he didn't describe it as a separate building or anything like that."

"But *why?*"

"I don't know. Maybe someone has it in for the Swansons; *really* in for them, a quarter of a million dollars' worth. Or . . ."

"But, Andy," Phyllis interrupted, remembering and choosing her words carefully. "The man who called used Pam's name. Not Jean Swanson's."

"Sure. But the heroin was left on the Swansons' property."

"I see."

"Well, I don't," said Trevayne, raising his glass to his lips. "It's all guesswork. Walter's probably right. Whoever it was was probably caught in the middle of two transactions and panicked. The girls came along; on the surface, rich, spoiled, easy scapegoats for an alibi."

"I can't think like that."

"I can't either, really. I'm quoting Walter."

The sound of an automobile could be heard in the circular driveway in front of the house.

"It must be Steve," said Phyllis. "I told him not to be too late."

"Which he is," added Trevayne, looking at the mantel clock. "But no lectures, I promise. I liked the way he behaved himself tonight. His language left something to be desired, but he wasn't intimidated. He might have been."

"I was proud of him. He was his father's son."

"No, he was just calling it as he saw it. I think the word is 'bummer.'"

The front door opened, and Steven Trevayne walked in, closing it slowly, firmly behind him. He seemed disturbed.

Phyllis Trevayne started toward her son.

"Wait a minute, Mom. Before you come near me, I want to tell you something. . . . I left the Swansons' around ten-forty-five. The cop took me downtown for my car. I drove over to Ginny's, and we both went to the Cos Cob Tavern. We got there about eleven-thirty. I had three bottles of beer, no grass, nothing else."

"Why are you telling us this?" asked Phyllis.

The tall boy stammered, unsure of himself. "We left the place about an hour ago and went out to the car. The front seat was a mess; someone had poured whiskey or wine or something all over it; the seat covers were ripped, ashtrays emptied. We figured it was a lousy joke, a really lousy joke. . . . I dropped off Ginny and started for home. When I got near the townline intersection, I was stopped by a police car. I wasn't speeding or anything; no one chased me. This patrol car just flagged me down at the side of the road. I thought maybe he was stuck, I didn't know. . . . The cop came over and asked me for my license and registration, and then he smelled the inside and told me to get out. I tried to explain, but he wasn't buying any of it."

"Was he from the Greenwich police?"

"I don't know, Dad. I don't think so; I was still in Cos Cob."

"Go on."

"He searched me; his partner went over the car like it was the French Connection. I thought they were going to haul me in. I sort of hoped they would; I was sober and everything. But they didn't. They did something else. They took a Polaroid shot of me with my arms against the car—they made me stretch out so they could search my pockets—and then the first cop asked me where I'd come from. I told him, and he went to his patrol car and called someone. He came back and asked me if I'd hit an old man on the road about ten miles back. I said of course not. Then he tells me this old guy is in critical condition in the hospital. . . ."

"What hospital? What *name?*"

"He didn't say."

"Didn't you *ask?*"

"No, Dad! I was scared to death. I didn't *hit* anyone. I never even saw anyone walking on the road. Just a couple of cars."

"Oh, my God!" Phyllis Trevayne looked at her husband. "What happened then?"

"The other policeman took more pictures of the car and a close-up shot of my face. I can still see the flash-bulb. . . . Christ, I was scared. . . . Then, just like that, they told me I could go." The boy remained in the hall-way, his shoulders slumped, the frightened bewilderment obvious in his eyes.

"You've told me everything?" asked Trevayne.

"Yes, sir," replied the son, his fear clouding his nearly inaudible voice.

Andrew walked to the end table by the couch and picked up the telephone. He dialed the operator and asked for the number of the Cos Cob Police Department. Phyllis went to her son and led him into the living room.

"My name is Trevayne, Andrew Trevayne. I understand one of your patrol cars stopped my son on . . .
where, Steve?"

"Junction Road, at the intersection. About a quarter
of a mile from the railroad station."

". . . Junction Road, near the station at the intersection; no more than a half-hour ago. Would you mind
telling me what the report says? Yes, I'll hold."

Andrew looked at his son, sitting in a chair, Phyllis
standing beside him. The boy shivered and took several deep
breaths. He watched his father, afraid, not understanding.

"Yes," said Trevayne impatiently into the telephone.
"Junction Road, Cos Cob side. . . . Of course I'm sure.
My son is right here! . . . Yes. Yes. . . . No, I'm not
positive. . . . Just a minute." Andrew looked at the boy.
"On the police car; did you see the Cos Cob name?"

"I . . . I didn't actually look. It was off on the side.
No, I didn't see it."

"No, he didn't, but it would have to be yours, wouldn't
it? He was in Cos Cob. . . . Oh? . . . I see. You couldn't
check it out for me, could you? He was stopped in your
township, after all. . . . Oh? All right, I understand. I
don't *like* it, but I see what you mean. Thanks."

Trevayne replaced the telephone and took a pack of
cigarettes out of his pocket.

"What is it, Dad? Wasn't it them?"

"No. They have two patrol cars, and neither one has
been near Junction Road for the past two hours."

"Why didn't you 'like' but 'understand'?" asked Phyllis.

"They can't check the cars of the other towns. Not
without a formal request, which has to be recorded in the
violations file. They don't like to do that; they have arrangements. In case police cars cross municipal lines going
after someone, they just haul them back informally."

"But you've got to find out! They took photographs,
they said Steve *hit* someone!"

"I know. I will. . . . Steve, go on up and take a
shower. You smell like an Eighth Avenue bar. And relax.
You didn't do anything wrong."

Trevayne moved the telephone to the coffee table and
sat down.

Westport, Darien. Wilton. New Canaan. Southport. Nothing.

"Dad, I didn't dream it up!" Steven Trevayne shouted; he was in his bathrobe.

"I'm sure you didn't. We'll keep trying; we'll call the New York stations."

Port Chester. Rye. Harrison. White Plains. Mamaroneck.

The picture of his son stretched forward, hands clamped to the hood of an automobile soaked with alcohol, being questioned by untraceable police on a dark road about an unknown man struck down—photographs, accusations. It made no sense; there was an abstract quality of unbelievability. As unbelievable, as unreal as his daughter and her friends and two hundred and fifty thousand dollars' worth of uncut heroin found in a milk box on the Swansons' guest-house porch.

Insanity.

Yet it all had happened.

"The girls finally fell asleep," said Phyllis, walking into the living room. It was nearly four o'clock. "Anything?"

"No," replied her husband. He turned to his son, who sat in a chair by the large wall window. The boy was staring outside, his fear intermittently replaced with angry bewilderment. "Try to recall, Steve. Was the patrol car some other color than black? Perhaps dark blue or green?"

"Dark. That's all. I suppose it could have been blue or green. It wasn't white."

"Were there any stripes? Any kind of insignia, no matter how vague."

"No. . . . Yes, I guess so. I just didn't look. I didn't think . . ." The boy brought his hand to his forehead. "I didn't *hit* anyone! I *swear* I didn't!"

"Of course you didn't!" Phyllis went to him and bent down, touching her cheek to his. "It's a terrible mistake, we know that."

"On top of a terrible joke," added Trevayne, puzzled.

The telephone on the coffee table rang. Its effect was frightening, a jarring intrusion on private fears. Trevayne swiftly picked it up.

"Hello! . . . Yes, yes. This is his residence; I'm his father."

Steven Trevayne leaped out of the chair and walked rapidly to the back of the couch. Phyllis remained by the window, afraid of the immediate moment.

"My God! I've been phoning all over Connecticut and New York! The boy's a minor, the car's in my name! I should have been called immediately! I'd like an explanation, please."

For the next several minutes Trevayne listened without comment. When finally he spoke, it was five words.

"Thank you. I'll expect them."

He hung up the telephone and turned to his wife and son.

"Andy? Is everything all right?"

"Yes. . . . The Highport Police Station; it's a small village about fifteen miles north of Cos Cob. Their patrol car was following an automobile down Coast Road, a robbery suspect they were checking out over their radio before an arrest. They lost him and swung west on Briarcliff Avenue, when they saw a man run down by a car that looked like yours, Steve. They radioed for an ambulance, informed the Cos Cob police, and after everything was taken care of, started back for Highport. They spotted you on Junction, swung onto a parallel street, and caught up with you a mile down the road by the intersection. . . . They could have let you go the minute they checked with Cos Cob; the hit-and-run had turned himself in. But they smelled the car and thought they'd give you a scare. . . . They're sending us the photographs."

The terrible night was over.

Steven Trevayne lay on his bed looking up at the ceiling; the radio was tuned to one of those endless all-night talk shows where everyone shouted over everyone else. The boy thought the cacophony might help him sleep.

But sleep would not come.

He knew he should have said something; it was stupid *not* to say anything. But the words wouldn't come, any more than sleep came now. The relief had been so total, so complete, so needed; he hadn't dared resurrect a doubt.

His father had first mentioned the words, unknowingly.
Try to recall, Steve. Was the patrol car some other color than black. . . .

Maybe. Maybe a dark blue or green.

But it was a *dark* color.

That's what he should have remembered when his father said "Highport."

Highport-on-the-Ocean was the name on the sign on Coast Road. Highport *was* a small village; tiny, actually. It had two or three great beaches—off by themselves, and privately owned. During hot summer nights he and a few friends—never more than a few—often parked a couple of hundred yards down Coast Road and crept through the private property to reach one of the beaches.

But they had to be careful; they always had to keep an eye out for the Yellowbird.

That's what they called it. *The Yellowbird.*

The village of Highport-on-the-Ocean's single patrol car.

It was bright yellow.

4

Andrew Trevayne boarded the 707 jet at John F. Kennedy Airport for the hour's flight to Washington.

He unlatched the seat belt once the aircraft completed its ascent and the warning lights were extinguished. It was three-fifteen, and he'd be late for his meeting with Presidential Assistant Robert Webster. He'd had his office at Danforth call Webster at the White House; say he was detained and that if because of the delay Webster wished to change the meeting place, he should leave instructions for him at Dulles Airport. It didn't matter to Trevayne; he'd accepted the fact that he'd have to stay overnight.

He reached for the vodka martini from the pretty young stewardess and took a long sip. Placing the glass on the small tray in front of him, Trevayne latched the seat halfway back and spread a hastily purchased *New York* magazine on his lap.

Suddenly he was aware that the passenger next to him was staring at him. He returned the man's look and immediately realized he knew the face. The man was large, his head enormous, his complexion deeply tanned— more from birth than from the sun. He was, perhaps, in his early fifties, and wore thick horn-rimmed glasses. The man spoke first.

"Mr. Trevayne, isn't it?" The voice was soft but deep, with a trace of a rasp. It was a gentle voice, however.

"That's right. I know we've met, but forgive me, I don't remember . . ."

"De Spadante. Mario de Spadante."

"Of course," said Trevayne, his memory instantly activated. Mario de Spadante went back to the New Haven days, the latter part, at any rate, about nine years ago. De Spadante had represented a construction firm involved with some buildings Trevayne and his brother-in-law were financing. Trevayne had rejected the bid—the builders had an insufficient history. But Mario de Spadante had gone a long way since those days a brief nine years ago. That is, if the newspapers were to be believed. He was reputed to be a power in the underworld now. "Mario the Spade" was the name often used—referring to his swarthy complexion and the fact that he had buried a number of enemies. He was never convicted of the latter, however.

"Must be nine, ten years ago, I'd say," said De Spadante, smiling pleasantly. "You remember? You turned me down on a construction job. And you were absolutely correct, Mr. Trevayne. Our company didn't have the experience for it. Yes, you were right."

"At best, it's always an educated guess. Glad you don't resent it."

"Of course not. Never did, to tell you the truth." De Spadante winked at Trevayne and laughed quietly. "It wasn't my company. Belonged to a cousin. . . . Him I resented, not you. He made me do his work. But everything always equals out. I learned the business, his business, better than he did. It's my company now. . . . Look, I interrupted your reading. Me, I got to go over some reports—a bunch of long-winded, eight-cylinder paragraphs with figures way beyond any math I ever took at New Haven High. If I get stuck on a word, I'm going to ask you to translate. That'll make up for your turning me down ten years ago. How about it?" De Spadante grinned.

Trevayne laughed, taking his martini off the miniature shelf. He raised the glass an inch or two toward De Spadante. "It's the least I can do."

And he did. About fifteen minutes before landing at Dulles, Mario de Spadante asked him to clarify a particularly complex paragraph. It was so complicated that Trevayne read it several times before advising De Spadante to have it simplified, put in cleaner form before accepting it.

"I really can't make much more sense out of this than to tell you they expect you to figure the large items first before tackling the smaller ones."

"So what else is new? I use a square-foot unit plus profit, which includes the whole thing."

"I think that's what this means. I gather you're a subcontractor."

"That's right."

"That general contractor wants it done in stages. At least, I think that's what it means."

"So I build him half a door, or maybe just the frame, and he buys the rest from somebody else?"

"I'm probably wrong. You'd better get it clarified."

"Maybe I won't. Cost him double with that kind of bidding. Nobody wants to do half of somebody else's job. . . . You just made up for ten years ago. I'll buy you a drink."

De Spadante took the papers from Trevayne and signaled the stewardess. He placed the papers in a large manila envelope and ordered drinks for Trevayne and himself.

As Trevayne lit a cigarette, he felt the plane gradually descend. De Spadante was looking out the window, and Trevayne noticed the printing—upside down—on the large manila envelope on De Spadante's lap. It read:

Department of the Army
Corps of Engineers

Trevayne smiled to himself. No wonder the language was so obscure. The Pentagon engineers were the most exasperating men in Washington when it came to doing business.

He should know.

The message at the reservation desk consisted of Robert Webster's name and a Washington telephone number. When Trevayne called, he was surprised to learn that it was Webster's private line at the White House. It was only a little after four-thirty; he could have telephoned the switchboard. In Trevayne's government days presidential aides never gave out their private numbers.

"I wasn't sure when you'd get in; the stack-ups can be terrible," was Webster's explanation.

Trevayne was confused. It was a minor point, not worth mentioning, really, but Trevayne was bothered. The White House switchboard didn't have hours.

Webster suggested they meet after dinner in the cocktail lounge of Trevayne's hotel. "It'll give us a chance to go over a few things before tomorrow. The President wants to chat briefly with you around ten or ten-thirty in the morning. I'll have his firm schedule in an hour or so."

Trevayne left the telephone booth and walked toward the main exit of the airport terminal. He'd packed only a change of shirt, shorts, and socks; he would have to ascertain the swiftness of the hotel's cleaning and pressing facilities if he was going to have a White House audience. He wondered why the President wished to see him. It seemed a little premature, the formalities of his acceptance not having been completed. It was possible that the President simply wished to reaffirm personally Franklyn Baldwin's statement that the highest office in the country was behind the proposed subcommittee.

If so, it was generous and meaningful.

"Hey, Mr. Trevayne!" It was Mario de Spadante standing by the curb. "Can I give you a lift into town?"

"Oh, I don't want to inconvenience you. I'll grab a cab."

"No inconvenience. My car just got here." De Spadante gestured at a long, dark-blue Cadillac parked several yards to the right.

"Thanks, I appreciate it."

De Spadante's chauffeur opened the back door, and the two men got in.

"Where are you staying?"

"The Hilton."

"Fine. Just down the street. I'm at the Sheraton."

Trevayne saw that the interior of the Cadillac was appointed with a telephone, miniature bar, television set, and a back-seat stereo cassette machine. Mario de Spadante had, indeed, come a long way since the New Haven days.

"Quite a car."

"You press buttons and dancing girls come out of the dashboard. Frankly, it's too ostentatious for my taste. I called it my car, but it's not. It belongs to a cousin."

"You have a lot of cousins."

"Big family. . . . Don't misunderstand the term. I'm a construction boy from New Haven who made good." De Spadante laughed his soft, infectious laugh. "Family! What they *print* about me! Holy Christ! They should be writing movies. I don't say there's no mafiosi; I'm not that dumb, but I wouldn't know one if I fell over him."

"They have to sell papers." It was the only thing Trevayne could think of saying.

"Yeah, sure. You know, I got a younger brother, about your age. Even *him*. He comes up to me and says 'What about it, Mario? Is it true?' . . . 'What about what?' I ask. 'You know me, Augie. You know me forty-two years. I got it so easy? I don't have to spend ten hours a day cutting costs, fighting the unions, trying to get paid on time?' . . . Hah! If I was what they say, I'd pick up a phone and scare the bejesus out of them. As it is, I go to the banks with my tail between my guinea ass and plead."

"You look like you're surviving."

Mario de Spadante laughed once more and winked his innocent, conspiratorial wink, as he had done on the plane. "Right on, Mr. Trevayne. I survive. It's not easy, but with the grace of God and a lot of hard work, I manage. . . . Your foundation got business in Washington?"

"No. I'm here on another matter, just meeting some people."

"That's Washington. Greatest little meeting place in

the Western Hemisphere. And you know something? Whenever anyone says he's 'just meeting people,' that's the sign not to ask who he's meeting."

Andrew Trevayne just smiled.

"You still live in Connecticut?" asked De Spadante.

"Yes. Outside of Greenwich."

"Nice terriitory. I'm doing some residential work down there. Near the sound."

"I'm on the sound. South shore."

"Maybe we'll get together sometime. Maybe I can sell you a wing on your house."

"You can try."

Trevayne walked through the arch into the lounge and looked around at the various people seated in the soft easy chairs and low couches. A headwaiter, dressed in a tuxedo, approached.

"May I help you, sir?"

"Yes. I'm to meet a Mr. Webster here. I don't know if he made a reservation."

"Oh, yes. You're Mr. Trevayne."

"That's right."

"Mr. Webster telephoned that he'd be a few minutes late. I'll show you to a table."

"Thank you."

The tuxedoed waiter led Trevayne to a far corner of the lounge that was conspicuous by its lack of customers. It seemed as if this particular location was roped by an invisible cordon to isolate it. Webster had requested such a table, and his position guaranteed it. Trevayne ordered a drink and let his memory wander back to his days in the State Department.

They had been challenging, exciting, almost as stimulating as the early years with the companies. Primarily because few people believed he could accomplish the major assignment given him. It had been to coordinate trade agreements with several eastern satellite countries—guaranteeing the business sectors of each country the most favorable conditions possible—without upsetting political balances. It hadn't been difficult. He remembered that at the very first conference he had disarmed both sides by suggesting that the U.S. State Department and its Communist counterpart hold an international press conference in one room categorically rejecting everything the other side stood for, while in the next room the businessmen negotiated their agreements.

The ploy had its effect; the laughter had been sincere, and the tone set for future meetings. Whenever the negotiations got heated, someone would playfully suggest that his adversary belonged in that "other room"—with the propagandists.

He had enjoyed his Washington days. There had been the exhilaration of knowing he was close to corridors of real power, that his judgments were listened to by men of great commitments. And they *were* men of commitment, regardless of their individual political affiliations.

"Mr. Trevayne?"

"Mr. Webster?" Trevayne stood up and shook the hand of the presidential assistant. He saw that Webster was about his own age, perhaps a year or two younger, a pleasant-looking man.

"Sorry as hell to be late. There was a flap over tomorrow's schedule. The President told the four of us to lock ourselves in a room and not come out till we got it in order."

"I gather that was accomplished." Trevayne sat down as Webster did the same.

"Damned if I know." Webster laughed, flagging a waiter. "I got you cleared for eleven-fifteen and let the rest of them figure out the afternoon." He gave his order and collapsed back into the chair, sighing audibly. "What's a nice Ohio farmboy like me doing a job like this?"

"I'd say it was a quite a leap."

"It was. I think they got the names mixed up. My wife keeps telling me there's a guy named Webster wandering around the streets of Akron wondering why he spent all that money for campaign contributions."

"It's possible," replied Trevayne, knowing well that Webster's appointment was no mistake. He had been a bright young man who had risen rapidly in Ohio State House politics, credited with keeping the governorship in

the President's column. Franklyn Baldwin had told Trevayne that Webster was a man to watch.

"Did you have a good flight?"

"Yes, thanks. Much smoother than your afternoon, I
think."

"I'm sure of that." The waiter returned with Webster's drink; the two men remained silent until he left.
"Have you talked with anyone but Baldwin?"

"No, I haven't. Frank suggested that I don't."

"The Danforth people have no idea?"

"There wasn't any point. Even if Frank hadn't cau-
tioned me, nothing's definite yet."

"It is as far as we're concerned. The President's delighted. He'll tell you that himself."

"There's still the Senate hearing. They may have
different ideas."

"On what possible grounds? You're houndstooth material. The only thing they might spring on you is your
favorable press in Soviet publications."

"My what?"

"They like you over at Tass."

"I wasn't aware of it."

"It doesn't matter. They like Henry Ford, too. And
you were doing a job for State."

"I have no intention of defending myself against something like that."

"I said it doesn't matter."

"I would hope not. . . . However, there *is* something
else, from my point of view. I've got to have certain . . .
well, I guess you'd call them understandings. They've got
to be clear."

"What do you mean?"

"Basically, two things. I mentioned them to Baldwin.
Cooperation, and no interference. Both are equally important to me. I can't do the job without them. I'm not even
sure I can do it *with* them; without them, impossible."

"You won't have any trouble there. That's a condition
anyone would make."

"Easily made, difficult to get. Remember, I worked
in this town once."

"I don't follow you. How could anyone interfere?"

"Let's start with the word 'classified.' Then jump to 'restricted.' Along with which can be found 'secret,' 'top-secret,' even 'priority.' "

"Oh, hell, you're cleared for all that."

"I want it spelled out up front. I insist on it."

"Then ask for it. You'll get it. . . . Unless you've managed to fool everyone, your dossier's a study in respectability; they'd let you carry around the little black box."

"No, thanks. It can stay right where it is."

"It will. . . . Now, I wanted to brief you on tomorrow."

Robert Webster spelled out the routine for a White House audience, and Trevayne realized how little had changed since his past appearances. The arrival time half an hour to forty-five minutes before admittance to the Oval Room; the specific entrance to be used; the pass supplied by Webster; the suggestion that Trevayne carry no metallic objects larger than a key ring; the realization that the meeting was restricted to just so many minutes and might well be cut short—if the Chief Executive had said what he wanted to say or heard what he wanted to hear. If time could be saved, it should be.

Trevayne nodded his understanding and approval.

Their business nearly finished, Webster ordered a second and final drink. "I promised you on the phone a couple of explanations; I'm flattered you haven't pressed me for them."

"They weren't important, and I assumed the President would answer the one uppermost in my mind."

"That being . . . why he wants to see you tomorrow?"

"Yes."

"It's all related. It's why you have my private number and why you and I will make arrangements so that you'll be able to reach me anytime of day or night, no matter where I am, here or overseas."

"Is that necessary?"

"I'm not sure. But it's the way the President wants it. I'm not going to argue."

"Neither am I."

"The President naturally wants to convey his support for the subcommittee, and his personal endorsement of you. That's primary. And there's another aspect—I'll put it in my words, not his; if I make a mistake, it's *my* mistake, not his."

Trevayne watched Webster carefully. "But you've discussed what you're about to tell me, so the variation would be minor."

"Naturally. Don't look so concerned; it's for your benefit. . . . The President has been through the political wars, Trevayne. He's a savvy old duck. The State machine, the House, the Senate—he's been where the action is, and he knows what you're going to face. He's made a lot of friends and I'm sure that slate is balanced by an equal number of enemies. Of course, his office removes him from those battles now, but it also allows him certain latitudes, certain pressure points. He wants you to know they're at your disposal."

"I appreciate it."

"But there's a catch. You're never to try to reach him by yourself. I'm your sole contact, your only bridge to him."

"It would never occur to me to try to reach him personally."

"And I'm sure it never occurred to you that the official weight of the presidency was behind you in the most practical way. Namely, at the moment you may need it."

"No, I guess it didn't. I'm a corporation man; I'm used to the structures. I see what you mean. I *do* appreciate it."

"But he's never to be mentioned, you understand that." Webster's statement was spoken firmly. He wanted no room for doubt.

"I understand."

"Good. If he brings it up tomorrow, just tell him we've discussed everything. Even if he doesn't, you might volunteer that you're aware of his offer; you're grateful, or however you want to put it."

Webster finished his drink and stood up. "Wow! It's not even ten-thirty yet. I'll be home before eleven; my wife won't believe it. See you tomorrow." Webster reached down to shake Trevayne's hand.

"Fine. Good night."

Trevayne watched the younger man dodge between the armchairs, making his way rapidly toward the arch. Webster was filled with that particular energy which was at once the fuel he needed and the sustenance he took from his work. The exhilaration syndrome, Trevayne reflected. This was the town for it; it was never really the same anywhere else. There were semblances of it in the arts, or in advertising, but the rates of failure were too pronounced in those fields—there was always an underlying sense of fear. Not in Washington. You were either in or out. If you were in, you were on top. If you were at the White House, you were standing on the summit.

The electorate got a lot of talent for the money it paid, Trevayne had long ago decided. All in exchange for the syndrome.

He looked at his watch; it was too early to try to sleep, and he didn't feel like reading. He'd go up to his room and call Phyllis and then look at the newspaper. Perhaps there was a movie on television.

He signed the check and started out, feeling his coat pocket to make sure the room key was there. He walked through the arch and turned left toward the bank of elevators. As he passed the newsstand he saw two men in neat, pressed suits watching him from the counter. They started toward him, and when he stopped in front of the first elevator, they approached.

The man on the right spoke, while taking a small black identification case from his pocket. The other man also removed his identification.

"Mr. Trevayne?"

"Yes?"

"Secret Service, White House detail," said the agent softly. "May we speak with you over here, sir?" He indicated an area away from the elevators.

"Of course."

The second man held his case forward. "Would you mind confirming, Mr. Trevayne? I'm going outside for a minute."

Trevayne checked the photograph against the man's face. It was authentic, and he nodded. The agent turned and walked away.

"What is this?"

"I'd like to wait until my partner returns, sir. He'll make sure everything's clear. Would you care for a cigarette?"

"No, thank you. But I would like to know what this is all about."

"The President would like to see you tonight."

5

The brown Secret Service car was parked at the side entrance of the hotel. The two agents rushed Trevayne down the steps while the driver held the rear door open. They sped off down the street, turning south on Nebraska Avenue.

"We're not going to the White House, Mr. Trevayne. The President's in Georgetown. His schedule is such that it's more convenient this way."

After several minutes the car bounced along the narrow cobblestone streets that marked the residential area. Trevayne saw that they were heading east toward the section with the large, five-story townhouses, rebuilt remnants of a gracious era. They drove up in front of a particularly wide brownstone structure with many windows and sculptured trees on the sidewalk. The Secret Sevice man on the curb side got out, signaling Trevayne to do the same. There were two other plainclothesmen at the front door, and the minute they recognized their fellow agent, they nodded to each other and removed their hands from their pockets.

The man who first had spoken to Trevayne in the hotel led him inside through the hallway to a tiny elevator at the end of the corridor. They entered; the agent pulled the brass grille shut and pushed the automatic button: four.

"Close quarters in here," said Trevayne.

"The Ambassador says his grandchildren play in it for hours when they visit. I think it's really a kiddie elevator."

"The Ambassador?"

"Ambassador Hill. William Hill. This is his house."

Trevayne pictured the man. William Hill was in his seventies now. A wealthy eastern industrialist, friend-to-Presidents, roving diplomat, war hero. "Big Billy Hill" was the irreverent nickname given by *Time* magazine to the articulate, soft-spoken gentleman.

The elevator stopped, and the two men got out. There was another hallway and another plainclothesman in front of another door. As Trevayne and the agent approached him, the man unobtrusively withdrew a small object from his pocket, slightly larger than a pack of cigarettes, and made several crisscross motions in Trevayne's direction.

"Like being given a benediction, isn't it?" said the agent. "Consider yourself blessed."

"What is it?"

"A scanner. Routine, don't be insulted. Come on." The man with the tiny machine opened the door for them.

The room beyond the door was an immense library-study. The bookcases were floor-to-ceiling, the Oriental carpets thick, the furniture heavy wood and masculine. The lighting was indirect from a half-dozen lamps. There were several leather armchairs and a large mahogany table which served as the desk. Behind the table sat Ambassador William Hill. In an armchair to the right sat the President of the United States.

"Mr. President. Mr. Ambassador. . . . Mr. Trevayne." The Secret Service man turned and walked out, closing the door behind him.

Hill and the President rose as Trevayne approached the latter, gripping the hand extended to him. "Mr. President."

"Mr. Trevayne, good of you to come. I hope I didn't inconvenience you."

"Not at all, sir."

"You know Mr. Hill?"

Trevayne and the Ambassador shook hands. "A pleasure, sir."

"I doubt it, at this hour," William Hill laughed, coming around the table. "Let me get you a drink, Trevayne.

Nothing in the Constitution says you have to be abstemious during any meeting called after six o'clock."

"I wasn't aware that there were any strictures before six, either," said the President.

"Oh, I'm sure there are some eighteenth-century phrases which might apply. What'll you have, Trevayne?" asked the old gentleman.

Trevayne told him, realizing that the two men were trying to put him at ease. The President gestured for him to sit down and Hill brought him his glass.

"We met once before, but I don't suppose you recall, Mr. Trevayne."

"Of course, I do, Mr. President. It was four years ago, I think."

"That's right. I was in the Senate, and you had done a remarkable job for State. I heard about your opening remarks at the trade conference. Did you know that the then-Secretary of State was very annoyed with you?"

"I heard rumors. He never said anything to me, though."

"How could he?" interjected Hill. "You got the job done. He'd boxed himself into a corner."

"That's what made it so amusing," added the President.

"At the time, it seemed the only way to thaw the freeze," said Trevayne.

"Excellent work. Excellent." The President leaned forward in the armchair, looking at Trevayne. "I meant what I said about inconveniencing you this evening. I know we'll meet again in the morning, but I felt tonight was important. I won't waste words; I'm sure you'd like to get back to your hotel."

"No hurry, sir."

"That's kind of you." The Chief Executive smiled. "I know you met with Bobby Webster. How did it go?"

"Very well, sir. I think I understand everything; I appreciate your offer of assistance."

"You're going to need it. We weren't sure we were going to ask you to come out here tonight. It depended on Webster. . . . The minute he left you he telephoned me here. On my instructions. Then we knew we had to get you over."

"Oh? Why was that?"

"You told Webster that you'd spoken with no one but Frank Baldwin about the subcommittee. Is that correct?"

"Yes, sir. Frank indicated that I shouldn't. At any rate, there was no reason to talk to anyone about it; nothing was set."

The President of the United States looked over at William Hill, who stared intently at Trevayne. Hill returned the Chief Executive's look, then pulled his attention back to Trevayne. Hill spoke softly, but with concern.

"Are you *absolutely sure?*"

"Of course."

"Did you mention it to your wife? Could she have said anything?"

"I did, but she wouldn't. I'm positive about that. Why do you ask?"

The President spoke. "You're aware that we sent out rumors that you were being approached for the job."

"They reached me, Mr. President."

"They were meant to. Are you also aware that the Defense Commission is composed of nine members—leaders in their respective fields, some of the most honored men in the country?"

"Frank Baldwin said as much."

"Did he tell you that they agreed to a man not to reveal any decisions, any progress, any concrete information?"

"No, he didn't, but I can understand it."

"Good. Now, I must tell you this. A week ago we sent out another rumor. An authenticated rumor—agreed to by the commission—that you had categorically rejected the post. We left no room for doubt as to where you stood. The rumor was that you violently objected to the whole concept, considered it a dangerous encroachment. You even accused my administration of police-state tactics. It was the sort of suppressed information that experience tells us is most readily believed, because it's embarrassing."

"And?" Trevayne did not try to conceal his annoyance. Not even the President of the United States had the right to attribute such judgments to him.

"Word came back to us that you had not rejected, but, instead, accepted the post. Civilian and military intelligence established the fact that in certain powerful sectors it was common knowledge. Our denial was ignored."

The President and the Ambassador remained silent, as if to let the importance of their revelation have an effect on Trevayne. The younger man looked bewildered, unsure of his reaction.

"Then my 'refusal' wasn't believed. That doesn't surprise me. Those who know me probably doubted it—the way it was phrased, at any rate."

"Even when personally confirmed to selected visitors by the President?" asked William Hill.

"Not simply *me*, Mr. Trevayne. The *office* of the President of the United States. Whoever that man is, he's a tall fellow to call a liar. Especially in an area like this."

Trevayne looked over at both men. He was beginning to understand, but the picture was still out of focus. "Is it . . . was it necessary to create the confusion? Does it matter whether I take the job, or someone else?"

"Apparently it does, Mr. Trevayne," answered Hill. "We know the proposed subcommittee is being watched; that's understandable. But we weren't sure of the intensity. We surfaced your name and then proceeded to deny—vehemently deny—your acceptance. It should have been enough to send the curious out speculating on other nominees. It wasn't. They were sufficiently concerned to dig further, dig until they learned the truth."

"What the Ambassador means—forgive me, Bill—is that the possibility of your heading up the subcommittee was so alarming to so many people that they went to extraordinary lengths to ascertain your status. They had to make sure you were out. They discovered otherwise, and rapidly spread the word. Obviously in preparation."

"Mr. President, I assume this subcommittee, if it functions properly, will touch a great many people. Of course, it'll be watched. I expected that."

William Hill leaned forward over his desk. "Watched? . . . What we've described goes far beyond the meaning of the word 'watched' as I understand it. You may be assured that large sums of money have been exchanged, old debts called in, a number of dangerous embarrassments threatened. These things had to happen, or a different conclusion would have been arrived at."

"Our purpose," said the President, "is to make you aware, to alert you. This is a frightened city, Mr. Trevayne. It's frightened of you."

Andrew slowly put down his glass on the small table next to the chair. "Are you suggesting, Mr. President, that I reconsider the appointment?"

"Not for a minute. And if Frank Baldwin knows what he's talking about, you're not the sort of man who'd be affected by this kind of thing. But you have to understand. This isn't an interim government appointment made to a respected member of the business community for the sake of mollifying a few outraged voices. We are committed—I am committed—to see it produce results. It must follow that there will be a considerable degree of ugliness."

"I think I'm prepared for that."

"Are you?" asked Hill, leaning back once again in his chair. "That's very important, Mr. Trevayne."

"I believe so. I've thought it over, talked it out at length with my wife . . . my very discreet wife. I have no illusions that it's a popular assignment."

"Good. It's necessary you understand that . . . as the President says." Hill picked up a file folder from the large maroon blotter on his table-desk. It was inordinately thick, bulky, and held together by wide metal hasps. "May we dwell for a minute on something else?"

"Of course." Trevayne looked at Hill as he answered, but he could feel the President's stare. He turned, and the President instantly shifted his eyes to the Ambassador. It was an uncomfortable moment.

"This is your dossier, Mr. Trevayne," said Hill, holding the file horizontally, as if weighing it. "Damned heavy, wouldn't you say?"

"Compared to the few I've seen. I can't imagine its being very interesting."

"Why do you say that?" asked the President, smiling.

"Oh, I don't know. . . . My life hasn't been filled with the sort of events that make for exciting fiction."

"Any man who reaches the level of wealth you did before he's forty makes fascinating reading," said Hill.

"One reason for the size of this file is that I kept requesting additional information. It's a remarkable document. May I touch on a few points I found salient, several not entirely clear?"

"Certainly."

"You left Yale Law within six months of your degree. You never made any attempt to finish or pursue the bar. Yet your standing was high; the university officials tried to convince you to stay, but to no avail. That seems odd."

"Not really. My brother-in-law and I had started our first company. In Meriden, Connecticut. There was no time for anything else."

"Wasn't it also a strain on your family? Law school?"

"I'd been offered a full scholarship. I'm sure that's listed."

"I mean, in the sense of contributing."

"Oh. . . . I see what you're driving at. I think you're giving it more significance than it deserves, Mr. Ambassador. . . . Yes. My father declared bankruptcy in nineteen fifty-two."

"The circumstances were untidy, I gather. Would it bother you to describe them?" asked the President of the United States.

Trevayne looked alternately at both men. "No, not at all. My father spent thirty years building up a medium-sized woolens factory—a mill, actually—in Hancock, Massachusetts; it's a town outside of Boston. He made a quality product, and a New York conglomerate wanted the label. They absorbed the mill with the understanding—my father's understanding—that he'd be retained for life as the Hancock management. Instead, they took the label, closed the factory, and moved south to the cheaper labor markets. My father tried to reopen, illegally used his old label, and went under. Hancock became a New England mill-town statistic."

"An unfortunate story." The President's statement was made quietly. "Your father had no recourse in the courts? Force the company to make restitution on the basis of default?"

"There was no default. His understanding was predicated on an ambiguous clause. And talk. Legally, he had no grounds."

"I see," said the President. "It must have been a terrible blow to your family."

"And to the town," added Hill. "The statistic."

"It was an angry time. It passed." Andrew recalled only too well the anger, the frustration. The furious, bewildered father who roared at the silent men who merely smiled and pointed to paragraphs and signatures.

"Did that anger cause you to leave law school?" asked William Hill. "The events coincided; you had only six months to go for your degree; you were offered financial aid."

Andy looked at the old Ambassador with grudging respect. The line of questioning was becoming clearer. "I imagine it was part of it. There were other considerations. I was very young and felt there were more important priorities."

"Wasn't there really just one priority, Mr. Trevayne? One objective?" Hill spoke gently.

"Why don't you say what you want to say, Mr. Ambassador? Aren't we both wasting the President's time?"

The President offered no comment; he continued to watch Trevayne, as a doctor might study a patient.

"All right, I will." Hill closed the file and tapped it lightly with his ancient fingers. "I've had this dossier for nearly a month. I've read it and reread it perhaps twenty times over. And as I've told you, I repeatedly asked for additional data. At first it was merely to learn more about a successful young man named Trevayne, because Frank Baldwin was—and is—convinced that you're the only man to chair that subcommittee. Then it became something else. We had to find out why, whenever your name was mentioned as a possible nominee, the reactions were so hostile. Silently hostile, I might add."

" 'Dumbstruck' might be more appropriate, Bill," interjected the President.

"Agreed," said Hill. "The answer had to be here, but I couldn't find it. Then, as the material was processed—and I placed it in chronological order—I found it. But I had to go back to March of nineteen fifty-two to understand. Your first compulsive, seemingly irrational action. I'd like to capsule . . ."

As Ambassador William Hill droned on, summarizing his conclusions point by point, Andrew wondered if the old man really did understand. It was all so long ago; yet yesterday. There had been only one priority, one objective. To make a great deal of money; massive amounts that once and for all would eliminate the remotest possibility of ever having to experience what he witnessed his father living through in that Boston courtroom. It wasn't so much a sense of outrage—although the outrage was there—as it was a feeling of waste; the sheer waste of resources—financial, physical, mental: that was the fundamental crime, the essential evil.

He saw his father's productivity thwarted, warped, and finally stopped by the inconvenience of sudden poverty. Fantasy became the reality; vindication an obsession. At last the imagination lost all control, and a once proud man—moderately proud, moderately successful—was turned into a shell. Hollow, self-pitying, living through each day propelled by hatreds.

A familiar, loving human being had been transformed into a grotesque stranger because he hadn't the price of survival. In March of 1952 the final gavel was sounded in a Boston courtroom and Andrew Trevayne's father was informed that he was no longer permitted to function in the community of his peers.

The courts of the land had upheld the manipulators. The *best-efforts, endeavors, whereases,* and *therebys* buried forever the work of an adult lifetime.

The father was rendered impotent, a bewildered eunuch appealing in strained, falsely masculine roars to the unappealable.

And the son was no longer interested in the practice of law.

As with most histories of material success, the factor of coincidence, of timing, played the predominant role. But whenever Andrew Trevayne gave that simple explanation, few believed it. They preferred to look for deeper, more manipulative reasons.

Or in his case an emotional motive, based on revulsion, that lucked in.

Nonsense.

The timing was supplied by the brother of the girl who became his wife. Phyllis Pace's older brother.

Douglas Pace was a brilliant, introverted electronics engineer who worked for Pratt and Whitney in Hartford; a painfully shy man happiest in the isolation of his laboratory, but also a man who knew when he was right and others were wrong. The others in his case were the Pratt and Whitney executives who firmly refused to allocate funds for the development of close-tolerance spheroid discs. Douglas Pace was convinced that the spheroid disc was the single most vital component of the new high-altitude propulsion techniques. He was ahead of his time—but only by about thirty-one months.

Their first "factory" consisted of a small section of an unused warehouse in Meriden; their first machine a third-hand Bullard purchased from a tool-and-die company liquidating its assets; their first jobs odd-lot assignments of simple jet-engine discs for the Pentagon's general contractors, including Pratt and Whitney.

Because their overhead was minuscule and their work sophisticated, they took on a growing number of military subcontracts, until second and third Bullards were installed and the entire warehouse rented. Two years later the airlines made an industry decision: the way of the jet aircraft was the way of the commercial future. Schedules were projected calling for operational passenger carriers by the late fifties, and suddenly all the knowledge acquired in the development of the military jet had to be adapted to civilian needs.

And Douglas Pace's advanced work in spheroid discs was compatible with this new approach; compatible and far ahead of the large corporate manufacturers.

Their expansion was rapid and paid for up front, their backlog of orders so extensive they could have kept ten plants working three shifts for five years.

And Andrew discovered several things about himself. He had been told he was a major salesman, but it didn't take a high degree of salesmanship to corner markets in which the product was so sought after. Instead, other gifts came into play. The first, perhaps, was the soft-science of administration. He wasn't just good; he was superb, and he knew it. He could spot talent and place it under contract—at some other company's loss—in a matter of hours. Gifted men believed him, wanted to believe him, and he was quick to establish the weaknesses of their current situations; to hammer at them and offer viable alternatives. Creative and executive personnel found climates in which they could function, incentives which brought out their best work under his aegis. He could talk to union leadership, too. Talk in ways it readily understood. And no labor contract was ever signed without the precedent he'd fought for in the company's first expansion in New Haven—the productivity clause that locked in wages with the end result of assembly-line statistics. The wage scales were generous, outstripping competition, but never isolated from the end results. He was called "progressive," but he realized that the term was simplistic, misleading. He negotiated on the theory of enlightened self-interest; and he was totally convincing. As the months and years went by, he had a track record to point to; it was irrefutable.

The most surprising asset Andrew found within himself was completely unexpected, even inexplicable. He had the ability to retain the most complex dealings without reference to contracts or notes. He had wondered briefly if he possessed a form of total recall, but Phyllis shot down that conceit by pointing out that he rarely remembered a birthday. Her explanation was, he felt, nearer the truth. She said he never entered any negotiation without absolute commitment, exhaustive analysis. She gently implied that this pattern might be traced to his observation of his father's experience.

It all would have been enough—the airlines, the expansion, the production network that began to extend throughout the Atlantic seaboard. On balance, it should have appeared that they had gone as far as they could hope for; but, suddenly again, the end was nowhere in sight.

For on the night of October 4, 1957, an announcement was made that startled mankind.

Moscow had launched Sputnik I.

The excitement started all over again. National and industrial priorities were about to be altered drastically. The United States of America was relegated to second status, and the pride of the earth's most inventive constituency was wounded, its people perplexed. Restoration to primacy was demanded, the cost inconsequential.

On the evening of the Sputnik news, Douglas Pace had driven out to Andy's home in East Haven, and Phyllis kept the coffee going until four o'clock in the morning. A decision was reached that ensured the Pace-Trevayne Company's emergence as the Space Administration's largest independent contractor of spheroid discs capable of sustaining rocket thrusts of ultimately six hundred thousand pounds. The decision was to concentrate on space. They would maintain a bread-and-butter margin with the airlines, but retool with space objectives, anticipating the problems to merge with the larger aircraft surely to be demanded in the late sixties.

The gamble was enormous, but the combined talents of Pace and Trevayne were ready.

"We reach a remarkable period in this . . . most remarkable document, Mr. Trevayne. It leads directly into the area of our concerns—the President's and mine. It is, of course, related to March of nineteen-fifty-two."

Oh, Christ, Phyllis. They've found it! The "game," you called it. The game that you despised because you said it made me "dirty." It began with that filthy little bastard who dressed like a faggot tailor. It began with Allen. . . .

"Your company made an audacious move," continued Big Billy Hill. "Without guarantees, you restructured seventy percent of your factories—nearly all of your laboratories—to accommodate an uncertain market. Uncertain in the sense of its realistic demand."

"We never doubted the market; we only underestimated the demand."

"Obviously. And you proved correct. While everyone else was still on the drawing board, you were ready for production."

"With respect, Mr. Ambassador, it wasn't that simple. There was a two-year period when the national commitment was more rhetorical than financial. Another six months, and our resources would have been exhausted. We sweated."

"You needed the NASA contracts," said the President. "Without them, you were on dangerous ground; you were in too far to reconvert."

"That's true. We counted on our preparation schedules, our timing. No one could compete with us; we banked on that."

"But the extent of your conversions was known within the industry, wasn't it?" asked Hill.

"Unavoidable."

"And the risks?" Hill again.

"To a degree. We were a privately owned company; we didn't broadcast our financial statement."

"But it could be assumed." Hill was centering in.

"It could."

Hill removed a single sheet of paper from the top of the file, turning its face toward Andrew. "Do you recall this letter? It was written to the Secretary of Defense, with copies to the Senate Appropriations and House Armed Services committees. Dated April 14, 1959."

"Yes. I was angry."

"In it you stated categorically that Pace-Trevayne was wholly owned and in no way associated with any other company or companies."

"That's right."

"When questioned privately, you said you'd been approached by outside interests who implied that their assistance might be necessary to obtain the NASA contracts."

"Yes. I was upset. We were qualified on our own."

Ambassador Hill leaned back and smiled. "This letter, then, was really a highly strategic device, wasn't it? You scared hell out of a lot of people. In essence, it assured you of the work."

"That possibility occurred to me."

"Yet in spite of your proclaimed independence, during the next several years, when Pace-Trevayne became the acknowledged leader in its field, you actively sought outside associations. . . ."

Do you remember, Phyl? You and Doug were furious. You didn't understand.

"There were advantages to be gained."

"I'm sure there were, if you had been serious in your intentions."

"Are you implying that I wasn't?"

Oh, Lord, I was serious, Phyl! I was concerned. I was young and angry.

"I arrived at that conclusion, Mr. Trevayne. I'm sure others did also. . . . You let the word out that you'd be interested in exploratory talks of merger. One by one you held successive conferences with no less than seventeen major defense contractors over a three-year period. A number of these were written up in the newspapers." Hill flipped through the file and removed a sheaf of clippings. "You certainly had an impressive assortment of suitors."

"We had a great deal to offer."

Only "offer," Phyl. Nothing else; never anything else.

"You even went so far as to arrive at tentative agreements with several. There were a number of startling fluctuations on the New York Exchange."

"My accountants will confirm that I was not in the market then."

"With reason?" asked the President.

"With reason," answered Trevayne.

"Yet none of the exploratory conferences, none of these tentative agreements, was ever satisfactorily concluded."

"The obstacles were insurmountable."

The people were insurmountable. The manipulators.

"May I suggest, Mr. Trevayne, that you never intended to reach any firm agreements?"

"You may suggest that, Mr. Ambassador."

"And would it be inaccurate to suggest further that you gained a relatively detailed working knowledge of the financial operations of seventeen major corporations involved in defense spending?"

"Not inaccurate. I'd stress the past tense, however. It was over a decade ago."

"A short period of time when you're talking about corporate policy," said the President. "I imagine that most of the executive personnel remain the same."

"Probably so."

William Hill rose from his chair and took several steps to the edge of the mahogany table. He looked down at Trevayne and spoke quietly, good-naturedly. "You were exorcising a few demons, weren't you?"

Andrew met the old gentleman's eyes and couldn't help himself; he smiled slowly, with a marked degree of defeat. "Yes, I was."

"You were repaying the sort of people who destroyed your father. . . . March, nineteen fifty-two."

"It was childish. A hollow kind of revenge; they weren't responsible."

Remember, Phyl? You told me: "Be yourself. This isn't you, Andy! Stop it!"

"Satisfying, however, I would think." Hill walked around the desk and leaned against the front edge between Trevayne and the President. "You forced a number of powerful men to make concessions, lose time, become defensive; all for a young man barely in his thirties who held a large carrot in front of their faces. I'd say that was very satisfying. What I can't understand is why you so abruptly stopped. If my information is correct, you were in a position of extreme strength. It's not inconceivable that you might have emerged as one of the world's richest men. Certainly possible that you could eventually have ruined a number of those you considered the enemy. Especially in the market."

"I suppose I could say I got religion."

"It's happened before, I'm told," said the President.

"Then let's call it that. . . . It occurred to me—with my wife's help—that I had involved myself in the same form of waste I found so appalling in . . . March of nineteen fifty-two. I was on the other side, but the waste was the same. . . . And that, Mr. President, Mr. Ambassador, is all I care to say about it. I sincerely hope it's acceptable."

Trevayne smiled as best he could, for he *was* sincere.

"Entirely." The President reached for his highball as Hill nodded and returned to his chair. "Our questions have been answered; as the Ambassador said, we were curious, we had to know. Among other things, your state of mind—which, frankly, we never doubted."

"We assumed it to be healthy." Hill laughed as he

spoke. "Anyone who leaves his own company to take on a thankless State Department job and then assumes the headaches of a philanthropic foundation is no ruthless Caesar of the financial world."

"Thank you."

The President leaned forward, locking his eyes with Andrew's. "It's of paramount importance that this job be carried out, Mr. Trevayne; go the distance. The specter of financial and political collusion is always ugly; it becomes worse if it's suspected of being covered up. In other words, once you commit yourself, that's it. There's no turning back."

Andrew realized that the President was giving him his last opportunity to reconsider. But the decision had really been made when he'd first heard the rumors. He knew he was the man to do it. He *wanted* to do it. For many reasons.

Among them, the memory of a Boston courtroom.

"I'd like the post, Mr. President. I won't quit."

"I believe you."

6

Phyllis Trevayne wasn't often annoyed with her husband. He was careless, but she attributed that to his extraordinary concentration on whatever project he currently undertook, not to indifference. He had little patience with the niceties, but he was a nice person, time permitting. Abrupt, but gentle in his relationships. Abrupt even with her sometimes, but always considerate. And he had been there when she needed him most. The awful years.

She was annoyed with him this evening, however.

He had told her—asked her, really—to meet him in town. In the Palm Court at the Plaza Hotel. He specifically had said seven-thirty; there was no reason why he should be late, he'd expressly pointed that out.

It was eight-fifteen, and no message had arrived to explain his absence. She was hungry as hell, among other things. And besides, she had had her own plans for the evening. Both children were leaving for their respective schools within the week; Pamela back to Miss Porter's, Steve to Haverford. Husbands never understood the preparations; there were as many logistic decisions to be made prior to sending children away for three months as there were in most business dealings. Probably more. She had wanted to spend the evening making a few of those decisions, not driving into New York.

Besides, she had a lecture to prepare. Well, not really; that could wait.

She was going to talk to Andy about getting a chauffeur. She hated that goddamned Lincoln. She hated the idea of a chauffeur, too, but she hated the Lincoln more. And Andy wouldn't let her drive a smaller car into New York. When she objected, he produced statistics about the vulnerability of small cars on the highway.

Oh, *damn! damn! damn!* Where was he?

It was eight-twenty now. Carelessness was rapidly becoming rudeness.

She'd ordered a second vermouth-cassis and nearly finished it. It was an innocuous drink, a feminine drink, and the best to sip while waiting, because she didn't really like it. And of course it was necessary that she didn't like it. She was flattered that several men had passed her table and given her second looks. Not at all bad for forty-two— about to be forty-three—and two grown children. She must remember to tell Andy about them. He'd laugh and say something like: What did you expect, you think I married a mongrel?

She had a good sex life, Phyllis reflected. Andy was a passionate man, an inquisitive man. They both enjoyed the bed. What had Tennessee Williams said? Was it Williams? Yes, it had to be. . . . Some character in an early play, a play about Italians . . . Sicilians, had said it. *If the bed's okay, the marriage's okay!* . . . Something like that.

She liked Tennessee Williams. He was a poet as much as a playwright. Perhaps more of a poet.

Suddenly Phyllis Trevayne felt sick, terribly sick. Her eyes lost their focus, the entire Palm Court seemed to spin around and around. And then she heard voices above her.

"Madame, madame! Are you ill? Madame! Boy! Boy! Get smelling salts!"

Other voices, crescendos of volume, a blurring of words . . . nothing made sense, nothing was real. There was a hardness against her face, and she vaguely knew it was the marble floor of the room. Everything began to go dark, black. And then she heard the words.

"I'll take care of her! It's my wife! We've a suite upstairs! Here, give me a hand! It's all right!"

But the voice wasn't that of her husband.

Andrew Trevayne was furious. The taxi he'd taken from his office at Danforth had rammed into a Chevrolet sedan, and the policeman had insisted he remain on the scene until all the statements were taken. The wait was interminable. When he told the police officer he was in a hurry, the patrolman replied that if the passenger in the Chevrolet could wait, prone on his back, for an ambulance, the least Trevayne could do was wait for the statements to be taken.

Twice Trevayne had gone to a corner pay phone to call his wife at the Plaza and explain, but each time he reached the bell captain to have her paged, he was told she wasn't in the Palm Court. The traffic down from Connecticut was probably lousy, and she'd be doubly upset if she arrived late and found him not there.

Goddamn it! Goddamn it!

Finally, at eight-twenty-five, he'd given his statement to the police and was allowed to leave the scene.

As he flagged down another cab, he vaguely thought about the fact that the second time he'd called the Plaza, the bell captain seemed to recognize his voice. Or, at least, the time span between his requesting the paging of his wife and the answer seemed much shorter than on the first call. But Trevayne knew his impatience was heightened when he was angry. Perhaps that was it.

And yet, if that were so, why didn't it seem longer? Not shorter.

*   *   *

"Yes, sir! Yes, sir! The description is the same! She sat right there!"

"Then where *is* she?"

"Her husband, sir! Her husband took her upstairs to their rooms!"

"*I'm* her husband, you goddamned idiot! Now, *tell* me!" Trevayne had the waiter by the throat.

"Please, sir!" The waiter screamed, as most of the Palm Court turned in the direction of the loud voices, heard above the punctuated strains of the violin quartet. Two Plaza house detectives pulled Trevayne's hands away from the pleading waiter. "He said they had rooms—a suite upstairs!"

Trevayne threw the arms off him and raced to the desk. When one of the detectives came up behind him, he did something he wouldn't have thought he was capable of doing. He slammed his fist into the man's neck. The detective fell backward as his fellow officer withdrew a pistol.

Simultaneously, the frightened clerk behind the desk spoke hysterically.

"Here, sir! Trevayne! Mrs. A. Trevayne. Suite Five H and I! The reservation was made this afternoon!"

Trevayne didn't think about the man behind him. He ran to the door marked "Stairs" and raced up the concrete steps. He knew the detective followed; the shouts came at him to stop, but he refused. It was only necessary to reach a suite at the Plaza Hotel marked "Five H and I."

He pushed his full weight into the corridor door and emerged on the thin rug that bespoke of better times. The doors in front of him read "Five A," then "B," then "Five C and D." He rounded the corner and the letters stared him in the face.

"H and I."

The door was locked, and he threw himself against it. It gave only slightly under his weight. Trevayne moved back several feet and slammed the heel of his foot against the lock area.

It cracked, but did not open.

By now the winded, middle-aged house detective approached.

"You goddamn son-of-a-bitch! I could have shot you! Now, get away from there or I *will!*"

"You will *not!* My wife's in there!"

The strident urgency of Trevayne's command had its effect. The detective looked at the panicked husband and lent his own foot to Trevayne's next assault. The door came off the upper left hinge, crashing down obliquely into the short foyer. Trevayne and the detective rushed into the room.

The detective saw what he had to see and turned away. He'd seen it before. He'd wait in the doorframe, both eyes on the husband, to make sure there was no violence.

Phyllis Trevayne was naked in the white sheets of the bed; the covers were at the foot, lumped as if thrown off carelessly. On the night table, on the left side, was a bottle of Drambuie, two glasses half-full.

On Phyllis Trevayne's breasts were lipstick marks. Phalluses outlined toward the nipples.

The detective assumed that somebody had had a ball. He hoped to Christ the third party had left the premises. Goddamn fool if he hadn't.

Phyllis Trevayne sat up in the bed drinking coffee, wrapped in towels. The doctor had finished his examination and motioned to Trevayne to come into the other room.

"I'd say a very powerful sedative, Mr. Trevayne. A Mickey Finn, if you like. There won't be much aftereffect, perhaps a headache, upset stomach."

"Was she . . . was she assaulted?"

"Debatable, without a more thorough examination than I can perform here. If she was, it was a struggle; I don't believe there was penetration. . . . But I think an attempt was made, I won't disguise that."

"She's not aware of the . . . attempt, is she?"

"I'm sorry. Only she can answer that."

"Thank you, doctor."

Trevayne returned to the front room of the suite and took his wife's hand, kneeling down beside her.

"You're a rough old lady, you know that?"

"Andy?" Phyllis Trevayne looked at her husband calmly, but with a fear he rightfully had never seen before. "Whoever it was tried to rape me. I remember that."

"I'm glad you do. He didn't."

"I don't think so. . . . Why, Andy, why?"

"I don't know, Phyl. But I'm going to find out."

"Where *were* you?"

"In a traffic accident. At least, I thought it was an accident. I'm not sure now."

"What are we going to do?"

"Not we, Phyl. Me. I have to reach a man in Washington. I don't want any part of them."

"I don't understand you."

"Neither do I, really. But I think there's a connection."

"The President's in Camp David, Mr. Trevayne. I'm sorry, it wouldn't be convenient to reach him now. What's the matter?"

Trevayne told Robert Webster what had happened to his wife. The presidential aide was speechless.

"Did you hear what I said?"

"Yes. . . . Yes, I did. It's horrible."

"Is that all you can say? Do you know what the President and Hill *told* me last week?"

"I have a good idea. The chief and I discussed it; I explained that."

"Is this connected? I want to know if this is part of it! I have a right to know!"

"I can't answer you. I don't think he could, either. You're at the Plaza? I'll call you back in a few minutes."

Webster hung up, and Andrew Trevayne held the disconnected telephone in his grip. They could all go *screw!* The Senate hearing was scheduled for two-thirty the next afternoon, and he'd tell them all to go to hell! Phyllis was no part of the bargain! It was one thing to go after him; he could handle that. Not his family. He'd level those bastards at two-thirty tomorrow as they'd never been leveled! And he'd hold a press conference afterward. He'd let the whole goddamn country know what kind of pigs inhabited a town called Washington, D.C.! He didn't need it! He was *Andrew Trevayne!*

He replaced the telephone in its cradle and walked over to the hotel bed. Phyllis was asleep. He sat down on a chair and stroked her hair. She moved slightly, started to open her eyes, and then shut them again. She'd been through so much. And now this!

The telephone rang, its bell causing him to jerk his head up, frightened, furious.

He ran to it.

"Trevayne! It's the President. I've just heard. How's your wife?"

"Asleep, sir." Trevayne was amazed at himself. In the midst of his anguish he still found the presence of mind to say "Sir."

"Christ, boy! I haven't any words! What can I say to you? What can I do?"

"Release me, Mr. President. Because if you don't, I'm going to have a great deal to say tomorrow afternoon. Inside the hearing and out."

"Of course, Andrew. It goes without saying." The President of the United States paused before speaking further. "She's all right? Your wife *is* all *right?*"

"Yes, sir. . . . It was a . . . terror tactic, I guess. An obscene . . . *obscene* thing." Trevayne had to hold his breath. He was afraid of the words that might come out of his mouth.

"Trevayne, listen to me. Andrew, listen! You may never forgive me for what I am about to say to you. If you feel strong enough, I'll accept the consequences and expect your roughest condemnation tomorrow. I won't rebut you . . . But you must think now. With your *head*. I've had to do it hundreds of times—granted, not like this—but, nevertheless, when it hurt badly. . . . The country knows you've been chosen. The hearing is only a formality now. If you tell them to shove it up their ass, how are you going to do it without paining your wife further? . . . Don't you see? This is exactly what they want!"

Trevayne took a deep breath and replied evenly. "I have no intention of paining my wife further or of allowing any part of you to touch us. I don't need you, Mr. President. Do I make myself clear?"

"You certainly do. And I agree with you completely. But I have a problem. I need *you*. I said it would be ugly . . ."

Ugly! Ugly! That goddamn terrible word!

"Yes, ugly!" Trevayne roared viciously into the telephone.

The President continued as if Trevayne had not shouted. "I think you should think about what's happened. . . . If it can happen to you, and by all our estimates you're one of the better ones, think what can happen to others. . . . Are we to stop? Is that what we should do?"

"Nobody elected me to anything! I'm not beholden, and you know damn well I'm not! I don't want it to concern me."

"But you know it does. Don't answer me now. Think. . . . Please, talk to your wife. I can postpone the hearing for several days—on illness."

"It won't do any good, Mr. President. I want out."

"Think about it. I ask you to give me a few hours. The *office* asks you that. Speaking as a man and not as your President, however, I must tell you that I'm pleading. The lines are drawn now. We can't turn back. But as a man, I'll understand your refusal. . . . My greatest sympathy and well-wishes to your wife. . . . Good night, Andrew."

Trevayne heard the click of the disconnection and slowly replaced the telephone. He reached into his shirt pocket for his cigarettes, and extracting one, lit it with the all-maroon matches labeled "The Plaza." There wasn't much to think about. He wasn't about to change his mind for the tactics of a very persuasive President.

He was Andrew Trevayne. Every once in a while he had to remind himself of that. He didn't need anyone. Not even the President of the United States.

"Andy?"

Trevayne looked over at the bed. His wife's head was propped sideways against the pillow, and her eyes were open.

"Yes, darling?" He got out of the chair and walked rapidly to the bedside. His wife was only half-conscious.

"I heard. I heard what you said."

"Just don't worry about a thing. The doctor'll be back in the morning; we'll head up to Barnegat first thing. You're fine. Sleep now."

"Andy?"

"What, sweetheart?"

"He wants you to stay, doesn't he?"

"It doesn't make any difference what he wants."

"He's right. Don't you see that? If you quit . . . they've beaten you."

Phyllis Trevayne shut her eyes deliberately. Andrew felt deeply for the pained expression on her exhausted face. Then he realized as he watched his wife that her pain was mixed with something else.

With loathing. With anger.

Walter Madison closed the door of his study and turned the brass knob, locking himself in. He'd gotten the call from Trevayne at the restaurant, and in spite of his panic, had followed Andy's instructions. He'd reached the Plaza security man and made sure no police report would be filed. Trevayne was adamant that Phyllis be spared— the family, the children, spared—any press coverage of the assault. Phyllis couldn't help with descriptions of either the man or the event; everything had been blurred for her, incoherent.

The Plaza security man had read something else into Madison's instructions—the explicit instructions of the powerful attorney for the more powerful Andrew Trevayne— and didn't bother disguising his interpretation. For several minutes Madison had considered offering the man money, but the lawyer in him prevented that; retired police officers adding to their pensions in stylish hotels had a proclivity for stretching out such understandings.

Better the man believe what he wanted to believe. There was nothing criminal involved, so long as the hotel property was paid for.

Madison sat down at his desk; he saw that both his hands shook. Thank God his wife was asleep. Asleep or passed out, what difference?

He tried to understand, tried to put everything into perspective, into some kind of order.

It had begun three weeks ago, with one of the most lucrative offers of his career. A silent retainer, conceived and executed in confidence. With him alone, unrelated to his partners or his firm. It wasn't an unusual practice, although he had entered into very few such agreements. Too often they weren't worth the strain—or the secrecy.

This agreement was. Seventy-five thousand dollars a year. Untaxable, untraceable. Paid out of Paris into a Zurich account. Length of contract: forty-eight months. Three hundred thousand dollars.

Nor was there any attempt to hide the reasons behind the offer.

Andrew Trevayne.

He, Walter Madison, was Trevayne's attorney; he had been for over a decade.

The conflict—so far—was minor. As Trevayne's lawyer he was to advise his new clients of any startling or extraordinary information related to Andrew and this proposed subcommittee—which wasn't even in existence as yet. And there was no guarantee that Andrew would advise *him*.

That was understood.

The risk was undertaken solely by the clients; they understood that.

It was entirely possible that no conflict would ever arise. Even if it did, whatever information he might transmit *could* be unearthed from a dozen sources. And in his bracket, it would take him a considerable length of time to bank three hundred thousand dollars.

But his agreement tolerated nothing in the area of what happened that evening at the Plaza.

Nothing!

To associate him with such an act was beyond imagination.

He unlocked the top drawer of his desk and withdrew a small leather notebook. He thumbed to the letter "K" and wrote the number on a scratch pad.

He picked up his telephone and dialed.

"Senator? Walter Madison. . . ."

A few minutes later the attorney's hands stopped trembling.

There was no connection between his new clients and the events of the evening at the Plaza Hotel.

The Senator had been horrified. And frightened.

7

The closed hearing comprised eight senators, as diversified as possible within the opposing camps, and the candidate for confirmation, Andrew Trevayne.

Trevayne took his seat, Walter Madison beside him, and looked up at the raised platform. On the platform was the usual long table with the necessary number of chairs, microphones in their places in front of each chair, and the flag of the United States centered against the wall. A small desk with a stenotype machine was below the platform on the main level.

Men were standing around in groups talking with one another, gesturing with quiet intensity. The clock reached two-thirty, and the groups began to disperse. An elderly man Trevayne recognized as the senior Senator from Nebraska—or was it Wyoming—climbed the three steps of the platform and walked to one of the two center chairs. His name was Gillette. He reached over for a gavel and lightly tapped it.

"May we clear the room, please?"

It was the sign for those not part of the hearing to leave quickly. Last-second instructions were given and received, and Trevayne was aware that he was the object of a great many looks. A youngish man dressed in a sober, dark suit approached the table and put an ashtray in front of Trevayne. He smiled awkwardly, as if he wished he could say something. It was a curious moment.

The panel of senators began assembling; cordialities were exchanged. Trevayne saw that the smiles were abrupt, artificial; a taut atmosphere prevailed. It was emphasized by an incident that would have gone unnoticed under more relaxed conditions. Senator Alan Knapp, mid-forties, straight black hair combed carefully back from his wide forehead, pressed the button on his microphone and blew through the meshed globe. The amplified rush of air caused a number of the panel to react sharply. They looked—

apprehensively, perhaps—at their colleague. It might have been Knapp's reputation for uncompromising investigation, even rudeness, that made the reactions so totally serious. Another curious moment.

Old Senator Gillette—Wyoming? No, it was Nebraska, thought Trevayne—perceived the tension and rapidly, softly tapped the gavel. He cleared his throat and assumed the responsibility of the chair.

"Gentlemen. Distinguished colleagues, Mr. Undersecretary. Senate hearing number six-four-one commences session on this date at the hour of two-thirty; so let the record state."

As the stenotypist, staring at nothing, effortlessly touched the muted keys, Trevayne realized that the "Undersecretary" was himself. He had been "Mr. Undersecretary"; *an* undersecretary, one of many.

"Having been appointed generously by my colleagues as chairman of this hearing, I shall open with the usual statement outlining the purposes of our gathering. At the conclusion of this brief statement I welcome any additions or clarifications—I hope no contradictions, as our objective is fully bipartisan."

There were perceptible nods of agreement, several unhumored smiles, one or two deep breaths signifying the start of Senate hearing six-four-one. Gillette reached for a folder in front of him and opened it. His voice had the drone of a court-martial charge.

"The state of the defense economy is appalling; an opinion shared by every knowledgeable citizen. As elected representatives, it is our duty-by-oath to use the powers granted us by the Constitution to ascertain these deficiencies and correct them wherever possible. We can and should do no less. We have made provision for the forming of an investigative subcommittee, so requested by the Defense Allocation Commission—a subcommittee the purpose of which is to make a thorough study of the major contracts now existing and submitted for congressional approval between the Department of Defense and those corporations doing business with Defense. To limit the scope of the inquiry—and surely it must be limited, for reasons of time—an arbitrary contractual figure of one-point-five million has been suggested for the subcommittee's guidelines. All Defense agreements in excess of this amount are subject to the scrutiny of the subcommittee. It will, however, be at the discretion of the subcommittee to make all such investigatory decisions.

"Our purpose this afternoon is to examine and confirm or deny the appointment of Mr. Andrew Trevayne, formerly Undersecretary of State, to the position of chairman of the above-mentioned subcommittee. This hearing is closed, and the record will remain classified for an indeterminate period, so I urge my colleagues to search their consciences, and where doubts exist, should they exist, express them. Again, further—"

"Mr. Chairman." Andrew Trevayne's soft-spoken, hesitant interruption so startled everyone in the room that even the stenotypist lost his appearance of uninterest and looked over at the man who had dared to interrupt the opening remarks of the chair. Walter Madison instinctively reached out and put his hand on Trevayne's arm.

"Mr. Trevayne? . . . Mr. Undersecretary?" asked the bewildered Gillette.

"I apologize. . . . Perhaps this isn't the time; I'm sorry."

"What is it, sir?"

"It was a matter of clarification; it can wait. My apologies again."

"Mr. Chairman!" It was the aquiline Senator Knapp. "The Undersecretary's lack of courtesy to the chair is strange, indeed. If he has anything to say in the nature of clarification, it certainly *can* wait for the proper time."

"I'm not that familiar with procedures, Senator. I didn't want it to slip my mind. You're right, of course." Trevayne reached for a pencil, as if to write a note.

"It must have struck you as most pertinent, Mr. Undersecretary." It was the Senator from New Mexico who now spoke; a man in his fifties, a respected chicano. It was apparent that he disliked Alan Knapp's intimidating rebuke.

"It did, sir." Trevayne lowered his eyes to the paper. There was a momentary silence in the room. The interruption was now complete.

"Very well, Mr. Trevayne." Senator Gillette seemed unsure of himself. "It's quite possible that you are correct, though unorthodox. I've never held to the theory that the chair's remarks were sacrosanct. I've been tempted far too often to cut them short myself. Please. Your clarification, Mr. Undersecretary."

"Thank you, sir. You stated that it was the responsibility of this panel to search for and express doubts. . . . I'm not sure how to say it, but I feel that a similar responsibility is shared by this table. Quite honestly, I've had doubts myself, Mr. Chairman."

"Doubts, Mr. Trevayne?" asked Mitchell Armbruster, the small, compact Senator from California whose wit was as much a part of his reputation as his judgment. "We're born with doubts; at least, we grow to recognize them. What doubts do you refer to? Pertinent to this hearing, I mean."

"That this subcommittee will be given the degree of cooperation it needs in order to function. I sincerely hope the panel will consider the implications of this question."

"That sounds suspiciously like an ultimatum, Mr. Trevayne." Knapp spoke.

"Not at all, Senator; that would be totally unwarranted."

"It nevertheless strikes me that your 'implications' are insulting. Is it your intention to put the Senate of the United States on trial here?" continued Knapp.

"I wasn't aware that this was a trial," replied Trevayne pleasantly, without answering the question.

"Damn good point," added Armbruster with a smile.

"Very well, Mr. Undersecretary," said Gillette. "Your clarification has been placed into the record and duly noted by this panel. Is that satisfactory?"

"It is, and thank you again, Mr. Chairman."

"Then I shall conclude my opening remarks, and we may proceed."

Gillette droned on for several minutes, outlining the questions which should be raised and answered. They fell into two categories. First, the qualifications of Andrew Trevayne for the position under consideration, and second, the all-important factor of conceivable conflicts of interest.

At his conclusion, the chairman made the customary statement. "Any additions or clarifications, beyond Mr. Trevayne's previous inclusions?"

"Mr. Chairman?"

"The Senator from Vermont is recognized."

James Norton, early sixties, close-cropped gray hair, down-easter accent very pronounced, looked at Trevayne. "Mr. Undersecretary. The distinguished chairman has described the areas of this inquiry in his usual clear and forthright manner. And we certainly will raise the questions of competence and conflict. However, I submit there is a third territory that should be explored. That is your philosophy, Mr. Undersecretary. You might say, where you *stand*. Would you grant that privilege to us?"

"No objections, Senator." Trevayne smiled. "I might even hope that we could exchange such views. My own and the panel's collective position, of course, relative to the subcommittee."

"*We* are not standing for confirmation!" Alan Knapp's voice crackled harshly through the speakers.

"I respectfully refer the Senator to my previous remarks," answered Trevayne softly.

"Mr. Chairman?" Walter Madison placed his hand once more on Trevayne's arm and looked up at the platform. "May I have a word with my client, if you please."

"Certainly, Mr. . . . Madison."

The Senate panel, in the courtesy of such hearings, talked among themselves and shuffled papers. Most, however, kept their eyes on Trevayne and Walter Madison.

"Andy, what are you doing? Are you trying to deliberately confuse the issues?"

"I made my point. . . ."

"Unforgettably. Why?"

"I want to make sure there's no misunderstanding. I want this record to specify—not indicate, but *specify*—that I'm putting everyone on notice. If they clear me, they do so knowing what I expect from them."

"For God's sake, man, you're reversing the function of the hearing. You're confirming the *Senate!*"

"I guess I am."

"What's your point? What are you trying to do?"

"Setting up the battleground. If they take me, it won't be because they want to; they'll have to. It'll be because I've challenged them."

"Challenged them? What for? What about?"

"Because there's a profound difference between us."

"What does *that* mean?"

"It means we're natural enemies." Trevayne smiled.

"You're crazy!"

"If I am, I'll apologize. Let's get this over with." Trevayne looked up at the panel. He took the time to rest his eyes on each place, each member. "Mr. Chairman, my attorney and I have concluded our discussion."

"Yes. Yes, of course. . . . I believe the Senator from Vermont submitted an addition in the form of the Undersecretary's . . . basic philosophy. The chair assumes that to mean *fundamental* political beliefs—not *partisan*—but of a more general application. None other are pertinent to this hearing." Gillette looked over his glasses at Vermont's Norton, so to be sure he understood his meaning.

"Perfectly acceptable, Mr. Chairman."

"I was hoping it would be, Senator," added California's Armbruster with a chuckle. Armbruster and Norton were not only from different sides of the aisle, but as separated in partisan politics as their states were in geography.

Knapp spoke without petitioning the chair. "If I'm not mistaken, the Undersecretary countered our colleague's addition with one of his own. I think he said he reserved the right to raise similar questions with the members of this panel. A right I seriously doubt should be granted."

"I don't believe I made such a request, Senator." Trevayne spoke softly but with firmness into his microphone. "If it was so construed, I apologize. I *have* no right—or reason—to question your individual persuasions. I'm concerned only that this panel, as one deliberative body, assure me, as I must assure it, of a sense of commitment. A *collective* commitment."

"Mr. Chairman?" The petitioner was the elderly Senator from West Virginia, a man named Talley. He was little known outside the club, but within it was well liked, as much for his easygoing temperament as for his intelligence.

"Senator Talley."

"I'd like to ask Mr. Trevayne why he even raises the issue. We want the same thing; none of us would be here otherwise. Frankly, I thought this would be one of the shortest hearings on record. Speaking personally, I have great confidence in you, sir. Isn't that confidence returned? If not personally, at least collectively—to use your term, sir?"

Trevayne looked over at the chairman, silently requesting permission to answer the question. Senator Gillette nodded.

"Of course, it is, Senator Talley. And immense respect. It's precisely because of my confidence *in* you, my respect *for* you, that I wish to be able to refer to this transcript and have it specify that we've understood each other. The subcommittee for the Defense Commission will be impotent unless it has the responsible backing of such impartial and influential men as yourselves." Trevayne paused and ingenuously looked from one side of the panel table to the other. "If you confirm me, gentlemen, and incidentally, I hope that you do, I'm going to need help."

The West Virginian did not notice the discomfort of several colleagues. "Let me then rephrase my supplication, Mr. Undersecretary. I'm old enough, or naïve enough, or perhaps both, to believe that men of good will—albeit different opinions—can join together in a common cause. The confidence you seek in us I might hope would be documented by what we say to one another in this room. Should it not be to your satisfaction, you have every right to bring it up. Why not find out first?"

"I couldn't hope for sounder advice, Senator Talley. I'm afraid my initial nervousness clouded my perspective. I'll try not to raise the issue again."

Gillette, peering once more over his glasses, looked at Trevayne, and when he spoke, it was clear that he was annoyed. "You may raise whatever issues you wish, sir. As will this panel." He looked down at the legal pad in front of him, at his own notations. "Senator Norton. You brought up the aspect of Mr. Trevayne's general philosophy. Would you amplify—briefly, if you please—so we may clear the question and get on. I presume you wish to be satisfied that our guest at least nominally endorses the fundamental laws of the land."

"Mr. Undersecretary." Norton's heavy Vermont dialect seemed more pronounced than necessary as he eyed the candidate. Norton always knew when to use the Yankee approach. It had served him well in many such Senate hearings—especially when television cameras were on the premises. It made him seem so bound-to-the-earth American. "I shall be brief; for both our sakes. . . . I'd like to ask you if you *do* subscribe to the political system under which this country lives?"

"Of course, I do." Trevayne was surprised by the naïveté of the question. But not for long.

"Mr. Chairman . . ." Alan Knapp spoke as if on cue. "I, for one, am frankly disturbed by an aspect of the Undersecretary's political history. Mr. Undersecretary, you're what is known as an . . . independent, if I'm not mistaken."

"That's correct."

"That's interesting. Of course, I'm aware that in many sectors the term 'political independent' is revered. It has a nice, rugged sound to it."

"That's not my intention, Senator."

"But there's another aspect of such a posture," continued Knapp without acknowledging Trevayne's answer. "And I don't find it particularly independent. . . . Mr. Trevayne, it's true, is it not, that your companies profited considerably from government contracts—especially during the maximum space expenditures?"

"True. I think we justified whatever profits we made."

"I would hope so. . . . I wonder, however, if your lack of partisanship wasn't perhaps shaped by other than ideological motivations. By being neither on one side nor the other, you certainly removed yourself from any political conflict, didn't you?"

"Again, not my intention."

"I mean, it would be difficult for anyone to take issue with you on political grounds, since your opinions were . . . are . . . buried under the classification of 'independent.' "

"Just one minute, Senator!" The chairman, visibly upset, spoke sharply.

"I'd like to comment, if I may—"

"You *may*, Mr. Trevayne, after my own observations. Senator Knapp, I thought I'd made it clear that this is a bipartisan hearing. I find your remarks irrelevant and, frankly, distasteful. Now, you may comment, Mr. Undersecretary."

"I'd like to inform the Senator that anyone, at any time, may ascertain my political opinions by simply asking for them. I'm not shy. On the other hand, I wasn't aware that government contracts were granted on the basis of political affiliations."

"Exactly my point, Mr. Trevayne." Knapp turned toward the center of the table. "Mr. Chairman, in my seven years in the Senate I have many times supported those whose politics differed from my own and, conversely, denied support to members of my own party. In such cases my approval or disapproval was based on the specific questions on the floor. As men of conscience, we all practice the same ethics. What bothers me about our candidate is that he elects to be called 'non-partisan.' That worries me. I fear such people in places of power. I wonder at their so-called *independence*. I wonder, if, instead, it's merely a convenience to be a companion of the strongest wind?"

There was a momentary silence in the room. Gillette removed his glasses and turned toward Knapp.

"Hypocrisy is a most serious insinuation, Senator."

"Forgive me, Mr. Chairman. You asked us to search our consciences. . . . As was pointed out by Justice Brandeis, honesty by itself is not enough. The appearance of integrity must be concomitant. Caesar's wife, Mr. Chairman."

"Are you suggesting, Senator, that I join a political party?" asked Trevayne incredulously.

"I'm not suggesting anything. I'm raising doubts, which is the function of this panel."

John Morris, Senator from Illinois, broke his silence.

He was the youngest man on the panel, in his mid-thirties, and a brilliant attorney. Whenever Morris was assigned to a committee, he was invariably called the "house teenager." It was a substitute for another phrase. For Morris was black, a Negro who had swiftly worked his way up within the system. "You haven't . . . Oh, Mr. Chairman?"

"Go ahead, Senator."

"You haven't raised a doubt, Mr. Knapp. You've made an accusation. You've accused a large segment of the voting public of potential deceit. You've relegated it to a position of . . . of a second-class franchise. I understand the subtleties you employ, even grant their validity in certain situations. I don't think they apply here."

The Senator from New Mexico, the admired chicano, leaned forward and looked at Morris as he spoke. "There are two of us here who understand only too well the meaning of a second-class franchise, Senator. In my opinion, the issue is valid—to be raised, that is. One always looks for checks and balances; that's the meaning of our system. However, I think, also, that once having been raised, the issue can be put to rest by a succinct answer from the man standing for confirmation. . . . Mr. Undersecretary? For the record, may we assume that you are not a . . . sworn companion of the wind? That your judgments are, indeed, as independent as your politics?"

"You may, sir."

"That's what I thought. I have no further questions on this subject."

"Senator?"

"Yes, Mr. Trevayne?"

"Are yours?"

"I beg your pardon?"

"Are yours? Are your judgments—and the judgments of every member of this panel—independent of external pressures?"

Several senators started talking angrily at once into their microphones; Armbruster of California laughed, Senator Weeks of Maryland's Eastern Shore stifled a smile by withdrawing a handkerchief from his well-tailored blazer, and the chairman reached for the gavel.

As order was restored by the rapid clatter of Gillette's hammer, Vermont's Norton touched the sleeve of Senator Knapp. It was a sign. Their eyes met, and Norton shook his head—imperceptibly, but the message was clear.

Knapp lifted up the pad in front of him and unobtrusively removed a file folder. He reached down for his briefcase and opened it, slipping the folder inside.

On the top of the folder was a name: "Mario de Spadante."

8

The recess was called at four-fifteen, the hearing to be resumed at five o'clock. The forty-five minutes would give everyone a chance to call home, rearrange minor schedules, confer with aides, dismiss assistants outside.

Since the eruption of Andrew's polite but explosively unexpected question, Gillette had managed to steer the inquiry rapidly through the ensuing invective and reach less abstract ground in Trevayne's qualifications.

Andrew was prepared; his answers were quick, concise, and complete. He surprised even Walter Madison, who was rarely surprised by his extraordinary client. Trevayne had no need of the numerous pages and charts filled with past figures and long-ago estimates. He rattled off facts and explanations with such assurance that even those who tried to sustain their antagonism found it difficult.

His total command of his own past economic relationships frequently left the panel speechless—and led Senator Gillette to voice the opinion that following a recess, they might conclude the hearing by seven that night—at the latest.

"You're hot on all burners, Andy," said Madison, stretching as he rose from his chair.

"I haven't begun, counselor. That's in act two."

"Don't revert to Charlie Brown, *please*. You're doing fine. We'll be out of here by six o'clock. They think you're a computer, with a human thought process; don't louse it up."

"Tell *them,* Walter. Tell them not to louse it up."

"Jesus, Andy! What are you—"

"Very impressive performance, young man." The elderly Talley, the former county judge from the state of West Virginia, walked up to the two of them, unaware that he was intruding.

"Thank you, sir. My attorney, Walter Madison."

The men shook hands.

"You must feel somewhat unnecessary, I should think, Mr. Madison. It's not often you high-powered New York lawyers get off so easy."

"I'm used to it with him, Senator. It's the most undeserved retainer in legal history."

"Which means it isn't, or you couldn't afford to say so. I was on the bench for damn near twenty years."

Alan Knapp joined the group, and Trevayne felt himself grow tense. He didn't like Knapp, not only because of his unwarranted rudeness, but because Knapp had about him the unhealthy look of an inquisitor. What had Ambassador Hill said? What were Big Billy's words? " . . . we don't want an inquisitor . . ."

But the Knapp now standing in front of Trevayne did not seem to be the same man who sat so coldly on the dais. He was smiling affably, infectiously, as he shook Trevayne's hand.

"You're doing splendidly! You really are. You must have boned up for this like the chief does for a televised press conference. . . . Senator? Mr. Madison?"

Hands were again shaken, the camaraderie so opposed to the atmosphere of five minutes ago. Trevayne felt uncomfortable, artificial; and he didn't like the feeling.

"You're not making it any easier for me," he said, smiling coldly at Knapp.

"Oh, Lord, don't personalize it, man. I do my job; you do yours. Right, Madison? Isn't that right, Senator?"

West Virginia's Talley did not agree as quickly as Madison. "I suppose so, Alan. I'm not a scrapper, so I don't cotton to the unpleasantness. Must admit, though, it doesn't bother most of you."

"Never think about it. . . ."

"I'll substantiate that, gentlemen." It was Armbruster of California, who spoke between puffs on his pipe. "Nice work, Trevayne. . . . Tell you all something. Knapp was in the process of crucifying his—the President's—H.E.W. man, I mean nailing him hands and feet, and yet when the hearing was over, the two of them couldn't wait to talk to each other. I thought, 'God damn, they're young enough to start throwing punches!' Instead, they were hurrying out to get a taxi. Their wives were waiting for them at a restaurant. You're an original, Senator."

Knapp laughed. "Did you know he was an usher at my wedding fifteen years ago? The President's H.E.W. appointment?"

"Mr. Undersecretary?" At first the title didn't register on Trevayne. Then a hand was placed on his shoulder. It was Norton of Vermont. "May I see you a minute?"

Trevayne stepped away from the group as Madison and Knapp argued a fine point of law and Armbruster questioned Talley as to the upcoming autumn hunting in West Virginia.

"Yes, Senator?"

"I'm sure everyone's told you by now. You're tacking right through the rough waters, and a port's in sight. We'll be outta here by twelve bells. . . ."

"I'm from Boston, Senator, and I like sailing, but I'm not a whaling man. What is it?"

"Very well. We'll eliminate the compliments—though you deserve them, let me tell you. I've conferred briefly with several of my colleagues; as a fact, we also spoke at length before the hearing. We want you to know that we feel as the President does. You're the very best man for the job."

"You'll forgive me if I find the methods of endorsement a little strange."

Norton smiled the thin-lipped smile of a Yankee tradesman—and he was trading now, no doubt about it. "Not strange, Trevayne. Merely necessary. You see, young fella, you're in the hot spot. In case anything goes wrong—which nobody thinks will, by the way—this hearing's got to be one of the strongest on record. Try to understand that; it's nothing personal."

"That's what Knapp said."

"He's right. . . . I don't suppose old Talley understands, though. Hell, down in West Virginia they don't even put up a man to run against him. Not seriously, that is."

"Then Talley isn't one of the colleagues you met with."

"Frankly, no."

"And you still haven't said what you wanted to say, have you?"

"Goddamn, fella, just slow down! I'm trying to explain a point of procedure so you'll understand. The confirmation's yours. . . . That is, it will be, unless you force us into opposition. None of us would like that."

Trevayne looked hard at Norton; he'd seen many lean and wrinkled men like this bending over farm fences or squinting beyond the dunes out at the sea in Marblehead. One never knew how much perception was hidden in those weathered eyes. "Look, Senator, all I want from this panel is the assurance that the subcommittee will act as a free agent. If I can't get your active assistance, I at least need your guarantee that you'll protect the subcommittee from interference. Is that so much to ask?"

Norton spoke laconically, the Yankee peddler fingering his merchandise. "Free agent? Eheah. . . . Well, let me tell you, son. Some people get a touch nervous when a man insists that he's got to be a . . . free agent; that he won't tolerate pressures. You can't help but wonder. There's good pressures and not-so-good pressures. Nobody likes the latter, but good pressures, that's something else again. It's comforting to know that a man is accountable to somebody other than God, isn't that so?"

"Certainly, I'd be accountable. I never expected otherwise."

"But it's kind of a second thought, isn't it? . . . The intent of this subcommittee is not to satisfy the personal ego of any one man, Trevayne. It has a job to do that's bigger than any one person. You may not have the tem-

perament for it. That's what I mean by 'intent.' We don't
want a Savonarola."

Norton held Trevayne's eyes with his own. The Yankee was trading abstractions as though they were horse-
flesh, and he was good at it. He never once hinted that he
was anything but the philosophical salt of the good brown
earth.

Trevayne stared back, trying to pry loose the hypocrisy he felt was behind Norton's words. It wasn't possible.

"You'll have to make that decision, Senator."

"Do you mind if I have a word with your attorney?
What's his name?"

"Madison. Walter Madison. No objection at all. However, I think he'll tell you that I'm a terrible client. He's
convinced I never pay attention when I should."

"No harm trying, young fella. You're obstinate. But I
like you." Norton turned and walked toward Madison and
Knapp.

Trevayne looked at his watch. In twenty minutes the
hearing would resume. He'd try the hotel and see if
Phyllis was back from shopping. The President had urged
him to bring her down. He wanted Phyllis to come to the
White House with her husband after the hearing. Another
photograph would be taken showing the President endorsing Trevayne personally—this time with Trevayne's wife
by his side. Phyllis had understood.

James Norton extended his hand to Madison and if
anyone in the room had been watching them it would
have been assumed that the Senator was merely introduc-
ing himself.

It wasn't the case.

"Goddamn, Madison! What the hell *is* this!?" Norton
spoke with quiet urgency. "He smells something! You
didn't tell us that!"

"I didn't *know* it! I just told Knapp, I don't know
what's going on."

"You'd better find out," said Alan Knapp coldly.

The hearing resumed at seven minutes past five, the
delay due to three senators unable to complete their outside business. The seven minutes, however, gave Walter

Madison a chance to speak with his client alone at the table.

"That fellow Norton talked to me."

"I know; he asked permission." Trevayne smiled.

"Andy, there's a logic in what he says. They're not going to confirm you if they think you're going to play power broker. If you were in their shoes, you wouldn't either. You'd be rougher than they are, and I think you know that."

"Agreed."

"What's bothering you, then?"

Trevayne spoke, looking straight ahead. "I'm not that sure I want the job, Walter. I certainly don't want it if I can't do it my way. I told you that; I said it to Baldwin and Robert Webster, too." Trevayne now turned to his attorney. "There're nothing in my record that gives credence to the Savonarola charge."

"The what?"

"That's what Norton threw at me. Savonarola. You called it 'power broker.' That's not me, and they know it. . . . If I'm confirmed, I've got to be able to walk into the office of every senator on this panel, and if I need assistance, get it without argument. I *must* be able to do that. . . . This panel wasn't chosen indiscriminately, by straws. Each of these men's states is heavily committed to Pentagon contracts; a few less than the others, but they're a minority—window dressing. The Senate knew exactly what it was doing when it put this crowd together. The only way I can make sure that subcommittee isn't interfered with by the Senate is to force these watchdogs of their own constituencies on the defensive."

"What?"

"Make them justify themselves to me . . . in the transcript. This panel will have to go on record as being a necessary adjunct to the subcommittee. A working partnership."

"They won't do it! The purpose here is to confirm you, that's all. There're no other requirements."

"There is if I make perfectly clear that the subcommittee can't function without the cooperation of the Senate, the active participation of this panel in particular. If I can't get a commitment from *them,* there's no point in continuing."

Madison stared at his client. "And what'll you gain by this?"

"They become a working part of the . . . inquisition. Each man an inquisitor himself, none sure of the extent of his 'distinguished colleague's' involvement . . . Share the wealth, share the responsibility."

"And share the risks?" asked Madison softly.

"You said it; I didn't."

"What happens if they turn you down?"

Trevayne looked up at the gathering panel of senators. His eyes were remote, his voice flat and cold. "I'll call a press conference tomorrow morning that will rip this goddamn city apart."

Walter Madison knew there was nothing more to be said.

Trevayne knew it had to come out of the proceedings. Come as a slowly revealed necessity; logically, without stress. He wondered who would say the words first and force the question.

Not surprisingly, it was old Senator Talley, the gnarled county judge from West Virginia; a minority member, window dressing. Not one of Norton's "colleagues."

It happened at five-fifty-seven. Talley leaned forward, looking at the chair; receiving the floor, he turned to the candidate and spoke.

"Mr. Trevayne, if I understand you, and I think I do, your primary concern is the degree of practical cooperation you'll get from those of us who can offer it. I can understand that; it's a valid point. . . . Well, you should know, sir, that the Senate of the United States is not merely a great deliberative body, but a coming together of dedicated gentlemen. I'm sure I speak for all when I tell you that *my* office is open to you, sir. There are a number of government installations in the state of West Virginia; I hope you'll use whatever information my office can provide."

My God, thought Trevayne, he's utterly sincere. Government installations!

"Thank you, Senator Talley. Not only for your offer,

but for clarifying a practical issue. Thank you again, sir. I would hope that you speak for all."

California's Armbruster smiled and spoke slowly. "Would you have any reason to think otherwise?"

"None whatsoever."

"But you'd feel more confident," continued the Californian, "more desirous of our endorsement, if the proceedings this afternoon included a joint resolution to aid your subcommittee in every way we can."

"I would, Senator."

Armbruster turned to the center of the table. "I find nothing objectionable in that request, Mr. Chairman."

"So be it." Gillette had been staring at Trevayne. He rapped his gavel harshly, just once. "Let the record state . . ."

It happened. One by one the senators made their individual statements, each as sincere, each as genuine as the preceding declaration.

Trevayne sat back in his chair and listened to the well-chosen words, abstracting phrases he knew he would soon commit to memory. He had managed it; he had maneuvered the panel into its voluntary resolution. It made little difference that few, if any, would honor the words. It would be nice but it didn't really matter. What mattered was the fact that he could point to them, quote them repeatedly.

Webster at the White House had promised him a copy of the transcript; it would be a simple thing to leak isolated sections to the press.

Gillette looked down from his perch of sanctum sanctorum at Trevayne. His voice was flat, his eyes—enlarged behind the bifocal lenses of his glasses—cold and hostile.

"Does the candidate wish to make a statement before he is excused?"

Andrew returned the chairman's stare. "I do, sir."

"I might hope it could be brief, Mr. Undersecretary," said Gillette. "The panel must try to conclude its business —at the President's request—and the hour is late."

"I'll be brief, Mr. Chairman." Trevayne separated a page from the papers in front of him and looked up at the senators. He did not smile; he did not convey any measure of emotion whatsoever. He spoke simply. "Before you conclude the business of confirming or denying my appointment, gentlemen, I think you should be aware of the results of the preliminary studies I've made. They will serve as the basis for my approach—the subcommittee's approach—should confirmation be granted. And since this is a closed hearing, I'm confident that my remarks will go no farther. . . . I have spent the past several weeks—courtesy of the Controller General's office—analyzing the defense commitments with the following companies and corporations: Lockheed Aircraft, I.T.T. Corporation, General Motors, Ling-Tempco, Litton, and Genessee Industries. It is my judgment that one, two or possibly three have acted either individually or in concert to achieve extraordinary authority within the decision-making processes of the federal government; this is malfeasance in the extreme. From everything I've been able to fit together, I must tell you now that I firmly believe it is one company that has been primarily involved in this malfeasance. I recognize the severity of the charge; it will be my intention to justify it, and until I do, I will not name that company. That is my statement, Mr. Chairman."

The room was silent. Each member of the panel kept his eyes on Andrew Trevayne; none spoke, none moved.

Senator Gillette reached for the gavel, then stopped and withdrew his hand. He spoke quietly.

"You are excused, Mr. Undersecretary. . . . And thank you."

9

Trevayne paid the taxi and got out in front of the hotel. It was warm, the night breeze tepid. September in Washington. He looked at his watch; it was nearly nine-thirty, and he was starved. Phyllis had said she would order dinner in their rooms. She claimed to be exhausted from shopping; a quiet dinner upstairs was just what she wanted. A quiet dinner with two round-the-clock guards—courtesy of the White House—in the hotel corridor. A goddamned hotel corridor.

Trevayne started for the revolving door on the right when a chauffeur who'd been standing by the main entrance came up to him.

"Mr. Trevayne?"

"Yes?"

"Would you be so kind, sir?" The man gestured toward the curb, to a black Ford LTD, obviously a government-rented automobile. Trevayne approached the car and saw Senator Gillette, his glasses still on the bridge of his nose, his expression still half-scowling, seated in the back. The window electronically rolled down, and the old gentleman leaned forward.

"Could you spare me five minutes, Mr. Undersecretary? Laurence here will just drive us around the block."

"Of course." Trevayne climbed into the back seat.

"Most everyone thinks spring in Washington is the best season," said Gillette as the car started off down the street. "I don't. I've always enjoyed autumn better. But then, I'm contrary."

"Not necessarily. Or maybe I'm contrary, too. September and October are the best months for me. Especially in New England."

"Hell, everybody says that. All your poets. . . . The colors, I imagine."

"Probably." Trevayne looked at the politician, and his expression carried the message.

"But I didn't ask you to take a drive in order to discuss your New England autumn, did I?"

"I wouldn't think so."

"No, no, of course, I didn't. . . . Well, you have your confirmation. Are you pleased?"

"Naturally."

"That's gratifying," said the Senator with disinterest, looking out the window. "You'd think the traffic would ease up by now, but it won't. Goddamn tourists; they should turn off the Mall lights. All the lights." Gillette turned to Trevayne. "In all my years in Washington, I've never seen such an insufferable display of tactical arro-

gance, Mr. Undersecretary. . . . Perhaps you were sub-
tler, with more honeybuckets, than Bloated Joe—I refer
to the deceased and not too distinguished McCarthy, of
course—but your objectives were every bit as censurable."

"I don't agree with you."

"Oh? . . . If it *wasn't* tactical, it was instinctive. That's
even more dangerous. If I believed that, I'd reconvene
the hearing and do my damnedest to have you denied."

"Then you should have made your feelings known
this afternoon."

"What? And hand you your issue wrapped in ribbons?
Come, Mr. Undersecretary, you're not talking to old Judge
Talley. Oh, no! I went right along with you. I gave every
one of us a very vocal opportunity to join your *holy crusade!*
Nothing else would *do!* No, *sir!* There was no alternative,
and you know it."

"Why would there be an alternative tomorrow? I
mean, if you reconvened and withdrew confirmation."

"Because I'd have eighteen hours to pull apart every
week of your life, young man. Pull it apart, rearrange a
number of ingredients, and put it all back together again.
When I got finished, you'd be on the Attorney General's
list."

It was Trevayne's turn to look out the window. The
President had said it; this was the town for it. It could
happen so easily because accusations always appeared on
page one, denials on page thirty, apologies on page forty-
eight, sandwiched between cheap advertisements.

That was the town; that was the way things were.

But he didn't need the town. He didn't have to
accept the way things were, and it was about time he let
people know it.

"Then why don't you do just that, Mr. Chairman." It
was not a question.

"Because I phoned Frank Baldwin. . . . And why don't
you call a halt to that arrogance? It doesn't become you, sir."

Trevayne was thrown by Baldwin's name. "What did
Baldwin say?"

"That you wouldn't have done what you did unless
you'd been provoked. Mightily provoked. He said he's
known you damn near ten years; he couldn't be mistaken."

"I see." Trevayne reached into his pocket for cigarettes and lit one. "And you accepted that?"

"If Frank Baldwin told me every astronaut was a fairy, I'd consider it holy writ. . . . What I want to know from you is, what happened?"

"Nothing. Nothing . . . happened."

"You didn't force every senator on that panel to *counter* your insinuations of guilt with protestations of innocence for no reason! Because that's what you did! You ridiculed the process of confirmation. . . . And I didn't appreciate it, sir."

"Do you people always add a 'sir' when you're pontificating?"

"There are a number of ways to deliver the word 'sir,' Mr. Undersecretary."

"I'm sure you're a master, Mr. Chairman."

"Was Frank Baldwin right? Were you provoked . . . mightily? And by whom?"

Trevayne tapped his cigarette carefully on the rim of the ashtray and looked at the older man. "Assuming there was provocation, what would you do about it?"

"Ascertain first whether it was provocation and not an incident or incidents magnified out of proportion, easily resolved. Should provocation prove to be the case, I'd call those responsible into my office and run them out of Washington. . . . This subcommittee is not to be tampered with."

"You sound as if you mean that."

"I do, sir. The time is due and overdue for this work to begin. If there's been any interference, any attempt to seek influence, I want it stopped in the strongest measures possible."

"I think I accomplished that this afternoon."

"Are you telling me there were senators in that hearing who tried to reach you improperly?"

"I have no idea."

"Then what *are* you saying?"

"There *was* provocation, I'll admit that; where it emanated from, I don't know. I just know that if it continues, I'm in the position of spreading it around. Or stopping it completely."

"If there was impropriety, it is incumbent upon you to report it."

"To whom?"

"To the proper authorities; there are any number!"

"Maybe I did."

"Then you were obliged to inform the panel!"

"Mr. *Chairman*, that hearing was loaded this afternoon. The majority of those men represent states whose economies are largely dependent on government installations and contracts."

"You've judged us all guilty!"

"I've judged no one. I'm only taking measures that seem appropriate under the circumstances. Measures to make sure these men cannot hinder me."

"You're wrong; you've misinterpreted." Old Gillette saw that the car had rounded another corner and was approaching Trevayne's hotel. He leaned forward in the seat. "Pull up, Laurence. We'll only be a few moments. . . . Trevayne, I find your judgment lacking. You make surface observations and proceed to draw erroneous conclusions. You deliver inflammatory insinuations and refuse to justify them. Most damaging, you withhold pertinent and, I gather, extraordinary information, setting yourself up as an arbitrary censor of what the Senate may be told. In my opinion, Frank Baldwin and his commission made a great mistake in recommending you; the President, too, is in error following their lead. . . . Tomorrow morning I shall insist upon a reconvening of the panel and use all the powers of my office to have your confirmation withdrawn. Your arrogance is not in keeping with the public interest; you'll have your chance to answer then. Good night, sir."

Trevayne opened the door and stepped out on the curb. Before closing it he bent down and spoke to the old man. "I assume you intend using the next eighteen hours to . . . what was it? Oh, yes. To pull apart my life week by week."

"I wouldn't waste my time, Mr. Undersecretary. You're not worth it. You're a damned fool." Gillette reached over to his left and touched a button. The car window rose as Trevayne pushed the door shut.

*   *   *

"Congratulations, darling!" Phyllis jumped up from the chair and dropped her magazine on the lamp table. "I heard it on the seven o'clock news."

Trevayne closed the door and walked into his wife's arms, kissing her lightly on the lips. "Well, don't go out and rent a house yet. It's not settled."

"What are you talking about? They interrupted some local story to read the bulletin. I was so proud; they said it was a bulletin. *You,* a *bulletin!*"

"I've got another flash for them. They may have a second bulletin tomorrow night. The confirmation may be withdrawn."

"What?"

"I've just spent a startling few minutes riding around the block with the distinguished chairman of the hearing. I'm leaving messages for Walter all over New York. I've got to talk to him."

"What in heaven's name are you saying?"

Trevayne had crossed to the telephone and picked it up. He gestured to his wife to hold her questions until he'd finished his calls. She was used to this; she went to the hotel window and looked out over the lighted city. Her husband spoke first to Madison's wife, and when the conversation ended, he pressed the button, holding the telephone in his hand. He hadn't been satisfied with Mrs. Madison's words—Mrs. Madison was not the most reliable woman after seven o'clock in the evening. He released the button and put through a call to La Guardia Airport, to the airline desk of the Washington shuttle.

"If he doesn't call back in an hour or so, I'll try his home again. His plane gets in at ten-something," he said, hanging up.

"What happened?" Phyllis saw that her husband was not only angry, but confused. Andy wasn't often confused.

"He surprised me. For the wrong reasons. He said my arrogance wasn't in keeping with the public interest; I withheld facts. Also, I was a damned fool."

"Who said it?"

"Gillette." Trevayne took off his jacket and threw it on a chair. "From his viewpoint, he's probably right. On the other hand, I know damned well *I'm* right. He may be the most honorable man in Congress; probably is, but that doesn't mean he can guarantee the rest of them. He may *want* to, but that doesn't mean it's so."

Phyllis understood her husband's non sequiturs; he'd told her what he intended doing that afternoon. At least, the objectives. "This was the man in the car?"

"Yes. The Senate's venerable Gillette. He says he's going to reconvene the panel and withdraw the confirmation."

"Can he do that? I mean, after they gave it to you?"

"I guess so. He'll call it new disclosures, or something. . . . Sure he can."

"Then you got them to agree, to work with you."

"Sort of. On the record, anyway. Webster was getting me the transcript tomorrow. But that's not it."

"This Gillette saw through what you were doing?"

"They all did!" Trevayne laughed. "Most of them looked like they'd swallowed mouthfuls of papier-mâché. . . . Oh, they'll be relieved as hell! Just the fact that I withheld information will be sufficient."

"What are you going to do?"

"First, see if my desk at Danforth can be salvaged. It's probably too late, but it's worth trying; I *do* like the job. Walter'll know better. . . . Then the important question: how far can I go tomorrow afternoon without being subject to a subpoena from the Justice Department?" He looked at his wife.

"Andy, I think you should tell them exactly what happened."

"I won't do that."

"You're far more sensitive about it than I am. How many times do I have to tell you. I am *not* embarrassed. I *will not* be a freak. Nothing *happened!*"

"It was ugly."

"Yes, it was. And ugly things happen every day. You think you're protecting me, and I don't need that kind of protection." She walked to the table where she'd put the magazine and spoke deliberately. "Has it occurred to you that the best protection I might have would be to tell what happened in headlines?"

"It has, and I reject it. That approach simply implants ideas. . . . Like kidnapping."

Phyllis knew there was no point in pursuing the subject. He didn't want to talk about it. "All right," she said, turning to him. "Tomorrow just tell them all to go to hell in a basket and you'll be happy to buy them the biggest basket made. Tax-deductible, of course."

He saw the hurt in her face and knew in some illogical way she held herself responsible. He went to her and took her into his arms. "We don't really like Washington, anyway. Last time, we couldn't wait for the weekends, remember? We found every excuse we could to get back to Barnegat."

"You're a sweet man, Andrew. Remind me to buy you a new sailboat." It was an old joke between them. Years ago when the company was struggling for existence, he once proclaimed that he'd feel successful only when he could go out and buy a small cat and not think about the price. It had come to mean all things.

He released her. "I'm going to order some dinner." He went to the coffee table, where there was a room-service menu.

"Why do you have to talk to Walter? What can he do?"

"I want him to describe the legal definitions between opinion and factual evaluation. The first gives me plenty of leeway to be angry; the second invites the Justice Department."

"Is it so important that you be angry?"

Trevayne was reading the menu, but his thoughts were on his wife's questions. He looked over at her. "Yes, I think it is. Not just for the satisfaction; I don't really need that. But because they all consider themselves so damned sacred. Whoever eventually chairs that subcommittee is going to need all the support he can get. If I shake them up a bit, maybe the next nominee will have it easier."

"That's generous, Andy."

He smiled, carrying the menu over to the telephone. "Not entirely. I'm going to enjoy watching those pompous bastards squirm; especially several . . . I extracted figures and percentages from the defense index. The most damaging thing I'll do tomorrow is simply read them off. All *eight states*."

Phyllis laughed. "That's terrible. Oh, Andy, that's devastating."

"It's not bad. If I don't say anything else, it'd be enough. . . . Oh, hell, I'm tired and hungry, and I don't want to think anymore. I can't do anything until I reach Walter."

"Relax. Have something to eat; take a nap. You look exhausted."

"Talking about exhausted warriors home from battle . . ."

"Which we weren't."

" . . . you look awfully attractive."

"Order your dinner. . . . You might include a nice bottle of red wine, if you've a mind to."

"I've a mind to; you owe me a sailboat."

Phyllis smiled warmly as Trevayne picked up the telephone and asked for room service. She went into the bedroom to change into a negligee. She knew her husband would have dinner and they'd both finish a bottle of Burgundy and then they'd make love.

She wanted that very much.

They lay in the hotel bed, Trevayne's arm around his wife, her head against his chest. Both still felt the warm effects of the lovemaking and the wine, and there was a splendid comfort between them. As there always was during such moments.

Trevayne removed his arm gently and reached for his cigarettes.

"I'm not asleep," said Phyllis.

"You should be; that's the way it is in the movies. Smoke?"

"No, thanks. . . . It's eleven-fifteen." Phyllis raised herself against the headboard, pulling the sheet over her naked body, looking at the travel clock. "Are you going to try Walter again?"

"In a few minutes. What with the stack-ups and the taxis, he's probably not home yet. I don't relish a conversation with Ellen Madison at this hour."

"She's very sad; I'm sorry for her."

"I still don't want to talk to her. And he obviously didn't get the message at the terminal."

Phyllis touched her husband's shoulder, then rubbed his arm affectionately, slowly. It was an unconscious but meaningful touch of ownership. "Andy, are you going to talk to the President?"

"No. I've kept my part of the bargain. I didn't quit. And I don't think he'd appreciate my running to him now. When it's over, I'll get the usual solicitous phone call. Probably breakfast, come to think of it, since I won't mention him tomorrow."

"He's going to be grateful for that. He should be. My God, when you think about it. You may lose a job you like; you're insulted; the waste of time . . ."

"I don't qualify as a charity case," interrupted her husband. "I was warned. Wow, was I warned!"

The phone rang, and Trevayne reached for it. "Hello?"

"Mr. Trevayne?"

"Yes?"

"I realize there's a 'do-not-disturb' on your room, but the messages are piling up, and—"

"A *what*? What do-not-disturb? I never gave those instructions! Phyllis?"

"Of course not," said his wife, shaking her head.

"The *d-n-d* is clearly marked, sir."

"It's a mistake!" Trevayne flung his legs over the side of the bed. "What are the messages?"

"The *d-n-d* was given to the board at nine-thirty-five, sir."

"Now, listen! We never requested it! I asked you, what messages?"

The operator paused for a moment; she wasn't going to be abused by forgetful guests. "As I started to say, sir, there's a Mr. Madison on the line who insisted that I ring through. He said it was urgent."

"Put him on, please. . . . Hello, Walter? I'm sorry; I don't know where that goddamned switchboard—"

"Andy, it's terrible! I knew you'd want to talk; that's why I insisted."

"What?"

"It's tragic. It's a tragedy!"

"How do *you* know? Where did you hear it?"

"Hear it? It's on every newscast. It's all over—radio, television."

Trevayne held his breath for a split second before speaking. His voice was calm, precise. "Walter, what are you talking about?"

"The Senator. Old Gillette. He was killed a couple of hours ago. Car went out of control over a Fairfax bridge. . . . What're *you* talking about?"

10

The account of the accident was bizarre enough to be real. According to the hospitalized chauffeur, Laurence Miller, he drove Gillette from midtown—no mention of the hotel, none of Trevayne—back to the Senate Office Building, where Miller was instructed to go to his employer's second-floor office and retrieve a forgotten briefcase. He returned to the car, drove across the Potomac River into Virginia, when the Senator insisted on taking a back route to his Fairfax home. The chauffeur had argued mildly—the back road was partially under construction, there were no street lamps—but the crusty old man was adamant; Laurence Miller didn't know why.

A mile or so from Gillette's property was one of those small offshoots of the Potomac which infiltrate the Virginia woods. A short, metal-ribbed bridge spanned the water and dipped sharply to the right before the Fairfax entrance. The Senator's car was at midpoint when another automobile came careening up from the other side approaching the bridge, its headlights at high beam, its speed enormous. Gillette's driver had no choice on the narrow bridge but to hug the right rail so as to avoid a direct collision. The opposing car skidded in its turn, and the chauffeur, again with no alternative but head-on impact, accelerated instantly, trying to race through the gap left by the onrushing car's skid. He managed the maneuver, and once over the planked entrance, hit the steep decline and slammed on his brakes. The LTD swerved to the left and descended sideways down the short, steep hill. Old Gillette was thrown bodily into the right window structure, crashing his head on the metal door frame with such force that the doctor said death was instantaneous.

The second automobile sped over the bridge and left the scene. The chauffeur could give no description of it; he'd been blinded by the lights, and his concentration was on survival.

The time of the accident was put at 9:55.

Andrew read the account in the Washington *Post* over breakfast in their suite. He read it several times, trying to find a false note, a variation not heard on the previous night's newscasts.

There was none. Except the drive to the Senate Office Building, the forgotten briefcase.

His eyes kept pivoting on the estimated time of the tragedy: 9:55.

Twenty minutes after someone—who?—had placed a "do-not-disturb" on his hotel telephone.

And why had it been done? For what purpose?

It certainly was no guarantee that he wouldn't hear of the accident. He or Phyllis might have had the radio or the television set on; they usually did, at least the radio.

Why, then?

Why would anyone want him incommunicado from 9:35 to—when did Madison get through—11:15. Nearly two hours.

Unless it was a mistake at the switchboard; that was entirely possible.

And he didn't believe it for a minute.

"I still can't get over it," said Phyllis, coming out of the bedroom. "It's scary! What are you going to do?"

"I don't know. I suppose I should call Webster and tell him about our conversation. How the old boy wanted me out."

"No! Why should you?"

"Because it happened. Also, on another level, Gillette may have said something to the others, told them he was going to put me on the spit. I'd hate to find myself confirming a conversation like that without volunteering it first."

"I think you ought to wait. On *both* levels, thank you. . . . You don't deserve being pilloried. I think that's what someone called it. You believe you're right; you said so last night."

Trevayne drank his coffee, buying a few seconds of time before answering his wife. He wanted above all else to keep his suspicions from her. She accepted Gillette's death as "scary" but nevertheless an accident; there was no reason to think otherwise. He wanted to keep it that way.

"Webster may agree with you; so might the President. But to keep it straight, I want them to know."

The President of the United States did, indeed, agree with Phyllis Trevayne. He instructed Webster to tell Andrew to say nothing unless the matter came up from other quarters, and even then, to be vague about specific aspects of his talk with Gillette until subsequent contact with the White House.

Webster also informed Trevayne that Ambassador Hill's considered opinion was that the old Senator was merely testing him. Big Billy had known the cantankerous war horse for years; it was a personal tactic. Hill doubted that Gillette would have reconvened the hearing. He simply would have let the candidate "stew," and if Trevayne stuck to his guns, let the confirmation stand.

It was a complicated rationalization.

And Trevayne didn't believe *it* for a minute, either.

Phyllis had promised herself a look at the NASA exhibition at the Smithsonian, and so, White House guard intact, she left Andrew at the hotel. The truth was that she realized he'd be on the telephone constantly; she knew he preferred being alone during such times.

Trevayne showered and dressed and had a fourth cup of coffee. It was nearly ten-thirty, and he'd promised to call Walter Madison before noon. He wasn't sure what he was going to say to him. He would tell him about the ride around the block; Walter should know about it in the event the hearing *was* reopened. It had crossed his mind to mention it during their tense conversation eleven hours ago. But everything had been so confused, the attorney inexplicably so agitated, that he decided not to complicate the already complex state of things. He recognized Madison's semihysteria and thought he knew what brought it about: a terrible afternoon in the Senate chamber; the return home to an ill wife—ill in the sense that he wasn't there to help her stay sober; and finally the bizarre account of the tragedy on a back-country Fairfax bridge. Even brilliant, sophisticated Manhattan lawyers had their thresholds of pressure.

He'd wait until noon before calling; everyone's head would be clearer then.

There was a knock at the hotel door; Trevayne looked again at his watch. It was probably maid service.

He opened the door and was greeted by the polite, formal smile of an Army officer, a major in a creased uniform with gleaming brass and three rows of ribbons.

"Mr. Trevayne?"

"Yes?"

"Major Paul Bonner, Department of Defense. I suppose you've been briefed; nice to meet you." The Major held out his hand, and Trevayne, by reflex, shook it.

"No, Major, I haven't been briefed."

"Oh. . . . That's a hell of a beginning. I'm your man Friday; at least until your office and staff are set up."

"Really? Well, come on in. I wasn't aware I was in business yet."

Bonner walked into the room with the assurance of a man used to command. He was, perhaps, in his late thirties or early forties, with close-cropped hair and the complexion of a man often outdoors.

"You're in business, all right. You want it; I get it. . . . Whatever. Those are my orders." He threw his hat on a chair and faced Trevayne with an infectious grin. "I understand you're happily married; maybe more to the point, your wife's here in Washington with you. So that rules out one area. . . . You're rich as Croesus, so there's nothing to be gained by offering you a boat ride on the Potomac; you probably own the river. Also, you've worked for State, so I can't intrigue you with D.C. gossip. You probably know more than I do. . . . So what's left? I drink; I assume you do, too. You sail; I try. I ski very well. You're at best on the intermediate slope; no sense in flying us to Gstaad. . . . So we find you a nice set of offices and start hiring."

"Major, you overwhelm me," said Trevayne, closing the door and approaching the officer.

"Good. I'm on target."

"You sound as though you'd read a biography I haven't written."

"You didn't; 'Big Uncle' wrote it. And you bet your life I read it. You're high-priority material."

"Also, you sound as if you didn't approve; am I correct about that, too?"

Bonner stopped smiling for the briefest of moments. "You may be, Mr. Trevayne. It wouldn't be fair for me to say it, though. I've heard only one side of the story."

"I see." Trevayne walked to the breakfast table and indicated the coffee.

"Thanks. It's too early for a drink."

"I've got that too, if you like."

"Coffee's fine."

Trevayne poured a cup, and Bonner crossed to the table and took it. No sugar, no cream.

"Why the come-on-strong, Major?"

"Nothing personal. I resented the assignment, that's all."

"Why? Not that I know what your assignment is; I still don't understand. Is there some combat situation somewhere that you're missing?"

"I'm not the late-late show, either."

"Neither am I."

"Sorry . . . again."

"You're blowing it, that's for sure; whatever it is."

"Sorry. For a third time." Bonner took his coffee and sat down in an armchair. "Mr. Trevayne, two days ago I was given your file and told that I was assigned to you. I was also told that you were a V.I.P. of the first water, and whatever I could do for you—*whatever* had no latitude or longitude, just *whatever*—I was to make sure you got it. . . . Then yesterday the word came through. You're out to nail us, hands and feet, with big, fat spikes. I'm a lousy go-between in this kind of a situation."

"I'm not out to nail anybody."

"Then my job's easier. I admit you don't look like a nut. Or sound like one, either."

"Thank you. I'm not entirely sure I can say the same."

Bonner smiled again, more relaxed than before. "Sorry. For a fourth time, or is it the fifth?"

"I lost count."

"Actually, I rehearsed that little speech. I wanted to give you a chance to complain; I'd be taken off."

"It's still possible. What's this 'nailing people' supposed to mean?"

"In short words, you're one of the virulent antimilitary. You don't like the way the Pentagon operates; incidentally, neither does the Pentagon. You think Defense spends zillions more than it has to; so does Defense. And you're going to spell it all out with a subcommittee, and our heads will roll. Is that fairly accurate, Mr. Trevayne?"

"Perhaps. Except, as with most such generalizations, you imply questionable accusations." Trevayne stopped for a moment, remembering that the dead Gillette had said pretty much the same thing to him in the car last night. He finished the Senator's spoken judgment with a feeling of irony. "I don't think they're justified."

"If that's so, then I'm relieved. We'll—"

"Major," interrupted Trevayne quietly, "I don't give a damn whether you're relieved or not. If you're going to stay on, we'd better have that clear. Okay?"

Paul Bonner took an envelope from his tunic. He opened it and removed three typewritten pages, handing them to Trevayne. The first was a listing of available government offices; it read like a real-estate prospectus. The second was a Xerox copy of the names Andrew had given Frank Baldwin almost two weeks ago—before the terrible events at the Plaza. They were the names of those men and women Andy wanted on his staff; the major positions. There were eleven: four lawyers, three accountants, two engineers—one military, one civilian—and two secretaries. Of the eleven, five had enigmatic checks beside their names. The third page was again a list of names—all unfamiliar to Trevayne. To the right of each was a one-word description of his or her employment classification and the previous government position held. Trevayne looked over at Major Bonner.

"What the hell is this?"

"Which?"

Andrew held up the last page. "This list here. I don't know any of these people."

"They've all been cleared for high-intermediate-level security employment."

"That's what I thought. And I assume these checks . . ." Trevayne held up the second page, his list. "They mean these people haven't been cleared?"

"No. As a matter of fact, they have."

"And six *haven't?*"

"That's right."

Andrew removed the first two pages and placed them on the coffee table. He took the last page and carefully folded it, then proceeded to tear the fold in half. He held out the torn paper for Bonner. The Major reluctantly approached and took it. "Your first job, Major, is to deliver this back to whoever gave it to you. I'll hire my own staff. Get those pretty little checks inked in for those other six people."

Bonner started to speak and then hesitated as Trevayne picked up the pages from the coffee table and sat down on the couch. Finally Bonner took a long breath and addressed the civilian.

"Look, Mr. Trevayne, nobody cares who you hire, but they've got to submit to security checks. This substitution list just makes it easier, quicker."

"I'll bet it does," mumbled Trevayne, marking off addresses on the office sheet. "I'll try not to employ anyone in the pay of the Presidium. . . . This suite at the Potomac Towers; isn't that an apartment building?"

"Yes. Government lease has fourteen months to run. It was rented last year for an engineering project, and then the funds were cut. . . . It's out of the way, though. It might be inconvenient."

"What would you suggest?"

"Someplace nearer Nebraska or New York Avenue. You'll probably be seeing a lot of people."

"I'll pay for the taxis."

"I hadn't thought of it that way. I just assumed they'd be calling on *you.*"

"Very good, Major." Trevayne rose from the chair and looked at the officer. "There're five places I've checked off. Look them over and tell me what you think." He crossed to Bonner and handed him the page. "I've some phone calls to make; I'll use the bedroom. Then we'll get going. Have some more coffee."

Trevayne went into the bedroom and closed the door. There was no sense in waiting any longer to call Madison. He'd have no place to make the call other than a government office or a pay phone. It was quarter to eleven; Madison should be routined and calm by now.

"Andy, I'm still shook up," said the attorney, sounding very much relaxed. "It's simply terrible."

"I think I should tell you the rest. That's pretty terrible, too."

He did, and Walter Madison was, as Trevayne expected, stunned.

"Did Gillette give you any indication that he'd spoken to the others?"

"No. I gathered he hadn't. He said he was going to call a reopening in the morning."

"He might have gotten too much resistance for that . . . . Andy, do you think the accident was anything else?"

"I keep wondering, but I can't come up with a reason that makes sense. If it wasn't an accident and he was killed because he was going to reopen the hearing—that means *they*, whoever they are, *if* they are, *want* me to chair the subcommittee. I can understand someone wanting me out; I can't understand anyone wanting to make sure I'm in."

"And I can't buy the theory that these extremes would be used. Money, persuasion, even outright influence; that's possible. Certainly not killing. As I gathered from the reports, that isn't feasible anyway. His car couldn't have gone into the water; the rail was too high. It couldn't have been forced into a roll; it simply slid sideways and threw the old man into the frame. . . . It was an accident, Andy. Simply terrible, but an accident."

"I think it has to be."

"Have you spoken to anyone about this?"

Trevayne was about to tell Madison the truth, that he'd been in touch with Webster at the White House.

Instead, he hesitated. Not for any reason related to Walter's confidence, only because he felt an obligation to the President. To mention Webster would mean involving the President of the United States—the office, if not the man.

"No. No, I haven't. Just to Phyllis, that's all."

"We may want to change that, but for the time being, telling me is sufficient. I'll phone around and let you know."

"Who are you going to call?"

For several seconds Walter Madison said nothing, and both men recognized the awkwardness of the moment. "I don't know yet. I haven't had time to think. Perhaps a couple of the men at the hearing, the ones I met. Easy enough to do; I'm solicitous, my client wants to know if he should make a statement. Anything. . . . I'll get the drift."

"Right. You'll call me back?"

"Of course."

"Make it late in the day. I've got my own major from the Defense Department. He's going to help me set up shop."

"Christ! They don't waste a minute. What's his name?"

"Bonner. First name, Paul, I think he said."

Madison laughed. It was a laugh of recognition, and not entirely pleasant. "Paul *Bonner?* They're not very subtle, are they?"

"I don't understand. What's so funny?"

"Bonner's one of the Pentagon's Young Turks. The original bad boy of Southeast Asia. Remember a few years ago? A half-dozen or so officers got thrown out of Indochina for some highly questionable activities beyond the borders, behind the lines?"

"Yes, I do. The inquiry was squashed."

"You *know* it. It was too damned hot. This Bonner was in command."

11

By two o'clock Trevayne and Bonner had scouted three of the five office suites. The Army liaison tried to maintain a neutral attitude, but he was too candid. Trevayne realized that in several ways Bonner was like himself; at close range, it was difficult for the officer to disguise his opinion.

It was obvious that Bonner felt all the locations they'd seen were satisfactory. He couldn't understand why Trevayne insisted on visiting the last two, both quite far from the central city. Why not pick one of the others?

Trevayne, on the other hand, had seen the first three out of courtesy, so it wouldn't appear that he was subject to snap decisions. Bonner had allowed that the offices at the Potomac Towers *did* look out on the river; Trevayne had suspected as much, and that fact, in itself, was enough to convince him.

His offices would be at the Potomac Towers.

But he would find other reasons than the river, the water. He wouldn't give Major Paul Bonner, the Young Turk of the Pentagon, the opportunity of saying that his V.I.P. had a thing about water. He wouldn't lend himself to the ridicule that might so easily come from the blunt observations of a man whose actions had frightened the Department of the Army a few short years ago.

"There's nothing against our taking a lunch break, is there, Major?"

"Christ, no. I'll get my ass chewed if it doesn't appear on my chit sheet. As a matter of fact, I'll get reamed anyway for letting you make this tour. Frankly, I thought you'd have someone else do it for you."

"Who, for instance."

"Hell, I don't know. Don't you people always have other people do these things? Get offices and stuff like that?"

"Sometimes. But not if it's a concentrated job that's going to require a lot of time on the premises."

"I forgot. You're a self-made millionaire, according to the reading material."

"Only because it was easier, Major."

They went to the Chesapeake House, and Trevayne was at first amused, then amazed, at Bonner's alcoholic capacity. The Major ordered double bourbons—three before lunch, two during, and one after. And they were generous singles to begin with.

Yet Bonner did not display the slightest indication of having had a drink.

Over coffee, Trevayne thought he'd try a more friendly approach than he'd shown throughout the morning.

"You know, Bonner, I haven't said it, but I do appreciate your taking on a thankless chore. I can see why you resent it."

"I don't mind, really. Not now. Actually, I pictured you as some kind of computerized . . . prick, if you'll forgive the expression. You know, a mincing slide-rule type who made his bread and thinks everyone else is worthless."

"Did the 'reading material' indicate that?"

"Yeah. I think it did. Remind me to show it to you in a couple of months. . . . If we're still speaking." Bonner laughed and drank the remainder of his bourbon. "It's crazy, but they didn't have any photographs of you. They never do with civilians, except in security cases. Isn't that nuts? In the field I'd never look at a file unless there were at least three or four photographs. Not just one; I'd never accept just one."

Trevayne thought for a moment. The major was right. One photograph was meaningless for a dozen reasons. Several were not.

"I read about your . . . field activity. You made a large impression."

"That's off-limits, I'm afraid. I won't talk about that, which means I'm not supposed to admit I was ever west of San Diego."

"Which strikes me as silly."

"Me, too. . . . So I've got a couple of programmed statements which don't mean a damn thing. Why bring them up?"

Trevayne looked at Bonner and saw that he was sincere. He didn't want to restate the programmed replies he'd been fed; yet there seemed to be something else he was perfectly willing to discuss. Andrew wasn't sure, but it was worth a try.

"I'd like a brandy. How about you?"

"Stick to bourbon."

"A double?"

"That's right."

The drinks came and were half-finished before Trevayne's observation proved out.

"What's this subcommittee all about, Mr. Trevayne? Why is everyone so uptight?"

"You said it this morning, Major. Defense is spending 'zillions' more than it should."

"I understand that; nobody would argue. But why are we the heavies right off the top? There are thousands involved. Why are *we* singled out as the prime targets?"

"Because you issue contracts. Simple as that."

"We issue contracts that congressional committees *approve*."

"I don't want to generalize, but it seems to me that Congress usually approves one figure and then is forced to approve another—the second being a lot higher than the first."

"We're not responsible for the economy."

Trevayne lifted his half-empty brandy glass and revolved it. "Would you accept that kind of reasoning in the field, Major? I'm sure you'd accept the fact that your intelligence teams had a margin for error, but would you tolerate a hundred-percent inaccuracy?"

"It's not the same."

"They're both information, aren't they?"

"I refuse to equate lives with money."

"I find that argument specious; you had no such consideration when your 'field activity' cost a great *many* lives."

"Horseshit! That was a statistical-combat situation."

"Double horseshit. There were an awful lot of people who thought the situation was totally uncalled for."

"Then why the hell didn't they do something about it? Don't cry *now*."

"As I recall, they tried," said Trevayne, staring at his glass.

"And failed. Because they didn't read their problem correctly. Their strategy was very un-pro."

"That's an interesting statement, Major. . . . Provocative, too."

"Look, I happen to think that particular war was necessary for all the reasons brighter men than me have stated time and again. I can also understand how a lot of those reasons could be rejected, traded off because of the price. That's what those people didn't concentrate on. They didn't emphasize it."

"You fascinate me." Trevayne finished his brandy. "How could . . . those people have done that?"

"Visual-tactical maneuvers. I could even break down the logistics of cost and geography."

"Please do," said Trevayne, returning the Major's smile.

"The visual: fifteen thousand coffins in three units of five thousand each. The real things—government issue, pine construction. Cost, two hundred dollars per item on bulk purchase. Geography: New York, Chicago, Los Angeles—Fifth Avenue, Michigan Avenue, Sunset Boulevard. Tactic: placing the coffins laterally at one-foot spacings, with every hundredth casket open and displaying a corpse. Mutilated, if possible. Personnel requirements: two men per coffin, with a side task force of one thousand per city employed to distract police or to prevent interference. Total troop requirements: thirty-three thousand . . . and a hundred and fifty corpses. . . . Three cities completely inmobilized. Two miles of corpses, real and symbolic, blocking major thoroughfares. Total impact. Revulsion."

"That's incredible. And you think it would have worked?"

"Have you ever seen civilians standing around on a street corner watching a hearse go by? It's the ultimate identification. . . . What I just described would have turned the stomachs of eight to ten million people on the scenes, and another hundred million through the media. A mass burial rite."

"It couldn't have been done. It would have been prevented. There's the police, national guard . . ."

"Logistics, again, Mr. Trevayne. Diversionary tactics; surprise, silence. The quiet grouping of personnel and equipment, say, on a Sunday morning or early Monday—minimum-police-activity hours. The execution of the maneuver so precisely timed that it could be accomplished in less than forty-five minutes in each city. . . . Only thirty-odd thousand men—women, too, probably. You had damn near a half-million in the Washington march alone."

"It's chilling." Trevayne was not smiling; he also was aware that Bonner had used the word "you" for the first time. Trevayne's position had been clear on Indochina, and the soldier wanted him to know he knew it.

"That's the point."

"Not only the maneuver, but that you could conceive of it."

"I'm a professional soldier. It's my job to conceive strategies. And once having conceived them, also to create countermeasures."

"You've created one for this?"

"Definitely. It's not very pleasant, but unavoidable. It's reduced to swift retaliation; immediate and complete suppression. Confrontation by force and superior weaponry so as to establish military supremacy. Suspension of all news media. Replace one idea with another. Fast."

"And spill a considerable amount of blood."

"Unavoidable." Bonner looked up and grinned. "It's only a game, Mr. Trevayne."

"I'd rather not play."

Bonner looked at his watch. "Gosh! It's almost four o'clock. We'd better check out those last two addresses, or they'll be locked up."

Trevayne got out of his chair just a little bit numbed. Major Paul Bonner had spent the last few minutes telling him something. Spelling out the harsh reality that Washington was inhabited by many Paul Bonners. Men who were committed—rightfully, justifiably, by their lights—to the promulgation of their authority and influence. Professional soldiers who were capable of outthinking their opponents because they were equally capable of thinking *for* them. Generous, too; tolerant of the hazy, muddled thinking of their soft civilian counterparts. Secure in the knowledge that in this era of potential holocaust there was no room for the indecisive or undecided. The protection of the nation was directly related to the enormity and effectiveness of its strike force. For such men as Bonner it was inconceivable that any should stand in the way of this goal. That they could not tolerate.

And it seemed incongruous that Major Bonner could say so ingenuously: *Gosh! It's almost four o'clock.* And not a little frightening.

The Potomac Towers provided its own reason for being selected, unrelated to the view of the river. Bonner accepted it. The other suites all had the normal five offices and a waiting room; the Towers included an additional kitchenette and a study. The latter was designed for quiet reading or conferences, even overnight accommodations by way of a huge leather couch in the main office. The Potomac Towers had been leased for an engineering crash program and outfitted to accommodate the pressurized schedule. It was ideal for Trevayne's purposes, and Bonner made the requisition, relieved that the tour was finished.

The two men returned to Trevayne's hotel.

"Would you care to come up for a drink?" asked Trevayne, getting out of the Army vehicle with the insignia on both doors that allowed for parking just about anywhere.

"Thanks, but I'd better report in. There are probably a dozen generals walking in and out of the men's room, watching my office, waiting for me." Bonner's face lit up, his eyes smiling; he was pleased with the image he'd just created. Trevayne understood. The Young Turk enjoyed the position he was in—a position undoubtedly assigned for reasons Bonner didn't like, and now, perhaps, could be turned on his superiors.

Trevayne wondered what those reasons were.

"Well, have fun. Ten in the morning?"

"Right on. I'll alert security; that list of yours will be cleared. If there are any real problems, I'll call you myself. You'll want others, though. I'll set up interviews."

Bonner looked at Andrew and laughed. "*Your* interviews, massa."

"Fine. And thanks." Trevayne watched the Army car start up and enter the congested flow of Washington's five-thirty traffic.

The hotel desk informed Trevayne that Mrs. Trevayne had picked up their messages at precisely five-ten. The elevator operator tipped three fingers to his visor and said, "Good evening," addressing him by name. The first guard, seated in a chair by the row of elevators on the ninth floor, smiled; the second guard, standing in the corridor several yards from his door, nodded his head in recognition. Trevayne had the feeling that he'd just passed through a hall of mirrors, his image reflected a thousandfold, but not necessarily for him. For the benefit of others.

"Hello, Phyl?" Trevayne closed the door and heard his wife speaking on the telephone in the bedroom.

"Be with you in a sec," she called out.

He took off his jacket, unloosened his tie, and went to the bar, where he poured himself a glass of ice water. Phyllis came out of the bedroom, and Trevayne saw a trace of concern in her eyes, beyond the smile.

"Who was that?"

"Lillian." She referred to their housekeeper, cook, aide-for-all-seasons at High Barnegat. "She had some electrical trouble; it'll be all right. The repairmen said they'd be out soon."

They kissed their customary kiss, but Trevayne was hardly aware of it. "What do you mean, trouble?"

"Half the lights went out. The north side. She wouldn't have known except for the radio; it went off."

"Didn't it go right back on again?"

"I guess not. It's all right, the men are coming."

"Phyl, we have an auxiliary generator. It cuts in when a circuit breaker fails."

"Darling, you don't expect us to know about *those* things. The men'll fix it. . . . How did everything go? Where *did* you go, incidentally?"

It was possible, Trevayne supposed, for there to be an electrical malfunction at Barnegat, but unlikely. Barnegat's entire electrical system was designed by Phyllis' brother; a labor of love and enormous sophistication. He'd call his brother-in-law later; ask him, jokingly perhaps, to check into it.

"Where did I go? . . . all over town with a nice young fellow whose late-night reading is restricted to Clausewitz."

"Who?"

"The science of . . . military supremacy will do."

"That must have been rewarding."

" 'Enlightening' would be more accurate. . . . We settled on the offices. Guess what? They're on the river."

"How did you manage that?"

"I didn't. They were just available."

"You haven't heard anything, then? About the hearing, the confirmation?"

"Nope. At least, not so far. The desk said you stopped for the messages. Did Walter call?"

"Oh, they're on the table. Sorry. I saw Lillian's and forgot."

Trevayne went to the coffee table and picked up the notes. There were an even dozen, mostly friends, a few quite close, others vaguely remembered. There was no message from Madison. But there was one from a "Mr. de Spadante."

"That's funny. A call here from De Spadante."

"I saw the name; I didn't recognize it."

"Met him on the plane. He goes back to early New Haven. He's in construction."

"And probably wants to take you to lunch. After all, you're a bulletin."

"I think, under the circumstances, I won't return the call. . . . Oh, the Jansens phoned. We haven't seen them in almost two years."

"They're nice. Let's suggest dinner tomorrow or Saturday, if they're free."

"Okay. I'm going to shower and change. If Walter calls and I'm in the john, get me, will you, please?"

"Sure." Phyllis absently took the remainder of her husband's ice water from the bar and drank it. She walked to the couch and sat down, reaching for the messages. Several names were completely unfamiliar to her; business friends of Andy's, she presumed. The rest only peripherally recognizable, except for the Jansens and two others, the Fergusons and the Priors. Old Washington cronies from the State Department days.

She heard the shower running and considered the fact that she, too, would have to dress when Andy was finished. They'd accepted a dinner invitation over in Arlington—a duty call, as Andy termed it. The husband was an attaché at the French embassy, a man who years ago had helped him during the conferences in Czechoslovakia.

The Washington carousel had begun, she reflected. God, how she hated it!

The telephone rang, and for a second Phyllis hoped it was Walter Madison and that he had to meet with Andy, thus canceling the Arlington dinner.

No, she thought further; that would be worse. Quickly called meetings were always terrible in Washington.

"Hello?"

"Mr. Andrew Trevayne, if you'd be so kind." The voice was a touch raspy, but soft, polite.

"I'm sorry, he's in the shower. Who's calling, please?"

"Is this Mrs. Trevayne?"

"Yes."

"I haven't had the pleasure; my name is De Spadante. Mario de Spadante. I've known your husband, not well, of course, for a number of years. We met again yesterday, on the plane."

Phyllis remembered that Andy had said he wouldn't return De Spadante's call. "Then I'm doubly sorry. He's way behind schedule, Mr. de Spadante. I'm not sure he'll be able to call you back right away."

"Perhaps I'll leave a number anyway, if it's not too much trouble. He may want to reach me. You see, Mrs. Trevayne, I was to be at the Devereaux's over in Arlington, *too*. I've done some work for Air France. Your husband might prefer that I find an excuse and not be there."

"Why in heaven's name would he do that?"

"I read in the papers about his subcommittee. . . . Tell him, please, that since I got into Dulles Airport I've been followed. Whoever it is knows he drove into town with me."

* * *

"What does he mean, he was followed? Why does your driving into town with him have any bearing on anything?" Phyllis spoke to her husband as he came out of the bathroom.

"It shouldn't—my driving in with him; he offered me a lift. If he says he was followed, he's probably right. And used to it. He's supposed to be in the rackets."

"At Air France?"

Trevayne laughed. "No. He's a builder. He's probably involved with air-terminal construction. Where's the number?"

"I wrote it on the blotter. I'll get it."

"Never mind." Trevayne, in undershirt and shorts, walked into the living room to the white desk with the green hotel blotter. He picked up the telephone and slowly dialed as he deciphered his wife's hastily scribbled numbers. "Is this a nine or a seven?" he asked her as she came through the door.

"A seven; there was no nine. . . . What are you going to say?"

"Straighten him out. I don't give a damn if he rents the rooms next door. Or takes pictures of me on May Day. . . . I don't play those games, and he's got a hell of a nerve thinking I do. . . . Mr. de Spadante, please."

Trevayne calmly but with obvious irritation informed De Spadante of his feelings and suffered through the Italian's obsequious apologies. The conversation lasted a little over two minutes, and when Trevayne hung up he had the distinct feeling that Mario de Spadante had enjoyed their dialogue.

Which was precisely the case.

Two miles away from Trevayne's hotel, in the Northwest section of Washington, De Spadante's dark-blue Cadillac was parked in front of an old Victorian house. The house, as the street—the area itself—had seen better, more affluent times. Yet there was a grandeur; decaying, perhaps, but still being clung to in spite of the declining values. The inhabitants of this particular section fell into roughly three categories: the dying elders whose memories or lack of money prevented their moving away; the youngish couples—usually early-rung-on-the-government-ladder—who could lease a fair amount of space for comparatively little rent; and finally—in sociological conflict—a scattering of subculture youth enclaves, groups of young nomads wandering into sanctuaries. The wail of Far Eastern sitars, the hollow vibrations of Hindu woodwinds continued long into the morning; for there was no day or night, only gray darkness and the moans of very personal survival.

Hard drugs.

The suppliers and the supplied.

The old Victorian house beyond De Spadante's Cadillac was recently taken over by a cousin, another cousin whose influence was felt in Washington's Police Department. The house was a substation in the subculture, a minor command post for narcotics distribution. De Spadante had stopped off with some colleagues to inspect the real-estate investment.

He sat in a room with no windows, the indirect lighting illuminating the psychedelic posters on the walls, covering the cracks. Except for one other person, he was alone. He replaced the telephone in its cradle and leaned back in his chair behind a filthy table.

"He's edgy; he just told me off. That's good."

"It would have been better if you goddamn fools had let things take their course! That hearing would have been reconvened and the confirmation withdrawn. Trevayne would have been out!"

"You don't think; that's your problem. You look for quick solutions; that's very dumb. It's especially dumb right now."

"You're wrong, Mario!" said Robert Webster, spitting out the words, the muscles in his neck tense. "You didn't solve anything, you only gave us a potentially dangerous complication. And a crude one!"

"Don't talk to me *crude!* I laid out two hundred thousand up in Greenwich; another five for the Plaza!"

"Also crude," blistered Webster. "Crude and unnecessary. Your out-of-date waterfront tactics damn near exploded in our faces! You watch your step."

The Italian leaped out of the chair. "Don't you tell

me, Webster! One of these days you pricks will kiss my
ass for what I got on him!"

"For God's sake, lower your voice. And don't use my
name. The biggest mistake we ever made was getting
mixed up with you! Allen's right about that. They all are!"

"I didn't ask for any engraved invitation, Bobby. And
you didn't get my name out of no telephone book. You
came to me, baby! You needed help, and I gave it to you.
. . . I've been helping you for a long time now. So don't
talk to me like that."

Webster's expression betrayed his reluctant acceptance of De Spadante's words. The mafioso had been
helpful, helpful in ways few others dared to be. And he,
Bobby Webster, had called upon him more than anyone
else. The day had long since come and gone when Mario
de Spadante could be so easily dismissed. It reduced itself
to controlling him.

"Don't you understand? We wanted Trevayne out. A
reconvened hearing would have accomplished that."

"You think so? Well, you're wrong, Mr. Lace Pants. I
talked to Madison last night; I told him to call me from the
airport before he boarded. I figured *someone* ought to
know what Trevayne was doing."

The unexpected information caused Webster to check
his hostility, replace it with a concern he hadn't anticipated.

"What did Madison say?"

"That's different, huh? None of you smart asses thought
of it, huh?"

"What did he say?"

De Spadante sat down again. "The esteemed attorney
was very uptight. He sounded like he was going to head
home and climb into a bottle with that lush wife of his."

"What did he *say?*"

"Trevayne figured that panel of senators for what it
was—a big roomful of loaded dice; he made that clear.
And Madison made no bones that he sweated out the
confirmation—not Trevayne, he didn't sweat piss—*Madison*
sweated. For a very goddamn good reason. Trevayne told
him if those bastards turned him down he wasn't leaving
town quietly. He was going to call in the newspapers,

television; he had a lot of things he wanted to say. Madison didn't guess any of it was too good."

"About what?"

"Madison doesn't know. He only knows it's very heavy. Trevayne said it would rip the city apart; those were the words. *Rip the city apart.*"

Robert Webster turned away from the mafioso; he breathed deeply to control his ire. The sour-sweet odor that permeated the old house was offensive. "It makes absolutely no sense. I've talked with him every day this past week. It doesn't make sense."

"Madison didn't lie, either."

Webster turned back to De Spadante. "I know. But what is it?"

"We'll find out," answered the Italian with quiet confidence. "Without having our asses in a sling over some press conference. And when you girls put it all together, you'll see I was right. If that hearing was reconvened and Trevayne thrown out, he would have shot off his cannon. I *know* Trevayne, from way back. He doesn't lie, either. None of us are ready for that; the old man had to die."

Webster stared at the heavyset man sitting so arrogantly in the filthy chair. "But we don't know what it was he was going to say. Has it crossed your Neanderthal mind that it might have been something as simple as the Plaza Hotel? We could have—and would have immediately—disassociated ourselves from anything like that."

De Spadante didn't look up at the White House aide. Instead he reached into his pocket, and while Webster watched apprehensively, with a certain unbelieving fear, De Spadante removed a pair of thick tortoiseshell glasses. He put them on and began scanning some papers. "You try too hard to get me pissed off, Bobby. . . . 'Might have,' 'could have'; what the hell is that? The fact is, we didn't know. And we weren't going to risk finding out on the seven-o'clock news. I think maybe you ought to go back to the lace parade, Bobby. They're probably sewing up a storm."

Webster shook his head, dismissing De Spadante's invective as he walked to the shabby door. Hand on the broken glass doorknob, he turned to look once again at the

Italian. "Mario, for your own good, don't make any more unilateral decisions. Consult us. These are complicated times."

"You're a bright boy, Bobby, but you're still very young, very green. You get older, things don't seem so complicated. . . . Sheep don't survive in the desert; a cactus doesn't grow in a wet jungle. This Trevayne, he's in the wrong environment. It's as simple as that."

12

The rambling white house, with the four Ionic pillars supporting an impractical balcony above the front porch, was situated in the middle of a landscaped three-acre plot. The driveway was as impractical as the balcony; it bordered the right side of a weedless, carpetlike front lawn and veered—inexplicably—again to the right, ending in a half-circle *away* from the house. The real-estate agent told Phyllis that the original owner had planned a garage apartment at the end of the semicircle, but before he could build it, he was transferred to Muscaton, South Dakota.

It was no High Barnegat, but it had a name—a name Phyllis wished she could obliterate. It was in raised lettering in the white stone beneath the impractical balcony.

Monticellino.

Since the year's lease did not entitle her to sandblast the letters, Phyllis decided the name would remain between God, the original owner, and Thomas Jefferson.

Tawning Spring, Maryland, was no Greenwich, although there were similarities. It was rich, ninety-eight percent white, and catered to the upward-mobility syndrome; it was essentially imitative—of itself—and insular; it was inhabited by people who knew exactly what they were buying: the penultimate rewards of the corporate dream. The ultimate—when admitted—was southeast: McLean or Fairfax, in the Virginia hunt country.

What the people who were buying the penultimate rewards didn't know, thought Phyllis, was that they were also getting, without additional charge, all of the unbearable problems that went with their purchases.

Phyllis Trevayne had had them. *Those* problems. Five years' worth; nearer six, really. Six years in a half-hell. It was no one's fault. And everyone's. It was the way things were. Someone once decreed that a day should have twenty-four hours—not thirty-seven or forty-nine or sixteen—and that was that.

It was too short. Or too long.

Depending.

In the beginning, of course, there were no such philosophical thoughts about time. The first exhilaration of love, the excitement, the unbelievable energies the three of them—Andy, Douglas, herself—put into the shabby warehouse they called a company; if there were any thoughts of time then, it was usually in the form of where-the-hell-did-it-go.

She did triple duty. She was the secretary so needed to keep Andy organized; she was the bookkeeper filling ledger after ledger with unpronounceable words and unbelievably complicated figures. And finally she was the wife.

Their marriage had been comfortably situated—as her brother phrased it—between a Pratt and Whitney contract and an upcoming presentation to Lockheed. Andy and Doug had agreed that a three-week honeymoon in the Northwest would be ideal. The couple could see the San Francisco lights, catch some late skiing in Washington or Vancouver, and Andrew could make a side trip to Genessee Industries in Palo Alto. Genessee was an enormous conglomerate—everything from trains to aircraft, prefabricated housing to electronics research.

She knew when they began—those awful years. At least, the day she saw the outlines of what was coming. It was the day after they got back from Vancouver.

She had walked into the office and met the middle-aged woman her brother had hired to fill in during her absence. A woman who somehow exuded a sense of purpose, who seemed so committed to accomplishing far more than eight hours would permit—before dashing home to husband and children. A delightful person without the slightest trace of competitiveness about her, only a profound gratitude at being permitted to work. She didn't actually need the money.

Phyllis would think of her often during the coming years. And understand.

Steven came; Andrew was ecstatic. Pamela arrived, and Andrew was the clichéd, bumbling father filled with love and awkwardness.

When he had the time.

For Andrew was also consumed with impatience; Pace-Trevayne was growing rapidly—too rapidly, she felt. There were suddenly awesome responsibilities accompanied by astronomical financing. She wasn't convinced her young husband could handle it all. And she was wrong. He was not only capable, but adaptable to the changing pressures, the widening pressures. When he was unsure or frightened—and he was often both—he simply stopped and made everyone else stop with him. He told her that his fear and uncertainty were the results of not understanding, not knowing. It was better to lose a contract—painful as it might be—than to regret the acceptance later.

Andrew never forgot the courtroom in Boston. That wouldn't happen to him.

Her husband was growing; his product filled a void that desperately needed filling, and he instinctively parried in point-counterpoint until he was assured of the advantage. A fair advantage; that was important to Andy. Not necessarily moral, just important, thought Phyllis.

But she wasn't growing; the children were. They talked, they walked, they filled uncountable pails of diapers and spewed out unmeasurable amounts of cereal and bananas and milk. She loved them with enormous joy and faced their beginning years with the happiness of the new experience.

And then it all began to slip away. Slowly at first, as with so many others. She understood that, too.

The schoolday was the initial shock. Pleasant to begin with—the abrupt cessation of the high-pitched, demanding voices. The silence, the peace; the wonderful first aloneness. Alone except for the maid, the laundry man, an occasional repairman. Essentially alone, however.

The few really close friends she'd known had moved

away—with husbands or with dreams of their own having little to do with the New Haven-Hartford environs. The neighbors in their upper-middle-class suburb were pleasant enough for an hour or two, but no more. They had their own drives—company drives; East Haven was the territory for them. And there was something else about the East Haven wives. They resented Phyllis Trevayne's lack of need and appreciation for their corporate strivings. That resentment—as resentment so often does—led to a form of quiet, progressive isolation. She wasn't one of them. And she couldn't help them.

Phyllis realized that she'd been thrust into a strange, uncomfortable limbo. The thousands of hours, hundreds of weeks, scores of months that she'd devoted to Andrew, Doug, and the company had been replaced by the all-day, everyday needs of her children. Her husband was more often away than at home; it was necessary, she understood that, too. But the combination of all things left her without a functioning world of her own.

So there was the first, free-of-cares, purposeful venturing out on a regular, daily basis; unencumbered by infant concerns. No patient explanations to impatient maids, no elaborate preparations for noontime, snacktime, playtime, friendtime. The children were in private schools. They were picked up at eight-thirty in the morning and returned conveniently at four-thirty, just prior to the rush-hour traffic.

The "eight-hour parole" was the term used by the other young, white, rich mothers of the white, rich youngsters attending the old, white, rich private schools.

She tried relating to their world and joined the proper clubs, including the Golf and Country; Andrew enthusiastically endorsed them but rarely set foot on the premises. They palled on her as rapidly as the members did, but she refused to admit the disenchantment. She began to believe the fault was hers, the inadequacy hers. Was there guilt? Then that was hers also.

What in God's name did she *want?* She asked that question of herself and found no answer.

She tried returning to the company—no longer a warehouse, now a sprawling complex of modern buildings,

one of several branches. Pace-Trevayne was running at
high speed on a very fast track in an extraordinarily complicated race. It wasn't comfortable for the wife of the energetic young president to be seated at a desk doing
uncomplicated chores. She left, and she thought Andrew
breathed easier.

Whatever it was she sought eluded her, but there was
relief to be found, starting at lunch. In the beginning it
was a delicate glass of Harvey's Bristcl Cream. Then grad-
uation to the single Manhattan, which swiftly became a
double. In several years her degree was awarded by the
switch to vodka—the no-telltale, very viable substitute.

*Oh, God! She understood Ellen Madison! Poor, bewil-
dered, rich, soft, pampered Ellen—hushed-up Ellen Madison. Never, never phone her after six p.m.!*

She recalled with painful clarity the late rainy afternoon Andy found her. She'd been in an accident, not
serious, but frightening; her car had skidded on the wet
pavement into a tree about a hundred yards from the
driveway. She'd been hurrying home from a very long
lunch. She'd been incoherent.

In her panic she'd raced from the smashed car to the
house, locked the front door, and run to her room, locking
that also.

A hysterical neighbor ran over, and Phyllis' maid
called the office.

Andrew convinced her to unlock their bedroom door,
and with five words her life was changed, the awful years
terminated.

"For God's sake, help me!"

"Mother!" Her daughter's voice intruded on the stillness of the new bedroom that opened on the impractical
balcony. Phyllis Trevayne had nearly finished unpacking;
it had been an early photograph of her children that had
triggered her silent reminiscing. "There's a special delivery letter from the University of Bridgeport for you. Are
you lecturing this fall?"

Pam's transistor radio filled the downstairs. Phyllis
and Andy had laughed when they met their daughter at
Dulles Airport the night before; Pam's radio was turned on

before she reached the passenger gate. "Only biweekly seminars, dear. Bring it up, will you, please?"

The University of Bridgeport.

The coincidence of the letter and her thoughts was appropriate, she considered. For the letter from such a place as Bridgeport was a net result of her "solution," as she called it.

Andy had realized that her drinking had become more than a social habit but had refused to accept it as a problem. He had more problems than he needed; he attributed her excess to the temporary condition of household pressures and too little outside activity. It wasn't uncommon; he'd heard other men speak of it. "Cooped up" was the phrase usually accompanying their rationalizations. It would pass. Further, he'd proved it to himself. For whenever they took vacations or were traveling with each other, there was no problem at all.

But that rainy afternoon they both knew there was a problem and they had to face it together.

The solution had been Andy's, although he let her think it was hers. It was to immerse herself completely in some project with a specific objective in view. A project in which she found a great deal of pleasure; an objective ambitious enough to make the time and energy worthwhile.

It didn't take her long to find the project; the fascination had been there since she was first introduced to medieval and Renaissance history. It was the chronicles: Daniel, Holinshed, Froissart, Villani. An incredible, mystical, marvelous world of legend and reality, fact and fantasy.

Once she began—cautiously at first, auditing graduate courses at Yale—she found herself as impatient as Andrew was with the expanding concerns of Pace-Trevayne. She was appalled by the dry academic approach to these vivid, full-bodied histories. She was infuriated with the musty, cobwebbed, overly cautious literateness given these —her—poetic novelist-historians of the ages. She vowed to open the rust-caked doors and let the fresh air of new appreciation circulate among the ancient archives. She thought in terms of contemporary parallels—but with the splendor of past pageantry.

If Andrew had his fever, she caught one, too. And the

more she immersed herself, the more she found everything else falling into organized place. The Trevayne household was a busy, energetic home again. In less than two
years Phyllis had her master's degree. Two and a half
years later, the once-described objective—now merely an
accepted necessity—was reached. She was formally conferred a Doctor of English Literature. Andrew threw a
huge party celebrating the event—and in the quiet love of
the aftermath told her he was going to build High Barnegat.

They both deserved it.

"You're almost finished," said Pamela Trevayne, coming through the bedroom door. She handed her mother the
red-stamped envelope and looked around. "You know,
Mom, I don't resent the speed you get things straightened
up in, but it doesn't have to be so organized, too."

The more she immersed herself, the more she found
everything falling into organized place.

"I've had lots of experience, Pam," said Phyllis, her
mind still on her previous thoughts. "It wasn't always so
. . . tidy."

"What?"

"Nothing. I said I've done a lot of unpacking." Phyllis
looked at her daughter as she rather absently thumbed
open the back of the envelope. Pam was growing so tall;
the light-brown hair fell loose, framing the sharp young
features, the wide brown eyes that were so alive. So
eager. Pam's face was a good face—a very feminine version of her brother's. Not quite beautiful, but much more,
much deeper than pretty. Pam was emerging as a most
attractive adult. And beneath the surface exuberance there
was a fine intelligence, a questioning mind impatient with
unsatisfactory answers.

Whatever the hang-ups of her immediate growth period—boys, transistor radios turned these days to mournful, back-country folk ballads, pop posters, poor marches
and Boone's Apple Farm—Pam Trevayne was part of the
vast "now." And that was fine for everybody, thought
Phyllis as she watched her daughter part the curtains over
the door of the impractical balcony.

"This is a crazy porch, Mother. With luck you could
get a whole folding chair out there."

Phyllis laughed as she read the letter from Bridgeport. "I don't think we'll use it for dinner parties . . . Oh, Lord, they've got me scheduled for Fridays. I asked them not to."

"The seminars?" asked Pam, turning from the curtains.

"Yes. I said any time from Monday through Thursday, so they assign me Fridays. I want Friday open for weekends."

"That's not very dedicated, Madame Professor."

"One dedicated member of the family is enough right now. Your dad's going to need the weekends—if he can take them off. I'll phone them later."

"Today's Saturday, Mom."

"You're right. Monday, then."

"When's Steve getting here?"

"Your father asked him to take the train up to Greenwich and drive the station wagon down. He has a list of things to bring; Lillian said she'd pack the wagon."

Pam uttered a short cry of disappointment. "Why didn't you tell me? I could have taken the bus home and driven down with him."

"Because I need you here. Dad's been living in a half-furnished house with no food and no help while I've been at Barnegat. We womenfolk have to put things to rights." Phyllis shoved the letter back in the envelope and propped it against the bureau mirror.

"I'm against your approach. In principle." Pam smiled. "Womenfolk are emancipated."

"Be against, be emancipated; and also go unpack the dishes. The movers put them in the kitchen—the oblong box."

Pam walked to the edge of the bed and sat down, tracing an imaginary crease on her Levi's. "Sure, in a minute. . . . Mom, why didn't you bring down Lillian? I mean, it would be so much easier. Or hire someone?"

"Perhaps later. We're not sure what our schedule will be. We'll be in Connecticut a lot, especially weekends; we don't want to close the house. . . . I didn't realize you were so maid-conscious." Phyllis gave her daughter a raised eyebrow of mock disapproval.

"Oh, sure. I get uptight when I can't find my ladies-in-waiting."

"Then why ask?" Phyllis rearranged some articles on

the bureau and looked casually at her daughter in the mirror.

"I read the article in the Sunday *Times*. It said that Dad had taken on a job that would keep him busy for ten years—with no time off—and then it would only be half-done; that even *his* well-known abilities were up against the impossible."

"Not impossible; they used the word 'incredible.' And the *Times* is prone to exaggerate."

"They said *you* were a leading authority on the Middle Ages."

"They don't always exaggerate." Phyllis laughed again and lifted an empty suitcase off a chair. "What is it, dear? You've got that I-want-to-say-something look."

Pam leaned back against the headboard; Phyllis was relieved to see that her daughter did not have shoes on. The bedspread was silk. "Not 'say.' 'Ask.' I've read the newspaper stories, the stuff in the magazines; I even saw that TV news thing of Eric Sevareid's—they called it a commentary. I was very big on campus; he's grooved these days. . . . Why is Dad taking this on? Everyone says it's such a mess."

"Precisely because it is a mess. Your father's a talented man. A lot of people think he can do something about it." She carried the suitcase to the doorway.

"But he can't, Mom."

Phyllis looked over at her daughter. She'd been only half-listening, parent-child listening, more concerned with the thousand and one things that needed to get done. "What?"

"He can't do anything."

Phyllis walked slowly back to the foot of the bed. "Would you mind explaining that?"

"He can't change things. No committee, no government hearing or investigation, can make things any different."

"Why not?"

"Because the government's investigating itself. It's like an embezzler being made the bank examiner. No way, Mom."

"That remark sounds suspiciously out of character, Pam."

"I admit it isn't mine, but it says it. We talk a lot you know."

"I'm sure you do, and that's good. But I think that kind of statement oversimplifies, to say the least. Since there's a general agreement that a mess exists, what's your solution? If you've arrived at a criticism you must have an alternative."

Pam Trevayne sat forward, her elbows on her knees. "That's what everyone always says, but we're not sure it's so. If you know someone's sick, but you're not a doctor, you shouldn't try to operate."

"Out of character . . ."

"No, that's mine."

"I apologize."

"There *is* an alternative. But it'll probably have to wait; if we're not too far gone or dead by then. . . . A whole big change. Top to bottom, a huge replacement. Maybe a *real* third party . . ."

"Revolution?"

"God, no! That's a freak-out; that's the violent-jocks. They're no better than what we've got; they're *dumb*. They split heads and think they're solving something."

"I'm relieved—I'm not condescending, dear. I mean that," said Phyllis, reacting to her daughter's sudden questioning look.

"You see, Mom, the people who make all the decisions have to be replaced with people who'll make other decisions. Who'll listen to the *real* problems and stop making up fake ones or exaggerating the little ones for their own benefit."

"Maybe your father can point out . . . things like that. If he backs them up with facts, they'll have to listen."

"Oh, sure. They'll listen. And nod; and say he's sure a great guy. Then there'll be other committees to look into *his* committee, and then a committee to look into *them*. That's the way it'll be; it's the way it always is. In the meantime, nothing changes. Don't you see, Mom? The *people* up there have to change *first*."

Phyllis watched her daughter's excited expression. "That's very cynical," she said simply.

"I guess it is. But I've got an idea you and Dad don't feel so differently."

"What?"

"Well, it seems to me everything's kind of . . . impermanent. I mean, Lillian's not here, this house isn't exactly the kind of place Dad digs . . ."

"There are good reasons for the house; there aren't many available. And Dad hates hotels, you know that." Phyllis spoke rapidly, offhandedly. She didn't care to spell out the fact that the small guest cottage in the back was ideally situated for the two Secret Service men assigned to them. The "1600 Patrol" was the name she'd read on a memorandum from Robert Webster.

"You said the place was only half-furnished . . ."

"We haven't had time."

" . . . you're still lecturing up in Bridgeport."

"I made the commitment; it was near home."

"You even said you weren't sure of your schedule."

"Darling, you're taking isolated, disconnected statements and making them support a preconceived judgment."

"Come on, Mother, you're not building a case against somebody's footnotes."

"I might as well be. I've seen an awful lot just as misleading. And extraneous. . . . What your father's doing is very important to him. He's made some agonizing decisions; they weren't easy, and they hurt. I don't like to hear you imply that he's not serious. Or part of a sham."

"Oh, wow! I'm sending out the wrong vibes." Pam rose from the edge of the bed and stammered, embarrassed that she'd so obviously upset her mother. "I'm not saying that, Mom. I'd never say that about Dad. Or you. I mean, you *level*."

"Then I misunderstood you." Phyllis walked aimlessly back to the bureau. She was annoyed with herself; there was no reason to pick at Pam for saying what men—and women—far more knowledgeable than her daughter were saying all over Washington. Not the sham; the aspect of futility.

The waste. And Andrew hated waste.

Nothing would change. That's what they were saying.

"I just meant that Dad maybe wasn't sure, that's all . . ."

"Of course," said Phyllis turning, showing her daughter an understanding smile. "And you may be right . . . about the difficulty of changing things. But I think we ought to give him a crack at it, don't you?"

The daughter, relieved by her mother's smile, returned one of her own. "Gosh, yes. I mean, he might switch the whole Navy around, make it a sailing fleet."

"The ecologists would approve. Go on, now, get those dishes out. When Steve arrives, he'll be hungry."

"He's always hungry." Pam went to the door.

"Speaking of your father, where is the elusive man? He conveniently disappears when chores are in order."

"He's out back. He was looking at that oversized doll house in the south forty. And that nutty driveway that looks like someone goofed with a cement mixer."

" 'Monticellino,' dear."

"Mom, what *does* that mean?"

"Monticello got pregnant, I guess."

"Oh, wow!"

Trevayne closed the door on the small guest cottage, satisfied once again that the equipment for the 1600 Patrol had been properly installed and was functioning. There were two speakers that picked up any sound from the main-house hallway and living room as soon as a switch underneath the living-room rug was stepped on. He had done so, and he'd just heard the front door open and a brief conversation between his daughter and a postman, followed by Pam's shouting to Phyllis that a special delivery had arrived. Further, he'd placed a book on the ledge of an open window in the downstairs rec room—so that it horizontally broke the vertical space—and noted, again with satisfaction, that a high, piercing hum was emanating from a third speaker beneath a numbered panel when he'd entered the cottage. Every room in the main house had a number that corresponded with one on the panel. No object or person could cross a window space without activating the electronic scanner.

He'd asked the two Secret Service men to wait in their car up the street during the day while the children were down for the weekend. Andy suspected that they had additional materials in their automobiles that were somehow connected with the guest-cottage equipment, but he didn't inquire. He'd find a way to tell the kids about the 1600 Patrol, but he didn't want them alarmed; under no circumstances were they to learn of the reasons for the protection. The two agents had worked out their own schedules with alternate men, and were sympathetic.

His agreement with Robert Webster—with the President—was simple enough. His wife was to be given around-the-clock safety surveillance; he learned that "safety surveillance" was the term, not "protection." For some reason the former gave "wider latitude" and was more acceptable to the Justice Department. His two children were to receive "spot-check surveillance" on a daily basis provided by local authorities through federal request. The schools were to be informed of the "routine" exercise and asked to cooperate.

It was agreed that Trevayne himself would be allocated the minimum "safety surveillance." A personal assault against him was considered unlikely, and he refused any formal association with Justice on the basis of conceivable conflict. Bobby Webster told him the President had laughed when informed that he objected to the "wider-latitude" phrase employed by the Justice Department.

A previous Attorney General named Mitchell had left his mark indelibly on such manipulative language.

Trevayne heard the sound of a horn and looked up. The station wagon, driven by his son, had gone partially beyond the entrance and was now in reverse, preparing to turn into the driveway. The back was filled practically to the roof, and Andy wondered how Steve could use the rear-view mirror.

The boy drove to the front path and accurately judged the parallel positioning of the tailgate so the unloading would be made easier. He climbed out of the front seat, and Andy realized—somewhat ruefully, but with amusement—that his son's long hair was now shaped almost biblically.

"Hi, Dad," said Steve, smiling, his shirt overlapping his flared trousers, his shoulders equal in height to the roof of the station wagon. "How's the nemesis of the incredible?"

"The who of the what?" asked Andy, shaking his son's hand.

"That's what the *Times* said."

"They exaggerate."

The house was "organized"—far more than Andy thought possible by late afternoon. He and his son had unloaded the wagon and then stood around in their shirt-sleeves, awaiting the next command from Phyllis, who had them shuffle furniture as though it were chess pieces. Steve announced that the hourly charges of the new moving company of Trevayne and Trevayne were going up rapidly, with double wages every time a heavy piece was moved back into a previous position. At one point he whistled loudly and stated with equal fervor that it was a union break for a can of beer.

His father, who had been relegated to vice-president by a unanimous vote of one, thought his shop steward a cunning negotiator. The beer break came between one couch and two armchairs—all out of place. For them to get back in position, the can of beer was a small additional price.

By five-thirty Phyllis was as satisfied as she'd be, the movers' cartons and sisal removed to the back of the house, the kitchen in order; and Pam came downstairs announcing that the beds were made—her brother's in a way she hoped he'd appreciate.

"If your IQ was one point lower, you'd be a plant," was Steve's only comment.

The original owner of Monticellino—or, as he was referred to without much affection, *him*—had installed one desirable appliance in the kitchen: a char-broil grate. The collective decision was reached for Andrew to drive into Tawning Spring, find a butcher shop, and come back with the largest sirloin steak he could buy. Trevayne thought it was a fine idea; he'd stop and chat with the 1600 Patrol on the way.

He did so. And not to his surprise but to his liking, he saw beneath the dashboard of the government automobile, the largest, most complicated assortment of radio dials he could imagine in one vehicle outside of a spacecraft.

That was fine, too.

The original owner's char-broil grate had one disadvantage: it smoked up most of the downstairs. As this required multiple windows to be opened, Trevayne remembered the rug switch to the guest-house panel, stepped on it, and loudly—if inexplicably to the children—complained redundantly about *him* and *his* char-broil fiasco.

"You know, Mom," said Steven Trevayne, watching his father open and close the front door, fanning the not currently overpowering smoke, "I think you'd better get him back on a sailboat. Dry land does something to his lobotomy."

"I think you'd better feed him, Mother," added Pam. "What did you say? He's been here for three weeks with no food."

Trevayne saw his wife and children laughing and realized the apparent ridiculousness of his actions, vocal *and* physical. "Be quiet or I'll cancel your subscriptions to *Child Life*."

The outsized steak was good, but no more than that. Several other decisions were made concerning the butcher shop and *his* char-broil grate. Pam and Phyllis brought on the coffee as Steve and Andy carried off the remaining dishes.

"I wonder how Lillian's doing?" asked Pam. "Up there all by herself."

"That's the way she likes it," said Steve, pouring a half-cup of heavy cream into his coffee. "Anyway, she can tell off the gardening service. She says Mom's too easy with them."

"I'm not easy or hard. I rarely see them."

"Lillian thinks you should look. Remember?" Steve turned to his sister. "She told us when we drove her into town last month that she didn't like the way they kept changing the crews. There was too much time wasted explaining, and the rock gardens were always loused up. She's a regular Louis the Fourteenth."

Andrew suddenly but unobtrusively looked up at his son. It was a small thing, if anything, but it caught his attention. Why had the gardening service changed personnel? It was a family business, and as the family was Italian and large, there was never any dearth of employees. At one time or another they'd *all* worked the grounds of

Barnegat. He'd look into the gardening service; he'd make some inquiries into the Aiello Landscapers. He would dismiss them.

"Lillian's protective," he said, backing off the subject. "We should be grateful."

"We are. Continuously," replied Phyllis.

"How's your committee coming, Dad?" Steve added some coffee to his heavy cream.

"Subcommittee, not committee; the difference is significant only in Washington. We've got most of the staff together now. The offices are in shape. Incidentally, very few beer breaks."

"Unenlightened management, probably."

"Positively." Andy nodded.

"When do you start blasting?" asked the son.

"Blasting? Where did you pick up that word?"

"Saturday morning cartoons," interjected Pam.

"Your father means relative to him," said Phyllis, watching her husband's concerned look.

"Well, aren't you going to out-Nader the raiders?" Steve smiled without much humor.

"Our functions are different."

"Oh? How so, Dad?"

"Ralph Nader's concerned with overall consumer problems. We're interested in specific contractual obligations pertaining to government agreements. There's a big difference."

"Same people," said the son.

"Not necessarily."

"Mostly," added the daughter.

"Not really."

"You're qualifying." Steve drank from his cup, his eyes on his father. "That means you're not sure."

"He probably hasn't had the time to find out, Steve," said Phyllis. "I don't think that's 'qualifying' anything."

"Of course it is, Phyl. A legitimate qualification. We're *not* sure. And whether they're the same people Nader's gone after or different people, that's not the issue. We're dealing in specific abuses."

"It's all part of the larger picture," said Steve. "The vested interests."

"Now hold it a minute." Trevayne poured himself more coffee. "I'm not sure of your definition of 'vested interests,' but I assume you mean 'well-financed.' Okay?"

"Okay."

"Heavy financing has brought about a lot of decent things. Medical research, I'd put first; then advanced technology in agriculture, construction, transportation. The results of these heavily financed projects help everyone. Health, food, shelter; vested interests can make enormous contributions. Isn't that valid?"

"Of course. When making contributions has something to do with it. And not just a by-product of making money."

"Your argument's with the profit motive, then?"

"Partially, yes."

"It's proved pretty viable. Especially when compared to other systems. The competition's built in; that makes more things available to more people."

"Don't mistake me," said the son. "No one's against the profit motive as such, Dad. Just when it becomes the only motive."

"I understand that," Andrew said. He knew he felt it deeply himself.

"Are you sure you do, Dad?"

"You don't believe I can?"

"I want to believe you. It's nice to read what reporters and people like that say about you. It's a good feeling, you know?"

"Then what prevents you?" asked Phyllis.

"I don't know, exactly. I guess I'd feel better if Dad was angry. Or angri*er*, maybe."

Andrew and Phyllis exchanged glances. Phyllis spoke quickly.

"Anger's not a solution, darling. It's a state of mind."

"It's not very constructive, Steve," added Trevayne lamely.

"But, Jesus! It's a starting point, Dad. I mean, *you* can *do* something. That's heavy; that's a real opportunity. But you'll blow it if you're hung up on 'specific abuses.'"

"Why? *Those* are *actual* starting points."

"No, they're not! They're the sort of things that clog

up the drains. By the time you get finished arguing every
little point, you're drowning in a sewer. You're up to your
neck—"

"It's not necessary to complete the analogy," interrupted Phyllis.

". . . in a thousand extraneous facts that high-powered
law firms delay in the courts."

"I think, if I understand you," said Andrew, "you're
advocating a spiked broom. That kind of cure could be
worse than the disease. It's dangerous."

"Okay. Maybe it's a little far out." Steven Trevayne
smiled earnestly without affection. "But take it from the
'guardians of tomorrow.' We're getting impatient, Dad."

Trevayne stood in his bathrobe in front of the miniature French door that opened on the impractical balcony.
It was one o'clock in the morning; he and Phyllis had
watched an old movie on the bedroom television set. It
was a bad habit they'd gotten into. But it was fun; the old
films were sedatives in their way.

"What's the matter?" asked Phyllis from the bed.

"Nothing. I just saw the car go by; Webster's men."

"Aren't they going to use the cottage?"

"I told them it was all right. They hedged. They said
they'd probably wait a day or so."

"Probably don't want to upset the children. It's one
thing telling them that routine precautions are taken for
subcommittee chairmen; it's quite another to see strangers
prowling around."

"I guess so. Steve was pretty outspoken, wasn't he?"

"Well . . ." Phyllis fluffed her pillow and frowned
before answering. "I don't think you should put too much
emphasis on what he said. He's young. He's like his
friends: they generalize. They can't—or won't—accept the
complications. They prefer 'spiked brooms.'"

"And in a few years they'll be able to use them."

"They won't want to then."

"Don't bank on it. Sometimes I think that's what this
whole thing's all about. . . . There goes the car again."

PART 2

13

It was nearly six-thirty; the rest of the staff had left over an hour ago. Trevayne stood behind his desk, his right foot carelessly on the seat of his chair, his elbow resting on his knee. Around the desk, looking at the large charts scattered over the top, were the subcommittee's key personnel, four men reluctantly "cleared" by Paul Bonner's superiors at Defense.

Directly in front of Trevayne was a young lawyer named Sam Vicarson. Andrew had run across the energetic, outspoken attorney during a grant hearing at the Danforth Foundation. Vicarson had represented—vigorously—the cause of a discredited Harlem arts organization reapplying for aid. The funds, by all logic, should have been denied, but Vicarson's imaginative apologies for the organization's past errors were so convincing that Danforth resubsidized. So Trevayne had made inquiries about Sam Vicarson, learned that he was part of the new breed of socially conscious attorneys, combining "straight," lucrative employment during the daytime with ghetto "storefront" work at night. He was bright, quick, and incredibly resourceful.

On Vicarson's right, bending over the desk, was Alan Martin, until six weeks ago the comptroller of Pace-Trevayne's New Haven plants. Martin was a thoughtful, middle-aged former stats analyst; a cautious man, excellent with details and firm in his convictions, once they were arrived at. He was Jewish and given to the quiet humor of ironies he'd heard since childhood.

On Vicarson's left, curling smoke out of a very large-bowled pipe, stood Michael Ryan, who, along with the man next to him, was an engineer. Both Ryan and John Larch were specialists in their fields—respectively aeronautical and construction engineering. Ryan was in his late thirties, florid, convivial, and quick to laugh but deadly serious when faced with an aircraft blueprint. Larch was contemplative, sullen in appearance, thin-featured, and always seemingly tired. But there was nothing tired about Larch's mind. In truth, each of these four minds worked constantly, at very high speeds.

These men were the nucleus of the subcommittee; if any were equal to the Defense Commission's objectives they were.

"All right," said Trevayne. "We've checked and rechecked these." He gestured wearily at the charts. "You've each had your part in compiling them; all of you studied them individually, without the benefit of one another's comments. Now, let's spell it out."

"The moment of truth, Andrew?" Alan Martin stood up. "Death in the late afternoon?"

"Bullshit." Michael Ryan took the pipe out of his mouth and smiled. "All over the arena."

"I think we ought to bind these and offer them to the highest bidder," said Sam Vicarson. "I could develop a penchant for the good life in Argentina."

"You'd end up in the Tierra del Fuego, Sam." John Larch moved slightly away from Ryan's pipe smoke.

"Who wants to begin?" asked Trevayne.

A quartet of statements was the reply. Each voice assertive, each expecting to dominate the others. Alan Martin, by holding up the palm of his hand, prevailed.

"From my point of view, there are holes in all the replies so far. But since the audits generally concern projects with subcontracting fluctuations, it's expected. Subsequent staff interviews are generally satisfactory. With one exception. In all cases of any real magnitude, bottom-line figures have been given. I.T.T. was reluctant, but they came over. Again, one exception."

"Okay, hold it there, Alan. Mike and John. You worked separately?"

"We cross-checked," said Ryan. "There was—and is—a lot of duplication; as with Alan, it's in the subcontracting areas. Ticking off: Lockheed and I.T.T. have been cooperative down the line. I.T.T. presses computer buttons, and out shoot the cards; Lockheed is centralized and still gets the shakes—"

"They should," interrupted Sam Vicarson. "They're using my money."

"They told me to thank you," said Alan Martin.

"GM and Ling-Tempco have problems," continued Ryan. "But to be fair about it, it's not so much evasion as it is just plain tracing who's responsible for what. One of our interviewers spent a whole day at General Motors—in the turbine engineering offices—talking to a guy who was trying to locate a unit design head. Turned out it was himself."

"There are also the usual corporation tremors," added John Larch. "Especially at GM; conformity and inquiry aren't happy bedfellows."

"Still, we generally get what we want. Litton is crazy. Smart-like-a-fox crazy. They finance; that puts them one to ten places removed from any practical application. I'm going to buy stock in those boys. Then we come to the big enigma."

"We'll get to it." Trevayne removed his foot from the chair and picked up his cigarette. "How about you Sam?"

Vicarson mocked a bow to Andrew. "I'd like to take this opportunity to thank the gods for bringing me in contact with so many prestigious law firms. My modest head is swimming."

"Translated," said Alan Martin, "he stole their books."

"Or the silver," said Ryan between puffs on his pipe.

"Neither. I have, however, juggled many offers of employment. . . . There's no point in recapping what's come in on a relatively satisfactory basis. I disagree with Mike; I think there's been a hell of a lot of evasion. I agree with John; corporation tremors—or delirium tremens—are everywhere. But with enough perseverance, you get the answers; at least enough to satisfy. With all but one. . . . It's Alan's 'exception' and Mike's 'enigma.' For me it's a legal jigsaw never covered in Blackstone."

"And there we are," said Trevayne, sitting down. "Genessee Industries."

"That's where it's at," replied Sam. "Genessee."

"Leopards and spots and nothing changes." Andrew crushed out his hardly smoked cigarette.

"What's that mean?" asked Larch.

"Years ago," answered Trevayne, "twenty, to be exact, Genessee waltzed Doug Pace and me around for months. One presentation after another. I'd just gotten married; Phyl and I traveled out to Palo Alto for them. We gave them everything they wanted. So well, they threw us out and used variations on our designs and went into production for themselves."

"Nice people," said Vicarson. "Couldn't you get them for patent theft?"

"Nope. They're better than that and you can't patent Bernoulli's principle. They made the variation in the metallurgical tolerances."

"Indigenous and unprovable." Michael Ryan tapped his pipe into an ashtray. "Genessee has laboratories in a dozen different states, proving grounds in twice as many. They could predate mockups with authenticated affidavits, and the courts wouldn't know what the hell was going on. They'd win."

"Exactly," agreed Andrew. "But that's another story, another time. We've got enough to think about. Where are we? What do we do?"

"Let me try to put it together." Alan Martin picked up the cardboard chart marked "Genessee Industries." Each chart was twenty-four inches by twenty-four: there were outlined boxes with headings above subdivisions. Underneath and to the right of every title was inserted—stapled—typewritten data pertaining to the areas of contractual commitment, engineering and construction, financial operations, and legal entanglements—usually concerning the financial operations. There were scores of index markings that referred the reader to this or that file. "The advantage of the financial picture is that it pervades all areas. . . . During the past weeks we've sent out hundreds of questionnaires—routine, all the companies got them. As you all know, they were coded, just like advertising coupons in newspapers. The codes gave us mailing times and locations. We then followed up with staff interviews. We found that with Genessee there was an abnormal amount of shifting. Answers we assumed would be sent from logically designated departments and locations were transferred to others—not so logical. Executive personnel our staff went out to interview *routinely* were suddenly no longer in their positions. Genessee had sent them to other divisions, subsidiaries; hundreds, even thousands of miles away. Some to overseas branches. . . . We began setting up conferences with union leadership. Same story, only less subtle. The word went out across the country—from one coast to the other—no local discussions. The nationals were deciding what to do about government interference. In short words, Genessee Industries has been engaged in a very efficient and massive cover-up."

"Not completely efficient, obviously," said Trevayne quietly.

"Pretty damned good Andrew," rejoined Martin. "Remember, Genessee has over two hundred thousand employees, multimillion-dollar contracts every fifteen minutes —under one name or another—and real estate rivaling the Department of the Interior. As long as those questionnaires kept coming back, and with Genessee's diversification, the shuffling might easily go unnoticed."

"Not with you, you financial raccoon." Vicarson sat on the arm of an easy chair and reached over, taking the Genessee chart from Martin.

"I didn't say they were *that* good."

"What struck me," continued Sam, "and it probably wasn't so great a shock to Mike and John or even Al here, was the sheer size of Genessee. Its subsidiary structure is goddamned unbelievable. Sure, we've all heard Genessee *this* and Genessee *that* for years, but it never really impressed me before. Like those one-page ads you see in magazines—institutional things; you figure, okay, it's a company. That's nice; it's a nice display. But this one! It's got more names than a telephone book."

"And no antitrust action," said Andrew.

"Gesco, Genucraft, SeeCon, Pal-Co, Cal-Gen, SeeCal . . . So help me, it's double crostics!" Sam Vicarson tapped his finger on the Genessee chart's "Subsidiary" heading. "What bothers me is that I'm beginning to think there are dozens more we haven't traced."

"Let them be," said John Larch with a pained expression on his thin face. "We've got enough to work with."

14

Major Paul Bonner parked in an empty space on the river side of the Potomac Towers lot. He stared out the windshield at the water, growing sluggish with the progressing fall season. It had been seven weeks to the day since he'd first driven into that parking area; seven weeks since he'd first met Andrew Trevayne. He had begun the liaison position with resentment—against both the man and the job. The resentment against the job remained, perhaps grew; he found it difficult to sustain any real dislike of the man.

Not that he approved of Trevayne's goddamn subcommittee; he didn't. It was all horseshit. Scattershot horseshit conceived by the pols on the Hill for the sole purpose of shifting—or at least diluting—the responsibility for that which was necessary. That's what made Major Paul Bonner so hostile; no one could dispute the necessity—no one! Yet everyone gave the appearance of shocked disbelief when dealing with acknowledged reality.

Time was the enemy. Not people. Couldn't they see that? Hadn't they learned that in the space program? Certainly Apollo 14 cost twenty million when it was launched in February of seventy-one. If, instead, it had been scheduled for seventy-two, it would have cost ten; six months later, probably five to seven and a half. Time was the ultimate factor in the goddamn civilian economics and since they, the military, had to reckon with time, they also had to accept the economic—civilian—penalties.

Over the weeks he'd tried to impress Andy Trevayne with his theory. But Trevayne only acknowledged it to be *a* factor, not *the* factor. Trevayne insisted that Bonner's theory was simplistic, then roared with laughter when Bonner reacted explosively to the term. Even the Major had smiled—"simplistic" was no less a code name for "idiocy" than his use of "civilian."

Checkmate.

But Trevayne did allow that if one eliminated time, a degree of corruption could be dispensed with; if there was all the time in the world, one could sit back and wait for reasonable prices. He agreed to that.

But it was only one aspect, he insisted. Trevayne knew the marketplace. Corruption went much further than the purchase of time.

And Bonner knew he was right.

Checkmate.

The fundamental difference between the two men was the importance each gave to the time factor, however. For Bonner it was paramount; for Trevayne it wasn't. The civilian held to the judgment that there was a basic international intelligence that would prohibit global holocaust. The Major did not. He'd seen the enemy, fought him, witnessed the fanaticism that propelled him. It filtered down from austere halls in national capitals through field commanders to battalions; from battalions down into the ranks of the half-uniformed, sometimes half-starved troops. And it was powerful. Bonner was not so simplistic, he felt, as to reduce the enemy to a political label; he'd made that clear to Andy. The enemy wasn't a Communist, or a Marxist, or a Maoist or a Lumumbaist. Those were merely convenient titles.

The enemy was three-fifths of the earth emerging from ignorance and thrust forward by the *idea* of revolution; the *idea* of finally—after centuries—possessing its own identity. And once possessing it, forcing its imprimatur on the rest of the world.

No matter the reasons, even the justifications; no matter the rationalizations, filled with motivational theories and diplomatic convolutions. The enemy was people. A few in control of millions upon millions; and these few, with their newly found power and technology, were subject to human weakness and their own fanatical commitments.

The rest of the world had to be prepared to deal decisively, emphatically, overpoweringly with this enemy. Paul Bonner didn't give a damn what it was called.

That it was, was enough.

And that meant time. Time had to be bought, no matter the price or the petty manipulations of the suppliers.

He got out of the Army car and started to walk slowly across the tarred surface toward the entrance of the apartment-office complex. He was in no hurry, no hurry whatsoever. If it were possible, he'd prefer not being there at all. Not today.

For today was the start of his real assignment, what he'd been primed for, maneuvered into. Today was when he was to begin bringing back concrete information to his superiors at Defense.

He'd known it all along, of course. He realized at the beginning that he hadn't been selected as Trevayne's liaison because of any outstanding qualifications. He had none for that type of work. He knew, further, that the constant but innocuous questioning he'd received to date was only a lead-in to what had to follow. His superiors weren't really interested in such mundane matters as: How are things going? Are the offices satisfactory? Is the staff up to snuff? Is Trevayne a nice fellow? . . . No, the colonels and the brigadiers had other things on their minds.

Bonner stopped by the steps and looked up. Three Phantom 40's, their jetstreams sharply defined in white against the blue sky, streaked west at an enormous altitude. There was no sound, only the barely visible outlines of three tiny triangles gracefully, like miniature silver arrowheads, piercing the air corridors of the horizon.

Strike force—bomb and rocket tonnage capable of obliterating five battalions; flight maneuverability—complete mastery of dynamics from ground zero to seventy thousand feet: speed—Mach three.

That's what it was all about.

But he wished it didn't have to happen *this* way.

He thought back to the morning, a brief three hours ago. He'd been sitting in his office trying to make sense out of some Light-colonel's appraisal of new installations at Benning. It was nonsense, the summation more concerned with the officer's egotistical evaluation of his own observations than with the equipment. The request had been for eighty-percent replacement; said request a put-down of the previous officer in charge. It was an Army game played by second-raters.

As Bonner had scribbled his negative recommendation across the bottom of the page, his intercom rang. He was ordered to report immediately to the fifth floor—"Brasswares," as all below the rank of colonel called it—to Brigadier General Cooper. Lester Cooper, a white-haired, tough, facile-tongued exponent of the Pentagon's requirements. An ex-commandant of West Point whose father had held the same position. A man of and for the Army.

The Brigadier had spelled it out. Not just what he was to do, but without using the specific words, why he was selected to do it. As most military strategies, it was simple—simplistic?—and to the point. Paul Bonner, for the sake of military necessity, was to be an informer. In the event any impropriety was charged, he was expendable.

But the Army would take care of him. As it had taken care of him once before in Southeast Asia; protected him once before and showed him its gratitude.

It was all a question of priorities; the Brigadier had made that clear. Ordered it to be clear.

"You must understand, Major. We support this Trevayne's efforts. The Joint Chiefs have requested that we cooperate in every way and we have. But we can't allow him to cripple vital production. You of all people should see that. . . . Now, you're on a friendly basis with him. You've . . ."

It was during the next five minutes that Brigadier General Cooper nearly lost his informer. He alluded to several get-togethers between Bonner and Trevayne that the Major had not listed in any report or spoken of in the office. There was no reason to; they were entirely social, in no way related to the Department of Defense. One had been a weekend he'd spent with the Trevaynes in Connecticut at High Barnegat. Another was a small dinner party Bonner's current mistress, a divorcée in McLean, had given for Andy and Phyllis. Still another, an afternoon of horseback riding and a fall barbeque in the Maryland hunt country. None was remotely connected with Trevayne's subcommittee or Bonner's liaison assignment; none was paid for with government funds. The Major was annoyed.

"General, why have I been under surveillance?"

"You haven't. Trevayne has."

"Is he aware of it?"

"He may be. He's certainly aware of the rotating patrols from Treasury. White House orders. He takes damn good care of them."

"Do they act as surveillance?"

"Frankly, no."

"Why not . . . sir?"

"That question may be beyond your province, Bonner."

"I don't wish to disagree with the General, but since I'm delegated to . . . act very closely with Trevayne, I think I should be informed of such matters. It was my understanding that the guards were assigned by '1600' for precautionary measures. Since they're in a maximum position for surveillance but they're not being used—at least not by us—and we assign additional personnel, it strikes me that we're either duplicating or at cross-purposes."

"Which means you object to my reading off information you haven't given this office."

"Yes, sir. That information had nothing to do with this office. If there was surveillance, I should have been informed. I've been placed in an unreasonably prejudiced position."

"You're a hard-nose, Major."

"I doubt I'd've been given this job if I wasn't."

The Brigadier got out of his chair and went to a long briefing table against the wall. He turned and leaned against it, facing Bonner. "All right, I'll accept 'cross-purposes.' I won't pretend that we have a solid working relationship with everyone in this administration. Nor will I deny that there are a number of people surrounding the President whose judgments we find lacking. No, Major, we're not about to let '1600' control our surveillance . . . or filter it."

"I understand that, General. I still think I should have been told."

"An oversight, Bonner. If it was anything else, my telling you now eliminates that, doesn't it?"

The two officers stared at each other briefly. The understanding was complete—Bonner was at that moment accepted into the highest echelons of Defense.

"Understood, General," said Bonner quietly.

The erect, white-haired Cooper turned back to the long table and opened a thick, plastic-bound notebook with huge metal rings. "Come here, Major. This is the book. And I mean *the* book, soldier."

Bonner read the typed words on the front page: "GEN-ESSEE INDUSTRIES."

Bonner entered the glass doors of the Potomac Towers and walked on the thick blue carpet toward the elevators. If he'd timed everything right, if his telephone calls had resulted in the correct information, he'd arrive at Trevayne's office at least a half-hour before Trevayne himself returned. That was the plan; over in the Senate Office Building, where Trevayne was in conference, others were also watching the clock.

He was such a familiar sight in Trevayne's suite of rooms that he was greeted now with complete informality. Bonner knew he was accepted by the small civilian staff because he seemed to be an anomaly. The professional soldier who possessed few of the unattractive military trappings; whose outlook, even his conversation, seemed easygoing, with a continuous undercurrent of humor. When civilians found a man in uniform—especially the sort of overdressed uniform required daily at the Pentagon—who seemed to contradict the accepted manifestations of his profession, they warmed quickly. It was standard procedure.

It would be no problem at all for him to wait in Trevayne's inner office. He would take off his tunic, and stand in the doorway, and joke with Trevayne's secretary. Then he might wander into one of the other rooms—his tie undone, his collar unbuttoned—and pass a few minutes with several of the staff. Men like Mike Ryan or John Larch. Perhaps the bright young attorney, Sam Vicarson. He'd tell them a couple of stories—stories which ridiculed a pompous, well-advertised general or two. Finally, he'd say he was going to stop bothering them and read the morning paper in Trevayne's office. They'd protest in good humor, of course, but he'd smile and suggest a few drinks after work, perhaps.

It would all take six or seven minutes.

He would then return to Trevayne's office, passing the secretary once again—this time complimenting her on her dress or her hair or whatever—and walk to the armchair by the window.

But he would not read the paper nor sit in the chair.

Instead he would go to the file cabinet on the right wall and open it. He would select the drawer that held the *G's.*

Genessee Industries, Palo Alto, California.

He would extract the folder, close the drawer, and return to the chair. He would have a safe maximum of fifteen minutes to make notes before replacing the information.

The entire operation would take less than twenty-five minutes, and there would be only one moment of risk. If Trevayne's secretary or a staff member walked in while the cabinet was open. In that event he would have to say he found it open and pass his actions off casually as "curiosity."

But of course the cabinet would never have been open; it was always locked. Always.

Major Paul Bonner would unlock it with a key given him by Brigadier General Lester Cooper.

It was all a question of priorities; and Bonner felt sick to his stomach.

15

Trevayne rushed up the steps of the Capitol Building, conscious of the fact that he had been followed. He knew it, because he had made two out-of-the-way stops from his office to the center of town: at a bookstore on Rhode Island Avenue, where the traffic was slight, and a spur-of-the-moment detour to Georgetown, Ambassador Hill's residence. The Ambassador wasn't home.

On Rhode Island Avenue he'd noticed a gray Pontiac sedan maneuver into a parking space half a block behind him—heard the Pontiac's rear tires scraping the curb.

Twenty minutes later, as he had walked to the front door of Hill's Georgetown house, he had heard the bells of a knife-sharpening truck, a small van driving slowly down the cobblestone street soliciting business from the uniformed maids. He had smiled, thinking the sight an anachronism, a throwback to his teen-age Boston memories.

Then he saw it again; there was the gray Pontiac. It was behind the slow-moving van, its driver obviously annoyed; the street was narrow, and the small truck was not accommodating. The Pontiac was unable to pass.

As Trevayne reached the top of the Capitol's steps he made a mental note to check with Webster at the White House. Perhaps Webster had assigned separate guards for him, although such precautions were unnecessary. Not that he was brave; he was simply too well known a figure now, and he rarely traveled alone. This afternoon was an exception.

He turned on the last step and looked down at the street. The gray Pontiac wasn't in sight, but there were dozens of automobiles—some parked, with drivers inside, some moving slowly past. Any one of them might have been radioed from Georgetown.

He entered the building and went immediately to the information desk. It was almost four o'clock, and he was expected at the office of National District Statistics before the end of the day. He wasn't sure what the N.D.S. information would prove; if, indeed, he could extract any information to begin with, but it was another alley, another possible connection between seemingly unrelated facts.

National District Statistics was a computerized laboratory that more logically should have been housed at Treasury. That it wasn't was merely another inconsistency in this town of contradictions, thought Trevayne. National District Statistics kept up-to-the-month records of regional employment directly affected by government projects. It duplicated the work of a dozen other offices but was somewhat different in the sense that its information was general; "projects" included everything from partial payment of state highways to federal participation in school construction. From aircraft factories to the renovation of

park areas. In other words, it was a catch-all for explaining
the allocation of tax money, and as such was used incessantly, prodigiously, by politicians justifying their exis-
tences. The figures could, of course, be broken down into
categories, if one preferred, but that was rarely the case.
The totals were always more impressive than their collective parts.

As he neared the N.D.S. door, Trevayne reconsidered
the logic of its location; it was, after all, quite proper that
N.D.S. be close to the offices of those who needed it most.
  In essence, why he was there.

  Trevayne put the papers down on the table. It was a
few minutes after five, and he'd been reading in the small
cubicle for nearly an hour. He rubbed his eyes and saw
that one of the minor custodians was looking through the
glass-paneled door; it was past closing, and the clerk was
anxious to shut the office and leave. Trevayne would give
him a ten-dollar bill for the delay.

  It was a ludicrous exchange. Information involving—at
a rough estimate—two hundred and thirty million for the
gratuity of ten dollars.

  But there it was—two increases of 148 million and 82
million respectively. Each increase predominantly the result of defense contracts—coded as "DF" in the schedules;
both "unexpected," if Trevayne's newspaper reading was
accurate. Sudden windfalls for each constituency.

  Yet both had been predicted with incredible accuracy
by the two candidates running for reelection in their respective states.

  California and Maryland.

  Senators Armbruster and Weeks. The short, compact
pipe-smoking Armbruster. And Alton Weeks, the polished
aristocrat from Maryland's Eastern Shore.

  Armbruster had faced a tough challenger for his incum-
bency. Northern California's unemployment was danger-
ously, if temporarily, high, and the polls indicated that his
opponent's attacks on Armbruster's failure to garner government contracts were having an effect on the voters.
Armbruster, in the last days of the campaign, suddenly
injected a subtle note that probably turned the election in

his favor. He insinuated that he was in the process of obtaining defense money in the neighborhood of one hundred and fifty million. A figure which even the state economists admitted was sufficient to prime the pumps of the state's northern recovery.

Weeks: also an incumbent, but faced not so much by competition as by a campaign deficit. Money was tight in the Maryland coffers, and the prestigious Weeks family reluctant to underwrite the entirety. According to the Baltimore *Sun*, Alton Weeks met privately with a number of Maryland's leading business figures and told them Washington's purse strings were loosening. They could be assured of a minimum of eighty million directed into Maryland's industrial economy. . . . Weeks's campaign resources were suddenly substantial.

Yet the election of both senators had taken place six months prior to each allocation. And although it was possible that both men had been huddling with defense appropriations, it wasn't logical that they could have been so precise as to the amounts. Not unless arrangements were made; arrangements more concerned with politics than with national security.

And both senators dealt with the same Defense contractor.

Genessee Industries.

Armbruster funded developments in Genessee's new high-altitude Norad interceptors, a questionable project from the outset.

Weeks had managed to finance an equally suspect undertaking with a Maryland subsidiary of Genessee's. A coastal radar network improvement "justified" by two isolated aircraft penetrating the coastal screen several years ago.

Trevayne gathered the papers together and stood up. He signaled the clerk through the glass panel and reached into his pocket.

Out on the street he considered going to a pay phone and calling William Hill. He had to see Hill about another "project," one that dealt with naval intelligence and might surface in a matter of days, perhaps hours, because of

Trevayne. It was why he'd driven out to Georgetown earlier; it was not the sort of conversation one had on the telephone.

The Navy Department had been authorized to equip four atomic submarines with the most sophisticated electronic intelligence instruments available, the equipment to be installed within twelve months of authorization. The due date had long since passed; two of the electronics firms contracted had declared bankruptcy; the four submarines were still in dry dock, essentially inoperable.

During his staff's preliminary work an angry lieutenant commander, one of the four submarine skippers, had openly criticized the operation. Word of the naval officer's complaints to an official audience had reached an aggressive Washington newsman named Roderick Bruce, who threatened to break the story in print. The Central Intelligence Agency and the Navy Department were in panic, genuine panic. Making public the undersea electronic installations was dangerous in itself; acknowledging the foulups compounded that danger, and admitting the current inoperability of the ships was an open invitation for Russian and Chinese saber-rattling.

It was a sensitive situation, and Trevayne's subcommittee was being blamed for creating risks far greater than any good it might achieve.

Trevayne knew that sooner or later the specter of "dangerous intrusion" would be raised. He had prepared himself for it, made clear his fundamental opposition to burying incompetence—or worse—under the label of "classified, top secret."

For such labels were too easily come by; even if sincerely arrived at, they were only judgments, singular positions.

There were other judgments, opposing positions. And he would not back off unless those opinions were analyzed as well. Once he did, once he retreated, his subcommittee would be emasculated. He could not allow that precedent.

And there was a side issue—unprovable, only rumor, but in line with everything they were learning.

Genessee Industries once again.

The back-room legal talk was that Genessee was preparing to submit bids to take over the electronics installation of the submarines. The gossip was that Genessee had brought about the bankruptcies; had created sufficient subcontracting problems for the remaining two, that their agreements with the Navy Department were as good as void.

Trevayne walked into a drugstore, to the telephone booth, and dialed Hill's number.

The Ambassador, of course, would see him immediately.

"To begin with, the CIA's assumption that the Russians and the Chinese are oblivious to the situation is ridiculous. Those submarines have been beached in New London for months; simple observation tells them their conditions."

"Then I'm right to press it?"

"I'd say so," answered Hill behind the mahogany table which served as his desk. "I'd also suggest that you give the Agency and the Navy the courtesy of talking to this newsman, this Bruce fellow; see if you can't get him to ease up a bit. Their fears are real to them, if only for their own skins."

"I've no objection to that. I just don't want to be put in the position of taking my staff off a project."

"I don't think you should. . . . I don't think you will."

"Thank you."

William Hill leaned back in his chair. His advice dispensed with, he wanted to chat. "Tell me, Trevayne. It's been two months. What do you think?"

"It's crazy. I know that's a frivolous word, but at this point it's the most descriptive. The economics of the biggest corporation in the world are run by lunatics. . . . Or, perhaps, that's the image that's meant to be projected."

"I assume you refer to the aspect of . . . 'you'll-have-to-check-with-someone-else.' "

"Exactly. Nobody makes a decision—"

"Responsibility's to be avoided at all costs," interrupted Hill with a benign smile. "Not much different from the outside. Each to his own level of incompetence."

"I'll accept that in the private sector. It's a form of survival-waste, if there's such a term. But it's controllable, when control is wanted. But that's private, not public

money. . . . Down here that theory shouldn't prove out.
This is civil service. Given a period of time—say, enough
so as to be in a decision-making position—a man's security
is automatic. The games aren't necessary. Or they shouldn't
be."

"You're oversimplifying."

"I know, but it's a starting point." Trevayne recalled
with amusement that he used his son's words.

"There are formidable pressures on people in this
town. The results often lead to ostracism, which can be as
important as security to all but the strongest. Scores of
departments, including the Pentagon, demand commitments in the name of national interest; manufacturers
demand the contracts and send highly paid lobbyists to get
them; organized labor plays them all off against each other
and threatens with strikes *and* votes. Finally, the senators
and congressmen—their districts cry out for the economic
benefits derived from the whole bundle. . . . Where do
you find the independent, or incorruptible, man within
such a system?"

Trevayne saw that Big Billy Hill was staring at the
wall. Staring at nothing anyone else would see. The Ambassador had not asked the question of his guest, but of
himself. William Hill was ultimately, after a long life, a
profound cynic.

"The answer to that, Mr. Ambassador, lies somewhere between our being a nation of laws, and the checks
and balances of a relatively free society."

Hill laughed. It was the tired laugh of an old man
who still possessed his juices. "Words, Trevayne, words.
You throw in the Malthusian law of economics—which can
be reduced to the human condition of wanting more, to
somebody else's less—and the pot goes to the man who
has raised the biggest bet . . . or bank. That's what our
friends in the Soviet Union have found out; why the
primary theories of Marx and Engels won't wash. You
can't change the human condition."

"I don't agree; not about the Russians, the human
condition. It changes constantly. We've seen that over and
over again, especially in times of crisis."

"Certainly, *crisis*. That's *fear*. Collective fear. The

member subordinates his individual wants to tribal survival. Why do you think our socialist co-earthlings continually cry 'emergency'? They've learned that much. . . . They've also learned that you can't project crises ad infinitum; that's against the human condition, too."

"Then I'd go back to the checks and balances . . . and a free society. You see, I really do believe it all works."

Hill leaned forward in his chair, putting his elbows on the table. He looked at Trevayne, and there was humor in his eyes. "Now I know why Frank Baldwin's on your side. You're like him in several ways."

"I'm flattered, but I never thought there was any similarity . . ."

"Oh, but there is. You know, Frank Baldwin and I often talk as we're talking now. For hours. We sit in one of our clubs, or in our libraries . . . surrounded by all this." Hill gestured with his right hand, including—somewhat derisively—the entire room. "There we are, two old men sitting around making pronouncements. Reaching for our very expensive brandies; servants checking out of the corners of their eyes to see if we're in need of anything. Comfort the prime consideration for our tired, breathing . . . rich corpses. And there we sit, dividing up the planet; each trying to convince the other what this part of the world *will* do and that part *won't* do. . . . That's what it all comes down to, you know. Anticipate the opposing interests; motives are no problem any longer. Just modus vivendis. The *whats* and *hows*; not the *whys*."

"Tribal survival."

"Precisely. . . . And Frank Baldwin, the toughest of the money lenders, a man whose signature can bankrupt small nations, tells me as you tell me now that underneath the frantic deceits—this global mendacity—there's a workable solution. And I tell him there isn't; not in his sense of the word. Nothing that can be set on a permanent course."

"There'll always be change, granted. But I side with him; there has to be a solution."

"The solution, Trevayne, is in the ever-present search for one. Cycles of build-up and retreat. That's your solution. *Paratus*, paratus."

"I thought you said that sort of thing was against the

human condition; nations couldn't project crises ad infinitum."

"Not inconsistent. Relief is constantly setting in. It's in the retreats. They're the breathing spells."

"That's too dangerous; there has to be a better way."

"Not in this world. We've gone beyond that."

"I disagree again. We've just arrived at the point where it's mandatory."

"All right. Let's take your present bailiwick. You've seen enough; how are you going to implement your checks and balances? Your problems aren't unlike the larger sphere of interacting nations; very similar in many ways. Where do you begin?"

"By finding a pattern. A pattern with designs common to all the rest; as near as possible, at any rate."

"The Controller General's done that, and so we formed the Defense Allocations Commission. The United Nations did the same, and we got the Security Council. The crises still exist; nothing much has changed."

"We have to keep looking—"

"The solution, then," interrupted Hill with a small triumphant smile, "is in the search. You see what I mean now? As long as the search goes on, we can breathe."

Trevayne shifted his position in the soft leather armchair. It was the same chair, he reflected, in which he had sat during the hastily summoned conference ten weeks ago. "I can't accept that, Mr. Ambassador. It's too impermanent, too subject to miscalculation. There's better machinery than half-constructed scaffolds. We'll find it."

"I repeat. Where do you begin?"

"I've begun. . . . I meant what I said about finding a pattern. A single enterprise, large enough to require enormous funding; complex enough to involve scores, hundreds of contractors and subcontractors. A project which reaches into a dozen states for its components. . . . I've found it."

William Hill brought the thin fingers of his right hand to his chin. He kept his eyes on Trevayne. "Is your point to concentrate on one venture; to make an example?" The tone of Hill's voice was unmistakably that of disappointment.

"Yes. Assistants will continue with the other work;

there'll be no loss of continuity. But my four top men and I are concentrating on one corporation."

Hill spoke quietly. "I've heard the rumors. Perhaps you'll find your enemy."

Trevayne lit a cigarette, watching the butane flame of his lighter reduce itself to a tiny yellow ball through the loss of fuel. "Mr. Ambassador, we're going to need help."

"Why?" Hill began doodling on a notepad. The scratches of the pencil were deliberate, controlled—and angry.

"Because a pattern is emerging that disturbs us very much. Let me put it this way: the clearer that pattern becomes, the more difficult it is to get specific information; we think we've nailed something, it eludes us. Explanations deteriorate to . . . what did you say a few minutes ago? 'Words.' 'Check here,' 'check there,' 'check somewhere else.' Specifics must be avoided at all costs, apparently."

"You must be dealing with a very diversified, spread-out organization." Hill spoke in a monotone.

"It has a subsidiary complex—to use one of my staff's phrases—that is 'goddamned unbelievable.' The major plants are centralized on the West Coast, but the Chicago offices run its administration. Its dictatorship is enormous and—"

"Read like a cross section of the West Point–Annapolis honor rolls." Hill interrupted rapidly, quietly, the humor fading from his eyes.

"I was going to include a number of highly placed—or once highly placed—residents of Washington. A few former senators and representatives, three or four cabinet appointments—going back over the years, of course."

William Hill picked up the notepad on which he'd been scratching, and put down his pencil.

"It strikes me, Trevayne, that you're taking on the Pentagon, both houses of Congress, a hundred different industries, organized labor, and a few state governments thrown into the bargain."

Hill turned the pad around toward Trevayne.

On it, hundreds of tiny lines converged to spell out two words. "Genessee Industries."

16

His name was Roderick Bruce, and its sound was as intelligently contrived as the man. An ear-catching, theatrical name; a fast tongue; and a hard stare were the extensions of his reporting personality.

He was syndicated in 891 papers across the country, had a standard lecture fee of three thousand dollars, which he invariably—publicly—donated to diverse charities, and, most surprising, was very much liked by his peers.

The reason for his popularity within the fourth estate was easily explained, however. Rod Bruce—of the "Washington-New York media axis"—never forgot that he was born Roger Brewster of Erie, Pennsylvania, and among his journalistic brothers, was generous and always humorous in a self-deprecating way about his public image.

In short, Rod was a nice guy.

Except when it came to his sources of information and the intensity of his curiosity.

He guarded the first zealously and was relentless in the second.

Andrew Trevayne had learned this much about Bruce and looked forward to meeting him. The columnist was perfectly willing to discuss the story of the four inoperable atomic submarines. But he'd made it clear that the subcommittee chairman would have to present an incredibly strong argument for the newsman to suppress the story. It was scheduled for release in three days.

And in what seemed an unusual courtesy, considering the situation, Bruce suggested that he come to Trevayne's suite at the Potomac Towers at ten in the morning.

When Trevayne saw the columnist enter his outer office, he was surprised by Bruce's appearance. Not the face; the face was familiar through years of newspaper photographs accompanying the man's columns—sharp features, deep-set eyes, longish hair before it was stylish. But his size. Roderick Bruce was a very short man, and this characteristic was accentuated by his clothes. Dark, conservative; seemingly overpressed. He looked like a little boy all dressed up for a Sunday-morning church service in a Norman Rockwell *Saturday Evening Post* cover. The longish hair being the one aspect of allowed independence, a little boy's independence, in a newspaperman well into his fifties.

Bruce followed the secretary through the door and extended his hand to Trevayne. Andrew was almost embarrassed to stand up and come around the desk. Bruce seemed actually shorter, smaller, at close proximity. But Roderick Bruce was no amateur at first meetings on a professional basis. He smiled as he gripped Trevayne's hand firmly.

"Don't let my size fool you; I'm wearing my elevator shoes. . . . Nice to meet you, Trevayne."

In this brief salutation Bruce took care of two objectives. He humorously smoothed the awkward, obviously unmentionable aspect of his size, and by the use of Trevayne's single last name, let Andy know they were on equal footing.

"Thank you. Please, sit down." Trevayne looked over at his secretary as she started out. "Hold my calls, will you, Marge? And close the door, please." He returned to his chair as Roderick Bruce sat down in front of the desk.

"These offices are certainly off the beaten track, aren't they?"

"I apologize; I hope the trip wasn't inconvenient. I'd have been happy to meet you in town; it's why I suggested lunch."

"No trouble. I wanted to scout this place for myself; a lot of people are talking about it. Funny, I don't see any racks or whips or iron maidens."

"We keep that equipment locked up in a back room. More centralized that way."

"Good answer; I'll use it." Bruce took out a small notebook—a *very* small notebook, as if scaled to his size—and jotted down several words as Trevayne laughed. "You never can tell when a good direct quote will come in handy."

"It wasn't particularly good."

"All right, then, humanizing. A lot of Kennedy's quips were just as much humanizing as they were bright, you know."

"Which one?"

"Jack's. Bobby's were labored, thought out. Jack was instinctively human . . . and humorous in a vulnerable way."

"I'm in good company."

"Not bad. But you're not running for anything, so it doesn't matter, does it?"

"You took out the notebook, I didn't."

"And it's going to stay out, Mr. Trevayne. . . . Shall we talk about four submarines, each costing roughly one hundred and eighty million apiece, currently boondoggled in dry dock? Seven hundred and twenty million dollars' worth of nothing. . . . You know it, I know it. Why shouldn't the people who paid for it know also?"

"Perhaps they should."

Bruce hadn't expected Trevayne's reply. He shifted his position in the chair and crossed his short legs. Andy wondered for a second if the newsman's feet were touching the floor.

"That's very good, too. I won't bother to write it down, because I'll remember it." Bruce folded the flap of his tiny notebook. "Then I assume you have no objection to my story."

"To be perfectly frank with you, I have no objections at all. Others have; I don't."

"Then why did you want to see me?"

"To . . . plead their case, I guess."

"I've turned them down. Why wouldn't I turn you down?"

"Because I'm a disinterested party; I can objectify. I think you have sound reasons for making public a very expensive fiasco, and if I were you, I'd probably release it without hesitation. On the other hand, I don't have your experience. I wouldn't know where to draw the line between a necessary reporting of incompetence and invading the areas of national security. I might shed light on that part."

"Oh, come on, Trevayne." Roderick Bruce uncrossed

his legs in annoyance. "I've heard that argument, and it won't wash!"

"You're sure of that?"

"For reasons more valid than you'd ever suspect."

"If that's the case, Mr. Bruce," said Trevayne, taking out a pack of cigarettes, "you should have accepted my offer of lunch. We could have spent the rest of the meal in pleasant conversation. You don't know it, but I'm an avid reader of yours. Cigarette?"

Roderick Bruce stared at Trevayne, his lower lip fallen from his mouth. Since he did not reach for a cigarette, Trevayne shook one out for himself and leaned back in his chair while lighting it.

"Jesus! You mean it," said Bruce quietly.

"I certainly do. I . . . suspect . . . the valid reasons you refer to cover the areas of security. If so, and I know damned well you didn't get where you are by lying in these matters, I can't offer any further argument."

"But my breaking it isn't going to help you, is it?"

"No, it's not. It'll be one bitch of a hindrance, to tell you the truth. But that's my problem, not yours."

Bruce leaned slightly forward, his miniature frame somewhat ludicrous in the large leather chair. "You don't have to have a problem. . . . And I don't *care* if the room is bugged."

"If it's what?" Trevayne sat up.

"I don't care if we're taped; I gather we're not. I'll trade you off, Trevayne. . . . No hindrance from me; no problems with the New London mess. Simple trade. I'll even give you a selection."

"What the hell are you talking about?"

"We'll start with yesterday." Bruce lifted the right flap of his coat jacket and slowly reinserted his notebook. He did so stylistically, as if the action were symbolic of confidence. He held his gold pencil in his hands and revolved both ends between his fingers. "You spent an hour and twenty minutes at National District Statistics yesterday; from shortly after four to past closing. You requested the volumes for the states of California and Maryland for the periods covering the past eighteen months. Now, given time, my office could easily go through the books and probably find what you were researching, but let's face it, there are several thousand pages and a couple of hundred thousand insertions. What interests me is that you did the legwork yourself. Not a secretary, not even an aide. You were playing close poker. What did you get?"

Trevayne tried to absorb Bruce's words, the implications behind his words.

"You were the gray Pontiac. You followed me in a gray Pontiac."

"Wrong, but interesting."

"You were on Rhode Island Avenue, and then you were in Georgetown. Behind a knife-sharpening truck."

"Sorry. Wrong again. If I want you followed, you'll never know it. What did you go after at N.D.S.? That's selection one. If it's worth it, I'll kill the sub story."

Trevayne's mind was still on the Pontiac. He'd call Webster at the White House as soon as he got rid of Bruce. . . . He'd nearly forgotten about the Pontiac.

"No deal, Bruce. It's not worth it, anyway. It was background."

"All right, I'll put my staff on the N.D.S. books. We'll find it. . . . Selection two. This is rougher. There's a rumor that six weeks ago, after your somewhat spectacular appearance at the Senate hearing, you met with the old boy from Nebraska a few hours before the Fairfax accident; that you had harsh words. Is it true, and what was the substance?"

"The only person who could have heard that conversation was a man named Miller . . . Laurence Miller, as I recall. The chauffeur. Ask him. He's told you this much, why not the rest?"

"He's loyal to the old man. He was also taken care of with a bequest. He won't say; claims he never listened to back-seat talk. There was too much of it."

"No deal again. It was an honorable disagreement. If Miller tells you anything else, I'd question it if I were you."

"You're not me. . . . One more selection; your last, Trevayne. If you cop out, I'll be a big hindrance. I may even mention your attempt to 'plead the case' for suppression. How about that?"

"You're a revolting little man. I don't think I'll read your column anymore."

"Your words."

"Followed by others; out of context."

"Tell me about Bonner."

"Paul Bonner?" Trevayne had an uncomfortable feeling that Roderick Bruce's last *selection* was the real reason he was there. Not that the first two choices were innocuous—they weren't, they were unacceptable—but the newsman's voice betrayed a degree of intensity absent from his other questions; his threat more direct.

"Major Paul Bonner, no-middle-initial, serial number 158-3288; Special Forces, Intelligence Section, currently attached to Department of Defense. Recalled from Indochina, nineteen seventy after spending three months' isolation in a military stockade—officer's quarters, of course—awaiting court-martial. No interviews permitted; no information available. Except a happy little descriptive phrase coined by a general in Eye Corps: the 'killer from Saigon.' That's the Bonner I'm referring to, Mr. Trevayne. And if you're the avid reader of my work you say you are, you know I've stated that the mad Major should be locked up in Leavenworth, not walking the streets."

"I must have missed that day's paper."

"*Those* days. What's Bonner's function? Why was he assigned to you? Did you know him before? Did you request him?"

"You talk awfully fast."

"I'm awfully interested."

"Taking your questions in order—if I can; Bonner's merely a liaison with Defense. If I need something he gets it. Those are his words, incidentally, and he's been damned efficient. I have no idea why he was assigned to me; I'm also aware that he's not particularly happy with the job. I didn't know him, so obviously I couldn't have requested him."

"Okay." Bruce kept his eyes on Trevayne. He made small rapid vertical motions with his gold pencil against the air, against nothing. Again it was a gesture, an irritating one. "That checks out; that's programmed. Now . . . do you believe it?"

"Believe what?"

"That the 'killer from Saigon' is simply a messenger boy? You really believe that?"

"Of course I do. He's been very helpful. These offices, arranging transportation, reservations all over the country. Whatever his opinions, they have no bearing on what he does around here."

"You mentioned your staff. Did he help you assemble it?"

"Of course not." Trevayne found himself raising his voice. His anger, he realized, was triggered because in the beginning Paul Bonner had tried to help him 'assemble' a staff. "To anticipate you, Major Bonner holds convictions which differ considerably from my own. We both understand that; neither expects to convert the other. Regardless, I trust him. Not that there's any reason to use the term; he's not involved with our work."

"I'd say he's very much involved. He's in a position to know what you're doing. Who you're talking to, which companies you're looking into—"

"That kind of information is hardly classified, Mr. Bruce," interrupted Trevayne. "Frankly, I'm not sure what you're driving at."

"It's obvious. If you're investigating a gang of thieves, you don't rely on one of the biggest crooks in town to help you out."

Trevayne recalled Walter Madison's initial reaction to Bonner. The attorney had observed that Defense wasn't practicing much subtlety. "I think I can relieve your anxiety, Mr. Bruce. Major Bonner is in no way responsible for any decisions here. We don't discuss our progress with him—except in the most general terms and if I'm not mistaken, usually with humor. He simply takes care of routine details; and as a matter of fact, far less so than at the beginning. My secretary has assumed most of those responsibilities and calls on Bonner only when she has problems. Defense is quite good at securing a difficult airlines reservation or locating a corporation man whose company has a Pentagon contract. I repeat he's been very helpful."

"You'll grant his being here on these premises is unusual."

"The military is not famous for its sensitivity, Mr. Bruce. I think that's perhaps a good thing. . . . Look, we're dealing with Defense economies; we need a liaison. Why the Army assigned Bonner, I can't presume to say. But it did, and he's been satisfactory. I won't say he's been inspired; I don't think he has much use for us. However, he's a good soldier. I believe he'd carry out whatever assignments given him, regardless of his personal feelings."

"Nicely said."

"There's no other way to say it."

"You're telling me he doesn't try to represent the Pentagon viewpoint?"

"On the few occasions when I've asked his opinion, he very *much* represents the military point of view. I'd be alarmed if he didn't. Wouldn't you be? . . . If you're attempting to unearth some kind of conspiracy, you're not going to find it. Using your own logic Mr. Bruce, we were aware of Bonner's reputation. Or became aware of it. Naturally, we were concerned. Those concerns proved unwarranted."

"You're not giving me what I want, Trevayne."

"It seems to me you want a headline for your column that says Bonner's impeding the subcommittee's progress. That he's been assigned here so he can transmit classified information to his superiors. I told you, I've read your by-line, Bruce. It was a nice try, very logical. But it's not true. It's too goddamned obvious, and you know it."

"What are some of his opinions? I might settle for that. What's he said that represents the 'military point of view'?"

Trevayne watched the diminutive columnist. He was becoming edgy; he was nervous now, as if he sensed he was about to lose something he wanted desperately. Andy recalled Paul Bonner's harrowing counterstrategy against the hypothetical peace march—the troops, the swift repression—and knew this was the sort of thing Roderick Bruce wanted to print.

"You're paranoid. You're willing to settle for just about anything that colors Bonner dirty, aren't you?"

"You got it, Trevayne. Because he *is* dirty. He's a mad dog who should have been gassed three years ago."

"That's a pretty strong indictment. If you feel that way, you've got the audience; tell them . . . if you can back it up."

"They cover for that son-of-a-bitch. They *all* cover for him. Up and down the line he's sacred territory. Even with those who hate his guts—from the Mekong to Danang—no one'll say a word. That bothers me. I'd think it would bother you, too."

"I don't have your information. I've got enough problems without creating more from half-truths or half-lies. Put plainly, I'm not that interested in Major Bonner."

"Maybe you should be."

"I'll think about it."

"Think about something else, too. I'll give you a couple of days. You've had conversations with Bonner; he spent a weekend with you in Connecticut. Call me and tell me about them. What he's said to you may seem inconsequential. But coupled with what I've got could be important. You might be doing yourself and the country considerable service."

Trevayne rose from the chair, looking down at the small reporter. "Take your Gestapo tactics somewhere else, Mr. Bruce. No sale here."

Roderick Bruce knew through experience the disadvantages of standing up. He remained seated, fingering his gold pencil. "Don't make an enemy of me, Trevayne. That's foolish. I can shape that submarine story in such a way as to make you untouchable. People'll run from you. Maybe worse; maybe they'll just be laughing."

"Get out of here before I throw you out."

"Intimidating the press, Mr. Chairman? Threatening physical violence on a man of my size?"

"Describe it any way you like. Just get out," said Trevayne calmly.

Roderick Bruce rose slowly, replacing the gold pencil in his breast pocket. "A couple of days, Trevayne. I'll expect your call. You're upset now, but things will clear up for you. You'll see."

Trevayne watched the little-boy/old-man walk firmly

with his short strides toward the office door. Bruce didn't look back; he grasped the knob, pulled the door, and walked out. The heavy door banged against a chair in its backward path and vibrated slightly.

Brigadier General Lester Cooper slammed his fist on the long briefing table. His face was flushed, the veins in his neck pronounced.

"That little *bastard*. That goddamned pygmy *prick!* What the hell is he after?"

"We don't know yet. Could be just about anything," answered Robert Webster from across the room. "Our guess is Bonner; we calculated that possibility when we put him on."

"*You* calculated it. We didn't want any part of it."

"We know what we're doing."

"I'd feel better if you could convince *me*. I don't like the possibility that everyone's expendable."

"Don't be ridiculous. Tell Bonner his old friend Bruce may be stalking him again, to be careful." Webster approached Cooper; there was a hint of a smile on his lips. "But don't lay it on too thick. We wouldn't want him overly careful; just tell him. He's aware of Trevayne's surveillance; don't let somebody else tell him first."

"I understand. . . . However, I think you people should find a way to force Bruce out of this. He shouldn't be anywhere near it."

"That'll come in time."

"It should be *now*. The longer you wait, the greater the risk. Trevayne's going after Genessee."

"That's exactly why we're not making any sudden moves. Especially not now. Trevayne won't get anywhere. Roger Brewster might."

17

Andrew Trevayne looked out the window at the rolling Potomac. Brown leaves now, brackish water; Saturday-afternoon football games, pro contests on Sunday. Congress filled the newspapers with more talk than achievement; middle autumn in Washington.

The meeting had gone well, his nucleus had confidentially compiled enough data to justify personal confrontations with a number of Genessee Industries' top management.

Especially one man. James Goddard. The one man at Genessee Industries who had the answers. San Francisco.

That was the next stop.

It had been a singularly effective effort on everyone's part, made more difficult by the unorthodox methods Andy had called for. Very little of the work was done in the offices, almost all of it accomplished in the basement recreation room of his rented house in Tawning Spring. And those involved were limited to Alan Martin, Michael Ryan, John Larch, and the irrepressible Sam Vicarson.

He initially conceived of these methods, this secrecy, for very uncomplicated reasons. When the last responses came in from Genessee plants and contractors across the country, the volume was enormous. File cabinets were filled in a matter of several weeks. Then as these reports proved consistently unsatisfactory and additional requests were sent to the company's offices, Trevayne realized that Genessee was going to crowd out everything else they were working on. Simple collating between the voluminous replies became a major complication, brought about by evasive responses.

Andrew found himself obsessed with the tactics of Genessee Industries. The only way to untangle the mess was to take each strand of the web and follow it through the myriad patterns to its source, adding up the misinformation and those responsible as one went along. It was a complex, gargantuan task, and it seemed logical to move this one area of the subcommittee's work to a single place, a comfortable environment conducive to late hours and long weekends.

From this unsophisticated reasoning, another, more concerning motive surfaced that further justified the move. Interference. Ryan and Larch were approached—indirectly, with extreme subtlety—and asked about the subcommittee's inquiries at Genessee. Veiled hints of payment were dropped; humorous allusions to Caribbean holidays made.

Only nobody was kidding. Ryan and Larch understood that.

Beyond these two half-explored contacts three other incidents occurred in which Genessee figured—again subtly, indirectly, in shadow conversation.

Sam Vicarson was invited to the country club at Chevy Chase by an apartment neighbor. What began as a small cocktail party for semi-acquaintances rapidly accelerated into a drinking bout of fairly hardcore dimensions. Acquaintances were suddenly close friends; a number of friends quickly developed enmities. The evening became alcoholically electric, and Sam Vicarson found himself on the golf course with the wife of a minor congressman from California.

As he related the story to Trevayne, and admittedly there were gaps brought on by the liquor, the young, ebullient lawyer and the girl commandeered a golf cart, drove several hundred yards, when the vehicle stopped, its charge diminished. The wife became frightened; it was a potentially bad scene, and she'd been the instigator, making it clear she was attracted to Sam. The two of them started back toward the clubhouse, when they were confronted by the Congressman and an unknown friend.

What followed was ugly, swift, and made indelible by the husband's final words. The Congressman was drunk to the edge of incoherence; he slapped his wife across the mouth and lurched at Vicarson. Sam stepped back, defending himself as best he could against the husband's onslaught, when the unknown man interceded, pinning the Congressman's arms and pushing him to the ground.

The stranger kept ordering the subdued man to be quiet, that he was making a fool of himself.

At which point the minor Congressman from California made a futile attempt to lunge upward, to free himself, then screamed at his subduer.

"Take your goddamn Palo Alto out of my life!"

The wife raced across the lawn toward the parking lot.

The unknown man lashed the back of his hand against the Congressman's mouth, pulled him to his feet, and shoved him after the girl.

Sam Vicarson had stood on the grass, aware through the liquor that in some strange, inexplicable way, a setup had just been aborted.

Palo Alto. Genessee Industries.

Trevayne agreed, knowing beyond a doubt that the young lawyer would be more circumspect in the future about invitations from neighbors.

The second incident was told to Trevayne by his own secretary. The girl was going through the last stages of a soured engagement. When, contrary to their agreed-upon separation, the ex-fiancé asked to move in again, she couldn't understand, the relationship was dead, amicably finished.

He said he needed to come back—just for a few days.

For appearances.

And if anyone ever inquired, she should remember he asked her a lot of questions.

Which he wouldn't ask. He didn't give a damn; he was getting out of Washington and just needed a few recommendations. Thanks to her, he got them.

On the day he left for Chicago and a new job, he phoned Trevayne's secretary.

"Tell your boss a lot of people on Nebraska Avenue are interested in G.I.C. They're very uptight."

And so she told him.

G.I.C. Genessee Industries Corporation.

The third and last incident that he *knew* about reached Trevayne through Franklyn Baldwin, the New York banker who'd recruited him.

Baldwin came to Washington for a granddaughter's wedding. The girl was being married to an Englishman, an attaché at the British embassy with a viscount somewhere in his family background. As Baldwin phrased it, "The dullest damned reception in nuptial history. Times don't change: tell an American mother her daughter's found a title, and she doesn't plan a wedding, she mounts a funereal coronation."

This introduction from Baldwin was his way of telling Trevayne that he'd left the reception the minute he received a likely invitation to do so. It came from an old friend, a retired diplomat who suggested they plead geriatric exhaustion and head for one of Virginia's better watering spots.

They did so. To the home of a mutual friend, a rear admiral, also retired, who, to Baldwin's surprise, expected them.

At first Baldwin said, he'd been delighted by the playful conspiracy of two old cronies; made him feel as though they were all youngsters again, ingenuously avoiding tiresome duties.

As the visit lengthened, however, Baldwin became upset. A supposedly pleasant get-together wasn't pleasant at all. The Admiral initiated the unpleasantness by referring to Roderick Bruce's article about the beached atomic submarines. From that point it was a short leap to Trevayne's understanding of military—especially Navy Department—problems: he obviously had none.

Finally, Baldwin continued, he found himself in a heated argument; after all, the Defense Commission was his responsibility. Trevayne's approval had been unanimous, not only within the commission itself, but with the President and the Senate as well. Those approvals stood; the military—including the Navy Department—had better damn well accept the fact.

However, the Admiral wouldn't. As Baldwin was leaving, the old Navy hand suggested that yesterday's approval might turn into today's revulsion. Especially if Trevayne continued to harass one of the great institutions—"*institutions*, mind you"—upon which the nation in large measure depended—"*depended*, goddamn it, that's what he said!"

That *institution* was Genessee Industries.

As Andrew continued to stare at the river, he reflected that these five fragments—the two guarded contacts with Ryan and Larch, Sam Vicarson in Chevy Chase, his secretary, and Franklyn Baldwin—these were what he *knew* about. How many others were there that he was not aware of? The subcommittee staff numbered twenty-one; had others been reached? Were there variations on the theme of interference that would remain silent?

He couldn't possibly hold a "team meeting" and ask; not only was such a tactic abhorrent to him, but it wouldn't work. If anyone had been contacted and hadn't spoken of it, he wasn't going to do so now. The delay would appear incriminating.

And if, in the remote but possible chance there was an informer inside the subcommittee, the information he carried back would be worthless. For until this afternoon the vital papers concerning Genessee Industries had been kept in Tawning Spring.

The office files on Genessee—all the pertinent ones— were clearly marked in plastic tape: "Status—Current. Complete. Satisfactory." Several which were minor Genessee transactions had another tape: "Status—Current. Pending." These were unimportant.

The coding of *"Satisfactory"* was not born of suspicion; instead, it was simply more convenient. Since only five people—the top four men and Trevayne—would have reason to use these files, each knew what the term meant. If anyone else, for any reason, came across them, there was no necessity for elaborate explanations.

"Satisfactory" was sufficient.

Andrew left the window and returned to his desk, where the three looseleaf notebooks were piled on top of one another. The Genessee notebooks, the partially unraveled threads of the web; a small clearing inside a labyrinth of very warped mirrors. He wondered where the hell they would lead?

He also wondered what a man like Roderick Bruce— Roger Brewster—would do if they were in his possession?

Roderick Bruce, diminutive slayer of dragons.

Yet he hadn't slain *him*. In spite of the columnist's threats, he'd been extraordinarily gentle about Andy's part of the submarine story.

No reasons given; none asked for.

There'd even been a kind of compliment:

> The tough, unresponsive chairman of the sub-
> committee remains unreachable by panicked high
> personnel of the intelligence departments. He
> leaves media relations to others—which may not
> be smart, but that kind of brightness isn't re-
> quired in his job. All they can do is dump him,
> and they probably will. Is that what he wants?

Trevayne wondered why Bruce had decided not to
expose his "plea for suppression." Not that it mattered.
He didn't give a goddamn about Roderick Bruce *or* his
readership. He wouldn't have called Bruce back under
any conditions. Whatever Paul Bonner stood for—and Christ
knew it was ponderously antediluvian—the man was authentic. His beliefs were profoundly arrived-at concerns,
not unthinking, blunt reactions to change. The Bonners of
this world had to be convinced, not sacrificed as goats in
ideological skirmishes.

Above all, *convinced*.

Trevayne picked up the top notebook, the plastic tape
on the right-hand corner imprinted with the Roman nu-
meral I. It constituted his immediate itinerary; the first
stop, San Francisco.

Routine. Nothing vital.

That's the way it was arranged. That's the way it was
described. The subcommittee chairman was merely making a personal tour of West Coast companies—a number
of them. If concerned executives took the trouble to check—
and it was certain they would—they'd be relieved to learn
that Andrew Trevayne was dropping in on a dozen or so
firms. Nothing much of any depth could be accomplished
with such a schedule.

It was even suggested off-handedly to several that the
subcommittee chairman wasn't averse to a game of golf or
a couple of sets of tennis—weather permitting.

The climate of his tour was therefore established.
There were rumors of an early demise of the subcommittee; that Trevayne's cross-country trip was a kind of fare-

well appearance, a symbolic finish to an impossible production.

That was fine; that was the way he wanted it.

It wouldn't be possible if a Roderick Bruce had access to the Genessee notebooks.

God forbid that should ever be the case! What had to be avoided at all costs now were blanket accusations, inclusive condemnations. It was far too complicated for simple conclusions.

The telephone interrupted his meandering thoughts. It was after five; he'd let everyone go early—five o'clock was early at the Potomac Towers. He was alone.

"Hello?"

"Andy? Paul Bonner."

"You're psychic. I was just thinking about you."

"Nice thoughts, I hope."

"Not particularly. How've you been? Haven't seen you in a couple of weeks."

"I've been out of town. In Georgia. Every six months or so the brass sends me down to Benning to run around obstacle courses, stay in shape. Or that's what they think."

"Probably nothing to do with it. They figure to beat out your hostilities, or give the Washington ladies a breather."

"Better than cold baths. What are you doing tonight?"

"I'm meeting Phyl for dinner at L'Avion. Care to join us?"

"Sure. If I'm not intruding."

"Not at all. Forty-five minutes?"

"Good. It'll give us a chance to go over this crazy tour of yours."

"What?"

"I'm back as your major-domo, massa. Whatever you want, snap your fingers or whistle; I'll scurry around and get it for you."

"I didn't know," said Trevayne hesitantly.

"I just got the orders. I understand we'll be hitting the links and a few tennis courts. You've loosened up."

"Sounds that way. See you at L'Avion."

Trevayne replaced the phone and looked at the Genessee notebook in his left hand.

No request had been made of the Defense Department for a military aide. As a matter of fact, the Pentagon had not been apprised of the trip.

At least not by his office.

18

Mario de Spadante stepped off the second-floor escalator at the San Francisco Airport and headed for the observation lounge. His gait was fast, remarkably agile for a man of his girth. He dodged and overtook passengers and clerks; he was impatient with a black porter who blocked his path with an unwieldy luggage dolly. He pushed open the glass door of the lounge and rapidly walked past the hostess, acknowledging her unspoken question with a gesture of his hand. His party was already seated; they were expecting him, two men at a corner table.

"If you don't mind my saying so, Mr. de Spadante, I think you're unnecessarily agitated."

"I do mind your saying it, Mr. Goddard. I mind very much, because I think you're a fucking idiot." De Spadante's voice remained gentle, only the rasp slightly more pronounced than usual. He turned to the other man, an older man somewhere in his sixties, stylishly tailored. A man named Allen. "Has Webster been in touch?"

"I haven't seen him or spoken with him since New York. Months ago, before Baldwin approached this Trevayne. We should have killed it then."

"The big machers didn't listen, because your suggestion was not only dumb but also hopeless. I took other measures; everything was under control—including emergency procedures. That is, it was until now." De Spadante reverted his look to Goddard. Goddard's cherubic face was still flushed with anger over the Italian's insult. Goddard was middle-aged, middle-fat, and middle brow, the essence of the pressurized corporate executive, which he was—for Genessee Industries. De Spadante purposely did not speak. He just stared at Goddard. It was the executive's turn, and he knew it.

"Trevayne gets in tomorrow morning, around ten-thirty. We've scheduled lunch."

"I hope you eat well."

"We have no reason to think the conference is anything more than what we've been told: a friendly meeting. One of many. He's scheduled conferences with half a dozen companies within a few hundred miles, all within several days."

"You kill me, Mr. Just-a-Minute. I mean, I'd be rolling on the floor laughing, except for the pain. . . . 'No reason to think'! You're beautiful! Like the kids say . . . very *heavy*, man."

"You're offensive, Mr. De Spadante." Goddard withdrew a handkerchief and blotted his chin.

"Don't talk to me 'offensive.' There's nothing more offensive on this earth than stupidity. Except maybe conceited stupidity." De Spadante spoke to Allen while his eyes remained on Goddard. "Where did you high types come up with this *capo-zuccone?*"

"He's not stupid, Mario," replied Allen softly. "Goddard was the best cost accountant G.I.C. ever had. He's shaped the company's economic policies for the past five years."

"A bookkeeper! A lousy bookkeeper who sweats on his chin! I know the type."

"I have no intention of taking your abuse any longer." Goddard moved his chair back, prepared to stand. However, Mario de Spadante's hand shot out, and with the grip of a man who was no stranger to hard work and coarse methods, he held the arm. The chair rocked to a stop as Goddard's legs went tense.

"You sit. You stay. We have problems bigger than your intentions. . . . Or mine, Mr. Bookkeeper."

"Why are you so sure?" asked Allen.

"I'll tell you. And maybe you'll understand some of my agitation. Also my anger. . . . For weeks all we've heard is that everything's just fine. No real problems; a number of items had to get straightened out, but they were taken care of. Then we get word that even the major questions are marked 'satisfactory.' Complete, finished, kaput . . . clear sailing. I even bought it myself." De Spadante released the chair but held the men with his eyes darting back and forth between them without shifting his head. "Only except a couple of very curious fellows in New York decide to run a check. They're a little nervous, because they're paid to solve problems. When they don't see any problems, they look for them; they figure it's better than missing them because of an oversight. . . . They take five—just five—very, very important inquiries which have been returned. All five have been accepted as satisfactory—we're told. They send supplementary information to Trevayne's office. Nothing that couldn't be explained but, by God, explanations were called for! . . . Do I have to tell you what happened?"

Goddard, who'd been holding his handkerchief in his hand, brought it once again to his chin. His look betrayed his fear. He spoke three words quietly, tensely. "Reverse double entries."

"If that fancy language means the office files were dummies, you're right on, Mr. Bookkeeper."

Allen leaned forward in his chair. "*Is* that what you mean, Goddard?"

"In essence, yes. Only I jumped a step. It would depend on whether the status of the office files was returned to 'pending.' "

"They weren't," said Mario de Spadante.

"Then there's a second set of files."

"Very good. Even us *tontos* figured that one out."

"But where?" asked Allen, his composure losing some of its confidence.

"What difference does it make? You're not going to change what's in them."

"It would be a great help to know, however," added Goddard, no longer hostile; instead, very much afraid.

"You should have thought about such things these last couple of months, instead of sitting with your thumb up your ass figuring you're so smart. 'Friendly meetings.' "

"We had no cause . . ."

"Oh, shut up! Your chin's all wet. . . . A lot of people may have to hang. But there are a lot of other people we won't let that happen to. We've still got certain emergency procedures. We did *our* work." Suddenly, with great but silent intensity, Mario de Spadante clenched his fist and grimaced.

"What is it?" The man named Allen stared at the Italian apprehensively.

"That son-of-a-bitch Trevayne!" De Spadante whispered hoarsely. "The Honorable—so fucking honorable— Undersecretary! Mr. Clorox! . . . That bastard's as dirty as any pig in the cesspool. I hadn't figured on it."

Major Paul Bonner watched Trevayne from across the aisle. Bonner had the window seat on the right side of the 707; Trevayne, flanked by Alan Martin and Sam Vicarson, sat directly opposite. The three of them were engrossed in a document.

Beavers, thought Bonner. Earnest, intense, chipping away at a thousand barks so the trees would fall and the streams would be dammed. Natural progression thwarted? Trevayne would call it something like ecological balance.

Horseshit.

It was far more important that the fields below be irrigated than a few earnest beavers survive. The beavers wanted to parch the land, to sacrifice the crops in the name of concerns only beavers cared about. There were other concerns, frightening ones that the smaller animals would never understand. Only the lions understood; they had to, because they were the leaders. The leaders stalked all areas of the forests and the jungles; they knew who the predators were. The beavers didn't.

Paul Bonner knew this jungle; had crawled on his bleeding stomach over the incredibly infested, ever-moving slime. He'd come face to face with the eyes, the commitment of pure hate. Had recognized the fact that he must kill the possessor of the hatred, put out the eyes. Or be killed.

His enemy.

Their enemy.

What the hell did the beavers know?

He saw that Trevayne and his two assistants began putting their papers back into their briefcases. They'd be

in San Francisco soon; the "fasten-your-seat-belts" light
was on, the no-smoking sign as well. Another five minutes.

And then what?

His orders were less specific, vaguer than they had
been before. Conversely, the atmosphere around Defense—
that part of it dealing with Trevayne—was infinitely tauter.
After his dinner with Andy and Phyllis, General Cooper
had interrogated him as though he were a *Charleysan*
guerilla with American dog tags around his neck. The
Brigadier was damned near apoplectic. *Why hadn't Trevayne
alerted Defense about this tour? What was the exact itinerary? Why so many stops, so many different conferences? Were they a smoke screen?*

Finally, Bonner had gotten angry. He didn't know
the answers, hadn't sought them. If the General needed
specific information, he should have briefed him on what
it was. Bonner reminded Cooper that he had brought out
over fifty separate reports from the Potomac Towers. Information *stolen* from Trevayne's private files, actions that
laid him wide open to civilian prosecution.

He understood the reasons, accepted them as well as
the risks, and relied on his superiors' judgment. But, goddamn it, he wasn't clairvoyant.

The Brigadier's reaction to his outburst stunned Bonner. Cooper had become hesitant, flustered; he started to
stutter, and for Bonner it was inconceivable that such an
old line man as Cooper would stutter. It was apparent that
Brigadier General Cooper was dealing with totally new,
unevaluated data.

And he was afraid.

Bonner had wondered what it was. What had produced the fear? The Major knew that he wasn't the only
one bringing information out of the Towers. There were
two others he knew about. One was a dark-haired stenogra-
pher, the nominal head of Trevayne's typing pool. He'd
seen her photograph and résumé on Cooper's desk with
several expense vouchers clipped underneath. Standard
procedure.

The second was a blond man, late twenties, a Ph.D.
from Cornell who, if he remembered correctly, Trevayne
had hired as a favor to an old friend. Bonner had left late

one night just as the blond man was going into the freight entrance. To the rear elevators invariably used by informers on scheduled runs. He'd looked up; Brigadier Cooper's fifth-floor office lights were still on.

Cooper had been too upset to be evasive or even subtle. So Bonner had been given his orders: Whatever Trevayne said, whatever either of the two aides traveling with him said—regardless of how inconsequential it might seem—commit it to memory and report by telephone direct on Cooper's private line. Try to find out the substance of any conference with anyone connected with Genessee Industries. Use whatever moneys might be needed, promise whatever immunities requested, but uncover facts.

Any facts.

Was he to look for specific . . .

Anything!

Bonner grudgingly admitted to himself that he'd caught a touch of the Brigadier's fever. He didn't like being fired up by someone else's anger—or panic—but he had been. Trevayne had no right meddling in Genessee. At least, not to the extent that caused Cooper's extraordinary degree of concern. Genessee Industries was, in its own way, a necessary line of the nation's defense. Certainly more important than any extraterritorial ally. Surely more reliable.

The fighters—rocket jets—better than anything in their class in the air; fourteen different styles of helicopters—from the massive troop-, vehicle-, and weapons-carrying jet combinations to the fast, silent "snakes" that hedged men like himself into tiny jungle locations; armor developed in dozens of Genessee laboratories that housed a hundred different types of protective cover saving thousands of square feet of human flesh from high-caliber shells and the refraction of napalm fire; even artillery—Genessee controlled scores of armaments plants, and thank God they did!—the finest, most destructive weaponry on earth.

Strike force! Power!

Goddamn it to goddamn hell! Couldn't "they" understand?

It wasn't just the *possession!* It was the *protection!*
Their protection!

What the hell did the beavers know?

What the hell did Trevayne know?

19

James Goddard walked out on his back lawn. The descending sun washed the Los Altos hills with misty hues of yellow and orange. As always, the view had a palliative effect on Goddard. It had been the primary reason he'd taken the gamble twelve years ago and bought the house in Los Altos. It had been far too expensive, but he'd reached that point at Genessee where either the future held such a home or there was no future at Genessee.

It really hadn't been much of a gamble. Twelve years ago he'd just begun his rapid ascendancy with *one* of the inner circles of Genessee Industries. The nature of his work ensured his survival, his eventual proprietorship of a corner office.

Finally, the penthouse. President, San Francisco Division.

But at times the pressure became too much.

Now was such a time.

The conference with Trevayne that afternoon had been nerve-racking. Nerve-racking because its objectives, at first, were totally unclear. A little of this, a little of that. A great deal of nodding-in-agreement, a fair amount of quizzical looks followed by further nods or just blank stares. Notes taken at seemingly inappropriate moments; innocuous questions asked by Trevayne's innocuous assistants. One Jewish; that was obvious. The other too young; that was insulting.

The whole meeting had been disjointed, without any discipline of agenda. As the immediate spokesman for Genessee, Goddard had tried to impose a sense of order, tried to elicit a schedule of inquiry. He'd been gently rebuffed by Trevayne; the subcommittee chairman uncon-

vincingly played the role of a patriarchal uncle—everything
would be covered sufficiently. The morning was only to
establish general areas of responsibility.

General areas of responsibility.

The phrase had hit James Goddard's brain like a bolt
of electricity.

But he had simply nodded as his three adversaries
had nodded and smiled. A ritual dance of deceit, he'd
decided.

When the meeting ended, around three-thirty or so,
he'd returned to his office from the conference room and
immediately pleaded a splitting headache to his secretary.
He had to get out, drive around, think over every aspect
of what had been said during the past two and a half
hours. For in spite of the nebulous approach, a great deal
had been said. The problem was that it hadn't been said in
figures. He understood figures. He could recite by rote
P-and-L statements from scores of divisions going back
years. He could take a handful of isolated numbers and
prepare projections that, given a variance of four percent,
would prove out. He astonished so-called economists—
academic theorists, usually Jewish—with the swiftness and
accuracy of his market analyses and employment stats.

Even the Senator, California's Armbruster, had called
upon him for advice last year.

He had refused any payment; after all, Armbruster
was his political choice, and Genessee wasn't going to get
hurt. However, he *had* accepted a token gift through a
friend of the Senator. A ten-year company pass on Trans
Pacific Airways.

His wife liked Hawaii, although he constantly had to
reassure her that cat meat wasn't part of the cooking.

He'd left the office and driven damn near fifty miles.
Along the ocean drive, over into Ravenswood, then across
to Fair Oaks.

What had Trevayne been after?

Whenever Goddard had attempted to explain a specific overrun or underestimated cost—and weren't those
explanations the essence of the subcommittee's function?
—he'd been discouraged from elaborating on them. Instead, there was only a general discussion of the items;

their validity, their functionability, their operational capacities, the engineering, the designs, the men who conceived the plans, those responsible for putting them into execution.

Abstractions and median-level personnel.

What in heaven's name could be the purpose of such a conference?

But as he approached the upward slope of the road leading to his isolated, view-calming house on his miniature mountain, James Goddard—cost-accountant-cum-division-president of Genessee Industries—saw with frightening clarity the purpose of Trevayne's conference.

Names.

Only names.

It explained the hastily written notes at seemingly inappropriate times, the innocuous questions from innocuous aides.

Names.

That was what they were after.

His own staff kept repeatedly going back into the papers. *This* engineering head, *that* design consultant; *this* labor negotiator, *that* stats analyst. Always buried under and sandwiched between unimportant judgments.

They weren't figures! They weren't numbers!

Only *people.*

Persons anonymous!

But that's what Trevayne was after.

And Mario de Spadante had said a lot of people might have to hang.

People.

Persons anonymous.

Was he one of them?

James Goddard watched a bird—a sparrow hawk—dip suddenly downward and just as swiftly come up from behind the trees and catch the wind, soaring to the sky, no quarry in his beak.

"Jimmy! . . . Jimmeee!"

His wife's voice—full-throated yet somehow nasal—always had the same effect on him, whether it was shouting from a window or talking over the dinner table.

Irritation.

"Yes?"

"Really, Jim, if you're going to commune, for God's sake put the telephone outside. I'm busy on *my* line."

"Who's calling?"

"Someone named de Spad . . . de Spadetti, or something; I don't know! Some *wop*. He's on 'hold.' "

James Goddard took a last look at his precious view and started for the house.

At least one thing was clear. Mario de Spadante would be given the very best efforts a "bookkeeper" could provide. He would tell him digit by digit the areas of inquiry Trevayne had asked for; no one could fault a "bookkeeper" for that.

But Mario de Spadante would not be privy to the "bookkeeper's" conclusions.

This "bookkeeper" was not for hanging.

Paul Bonner walked through the door of the cellar café. It was like a hundred other San Francisco basements-with-licenses. The amplified, ear-shattering sound from the tiny bandstand was an assault on his sensibilities—all of them—and the sight of the freaked-out, bare-breasted dancers no inducement.

The place was a mess.

He wondered what the effect might have been if he'd worn his uniform. As it was, he felt singularly out of place in a sport coat and denims. He quickly undid his paisley tie and stuffed it into his pocket.

The place was crazy with weed; more hash than "grass," at that.

He went to the far end of the bar, took out a pack of cigarettes—French, Gauloise—and held them in his left hand. He ordered a bourbon—shouted his request, actually—and was surprised to find that the drink was an excellent sour mash.

He stood as best he could in one spot, jostled continually by the bearded drinkers and half-naked waitresses, a number of whom took second glances at his clean-shaven face and close-cropped hair.

Then he knew he saw him. Standing about eight feet

away in tie-dyed Levi's and sandals, his shirt a variation of winter underwear. But there was something wrong with the hair, Bonner thought. It was shoulder-length and full, but there was something—a neatness, a sheen; that was it. The man's hair was a wig. A very good wig, but by the nature of its in-place effect, inconsistent with the rest of his appearance.

Bonner unobtrusively raised the pack of Gauloise and lifted his glass in greeting.

The man approached, and when he stood next to Paul he leaned over and spoke through the noise close to Bonner's ear.

"Nice place, isn't it?"

"It's . . . overwhelming. You look like you fit in, though. Are you sure you're the right guy? No intermediaries; I made that clear."

"These are my civilian clothes, Major."

"Very appropriate. Now, let's get out of here."

"Oh, no, man! We stay. We talk here."

"It's impossible. Why?"

"Because I know what these vibes do to a pickup."

"No tapes; no pickups. Come on, be reasonable. There's no call for that sort of thing. Christ, I'd be frying myself."

The unkempt mod with the neat hair looked closely at Bonner. "You've got a point, man. I hadn't thought of it that way. You've *really* got a point! . . . The bread, please."

Bonner replaced the Gauloises in his shirt pocket and then withdrew his wallet. He took out three one-hundred-dollar bills and handed them to the man. "Here."

"Oh, come on, Major! Why don't you write me a check?"

"What?"

"Get the bartender to change them."

"He won't do that."

"Try."

Bonner turned toward the bar and was surprised to see the bartender standing close by, watching the two of them. He smiled at the Major and held out his hand. Sixty seconds later Bonner was holding another assortment of bills—fives, tens, twenties. Three hundred dollars' worth. He gave them to the contact.

"Okay. Let's split, man. We'll walk the streets, just like cowboys. But we'll walk where *I* say, got it?"

"Understood."

Out on O'Leary Lane the two men headed south, slowly weaving their way among what was left of the Haight-Ashbury tribes. The sidewalk stalls and curbside vendors noisily proclaimed the tribes' acceptance of a laissez-faire economy. A lot of profit was being made on O'Leary Lane.

"I suppose, in line with your obvious cautions, you haven't written anything down for me."

"Of course not. Nothing to prevent *you* from taking notes, though. I remember everything."

"That conference lasted damn near three hours."

"I didn't get to be Genessee Jim's top accountant because of a bad memory, Major." The long-haired man gestured left, toward an alley. "Let's head in here. Not so frenetic."

They leaned against a brick wall covered with semi-pornographic posters, mostly torn, all marked with graffiti; the light from the street lamps on O'Leary Lane was just enough to illuminate their faces. Bonner maneuvered his contact so the light was shining on him. Paul Bonner always watched a man's face during interrogations—whether in the field or in a San Francisco alley.

"Where do you want to begin, man?"

"Forget the tea and cookies. Start with the major items; we'll work back to the less important."

"All right. In descending order. . . . The F-90's over-run—specifically, the design conversions of fan metals mandated by innovations called for in the Houston labs. They were first conceived of because of the flap at Rolls-Royce, if you recall."

"What about them?"

"What do you mean, what about them? Those inno's had a price tag of one-zero-five mill; that's what about them."

"That's no secret."

"I didn't say it was. But Trevayne's crowd wanted to know dates. Maybe there was a time lag you people haven't thought about. . . . But that's not my bag. I'm no J. Edgar; I provide data, you evaluate. Isn't that what that honky used to say?"

"Go on." Bonner had withdrawn a spiral notepad and began writing.

"Next. Down south, Pasadena. . . . The plants are eight months behind with the tool and dies for the big chopper armor plates. That's a bad one, man. They're so fucked up they'll never find ozone. Labor troubles, pollution complaints, blueprint alterations, base-metal compos; you name it, they fell over it. Armbruster's got to bail those plants out and still make it with the pure-breathers."

"What did Trevayne want with this one?"

"Funny. He was sort of sympathetic. Honest mistakes, environment concerns; that kind of thing. He didn't dwell on the bread; he seemed more interested in the boys who had the problems. . . . Next. Right here in our beloved Northwest Pack. The lines up south of Seattle. As you know, there's a little diversification going on; Genessee took over the Bellstar Companies and has thrown a mighty tax chunk into making them work. So far, it's a large pair of snake-eyes."

"Those are the rocket plants, aren't they?"

"Rockets, propulsion fuel, pads, launch tracks . . . the Peenemünde of the Pacific, as we affectionately call that mess."

"They're necessary. They've got to keep functioning . . ." Bonner caught himself.

"Ah, so, Mr. Moto! . . . Don't burden me with evaluations, man. Remember?"

"I know; not your bag. . . . So what about them?"

"So they're a loss leader, and I *do* mean the leader of the losses, Charlie. And for a very good reason that Trevayne suspects. Genessee has no business buying from itself."

"That was thrown out of court."

"My turn to evaluate." The long-haired, wigged accountant laughed. "The court was thrown out of court. Because a few other people made evaluations. . . . Trevayne wants more information on Bellstar. Only, here again, like Pasadena and Houston, he's mining some personnel files.

Frankly, I don't dig; they're not going to tell him anything. Wrong turn on his part. He doesn't pass 'Go.' "

Bonner wrote in his notebook. "Did he get any more specific?"

"No, man. He couldn't. Your Mr. Trevayne is either very dull or very cozy."

A drunk careened off the wall at the far end of the short alley. He was a tourist, obviously; dressed in a jacket, slacks, tie, and an American Legion barracks cap. He leaned against the brick, unzipped his trousers, and proceeded to urinate. The accountant turned to Bonner.

"Come on, let's get out of here. The neighborhood's going to hell. And if that's a tail, Major, I'll grant you're imaginative."

"You may not believe this, *man*, but I hate those professional heroes."

"I believe you, man. You look like you hate good. . . . I know a quiet mahogany a few blocks west. We'll finish up there."

"Finish up! We haven't begun! I figure you've got about two hundred and ninety dollars to go. . . . *Man!*"

"We'll make it, soldier-boy."

An hour and ten minutes later, Bonner had just about filled his small spiral pad with notes. He was getting his three hundred dollars' worth—at least in terms of the accountant's recollections. The man was amazing; he was capable—if he was to be believed—of recalling exact phrases, specific words.

What it all meant would be up to someone else, however. All Bonner could make of the information was that Trevayne and Company covered a lot of ground but didn't do much digging. However, again, that could be an erroneous conclusion on his part.

Others would know better.

"That about does it, Major," said the Genessee executive from under the long, false hair. "Hope it gets you a pair of 'birds'; that is, if you're really a soldier type and not some kind of crusading nut."

"Suppose I was the latter?"

"Then I hope you nail G.I.C."

"You can be flexible, I see."

"Pure rubber. I've got █████████
mongrel. *I'm* my cause."

"That must be nice to live wit██

"Very comfortable. . . . And I██
thank for that comfort."

"What?"

"Oh, yes, man! A few years ago I *really* d█
this. I mean, I meant it! Protests, peace marches,
thons for the dried-up Ganges, every man was my bro█
—black, white, and yellow; I was going to change the
world. . . . Then you mothers sent me to 'Nam. Bad scene,
man. I got half my stomach blown out. And for what? The
pious, plastic men with their square-jawed bullshit?"

"I'd think that kind of experience might have re-
newed your energies; to change the world, I mean."

"Maybe some, not me. I lost too much meat around
the middle; I paid my dues. The saints are pimps, and
Jesus Christ is not a superstar. It's *all* a bad scene. I want
mine."

Bonner rose from the small, dirty barroom table. "I'll
pass the word. Maybe they'll make you president of Genessee Industries."

"It's not out of the question. . . . And, soldier, I
meant what I said. I want mine. If Trevayne's in the
market, I'll let him bid; I want you to know that."

"It could be dangerous for you. I might have to blow
out the other half of your stomach. I wouldn't think twice
about it."

"I'm sure you wouldn't. . . . But I'm fair about such
things. I'll call you first and give you a chance to meet the
price. . . . If he's in the market, that is."

Bonner looked at the accountant's enigmatic smile
and the somewhat crazy expression on his face. The Major
wondered whether the evening was one hell of a mistake.
The Genessee man was toying with him in a very unhealthy way. Bonner leaned over, his hands gripping the
sides of the table, and spoke firmly but calmly.

"If I were you, I'd be awfully careful about fishing on
both sides of the river. The natives can get very unfriendly."

"Relax, Major. I just wanted to see you spin; you spin

eft of my stomach.

d he'd never have to
an again. He was the
the best at his job: a
unnels of filth and had
rtain disdain. His only

Trevayne
the objectives of a scavenging
got you boys to
essed like
walka-
ther
187

The young attorney, Sam Vicarson, had never seen Fisherman's Wharf. It was a silly thing to want to do, he supposed, but he'd promised himself. And now he had two hours to himself, before the five-thirty session in Trevayne's room. The subcommittee chairman had called the two hours a bonus for extraordinarily good behavior during the Genessee conference.

Sam Vicarson suggested they be given Academy Awards instead.

The taxi pulled up to a clam bar with baskets filled with seaweed and large hemp nets piled in front.

"This is where the wharf begins, mister. Straight north, along the waterfront. Do you want to go to someplace special? Di Maggio's maybe?"

"No, thanks; this'll be fine."

Vicarson paid the driver and climbed out of the cab. He was immediately aware of the heavy odor of fish, and wondered—since the whole area had a contrived appearance—if it was piped in. He smiled to himself as he started down the street with the curio shops and the "atmosphere" bars, the fishing boats bobbing up and down in their slips, nets everywhere. A half-mile travelogue prepared by a very knowledgeable Chamber of Commerce.

It was going to be fun. It was going to be a fun two hours.

He wandered into a number of shops, and for laughs sent postcards to several cynical friends—the most atrocious postcards he could find. He bought Trevayne and Alan Martin two grotesque little flashlights about three inches long and shaped like sharks; the mouths lit up by pressing the dorsal fins.

He strolled out to the far end of a pier, where the boats had an authentic look about them; or, more correctly, the men around them seemed intent on making their living from the water, not from the tourists. He started back, stopping every twenty yards or so to watch the various crews unload their catches, hose down the slicks. The fish were fascinating. Different shapes; odd speckling of colors amidst the predominant grays; the lidless eyes so wide, so blank, so dead yet knowing.

Vicarson looked at his watch. It was almost four-fifteen. The Mark Hopkins was a twenty-minute taxi ride, and he wanted to allow himself time for a shower. That left him just about fifteen minutes for a drink at one of the waterfront bars.

That had to be on his wharf agenda.

As he looked up from his watch for a second time and increased his calculations, he saw two men standing perhaps fifty feet away. They were looking at him. They quickly turned and began talking to each other—too rapidly, too artificially. Then Vicarson realized what he'd just done. The San Francisco sun had caused a glare on his watch, so he'd turned to recheck the time in his own shadow; he'd made the movement at the last second. The men hadn't expected it.

Vicarson wondered. Or was Trevayne's constant reminder of caution causing his imagination to overwork?

A group of Girl Scouts accompanied by a large contingent of adult guides began filling up the base of the pier. They were preparing an assault march to the far end amid squeals of laughter and parental reprimands. They started out; the tourists backed away to let Troop 36, Oakland Brownies, pass through.

Vicarson headed into the group, loudly apologizing as he worked his way through. He reached the last rows under the critical eyes of several adults and emerged within ten yards of the street. He dashed into the thoroughfare and turned right, entering the flow of human traffic on the waterfront side.

Two blocks south he saw a crowded café which advertised "Drinks on the Bay" and rapidly walked through the door. The bar was in the shape of a horseshoe, the open end by the front entrance, the bar itself following the odd contours of the building, extending out over the water.

"Drinks on the Bay," indeed.

Vicarson positioned himself halfway around the horseshoe so he could observe both the north side of the dock and the street. He ordered a Fisherman's Punch and waited, wondering if he'd see the two men again.

He did. Only when they came into view they'd been joined by a third man. A large, somewhat obese man in his fifties, or thereabouts.

Sam Vicarson nearly dropped his frosted glass of Fisherman's Punch.

He'd seen the third man before; he wasn't likely to forget, in spite of the circumstances of the meeting—perhaps because of them.

The last time—the only time—he'd seen the large man was on a golf course in the middle of the night three thousand miles away. At Chevy Chase in Maryland. This was the man who'd hammerlocked the drunken Congressman from California and slapped him to the ground.

Trevayne stood by the hotel window and listened to Vicarson's description but kept his own counsel. The young lawyer had described Mario de Spadante. And if he was correct, if De Spadante was in San Francisco, then there were side issues coming into play with Genessee Industries that he hadn't considered.

Mario de Spadante had to be scrutinized. The "construction boy from New Haven who, with hard work and the grace of God, had made good" bore immediate looking into. Trevayne hadn't made any such connection before. There had been no reason to look for one.

"I'm not mistaken, Mr. Trevayne. It was the same man. Who the hell is he?"

"I may be able to answer that after a few phone calls."

"No kidding?"

"I wish I were. . . . We'll go into it later. Let's talk about this afternoon." Trevayne crossed to an armchair; Alan Martin and Sam sat on the couch, papers on the coffee table in front of them. "We've had time to mull it over, get a little perspective. What's your opinion, Alan? How do you think it went?"

The middle-aged accountant glanced at his papers. He pinched the bridge of his nose and spoke first with his eyes shut. "Goddard was running scared but did his damnedest to conceal it." Martin opened his eyes. "He was also confused. He kept pressing his fingertips on the table; you could see the veins working. Here, I made some notes." Martin picked up a clipboard from the coffee table. "One of the first things that threw him was the Pasadena labor settlement. I don't think he expected it. He wasn't happy when Sam pushed his boys for the name of the AFL-CIO negotiator."

"What was his name?" asked Trevayne.

"Manolo. Ernest Manolo," answered Vicarson, looking down at his papers on the coffee table. "The contract wasn't too rough from a local-conditions viewpoint, but if it's used as any sort of national guideline, consider it a giveaway."

"Will it be?"

"That's up to Manolo and his crowd, I guess. Goose-and-gander reciprocity will be the issue," replied Vicarson.

"You mean the AFL-CIO delegates that kind of authority to this . . . Manolo?"

"Manolo was a medium-paced starter, but he's rising fast. Not much is delegated to him. He just takes. He's a firebrand—crusader type. Like Chavez; but with the benefit of an education. Economics, University of New Mexico."

"Go ahead, Al." Trevayne took an envelope out of his pocket.

"I think you fuzzed Goddard when you didn't pursue a number of Genessee's underestimates. He had the files on the Pittsburgh Cylinder Company; the Detroit armature run; the alloy steel—also Detroit; the Houston laboratories; the Green Agency, advertising, New York; and God knows what else. He was ready to throw volumes at us,

justifications. . . . I did get the design-unit head, though.
In Houston. His name never appeared in any of *our* files
before. Ralph Jamison. Goddard couldn't figure that one
out; a lousy lab man behind a one-hundred-and-five-mil-
lion-dollar conversion. . . . Then he practically put his
fingers through the table when we asked for the Bellstar
projections. That's understandable; Genessee had antitrust
problems with Bellstar."

"Speaking as the most brilliant practicing attorney
here," said Sam Vicarson with a grin, "if the Bellstar
decision had been rendered by anyone but old Judge
Studebaker, it would have been challenged months ago."

"Sam, why do you say that? I've heard it before."

"Oh, Lord, Mr. Trevayne, ask any trust lawyer who
knows his books. The Genessee-Bellstar brief was filled
with holes. But Joshua Studebaker was given the case.
Old Josh is a little-known bench tradition, but a tradition
nevertheless. He might have gone farther, but he prefers
to sit in his chambers up in Seattle. He's a quiet, up-from-
slavery legal diamond. He's black, Mr. Trevayne. When
you talk about little kids being whipped, and rickets, and
scratching the ground for a potato that's divided, you're
talking about old Josh. He's really been there. Even Justice would rather not challenge him."

"I never realized that." Alan Martin was fascinated by
this newly acquired information. "I never heard of him."

"Neither did I," said Trevayne.

"It's not surprising. Studebaker's assiduously devoted
to being a private person. No interviews, no books; articles involving only the most complex legalistics in superaca-
demic law journals. He's spent forty years or so complicating
and uncomplicating legal decisions. . . . Some say he's slipped
in recent years—they're beginning to understand him."

"You're saying he's untouchable?" Trevayne asked a
question.

"For a number of reasons. He's a genius; he's black;
he's eccentric-in-his-fashion; he's got a positively frightening grasp of legal abstractions; he's black. Do I draw a
picture?"

"He's black and he made it," said Alan Martin with
resignation.

"To the very-most top of the mountain."

"You're leaving out a pretty important piece of information . . . or judgment," said Trevayne.

"Why did he render the decision?" Sam Vicarson leaned forward on the couch. "I told you his rep is in legal complexities . . . abstractions. He used the phrase 'mass human endeavor' in balancing, then overriding, obvious Genessee irregularities. He justified certain questionable economic relationships by ascertaining the necessity of 'compatible motives' in large-scale financing. Lastly, he threw the hooker: in nothing words, the government hadn't proved the need for viable competition."

"What does that mean?" asked Alan Martin, his eyes betraying a complete lack of understanding. "Other than that you read the goddamn papers?"

"Nobody else had the loot."

"Which has nothing to do with the legality of the situation," said Trevayne.

"Conclusion?" Sam leaned back on the couch. "Either old Josh wandered back through the legal gymnastics to the essential truth with all of its human imperfections, or he had an ulterior motive. Frankly, I can't subscribe to the latter. No . . . 'compatible motive,' to use the judge's own words. Lastly, he's a stand-up legal encyclopedia. Even though a lot of us are convinced there are holes, he might just be able to fill every one."

"So much for Bellstar." Trevayne wrote a note to himself on the back of the envelope in his hand. "What else, Alan?"

"Goddard was angry—I mean he blinked and smiled and damn near tore his fingernails on the wood—when you skirted the question of Armbruster. The Senator's off-limits with him. I don't think he knew what you were driving at. Neither did I, to tell you the truth. . . . Armbruster's been a thorn to big corporations, especially monoliths like Genessee. He couldn't understand your question about Armbruster being consulted about employment statistics."

"Because Armbruster wasn't consulted. *He* did the consulting."

"I still don't understand."

"The liberal Senator did some rather illiberal cogitations during the last election."

"No kidding?" Vicarson's eyes were wide.

"I wish I were," answered Trevayne.

"The last thing I put down—I left the legal stuff to Sam—was the downright evasions they all gave us, in unison, on the aircraft lobby. They were primed on this one. By their percentage figures they're accountable for a maximum of twenty-two percent of the lobby's funding. Yet according to the lobby's own stats, Genessee's responsible for twenty-seven percent that we know about, and probably another twelve that's buried. If I really ran a subsidiary check and pulled in the Green Agency in New York, I swear I'd find an additional twenty percent. I know goddamned well Genessee plies a minimum of seven million into the lobby, but they refuse to admit it. I tell you, they've got more labels for public relations than Sears Roebuck has in a catalog."

Labels. A nation of labels, thought Andrew Trevayne.

"Who runs Green in New York?"

"Aaron Green," answered Sam Vicarson. "Philanthropist, patron of the arts, publisher of poetry at his own expense. Very high type."

"A co-religionist of mine," added Alan Martin. "Only he came from Birmingham's 'Our Crowd,' not from New Britain, Connecticut, where us yids ate Kielbasa or got rapped by Polack knuckles. . . . That's all I wrote down."

Labels, a nation of labels.

Andrew Trevayne unobtrusively made another notation on the back of the Mark Hopkins envelope. "Grade A, pass, Rabbi Martin. Shall we bar-mitzvah young Sam?"

"After all my erudition? You're a hard man, Mr. Chairman."

"We grant you're erudite, don't we, Alan? We also grant your exquisite taste in gifts." Trevayne picked up his shark lighter from the lamp table and pressed the dorsal fin. No light appeared in the mouth. "You owe me a battery. . . . Now, what has the learned counselor deemed to provide us?"

"Crap. . . . Funny, I don't even like the word, but I use it a lot. Now, it fits." Vicarson rose from the couch and walked toward the hotel television set and fingered the top.

"What's the crap?" asked Trevayne.

"The term is *no-volotore*. At least it's *my* term." Vicarson turned around and faced Martin and Trevayne. "Goddard had a lawyer there this afternoon, but he didn't know what the hell was transpiring. *No-volotore;* he couldn't *offer* anything. He was there to make sure no one contradicted himself legally—that's *all*. He wasn't allowed to know much of anything. It's one hell of a position."

"Christ, I'm repeating myself," said Martin, "but I don't understand."

"Dumb yiddle." Vicarson lobbed an empty ashtray at Martin, who caught it effortlessly with his left hand. "He was a front. A surface front who watched both sides like a biased referee. He kept picking us up on phrases, asking for classifications—*not* on substance, only on verbiage. You dig? . . . He made sure some future record was clean. And take my word for it, there was nothing said this afternoon that anyone could use in court." Vicarson leaned against the back of a chair and feigned a push-up on it.

"All right, Mr. Blackstone. Why does that disturb you so?" Trevayne shifted his position so he could give young Sam the benefit of his full attention.

"Simple, my leader. No one puts a lawyer, especially a *corporate* lawyer, in that kind of position unless he's frightened out of his tree. You *tell* him something! . . . That man didn't *know* anything. Believe me true, Mr. Trevayne, he was in a much darker area than we were."

"You're employing Judge Studebaker's tactics, Sam. Abstractions," said Trevayne.

"Not really; that's for openers." Vicarson suddenly stopped his juvenile gyrations and walked rapidly back to the couch. He sat down and picked up one of the pages on the coffee table. "I made a couple of notes, too. Not so elaborate as Al's—I was dodging the evil people—but I figured out a few things. . . . For a first raise, what would you say to collusion?"

Both listeners looked at each other, then at Vicarson.

"I thought nothing was said this afternoon that could be used in court." Trevayne spoke while lighting a cigarette.

"Qualification—not by itself. In conjunction with other information, and a lot of digging, there's a good possibility."

"What is it?" asked Martin.

"Goddard dropped the fact that he—'he' being Genessee Industries—hadn't been apprised of the steel quotas set by the President's Import Commission in March of last year before the official release date. The fact that Genessee had an armada of Tamishito ingot shipped from Japan just under the wire was ascribed to favorable market conditions and an astute purchasing board. Am I right?"

Trevayne nodded; Martin toyed with his grotesque little flashlight. "So?" he asked.

"In August, Genessee floated a bond issue. Some one hundred million dollars. . . . We lawyers keep an eye on such things; we always wish we were a member of the firm that gets the job. That's big-bonus time. I stray. . . . The firm which took on the bond issue was a Chicago office, Brandon and Smith; very big, very aristocratic. But why Chicago? There are a dozen tried-and-trues just down the street in New York."

"Come on, Sam," said Trevayne. "What's your point?"

"I have to tell it this way. I need the background. . . . Two weeks ago, Brandon and Smith took on a third principal partner. One Ian Hamilton, an irreproachable member of the bar and—"

It was as far as Vicarson got. Andrew sat forward, holding the envelope in his hand. "Ian Hamilton was on the President's Import Commission."

"The commission was formally adjourned after the report was given to the White House. In February; nine months ago. Although no one knew whether the President would accept the recommendations, the five members of the commission were expected—legally required—to keep silent about their findings."

Trevayne sat back and wrote another note on his envelope. "All right, Sam. . . . It's a traceable item. What else?"

"Minor stuff, mostly. You may pick up something though."

The three men talked for an additional forty-five minutes. Trevayne wrote nothing further on the back of the Mark Hopkins envelope. During the conversation Andy made martinis from the ingredients ordered from room service.

The dissection of the Genessee conference was nearly complete.

"You've picked our—laughingly called—brains, Mr. Trevayne," said Vicarson. "What did *you* think?"

Trevayne rose from his chair and held up the envelope. He approached the two aides on the couch and dropped it on the coffee table. "I think we've got what we came for."

Vicarson picked up the envelope and held it between himself and Martin. They read the carefully printed names.

ERNEST MANOLO—*Pasadena*

RALPH JAMISON—*Houston*

JOSHUA STUDEBAKER—*Seattle*

MITCHELL ARMBRUSTER—*D.C.*

AARON GREEN—*N.Y.C.*

IAN HAMILTON—*Chicago*

"Very well-rounded list, Andrew," said Alan Martin.

"Very. Each is intrinsic to a Genessee operation involving unusual and expensive circumstances. It's across the board; that's what makes it interesting. Starting with Manolo, there's a labor settlement; Jamison: project design, production; Studebaker: a highly questionable legal decision—federal, too; Armbruster: right into the Senate—there are others in that area, but none have dealt directly with Genessee in California; Aaron Green is distributing a large part of a national lobby's finances—courtesy of G.I.C. . . . Ian Hamilton? Who knows? But I get nervous when a man with his presidential ties is that close to a hundred-million-dollar bond issue with a major Defense contractor."

"What do you want to do?" Martin took the envelope from Sam. "We can get background material on each, I would think."

"Can we get it without arousing undue interest, though?"

"I think I can," said Sam Vicarson.

"I had an idea you could," replied Andy, smiling. "I want each of these people researched thoroughly, quickly. Then I want Manolo, Jamison, and Studebaker interviewed,

confronted with—in order—the AFL-CIO negotiation in
Pasadena, the design conversions at the Houston laboratories, and the Bellstar court decision in Seattle. We may
get nothing, each may be an isolated action, but I don't
think so. I think we'll find some sort of outline or pattern
of how Genessee operates. Even if they're not related,
we'll get a very good idea of Genessee's methods."

"What about the last three? The Senator, Green, and
Hamilton?" asked Martin.

"We'll hold on them until we interview the others,"
said Trevayne. "What's important now is that we move
quickly, without giving anyone a clue as to what we're
doing. To use a Bonnerism, a surprise pincer attack; no
one has the chance to create explanations. . . . We're on a
junket right now; the word is out that the three of us are
pulling routine drop-ins at various plants—from San Francisco to Denver. Okay, that's what the story remains. We
continue. Only there'll be some absenteeism."

"Absenteeism? What's that?" Sam Vicarson seemed
entranced by Andrew's rapid manipulations.

"Alan, I want you to go down to Pasadena; reach
Manolo. You've had experience in labor stats; you and I
negotiated union stuff all over New England years ago.
Find out how Manolo did it without any of the big labor
boys. And how come he's so quiet about it; why the
settlement hasn't developed as a union guideline. Manolo
should have been crowned and moved into the Washington headquarters. He hasn't."

"When do I go?"

"Tomorrow morning. If Sam here can come up with
enough Manolo biography to give you something to work
with."

Vicarson wrote on his notes. "It'll be a long night, but
I think I can."

"I'll get hold of Mike Ryan back east. He's an aero-
nautics engineer; that's close enough to this Jamison's
work in Houston. I want him to get to the Genessee labs,
find out how Jamison was able to get away with a conversion that cost one hundred and five million. What kind of
man is given that kind of responsibility. . . . Sam, if we

could find more hours for the night, could you dig up material on Jamison?"

Vicarson put down his pencil. "Someone in his position at the Genessee labs has to have clearance, doesn't he?"

"Definitely," answered Alan Martin.

"I know a disenchanted friend at the FBI. I went to school with him. He was never in the Hoover camp, but the Hoover contingent doesn't know it. He'll help us; no one will know."

"Good. And now you, Sam. Get out all the information you find on the Bellstar decision, Studebaker's decision. Read it until you can recite it backwards. As soon as Alan returns, I want you to go to Seattle. Studebaker's your assignment."

"It's my pleasure," said Vicarson. "That man's a giant; maybe some of his stuff will rub off."

"Let's hope it's the right stuff," answered Trevayne.

"Andrew?" Alan Martin seemed concerned. "You say you want this all to be done with no flak, no one knowing what we're doing. That's going to be difficult. How do you explain the absenteeism?"

"A few years ago, Henry Kissinger got the 'touristas' in Taiwan; instead of being in his hotel room, he was in Peking."

"Okay," answered Martin. "That part's okay. But he had rather special transportation. If anyone's watching us —and we know damned well they are— airline reservations are easily traced."

"Good point," answered Trevayne, addressing both men. "And we'll have special transportation, too. I'll call my brother-in-law, Doug Pace, in New Haven. He can arrange private planes here and in D.C. Ryan will be watched also."

"You haven't lost your touch, Andrew," said Martin. "Doug may have apoplexy, but he'll do it."

"He still hasn't forgiven me for kidnapping you, you know."

"My wife brings him chicken soup at the office. She's afraid he won't take me back." Martin smiled; Andrew laughed.

"Mr. Trevayne?" Sam Vicarson was staring at his notes. "Yes?"

"I see a problem."

"Only one?" asked Martin. "I'm relieved."

"I think it's a big one. How do we know that the minute these guys—Manolo, Jamison, Studebaker—see us, they won't throw panic switches and call the Genessee management?"

"That *is* a problem. I think the only way to solve it is to use concrete threats. The approach to each should be that he is a small part of a much, much larger concern. The interviews are confidential; to break that confidence could be indictable. Since Defense is involved, maybe we could use the National Security Act."

"Section three-five-eight!" Vicarson was impressed with himself. "I picked that up from Bonner during an argument."

"We'll try it. . . . Now, you've both got a lot to do, and I have calls to make. Was Paul going to have dinner with us?"

"No," answered Sam. "He said he was going out catting. The son-of-a-bitch didn't even ask me to come along."

"He'd be court-martialed for corrupting minors," said Martin, chuckling.

"Thanks, Father Ben-Gurion."

"We'll break, then." Trevayne reached down for the envelope. "The day after tomorrow we're in Boise, Idaho; that I.T.T. subsidiary. Try to coordinate and meet us there, Alan. I'll call your room after I talk to Doug. From Boise, Sam, you head up to Seattle."

"Join a subcommittee and see the world," said Sam Vicarson, finishing his martini.

Trevayne leaned back on the pillow and put his feet up on the bed. The telephone calls had been made. Phyllis missed him; she'd gone back to Barnegat while he was away. Life was uneventful. Pam and Steve were surviving at their schools. Pam had won some kind of award this semester in chemistry; how did she *ever* come by *that* talent? Phyllis was having the Swansons over for dinner tomorrow. They were still upset over the heroin episode;

Officer Fowler at Police Headquarters was no further along than before.

His brother-in-law would take care of the small-plane arrangements. Charter and flight plans would be in his, Pace's, name, and the first field would probably be the small private airport outside of Redwood City. Not San Francisco International. He'd call back. Further, his brother-in-law would discreetly, but thoroughly, check around the Hartford-New Haven area and uncover the whereabouts of Mario de Spadante. It wouldn't be difficult; De Spadante delegated very little authority in his company. Any number of problems could be raised—invented—that required his immediate attention.

Trevayne reached Michael Ryan, who was still in his office at the Potomac Towers. Ryan made the evening brighter by telling Andrew he knew Ralph Jamison. Knew him quite well, as a matter of fact. They'd both been called in on the SST mock-up at Lockheed—consulting specialists.

"He's a *crazy* bastard, Andy. But they don't come any better in metallurgy. He's a goddamn genius. And *man*, does he *live!* I'll pump him dry."

Ryan would be called directly by Doug Pace in New Haven; he understood the reasons for secrecy and felt certain he could handle Jamison in that area. Ryan would try to complete the job and meet them in Boise. If he wasn't able to make it by then, he'd get to Denver, the junket's next stop.

Andrew made a final telephone call to Washington. To Robert Webster on the White House aide's private line. He eventually reached him at home. He asked Webster to compile everything he could about Mario de Spadante.

Webster agreed to do so.

Trevayne looked down at the envelope in his hand. It was wrinkled, creased by his constant folding and unfolding. But the writing was still clear:

ERNEST MANOLO—*Pasadena*
RALPH JAMISON—*Houston*
JOSHUA STUDEBAKER—*Seattle*

MITCHELL ARMBRUSTER—*D.C.*
AARON GREEN—*N.Y.C.*
IAN HAMILTON—*Chicago*

This was the real itinerary. Six men who might help him understand the apparent majesty of Genessee Industries.

21

Sam Vicarson walked into the small passenger terminal at the Ada County airport, ten miles from Boise. Douglas Pace's Lear jet had brought him back from Tacoma; while in Tacoma he'd rented a car and driven to Seattle.

To see Judge Joshua Studebaker.

It was a meeting he'd remember for the rest of his life.

It was also a meeting he could describe only to Andrew Trevayne alone. Not with Alan Martin; not with Mike Ryan. It was too private, too terrible, somehow, for any ears but Trevayne's.

Vicarson knew that Mike had gotten into Boise from Houston several hours ago; Alan had returned from the Manolo interview two days ago, when he turned the Lear jet over for the Seattle run.

They were to meet that night in Trevayne's hotel room. They were to put it all together then.

Sam had to find Trevayne before the meeting. Trevayne would know what to do.

Vicarson felt tired, exhausted, and depressed; he thought about stopping off at a bar for a few drinks. But he knew he wouldn't.

He'd get roaring drunk, and that wouldn't do anyone any good.

Especially not Joshua Studebaker.

Alan Martin stared out of the car window. He was alone; Andrew had left the meeting with I.T.T.'s subsidiary early, without explanation. Sam Vicarson had called from the airport; something was the matter.

The sign on the highway read: "Boise, Idaho; State Capital; Population 73,000; Heart of the Columbia Basin."

It was difficult for Alan Martin to think of Boise, think of the unnecessary conferences they were holding, for cover.

He couldn't get his mind off Pasadena. Pasadena and a fiery little man named Ernest Manolo. An incredibly *young* fiery man. Andrew didn't want to discuss Manolo until they all got together that night. There was logic in that; save the information, don't lose details in the retelling. Andrew was right; they could all trigger each other.

It wasn't so much Manolo; Andrew was right again. Manolo was only a cog, a single spike in a frightening wheel.

Ernest Manolo, AFL-CIO negotiator for the entire district of southern California, had his own considerable fiefdom.

How many others were there across the country?

Michael Ryan sat at a booth in the hotel's coffee shop. He was annoyed with himself. He should have known better than to be so obvious; he should have gotten a room and just stayed there until Trevayne called him.

Goddamn!

He just wasn't thinking!

The first goddamn person he'd run into in the goddamn coffee shop was Paul Bonner!

Bonner was surprised, of course. And when he, Ryan, couldn't come up with a decent explanation, Bonner's surprise turned into something else.

It was there, in the soldier's eyes. That something else.

Goddamn!

His carelessness, Ryan realized, was due to an old friend, Ralph Jamison. Stupid, insane, crazy-head Jamison! Falsifying designs to get Genessee Industries a hundred and five million of Defense funds.

How could he have *done* it? How could he *do* it?

Sold lock, stock, and barrel to Genessee Industries. Jamison, with his three ex-wives, his four kids from who-knew-which, his middle-aged peccadilloes that were right out of some goddamn fifth-rate porno movie.

Genessee took care of Ralph Jamison. Jamison told him it was standard operating procedure. "Ma Gen" took care of its talent.

Bank accounts in Zurich!

Insane!

It had been three days since Trevayne and his subcommittee aides had left San Francisco, but James Goddard couldn't get them out of his mind. Something had gone wrong. The final two conferences were merely prolonged embarrassments.

Without the accountant. The accountant hadn't been there. And it didn't make sense for this Martin to be absent. Alan Martin was the cost man; just as he, Goddard, was a cost man. Without Martin, too many details were overlooked; Martin would have caught the details.

Trevayne had joked about his aide. The subcommittee chairman had laughed and said that Martin was holed up at the Mark Hopkins with a bad case of "San Francisco water."

After the last conference, Goddard decided to inquire. He could do so easily, even be solicitous. He called the hotel.

Alan Martin had checked out two days ago.

Why had Trevayne lied? Why had the other aide, Vicarson, lied? Where had Martin gone?

Had he suddenly gone to get follow-up data on information revealed during the conferences?

Revealed by him; revealed by James Goddard, president, San Francisco Division, Genessee Industries?

Which? What?

How could he find out what it was without others becoming alarmed?

That was important. Mario de Spadante said some might have to hang so that those farther up could remain untouched. Goddard knew he was considered vital. Good *Lord;* he *was* vital! He was the figure man. He arranged the numbers, created the projections upon which the decisions were made. Even he wasn't sure who ultimately made those decisions, but without *him* they couldn't be made.

He was the keystone . . . a keystone.

But he also knew that underneath the attention they gave him, the respect they surfacely rendered, there was a certain contempt. The contempt associated with a man who could only propose, never dispose.

A "bookkeeper."

But this bookkeeper wasn't for hanging.

Goddard signaled a cab, and as it pulled up to the curb he made his own decision. He'd return to his office and remove a number of highly confidential papers. He would carefully put them at the bottom of his briefcase and take them home.

Numbers. His numbers. Genessee's numbers. Not names.

He knew how to deal with numbers.

A man had to protect himself. Perhaps against names.

Andrew Trevayne jumped out of the cab and walked into the hotel lobby. He'd promised Sam Vicarson he'd meet him in Vicarson's room. But before he did, he knew it was time to talk to Bonner. Regardless of what was learned from Sam and Alan and Mike Ryan, he had to get on Pace's Lear jet tonight and go to Washington.

And depending on what was learned from his three aides about Manolo, Jamison, and Studebaker, he might well go from Washington to New York and on to Chicago.

Mitchell Armbruster. Aaron Green. Ian Hamilton.

Either way, it was time to use Paul Bonner.

Bonner was waiting for him in the cocktail lounge. The meeting would be brief.

Trevayne was of two minds. He knew he had to do what he was doing; by using Paul Bonner, Washington would be convinced of the "legitimacy" of his temporarily abandoning his subcommittee, but there was another aspect.

He was actively, willfully engaging in much the same type of manipulation he'd been recruited to expose—calculated deception. The difference, he rationalized, was the absence of financial profit, and for a while he accepted this rationalization as fundamentally justifiable. But there were other "profits," equally important rewards. He didn't need money. . . . Was he somehow applying the intensity others used for making money to reach something else?

He couldn't dwell on it; the decision had been made.

He was going to relive—for the record—one of the most difficult periods of his life. It would give flexibility to time.

Six years ago Phyllis had entered the hospital for an exploratory. It was before mammography had been perfected, and she had developed lumps on her breasts. He had been beside himself, trying his best to be outwardly confident, knowing the children suspected something far more serious than what they'd been told—perceiving his anguish.

Now, six years later, Paul Bonner was to be given a current variation of the incident. An unspecific account, clouded with doubt and filled with apprehension. And a request: would Paul sit in on the upcoming subcommittee conferences with two subcontractors of General Motors and Lockheed? They were in Denver the next few days. The conferences needed the "weight" of his, Bonner's, inclusion. Sam Vicarson was simply too young, Alan Martin seemingly too lacking in authority. The aides would fill him in.

So that he, Andrew Trevayne, could get home to his wife.

Phyllis was entering a private hospital Friday afternoon. No one knew anything about the exploratory other than Sam and Alan. Even the two men from 1600 who stayed on the Barnegat property knew only that Phyllis was going for a checkup. One way or the other Trevayne would return to Denver on Monday.

When the drinks were finished, Andy found it difficult to look at Paul Bonner. The Major was so genuinely concerned for him, he agreed to do anything, take whatever worries he could from Andy's mind.

Oh, God! thought Trevayne. *In this nation of labels this man is my enemy. Yet look at his eyes! They're frightened—for me.*

Paul Bonner walked slowly down the hotel corridor to his room. He unlocked the door, entered, and slammed it shut. He swung it with such force that two paintings—

poor reproductions selected by a tasteless Boise management—vibrated on the wall. He crossed to his bureau,
where there was the ever-present bottle of bourbon, and
poured himself a large drink.

He poured himself another and drank it rapidly.

It was entirely possible, he reflected, that he might
just stay in his room the remainder of the day, order
another bottle, and get quietly, thoroughly drunk.

But then, that would preclude the charade. He'd be
too hungover in the morning for his meeting with Alan
Martin and Sam Vicarson, during which time they were to
give him the background on the subcontractors in Denver.

Horseshit!

The beavers were so inept. And the head beaver was
playing a dirty game—a very personally dirty game—of
dam building. He hadn't thought Andrew Trevayne could
roll in that kind of filth. Even the possessors of hatred—
they might use their women to run guns and contraband,
alert the jungles, smuggle narcotics, but they wouldn't use
them *this* way. They wouldn't trade in painfully intimate
confidences. There was no dignity in that, no essential
strength.

Bonner carried his glass to his bed, sat down, and reached
for the hotel telephone. He gave the operator the private
Washington number of Brigadier General Lester Cooper.

It took Major Bonner less than a minute to get to the
basic information.

". . . the cover is his wife. He says he's flying east to
be with her. She's supposed to enter a quote—private
hospital—unquote; cancer exploratory. It's a lie."

"Are you sure?"

"Damned near positive," answered Bonner, swallow-
ing the remainder of the bourbon in his glass.

"Why? That's pretty hairy."

"Because it follows!" Bonner realized he spoke too
sharply to his superior; he couldn't help himself. His
anger with Trevayne was too personal. "Alan Martin disappeared for a day and a half; Vicarson was gone for two. No
explanation given, just subcommittee business. Then this
afternoon, who the hell do I run into. In Boise. . . . Mike
Ryan. Something's going on, General. It stinks."

Brigadier General Cooper paused before speaking. His fear carried over the wire. "We can't afford to be mistaken, Bonner."

"For God's sake, General, I'm an experienced man; I've interrogated the best of them. Trevayne's learning, I'm sorry to say, but he's still a bad liar. It hurt him to look at me."

"We've got to find out where the other three were. . . . I'll put out tracers with the airlines. We've got to know."

"Let me do that, General." Bonner didn't want the Pentagon amateurs coming on the scene. "There are only half a dozen lines coming in here. I'll find out where they flew in from."

"Call me as soon as you learn something. This is priority, Major. In the meantime, I'll put surveillance on his wife. To be sure; in case he shows up."

"You're wasting your time, sir. She's a cooperative girl. The '1600' team will vouch that she's going for a checkup. Trevayne's a rotten liar, but I'm sure he's methodical about this sort of thing. He's in new territory now; he'll be thorough."

22

Sam Vicarson leaned against the writing desk as Trevayne settled into an armchair.

"All right, Counselor," said Andrew, looking up, "why the private conference? What's the matter?"

"Joshua Studebaker made a mistake forty years ago. They're making him pay for it. He thinks thirty years of judicial decisions will go out the window if he's called. As he put it, the source of his decisions would become suspect in every court in the land."

Trevayne whistled softly. "What did he do? Shoot Lincoln?"

"Worse. He was a Communist. Not the radical-chic variety, but a real card-carrying, cell-organized, Kremlininstructed Marxist. . . . The country's first black judge west of the Rocky Mountains spent five years—again, as he put it—in dimly lit rooms preparing cases for his practicing colleagues that tied up the courts with manipulative language. For the cause."

"His practicing colleagues?"

"He was disbarred in Missouri. He'd won one appeal in the State Supreme Court; he wasn't welcome after that. He went underground, landed in New York, and became part of the movement. He got the Red fever; for five years he really believed it was the answer."

"What's that got to do with Genessee Industries? With the Bellstar decision?"

Vicarson pulled the chair out from under the writing desk and straddled it, his arms resting on the back. "The Genessee attorneys got to him. Very subtly. Veiled but explicit threats of exposure."

"And he sold out. He sold the bench."

"It's not that simple, Mr. Trevayne. That's why I wanted to see you alone, without the others. . . . I don't want to write up a report on Studebaker."

Andrew's voice was clipped, cold. "I think you'd better explain, Sam. That decision isn't yours to make."

And Sam Vicarson tried to explain.

Joshua Studebaker was in his seventies. A large, magnificently gifted Negro, he was the son of an itinerant crop hand named Joshua, as *his* father before him was Joshua. In 1907, during one of Theodore Roosevelt's last-gasp reform programs, young Joshua was selected to receive some minimum schooling.

Studebaker's government-sponsored education lasted an extraordinary seven years, six more than the counter-reformers anticipated. During those years the young boy crammed an equally extraordinary amount of knowledge into his previously illiterate head. But at sixteen he was told there was no more; he was to be grateful for what he'd been given. It was certainly no birthright, not in the year 1914 in the state of Missouri, U.S.A.

However, the tools had been provided, and Joshua Studebaker took care of the rest. He sought, begged, stole, and fought for the remainder of an education. The years were migrant years, but instead of following the crops, he went to where the classrooms were open for him. He lived in squalor, when it was available; more often in railroad yards and dump shacks with corrugated metal roofs and fires kindled by refuse. At twenty-two Joshua Studebaker found a small experimental college that prepared him for the law. At twenty-five he was a lawyer. At twenty-seven he'd astounded the bar in Missouri by successfully appealing a case before the State Supreme Court.

He was not welcome in Missouri.

He was soon thereafter without a practice in Missouri, disbarred over technical preparations. He'd been put in his proper place.

There followed years of running, eking out whatever living he could—teaching when possible in back-country schools, more often doing manual labor. His prized lawyer's certificate was next to worthless. Negro attorneys were not sought after in the twenties; a disbarred Negro attorney not at all.

Studebaker drifted north to Chicago, where he made contact with the disciples of Eugene Debs, living out his last years writing and lecturing among the socialist intelligentsia. Joshua's talents were perceived by the extremists in Debs's circles, and he was sent to New York—to the soft, hot core of the Communist party.

For the next five years of his adult life he was a vital, unknown legal manipulator, hidden by anonymity, doing the work of headlining radicals. He was getting even with the Eden that had cast him so unfairly from its garden.

Then Franklin Roosevelt was elected President, and the Marxists went into panic. For Roosevelt went about saving the capitalistic system by boldly implementing social reforms the Leninists held as their own.

Joshua Studebaker was approached by the Marxists to enter into another phase of operation. He was ordered to form an elitist subcell, the end result of which was the training of insurgent teams used for the physical disruption of government reform programs. Offices, job camps, food-distribution centers, were to be sabotaged; files stolen, welfare caseloads destroyed; any and all tactics employed that might cripple or make ineffective by delay the cures for the economic ills of the lingering Depression.

"It was appalling that they should have chosen me," Joshua Studebaker had said to Sam Vicarson. "They misunderstood my zeal. . . . As a thinker, a strategist, perhaps, I accepted the *principle* of violence. As an activist I could not accept participation. I specifically could not accept it when the first results were directed at those who were helpless."

Joshua Studebaker, after reading in a newspaper the aftermath of a life-taking fire at a CCC camp in New York State, went to the Justice Department.

It was the time of welcoming back errants; it was also a time of rewarding those who could help the Roosevelt administration wash off the taint of the Red brush. Joshua fit into both categories. He was quietly hired by the government, and all his legal privileges were restored. For the first time in his life Joshua Studebaker could stop running, stop scratching, stop lashing out at the horrors—real and unreal—that had pursued him. Eden became a productive, serpentless garden.

And finally, as if the circle of experimentation were complete, Joshua Studebaker was awarded the first black judgeship west of the Rocky Mountains. It was a safe experiment—a small appointment with a constituency generously peopled by transient lumbermen and Tacomack Indians, but a judgeship, nevertheless.

Ironically, it was later, during the McCarthy madness, that Studebaker received his "promotion," as it were, to Seattle. It was someone's sense of outrage that a once dangerous though anonymous radical was put forth. It balanced someone's scale.

"He's spent thirty years fighting vested advocacy, Mr. Trevayne. I guarantee you that; look at the law books, at the supportive adjudications used by thousands of Legal Aid attorneys in the ghettos, in the barrios. I know, sir. I've been there. From land condemnation to restraints, from undue process to abridged rights. Studebaker's been a one-man barricade against the self-interest groups. If we expose what he was, all that could be in jeopardy."

"*Why?*" Andrew was annoyed. "For something that happened forty years ago, Sam? You're unreasonable."

"No, I'm not, sir! He never recanted, there was no public confessional, no groveling for forgiveness. . . . His court decisions have been interpreted as ideologically left of center. If his past is brought up, they'll be labeled something else."

Labels. A nation of labels, thought Trevayne.

"Don't you see?" continued Vicarson. "He doesn't care about himself. He cares deeply about his work. And whatever the reasons—even justifications—he *was* a subversive. In the real meaning of the word. The prospects of ulterior motive *could* be attributed to every major decision he's ever made. It's called 'dishonorable source.' It usually overrides everything else."

"And that's why you don't want to write the report?"

"Yes, sir. You'd have to meet him to understand. He's an old man; I think a great man. He's not afraid for himself; I don't think the years he has left are important to him. What he's accomplished *is*."

"Aren't you forgetting something, Sam?" asked Trevayne slowly.

"What?"

"The Bellstar decision. Didn't you say it was full of holes? Are we to let the Genessee lawyers get away with the most corrupt sort of practice?"

Vicarson smiled sadly. "I have an idea they wasted their time. Studebaker might have reached the same decision without them. Of course, we'll never know, but he's pretty damned convincing."

"How?"

"He quoted Hofstader: antitrust is 'a faded passion of reform.' And Galbraith: modern technology has brought about the 'industrialized state.' Competition, per se, is no longer a viable, built-in regulator. The huge economic resources demanded by our technology bring about a concentration of financing. . . . Once this is accepted—and the law has to deal with practicalities—it's the government's responsibility, and the law's, to act as the regulator, the protector of the consumer. The civilizer, if you will. . . . Put in blunt terms, the country needed the

Bellstar products. The company was going under; there was no one else but Genessee Industries who had sufficient economic resources to assume the responsibility."

"He said that?"

"Almost verbatim. It wasn't so clear in the decision; at least, not to me. He told me I wasn't the best student he'd ever met."

"But if he believed that, why didn't he just say so? Why did he tell you all the rest of it?"

Sam Vicarson got out of the chair; there was a restless, uncomfortable expression on his face. "I'm afraid I forced him. I said that if I didn't understand the Bellstar decision, if I thought it was suspect—and for the record, I'm considered a bright bastard—then he had an obligation to make a public clarification. He flatly refused. No way; he was adamant. I felt awful, but I told him he was copping out, and I wouldn't buy it. I was going to subpoena him."

"I would have done the same thing."

Vicarson was by the hotel window, staring out at the Boise skyline. "He didn't expect that; I don't think he realized we had subpoena powers."

"Honored in the breach, I hope," said Trevayne. "We haven't used them."

Vicarson turned. "It shook him, Mr. Trevayne. It was a terrible sight. And it wasn't for *himself;* you've got to believe that."

Trevayne got out of the chair and stood facing the young man. He spoke quietly but firmly.

"Write the report, Sam."

"*Please . . .*"

"Don't file it. Give it to me. One copy." Andrew walked to the door. "See you at eight o'clock. My room."

23

The coffee table served as a communal desk. The reports and memoranda were in file folders in front of each man. The conference in Trevayne's room had begun with Alan Martin's description of Ernest Manolo, president of the Lathe Operators Brotherhood of the District of Southern California and the all-powerful negotiator of the AFL-CIO. According to Martin, Ernest Manolo looked like a twelve-year-old bullfighter.

"He travels with his own picadors; two big fellows, they're always flanking him."

"Are they guards?" asked Trevayne. "And if so, why?"

"They are, and he needs them. Fast Ernie—that's what he's called, Fast Ernie—has a goodly share of resentful brothers in his brotherhood."

"Good Lord, why?" Andrew was sitting next to Sam Vicarson on the couch. "He got them a hell of a settlement." Vicarson started to interrupt as Martin answered quickly.

"Sam knows. It was in his bio material. Incidentally, buddy," said Martin to the young attorney, "that was a good job."

"Thanks," answered a subdued Vicarson. "It wasn't hard. When he was running for office he had a lot of promotion material circulated. Easy to zero in on."

"That's why he travels with his two friends," continued Martin. "Fast Ernie's twenty-six years old. He had to jump over a lot of seasoned union stewards to get the job. Most of them don't like the way he did it."

"Which was how?" asked Mike Ryan, sitting across from Martin.

"A lot of the hard-hat brothers think he used dirty money. They figure it had to be dirty, because he had so much of it. He brought into office with him a whole new breed of union management. Young, bright, college-educated. They don't shout arguments in union halls, they issue position paper with lots of charts and logistics. The old-timers don't like it. They're suspicious of three syllables."

"Still," said Andrew, "he got them a decent contract. That's the name of the game, Alan."

"It's also the name of Fast Ernie's problem. It's both his best weapon and his highly suspect maneuver. . . . It was the quickest settlement Genessee ever made. No big fights, no all-night bargaining sessions; when it was concluded, there weren't any celebrations; no dancing in the streets. No words of congratulation from the old war horses like Meany and his boys on the Labor Council. Most important, the settlement in the Southern California District will *not* be used as a guideline anywhere else. It's isolated, jurisdictional."

Mike Ryan leaned forward in his chair. "I'm an engineer, not a union-watcher. Is that unusual?"

"You can bet your blueprints on it," answered Martin. "Any major labor contract serves as the basis for upcoming negotiations. But not this one."

"How do you know?" asked Trevayne.

"I backed Manolo into a corner. I told him I was surprised, even astounded, that he hadn't been given his proper due; that the D.C. Labor Council had brushed him off. I knew a few of those old buzzards, and I was going to raise the issue. . . . Manolo didn't want any part of my solicitousness. In fact, he was goddamned upset. He began retreating to his charts and employment stats relative to district conditions. He reiterated more times than I care to recall how the old-time labor clods couldn't understand the new jurisdictional economic theories. What was applicable to southern California wasn't to west Arkansas. . . . Do you begin to see?"

"He's Genessee's man. They put him in and bought him with the single contract," interjected Vicarson.

"They're doing it all over the country—including west Arkansas," said Martin. "Genessee Industries is well on its way to controlling its own labor markets. I made a surface check this afternoon, based on Manolo's districting pattern. It's surface, mind you, but I found similarities in Genessee companies and subsidiaries in twenty-four states."

"Jesus," said Mike Ryan softly.

"Will Manolo run to Genessee? That could be a problem for us right now." Andrew frowned as he asked the question.

"I don't think so. I can't guarantee it, but I think he's going to sit on the tightrope; at least for a while. I told him I was perfectly satisfied, and I think he bought it. I also implied that I'd be just as happy if our meeting was kept between the two of us. If others got involved—especially Genessee management—I'd have to spend a lot more time in Pasadena. . . . I think he'll keep quiet."

"So much for Manolo. What about this Jamison in Houston, Mike?"

Ryan seemed to hesitate as he reached for the folder on the coffee table. He looked over at Trevayne and for several moments said nothing. The expression on his face was questioning. Finally he spoke. "I'm trying to figure out a way to say this. I listen to Al's words here and find myself nodding my head, saying, 'Yes, sure, that's the way it is.' Because suddenly I realize he's describing Houston. And probably Palo Alto, Detroit, Oak Ridge, and twenty or so other Genessee design shops and laboratories in God knows how many places. Only you substitute 'scientific community' for 'labor markets,' dirty up the players a bit more, and it's the same ballgame."

Michael Ryan had flown into Houston International using a plane also chartered by Douglas Pace, flight plans filed under Pace's name. After checking the Genessee laboratories, he found Ralph Jamison, metallurgical specialist, at a yacht club on Galveston Bay. It was in Megans Point, a haven for oil-rich Texans, the Southwest's Riviera.

Ryan feigned an unexpected reunion, completely accepted by Ralph Jamison. The two men had become friends while they were at Lockheed; each an extrovert, each a lover of good times and a good deal of good liquor.

Each, too, a brilliant man.

Afternoon became evening and then, swiftly, the early-morning hours. Ryan found that Jamison continuously evaded questions about his projects at Genessee. It was frustrating, because it wasn't natural; shop talk among top aeronautical men—especially with both cleared for the highest classification—was the normal, anticipated, looked-forward-to indulgence.

"Then I got an inspiration, Andy," said Mike Ryan, interrupting his narrative. "I decided to offer Ralph a job."

"Where?" asked Trevayne, smiling. "Doing what?"

"Who the hell cared? We were both fried out of our skulls; him more than me, I'm happy to say. . . . I made it sound like I was a lab raider. I was with a company that was in a bind; we needed him. I'd actually come looking for him. I offered him three, maybe four times what I figured he was pulling down at Genessee."

"You were pretty damned generous," said Alan Martin. "What were you going to do if he accepted?"

Ryan stared down at the coffee table. His eyes had a sadness about them. "By then I'd accurately predicted that he wouldn't." Ryan looked up. "Or couldn't."

Ralph Jamison, faced with a firm, incredible offer made by a man who—drunk or sober—would not have made it without authorization, had to find explanations commensurate with his illogical refusal. The words, at first, came easily: loyalty, current projects that concerned him at Genessee, lab problems he couldn't leave, again loyalty, stretching back over the years.

Ryan countered each with growing irritation, until Jamison—by now nearly incoherent, and pressured by his total belief in Ryan's extraordinary offer—dropped the words.

"You can't understand. Genessee has taken care of us. All of us."

"Taken care?" Trevayne repeated the words reported by Mike Ryan. "All of them? . . . Who? What did he mean?"

"I had to piece it together. He never came out and made any blanket admissions . . . except one. But it's there, Andy. All the top talent—especially lab and design—are paid below the line."

"Under the table, I presume, is another, more accurate description," said Alan Martin.

"Yes," answered Ryan. "And not little driblets in expense vouchers. Fair-sized amounts, usually paid outside the country and wending their way to Zurich and Bern. Coded bank accounts."

"Unreported income," supplied Martin.

"Untraceable," added Sam Vicarson. "Because no one cries fraud. And no country's tax laws are recognized in Switzerland. Even when violated, it's not fraud as far as the Swiss are concerned."

"It starts early, as I understand it," said Ryan. "Genessee spots a comer, a real potential, and the loving begins. Oh, they check out the person; they work slowly, gradually. They find weaknesses—that was Ralph's admission, incidentally, I'll get to it—and when they find them they cross-pollinate them with plain, outright, hidden bonuses. In ten or fifteen years a guy has a sweet nest egg of a hundred, a hundred and fifty thousand salted away. That's mighty inducive."

"And he's inexorably bound to Genessee Industries," said Trevayne. "It's a collusion pact; he does what Genessee tells him to do. Because if he doesn't, that's conducive to something else. I assume payments are made by . . . let's say, expendable intermediaries."

"Right."

"A rough estimate, Mike: how many Ralph Jamisons are there?" asked Trevayne.

"Well, figure Genessee has a hundred installations—general and subsidiary—like the Houston labs. Not as big, certainly, but substantial. You can estimate between seven and ten top men at each site. Seven hundred to a thousand."

"And these people control project decisions, production lines?" Trevayne wrote on notepaper.

"Ultimately, yes. They're responsible."

"So for a few million a year, Genessee extracts obedience from a powerful sector of the scientific community," said Andrew, scratching over the figures he'd written. "Men who have control over, say, a hundred project installations, which in turn make the decisions for all of the Genessee plants and subsidiaries. Assembly lines and contracts involving billions."

"Yes. I'd guess it's growing every year; they start young." The dejected, questioning expression returned to Ryan's face. "Ralph Jamison's a sad casualty, Andy. He's better than that. He's got a big problem."

"He drinks with the Irish crazies," said Alan Martin gently, seeing the pain in Ryan's eyes.

Ryan looked at Martin, smiled, and paused before replying softly. "Hell no, Al, he's an amateur. He goes out New Year's Eve. . . . Ralph's at the real genius level. He's made great contributions to metallurgical research; we'd never have made the moon without him. But he burns himself out in the shops. He's been known to work seventy-two hours straight. His whole life is committed to the laboratory."

"Is that his problem?" asked Andy.

"Yes. Because he can't take the time for anything else. He runs from personal commitments; he's frightened to death of them. He's had three wives—quick selections. They gave him among them four children. The ladies have bled him in alimony and support. But he's nuts about the kids; he worries about them so because he knows himself and those girls. That was his admission to me. Every February he goes to Paris, where a Genessee small-timer gives him twenty thousand in cash, which he takes to Zurich. It's for his kids."

"And he's one of the men who put us on the moon." Sam Vicarson made the statement quietly and watched Trevayne. It was apparent to all in the room that Sam was referring to something—someone else.

And each knew that Sam had been to Seattle, Washington. To Joshua Studebaker.

Andrew accepted Vicarson's words and his unspoken appeal. He turned back to Ryan. "But you're not suggesting that we disregard Jamison's report, are you, Mike?"

"Christ, no." Ryan exhaled slowly. "I don't like nailing him, but what I've learned about Genessee Industries scares the hell out of me; I mean *really scares* me. I know what those design shops and laboratories are turning out."

"That's physical, not sociological," said Vicarson quickly, firmly.

"Sooner or later those two get together if they're not already, fella," answered Ryan.

"Thanks, Mike." Trevayne's voice indicated that he wanted no tangential discussions at the moment.

Vicarson leaned forward on the couch and picked up

his file folder. "Okay. I guess it's my turn," he said with a shrug that conveyed far more than resignation.

Andrew interrupted. "May I, please?"

Sam looked at Trevayne, surprised. "What?"

"Sam came to me earlier this evening. The Studebaker report isn't complete. There's no question that he was reached and threatened by Genessee, but we're not sure of the degree of influence that had on the antitrust decision regarding Bellstar. The judge claims that it didn't; he justifies the decision in legal and philosophical terms, using contemporary definitions. We *do* know the Justice Department had no real interest in pursuing the action."

"But he *was reached*, Andrew?" Alan Martin was concerned. "And threatened?"

"He was."

"Threatened with what?" asked Ryan.

"I'm going to ask you to let me wait before answering that."

"It's so filthy?" asked Martin.

"I'm not sure it's relevant," said Trevayne. "If it turns out to be, it'll be filed."

Ryan and Martin looked at each other, then at Vicarson. Martin spoke, addressing Trevayne. "I'd be a damn fool to start questioning your judgment after all these years, Andrew."

"So, what else is new?" said Ryan casually.

"I'm leaving tonight. For Washington. Paul Bonner thinks I'm going to Connecticut; I'll explain. . . . Genessee Industries is progressively eliminating all the checks and balances. It's time for Senator Armbruster."

24

Brigadier General Lester Cooper walked up the flagstone path toward the front door of the suburban home. The coach lamp on the lawn was lighted; the metal plate beneath it, suspended by two small chains from a crossbar, read: "The Knapps; 37 Maple Lane."

Senator Alan Knapp.

There'd be at least one other senator inside, too, thought Cooper as he walked up the steps. He switched the attaché case to his left hand and pushed the button.

Knapp opened the door, his irritation obvious. "For God's sake, Cooper, it's almost ten o'clock. We said nine!"

"I didn't *have* anything until twenty minutes ago." The General spoke curtly. He didn't like Knapp; he simply had to tolerate him, not be polite. "I didn't look upon this evening as a social call, Senator."

Knapp feigned a smile; it was difficult for him. "Okay, General, call off the artillery. Come on in. . . . Sorry, we're a little upset."

"With damned good reason," added Cooper as he stepped inside.

Knapp preceded the General into the living room. It was an expensive room, thought Cooper as he saw the French provincial furniture, the soft white rugs, and the ornate objets d'art scattered about. Knapp came from money; old money.

Vermont's Senator Norton looked out of place sitting in a delicate love seat. The craggy New Englander was not the sort of person for whom such pieces were designed. The other man, however—Cooper didn't know him— seemed very much at ease on the couch. His clothes looked English; dark, thin pinstripes and cut close.

The White House's Robert Webster was the fourth man.

"You know Norton and Webster, General. May I introduce Walter Madison. . . . Madison, General Cooper."

The men shook hands. Knapp indicated a chair for Cooper and said, "Mr. Madison is Trevayne's attorney."

"What?" The Brigadier looked questioningly at the Senator.

"It's all right, Cooper." Norton shifted in the stiffly upholstered love seat as he spoke. He didn't feel the need to add anything further.

Webster, standing by the piano, highball in hand, was more understanding. "Mr. Madison is aware of our problems; he's cooperating with us."

The Brigadier unlocked his attaché case, opened it,

and extracted several typewritten pages. Madison elegantly uncrossed and crossed his legs. He asked calmly, "How is Andrew? I haven't heard from him in weeks."

Cooper looked up from his papers. It was obvious that he thought Madison's question was foolish. "He's busy."

"What have you learned?" Norton was impatient. He rose and walked to the couch—to the opposite end from Madison. Knapp kept his eyes on Cooper; he sat down in an armchair to the right of the General.

"Major Bonner spent the better part of the afternoon and evening trying to find the subcommittee's airline reservations. There were none. Thinking they might have used false names, he ran tracers on all male passengers coming into and out of the Boise airport during the past several days. They all proved out. He went to private aircraft; same answer." Cooper paused briefly; he wanted the pols to recognize the thoroughness of Defense personnel. "He then questioned several pilots and learned there was another airfield used exclusively for noncommercial aircraft; runway, medium-sized. Five thousand feet; sufficient for small jets. On the other side of Boise, eight to ten miles out of town. It's called Ada County Airport."

"General?" It was Knapp who was impatient now. The military was usually circumlocutory about a problem it hadn't solved. "I'm sure Major Bonner is an efficient officer, but I wish you'd get to the point."

"I'll *do* that, Senator. But I'll get there by giving you this information, because you should have it. *We* should have it. It bears considerably on the subcommittee's actions."

"I stand corrected. Go ahead, if you please."

"Ada County has a lot of corporate traffic. The flight plans generally list only the pilot, the company, and, perhaps, the executive who ordered the aircraft. Rarely passengers. Bonner thought it might be a dead end. Trevayne knows a lot of people in companies that fly their own planes; his staff personnel could be unlisted passengers. . . . Then he found it. Two Lear jets chartered in the name of Douglas Pace."

Walter Madison abruptly uncrossed his legs and sat forward.

"Who the hell is Douglas Pace?" asked Norton.

Walter Madison answered. "He's Trevayne's brother-in-law."

Robert Webster whistled softly by the piano. General Cooper turned to Knapp. "Trevayne not only avoided all the commercial airlines, he also used an out-of-the-way field and flight plans under another name."

Knapp wasn't convinced that Trevayne's caution required Cooper's elaborate explanation, but Knapp decided to let him enjoy the moment. "Commendable job. . . . Where had they flown in from?"

Cooper looked down at the papers. "According to Flight Service Stations, the first Lear was traced back to San Francisco, where Air Traffic Control confirmed its destination as San Bernardino. No amended flight plan filed with ATC."

"What?" Senator Norton was constantly annoyed by the Army's use of short, staccato-sounding agencies and departments he'd never heard of or knew little about.

Webster, still by the piano, was once again understanding; this time on Norton's behalf. "Flight plans can be amended within several minutes after a plane leaves the field, Senator. The information is filed with Traffic Control, not FSS. Flight Service rarely gets the information for hours, if at all. It's one way to confuse tracers."

Norton looked over his shoulder at Webster with suspicious respect. He didn't know what Webster was talking about. Cooper continued.

"While the aircraft was in San Bernardino, Trevayne remained in San Francisco. Alan Martin did not."

"He's the comptroller from Pace-Trevayne in New Haven, isn't he?" asked Knapp.

"Yes," replied Cooper. "And San Bernardino's twenty minutes from Pasadena. Genessee plants; there've been a lot of problems down there."

Knapp looked at Norton. "Go on, General."

"The Lear left Thursday morning, destination Boise, Idaho. It remained at the Ada County field for only an hour and then took off for Tacoma, Washington. Bonner confirms that at that point Alan Martin returned, and the young lawyer, Sam Vicarson, was removed from the scene."

"Tacoma!" shouted Norton angrily. "What the hell is in Tacoma?"

Robert Webster drank his drink; he was getting drunk. He looked down at the disheveled New Englander. "Tacoma is in the state of Washington, Senator Norton. An hour's drive up the Puget is a city called Seattle. Just outside that city is a complex of buildings with ten-foot-high fences all around. By coincidence it has something to do with Genessee Industries. Its name is Bellstar."

"Oh, Jesus!" Norton did not look at the White House aide this time. He was staring at Knapp, who addressed General Cooper.

"What about the second Lear? Do you have anything on it?"

"Everything," answered Cooper. "Tracing the FP's back from Boise, the plane was flown from Houston International. Its point of origin was Dulles Airport. Our informants at the Potomac Towers tell us that an aeronautical engineer named Michael Ryan was absent from the offices. Bonner confirms that Ryan showed up in Boise."

Alan Knapp spoke quietly. "Then Ryan was in Houston. We can presume he was at the Genessee laboratories. They have check-in ledgers. Let's find out who he went to see." He rose from his chair and started for an antique desk with a French telephone on its sculptured top. "I know who to call."

"Don't bother, Senator. We called. Ryan never went to the labs."

Knapp stopped and turned to Cooper. "Are you sure? I mean, how can you be sure?"

"We also know who to call. *I* know who to call." Both men stared at each other. It was checkmate, and then some. The permanent career officer had made it clear to this elected—impermanent—official that there were doors the military could unlock effortlessly that the politicians might not be able to find. Knapp understood.

There were such doors.

"All right, General. Ryan wasn't at the labs. Where was he? Why did he go to Houston?"

"Since I learned within the hour that he wasn't on Genessee property, I haven't had time to find out."

"Can you?"

"Again, time."

"We don't *have* time!" interjected Norton from the couch. "Goddamn it! This is rough weather!"

"Oh, for God's sake, stow that crap!" yelled Knapp. Senator Alan Knapp had been a decorated naval officer, and Norton's excessive use of sea language maddened him.

"Now, just a minute!"

"All right, all right!" Knapp retreated. "Sorry, Jim. . . . What are you figuring on, General?"

"I thought we'd discuss that. . . . Along with a prior consideration."

Robert Webster moved from the piano and spoke. "Trevayne sends a top financial analyst to Pasadena. To see who? Why? . . . An aeronautical engineer—one of the best, by the way—to Houston. Ryan may not have been *in* the labs, but he sure as hell was in Houston to see someone connected with them. . . . And a lawyer to Bellstar; that's dangerous. I don't like it." Webster sipped his replenished drink and stared straight ahead, at nothing. "Trevayne's cutting near a jugular."

"I *think*"—Walter Madison stretched his arms through his fashionable sleeves and leaned back on the couch— "that you all should be reminded that Andrew could not, *can* not, come up with anything more than minor corruption. It's just as well that he finds it, if he does. It will satisfy his puritan streak."

"That's a pretty goddamn blanket statement, Madison." Knapp returned to his chair. He remembered how bewildered the lawyer had been at the hearing, months ago. He was astonished now at his calm.

"It's simply true. Legally, every overrun at Genessee has been substantially vindicated. And that's what he's looking into; that's what he's going after. I've spent weeks examining every congressional question. I've put my best staff on every problem. A little stealing, yes; and Andrew will nail it. Beyond that, nothing."

"You're supposed to be a good man," said Norton. "I hope you're as good as the supposers say you are."

"I can assure you I am, Senator. My fees might help to convince you."

"I still want to know what Trevayne's been after. You'll find out, General?" asked Senator Knapp.

"Within forty-eight hours."

25

Friday morning in Washington, and no one knew he was there. The Lear jet landed at Dulles at seven-thirty, and at ten minutes past eight Trevayne walked into the rented house in Tawning Spring. He showered, changed clothes, and allowed himself an hour to sit and collect his thoughts, let the pressures of the fast trip from Boise wear off. He was good at pacing himself, he believed. He worked well under tension, because he tried never to permit tension and exhaustion to be simultaneous—mental exhaustion. And he was aware that now, during these next few days, he had to be very careful. It would be so easy for his mind, his imagination, to work itself into such a state of anxiety that thinking clearly might be impossible.

He phoned for a Tawning Spring taxi and was driven into Washington to the Senate Office Building.

It was ten-twenty-five; Senator Mitchell Armbruster would be returning to his office within minutes. He had been on the floor for a quorum demanded by his party, but there was no other business of consequence. Armbruster was expected back by ten-thirty at the latest. For a routine Friday-morning meeting with his staff.

Andy stood in the corridor outside Armbruster's door and waited. He leaned against the wall and halfheartedly leafed through the Washington *Post*. The editorial once again was a scathing appraisal of Congress' progress; the House criticized for its indecisiveness, the Senate for its obfuscation of pertinent business.

Late November in Washington; perfectly normal.

Trevayne was aware of the fact that Armbruster had seen him first. The small, compact Senator had literally stopped walking; he stood motionless, as if momentarily frozen in astonishment. Indeed, it was this sudden break in the moving human traffic that caused Trevayne to look up from the newspaper.

Armbruster resumed his casual, relaxed posture as he approached Trevayne. He smiled his warm, laconic smile and held out his hand. The moment of silent revelation had passed, but it was absolute, and both men recognized it.

"Well, Mr. Trevayne, this is a delightful surprise. I thought you were out in my state, enjoying the scenic wonders of our Pacific."

"I was, Senator. Then Idaho. But I found it necessary to make a brief, unscheduled return. . . . To see you."

Armbruster, the handshake completed, looked questioningly at Trevayne as his smile diminished. "That's certainly direct. . . . I'm afraid I have a full calendar to-day. Perhaps tomorrow morning; or if you like, we could have drinks around five-thirty. Dinner's taken."

"May I suggest that it is most urgent, Senator. I'm seeking the help and advice of your office. Shall we say, on labor statistics in northern California?"

There was a short halt to Mitchell Armbruster's breathing. He was silent for a few moments, his eyes wandering from Trevayne's face. "I'd rather not speak with you here, in my office. . . . I'll meet you in an hour."

"Where?"

"Rock Creek Park. Near the outdoor pavilion. Do you know it?"

"Yes, I do. In an hour. . . . And, Senator, one more suggestion. Hear what I have to say before you get in touch with anyone. You don't *know* what I'm going to say, sir. It would be best."

"I said you were direct, Mr. Trevayne. . . . I'll keep my own counsel; because I also think you're an honorable man. But then, I said that before, too. During the hearing."

"Yes, you did. In an hour, sir."

The two men walked along the wooded path in Rock Creek Park, the shorter one intermittently lighting his pipe with fresh matches. Trevayne realized that Armbruster's pipe acted as some kind of psychological crutch, an anchor, for the Senator. He remembered during the hearing how Armbruster had toyed with it—fondled it, really— packing and repacking the bowl, scraping the burned-out contents into an ashtray with methodical precision. Now, here in Rock Creek Park, walking casually along a path, he clutched it, held it between his teeth with such force that the muscles of his jaw stood out.

"So you've concluded that I've taken advantage of my office for personal gain," said Armbruster calmly, his eyes staring straight ahead.

"I do, sir. I don't know any other way to put it. You determined the maximum funding Genessee Industries could handle; made sure it was sufficient for the unemployment recovery—at least, you had the economists back you up; and then guaranteed the amounts. You *had* to get both labor and management support. It won you the election."

"And that was bad?"

"It was a political manipulation engineered at considerable expense. The country will be paying for it for a long time to come. . . . Yes, I'd say it was bad."

"Oh, you rich Brahmins are too holy for words! What about the thousands of families I represent? In some areas unemployment had reached the levels of twelve, thirteen percent! It was a constituency priority, and I'm damned proud I was able to help. Do I have to remind you that I'm the senior Senator from the state of California, young man? . . . If you want to know the truth, Trevayne . . ." Armbruster paused and looked up at Andy, chuckling his pleasant, throaty laugh. "You sound faintly ridiculous."

Trevayne returned the good-humored laugh and saw that Armbruster's eyes weren't laughing at all. If anything, they were more probing than they had been in the corridor of the Senate Office Building.

"In other words, I'm ridiculous because I don't recognize that what you did was not only good politics—I mean 'good' in all senses of the word—but also sound economics? And in line with defense objectives."

"You're damned right. You're *goddamned* right, young man."

"It was a question of priorities? A constituency . . . emergency?"

"You're almost poetic. 'Course, you don't scan."

"It's done every day, that's what you're saying."

"It's done several *hundred* times a day, and you know it as well as I do. In the House, the Senate, every agency in Washington. What in heaven's name do you think we're in this town for?"

"Even with such extraordinary sums of money?"

"That description is relative."

"Contracts worth hundreds of millions are relative?"

"What in hell are you driving at? You sound like a ten-year-old."

"Only one question, Senator. How often are these politically sound, economically feasible arrangements made with Genessee Industries? All over the country."

Mitchell Armbruster stopped. They were on a small wooden bridge spanning one of Rock Creek Park's many streams. Armbruster stood by the gray-oak railing and looked down at the rushing water. He took his pipe from his mouth and tapped it against the wood.

"That's why you flew in on your . . . unscheduled detour." He made the statement without any emotion whatsoever.

"Yes."

"I knew it was. . . . Why me, Trevayne?"

"Because I was able to make the practical, provable connection. I think coincidence. Frankly, I wish it were somebody else; but I don't have the time."

"Is time that important?"

"If what I believe has happened, it is."

"I'm minor. I fight for political survival so I can present a point of view that's progressively disappearing. It's important that I do that."

"Tell me."

Armbruster slowly removed a tobacco pouch from his jacket pocket and began refilling his pipe. He looked up at Trevayne several times, as if searching, wondering. Finally he lit the pipe and leaned his short elbows against the railing.

"What's there to tell? You join an organization, you understand the bylaws, the fundamental rules. As you go on, you find that in order to achieve certain objectives, those bylaws have to be, must be, circumvented. Otherwise you can't get the job done. If you're dedicated, I mean *passionately committed*, to your objectives, you become a very frustrated human being. You begin to doubt your own capabilities, your political virility. You think you're a eunuch. . . . Then, after a while—at first very subtly—you're told that there *are* ways, if you stop shouting off your big, fat *liberal* mouth. Stop trying to turn everything upside down with rhetoric. Be a little more accommodating. . . . It's easy to assimilate; they call it the process of maturing. *You* call it at-last-achieving-something. You see the good you're doing; you give just a little, but you get so much more in return. . . . Goddamn it, it's worth it! Bills are given your name, amendments are named after you. You see the good . . . only the good. . . ."

Armbruster seemed to weary, to tire of his own logic, obviously circulated and recirculated throughout his ever-active brain. Trevayne knew he had to jar the man, make him respond.

"What about Genessee Industries?"

"It's the goddamned key!" Armbruster whipped his head around and stared at Andy. "It's the funnel. . . . It's *accepted;* what more can I tell you? It's the watering hole we constantly replenish, it never runs dry. . . . It's got Mother, God, Country, Liberal, Conservative, Republican, Democrat, Bullmoose, and so help me Christ, the Communes, all wrapped into *one!* It's the answer to every political animal's hunger. . . . And the strangest thing of all is that it does a good job. That's what's remarkable."

"I don't think you settle for that, Senator."

"Of course I don't, young man! . . . I've got two more years to go; I won't run again. I'll be sixty-nine years old, that's enough. . . . Then, perhaps, I'll sit back and wonder."

"With a Genessee directorship?"

"Probably. Why not?"

Trevayne leaned his back against the railing and took

out his cigarettes. Armbruster lit one for him. "Thank you. . . . Let me try to put this into perspective, Senator."

"Do more than that, Trevayne. Drop it from your schedule. Go after the profiteers; what you and your subcommittee *should* be doing. Genessee doesn't qualify. It may be too big, but it produces. It's borne scrutiny well."

It was Trevayne's turn to laugh, and he did. Out loud and derisively. "It's borne scrutiny because it's too damned big, too complicated to *scrutinize!* And you know it as well as *I* know what's happening in . . . what did you say? —'every agency in Washington.' That flag won't get up the pole, Senator. Genessee Industries, the 'watering hole,' is the fifty-first state. The difference being that the other fifty are beholden to it. Obligated, I think, in a very dangerous way."

"That's overstating the case."

"It's understating it. Genessee has no constitution, no two-party system, no checks and balances. . . . What I want to know from you, Senator, is who are the princes? Who rules this self-contained, self-sufficient, ever-expanding kingdom? And I don't refer to the corporate structure."

"I don't know that anybody . . . rules. Other than its management."

"Which management? I've met them; even the money man, Goddard. I don't believe it."

"Its board of directors."

"That's too easy. They're place cards at a dinner table."

"Then I can't answer you. Not 'won't,' 'can't.' "

"Are you implying that it just grew—a Topsy?"

"That may be more accurate than you realize."

"Who speaks for Genessee to the Senate?"

"Oh, Lord, scores of people. There are a dozen committees in which Genessee figures. It's the predominant factor in the aircraft lobby."

"Aaron Green?"

"I've met Green, of course. Can't say I know him."

"Isn't he the real account man?"

"He owns an advertising agency, if that's what you mean. Along with ten or twenty other companies."

"It wasn't a pun, Senator. The accounts I refer to go beyond advertising, although they may be considered part of it."

"I don't follow you."

"We've established that Aaron Green administers between seven and twelve million a year—conceivably more
—for the purposes of convincing the Washington bureaucracy of the patriotic validity of Genessee Industries and—"

"All registered—"

"Most buried. Anyone with that kind of fiscal responsibility generally has the authority that goes with it."

"You're speculating."

"I certainly am. Over unbelievable amounts of petty
cash. Year after year. . . . Does Green hold the reins?"

"Goddamn, son, you're looking for villains! 'Account
men,' 'rulers,' 'kingdoms,' 'holding reins'. . . . 'Fifty-first
state!'" Armbruster tapped his pipe violently against the
railing, clearing out the bowl. Several specks of burning
tobacco fell on the back of the Senator's hand, which
shook in anger, but Armbruster did not seem to feel the
pain. "Listen to me. For all my political life I've clashed
with the big boys! I haven't shrunk. Read over some of
those speeches I've made at conventions! I've *set* policy! If
you recall, a whole goddamn contingent of right-wingers
walked out on me—walked out—in the fifty convention! I
didn't waver; I was right!"

"I remember. You were quite a hero."

"I was right! That's the important thing. . . . But I
was also wrong. You didn't expect me to say that, did you?
I'll tell you where I was wrong. I didn't try to understand;
I didn't try hard enough to get to the roots of their
thinking, their fears. I didn't try to use the powers of
reason. I just condemned. I found my villains, raised my
sword of wrath, and smote the hordes of Lucifer. . . .
Some awfully good men went out of the hall that day.
They never came back."

"Are you drawing a parallel?"

"Of course I am, young man. You think you've found
your villain, your emissary from Lucifer. Your villain is a
concept—bigness. And you're prepared to impale anyone
who accepts any aspect of it with *your* sword of wrath.
. . . And that could be a tragic error."

"Why?"

"Because Genessee Industries has been responsible

for a great deal of social good. Very progressive accomplishments. Did you know, for example, that there are drug clinics, day-care centers, mobile medical units in the hearts of some of California's worst ghetto areas, thanks to Genessee? A retraining center for ex-convicts in Cape Mendocino that's considered a model rehabilitation operation? Genessee financing, Mr. Trevayne. There's even the Armbruster Research Cancer Clinic in San Jose. Yes, my name, Trevayne; I convinced Genessee to donate the land and much of the equipment. . . . Lower your sword, young man."

Trevayne turned away, just enough to avoid having to look at Mitchell Armbruster. To avoid watching a man who'd traded the voting strength of millions for tax-deductible marbles.

"Then there's no harm in bringing it all out in the open. Let the country know how it's twice blessed. It gets Genessee's superior products as well as its charity."

"You do that, and they'll phase out the programs."

"Why? For being publicly thanked?"

"You know as well as I do that whenever the business community takes on these projects it reserves the right to release only the information it wishes. They'd be swamped."

"They'd be suspect."

"Whatever. The losers are in the ghettos, the barrios. Do you want to be responsible?"

"For God's *sake*, Senator, I want *someone* to be responsible!"

"Not everyone's as fortunate as you, Trevayne. We can't all sit in our lofty perches and look down with such impunity—and, I suspect, no little disdain—at the struggle beneath us. Most of us join in that struggle and do the best we can. For others as well as ourselves."

"Senator, I'm not going to argue utilitarian philosophy with you. You're a debater, I'm not. Maybe we have no quarrel. I don't know. You said your term expires in two years; I've got about two months. Our report will be finished by then. For what it's worth, I think you've accommodated in good faith; you've contributed a great deal of good to a great many people. You may be on the side of the angels, while I'm the one making pacts with Lucifer. Maybe."

"We all of us do what we can. The best way we can."

"Again, maybe. Don't interfere with my two months, and I'll do my damnedest not to create any problems for your two years. A simple accommodation, Senator."

Trevayne's Lear jet climbed rapidly to its cruising altitude of thirty-eight thousand feet. He'd be landing at Westchester airport in a little over an hour. He had decided to surprise Phyllis at the Darien Hospital. He needed the rest, needed the comfort of her gentle humor, her essential reasonableness. And, too, he wanted to allay her fears; she'd been afraid but was too unselfish to burden him.

Then tomorrow morning or afternoon or evening there was Aaron Green.

Four down, two to go.

Aaron Green, New York.

Ian Hamilton, Chicago.

26

Major Paul Bonner found himself actually issuing orders to Brigadier General Lester Cooper. Orders to use only the best CID undercover men and have them span out through Pasadena, Houston, and Seattle. To reach Genessee or Bellstar personnel substantively related to any of the issues raised at the San Francisco conference. In Houston, since it was already established that Ryan hadn't gone to the labs, the agents should check with NASA high-level personnel. There had to be any number who knew Ryan; perhaps leads could be unearthed.

Bonner even suggested covers for the agents to use. The men should state that the subcommittee had received threatening communications—letters, telephone calls, et cetera.

It was the sort of cover that led easily into expansive conversations. Civilians were always eager to help the military when it was *protecting* someone. The mere confidence broke down reticence, especially when the inquiries had nothing to do with *them*.

Something was bound to turn up.

And if and when it did, Bonner asked the General to please alert him before taking action, before confronting anyone. He knew Andrew Trevayne better than Cooper did, better than anybody at Defense. He might have suggestions.

The Brigadier was delighted to share his responsibility with the Young Turk.

The last request Bonner made of his superior officer was to have a fighter jet sent down from the Air Force base at Billings, Montana.

If it became necessary, he was going to follow Andrew Trevayne.

It *would* become necessary if he could learn who Trevayne had gone to see. That he'd left for Washington, Bonner knew; the Lear flight plan had been filed with Ada County Traffic Control.

But who in Washington?

There was a chance of finding out, but it would have to wait until morning. He was having breakfast with Alan and Sam; he wondered if Mike Ryan would be there. After breakfast Martin and Vicarson had a final short meeting in Boise; they were all meeting at the airport for a noon plane to Denver.

During that hour or two, Major Paul Bonner would do some reconnoitering.

Paul watched Alan Martin and Sam Vicarson leave the hotel dining room, off to their final Boise conference.

He waited until they'd gone through the dining-room door, then rapidly left the table and followed them into the lobby. Martin stopped at the newsstand, while Vicarson went to the information desk. Bonner kept his back to them, pretending to look over the "Nightly Entertainment" case. Thirty seconds later Vicarson joined Martin at the newsstand, and the two men walked toward the front entrance. Bonner went to the lobby window and watched them get into a cab.

He'd try Vicarson's room first. Sam seemed closer to Trevayne—or at least the one Andy delegated more authority to. If the front desk balked, he'd give a simple explanation that Sam forgot important papers. The clerk was the one on duty when they'd checked in together. If the clerk proved difficult, Bonner would produce several plastic identifications that would scare the hell out of him.

But when Bonner asked for the key, the laconic clerk handed it to him without question.

Inside Vicarson's room he started with the bureau drawers. There was nothing in them, and Bonner smiled; Sam *was* young. He lived out of a suitcase and a closet.

The suitcase was filled with unlaundered shirts, socks, and underwear. Vicarson was not only young but sloppy, thought Bonner.

He closed the suitcase, lifted it off the bed, and since the desk was nearest, he sat down at it and opened the single top drawer. Stationery had been used, not the envelopes. He picked up the wastebasket and removed two pages of crumpled paper.

One had figures with dollar signs, and Bonner recognized the information as pertinent to a Lockheed subcontractor he'd heard them all talking about.

The other had numbers also, but not dollars. Times. And several notations: "7:30-8:00 Dls.; 10:00-11:30 S.A. Qu.; Data—Grn. N.Y."

Bonner looked at the paper. The "7:30-8:00" was Trevayne's arrival time; he'd learned that from Ada Traffic Control. The "10:00-11:30 S.A. Qu." was indecipherable. So, too, was the last line "Data—Grn. N.Y." He took out his ball-point pen and copied the words onto a fresh page, folded it, and put it in his pocket.

He recrumpled the stationery, threw it in the wastebasket, and put the receptacle back on the floor.

In Vicarson's closet he separated the trousers from the jackets and began going through the pockets. He found it in the breast pocket of the second jacket. It was a precisely folded, precisely lettered note from a small appointments book, and it was between several baggage claim-checks. It was the sort of reminder a bright but often careless man might jot down because the information seemed so vital. It read: "Armbruster. $178 Mill. Duplications. No Defense request. Six-month time lapse. Guarantees confirmed by J.G.'s top acct., L.R. Paid L.R. $300.

L.R. offers add'l. data on Pasadena, Bellstar, etc. Price—
4 figures."

Bonner stared at the note, his anger rising. Had Sam
Vicarson met "L.R." in a crowded, dimly lit San Francisco
cellar with a heavy odor of "hash" and a bartender only too
willing to exchange large bills for smaller ones? Had Sam
been told he could make whatever notes he wished as long
as he didn't ask "L.R." to write anything? Had "L.R." fed
Vicarson that garbage about a blown-out stomach and a
justifiable eagerness to steal from whoever was an ac-
cessible mark? Sam was not only young and sloppy, he
was also naïve and an amateur. He paid for conjectures,
for lies, and then forgot to destroy his notes. Bonner had
burned his own notebook. It was so easy to forget—if one
was an inept beaver.

The Major instantly made up his mind to carry out his
threat; he'd find "L.R." and blow out the rest of his
stomach.

Later.

Now he had to reach Trevayne. Andrew had to understand that the sewer rats, the double-a's, dealt in lies. Lies
and half-lies were their merchandise. Find opponents and
feed them—scraps, fragments, appetizers. Always with
the promise of vital, explosive information to follow.

Better, *create* opponents.

Trevayne wasn't standing by a possibly diseased wife—
such a cheap, undistinguished artifice; he was in Washington seeing the Senator from California. Armbruster was a
good man, a friend to Genessee, a powerful friend. But he
was a senator. Senators were easily frightened. They pretended not to be, but they always were.

Bonner put Vicarson's note in his pocket and left the
room. Down in the lobby he returned the key to the front
desk and went to a pay phone; he couldn't use the telephone in his room—hotels recorded numbers. He called
the airport and asked for Operations.

The stand-by fighter jet from Air Force, Billings,
Montana, was to be prepared immediately. Flight plan,
straight through to Andrews Field, Virginia. Priority clearance, Defense Department.

As he started for the elevator to go to his room, pack,

and check out, Paul Bonner had two reasons to reach
Trevayne. One professional, the other personal.

Trevayne had involved himself and his goddamned
subcommittee in a witch hunt that had to stop now. They
were playing games they didn't understand. They didn't
know the jungles. Beavers never did.

The other reason was the very personal lie.

That was sickening.

27

Phyllis Trevayne sat in the chair and listened to her husband as he paced the private hospital room. "It sounds
like an extraordinary monopoly, complete with state and
federal protection."

"Not just protection, Phyl. Participation. The active
participation of the legislative and the judicial. That makes
it more than a monopoly. It's some kind of giant cartel
without definition."

"I don't understand. That's semantics."

"Not when the election of a senior senator from the
country's most populous state is one result. Or when a
decision rendered by an eminent jurist is a Justice Department compromise. That decision—even if eventually ap-
pealed and overturned—will cost millions . . . billions,
before it gets through the courts."

"What will you learn from these last two? This Green
and Ian Hamilton?"

"Probably more of the same. At different levels. Armbruster used the term 'funnel,' referring to the Genessee
appropriations. I think it also applies to Aaron Green.
Green's the funnel in which enormous sums of house
money are poured, and he allocates it. Year after year. . . .
Hamilton's the one that scares me. He's been a presidential adviser for years."

Phyllis heard the fear in her husband's voice. He had
walked to the window by the bed and leaned against the

sill. his face next to the glass. Outside, the late-afternoon sky was overcast; there would be snow flurries by nightfall.

"It seems to me you should be careful before you make assumptions."

Andy looked over at his wife and smiled with affection, with relief. "If you knew how many times I've reminded myself of that; it's the toughest part."

"I should think it would be."

The telephone rang on the night table. Phyllis went to it. Andy remained by the window. The patrol from 1600 knew he was there, and the doctor. No one else.

"Certainly, Johnny," said Phyllis as she handed the telephone to her husband. "It's John Sprague."

Trevayne pushed himself away from the window. John Sprague, M.D., F.A.C.S., was an across-the-street boyhood friend from Boston. He was now as close a friend as he had been then. And their family physician.

"Yes, Johnny?"

"I don't know how far you want to go with this Hasty Pudding stuff, but the switchboard says there's a call for you. If you're not here, the call's supposed to be given to Phyl's doctor. I can handle it, Andy."

"Who is it?"

"Man named Vicarson."

"God, isn't he *something?*"

"He may be. He's also got the price of a toll call."

"I know. Denver. Can you have it switched here, or shall I go down to the board?"

"Please! With the contributions you make, my partners would fire me. Hang up. It'll ring in a couple of seconds."

"It's nice to know big shots."

"It's better to know money. Hang up, Croesus."

Trevayne pressed down on the telephone button while holding the instrument in his hand. He turned to Phyllis. "It's Sam Vicarson. I didn't tell him I was coming here. I was to call him later, after his meetings. He's in Denver now. I didn't think he'd be finished by now." Andy spoke disjointedly, and his wife realized that he was troubled.

The telephone rang; the sound was short, merely a signal.

"Sam?"

"Mr. Trevayne, I took a chance you might have driven over there; the airport said the Lear was going to West-chester."

"Is anything the matter? How did the meetings go with the GM and Lockheed subs?"

"Short and to the point. They've got to come up with better cost sheets, or we threatened penalties. That's not why I'm calling. It's Bonner."

"What happened?"

"He's gone."

"What?"

"Just blew. Never showed up for the meetings, checked out of the hotel in Boise this morning, and never met us at the airport. No word, no messages, nothing. We thought you ought to know."

Andy held the telephone firmly in his hand. He tried to think quickly; he realized that Vicarson expected instructions. "When did you last see him?"

"This morning at breakfast. In Boise."

"How did he seem?"

"Fine. A little quiet, but okay. I think he was tired, or hung. He was going to join us at the airport. He never showed."

"Did I come up in the conversation?"

"Sure; normal. Our concern for your wife, how well you were taking it; that sort of thing."

"That's all?"

"He did ask what flight you took out last night; fig-ured you had to make rotten connections. Said he might have been able to get you a Defense jet, so it—"

"How did you answer that, Sam?" interrupted Trevayne sharply.

"No problem. We told him we didn't know. We kind of laughed and said with your connections and . . . your money, you probably bought an airline. He took it fine."

Andy switched the telephone to his other hand and gestured Phyllis to light him a cigarette. He spoke quietly but with assurance to Vicarson.

"Listen to me, Sam. This is what I want you to do. Send a telegram, a very routine telegram, to Bonner's superior. . . . No. Wait a minute; we're not sure who that is. Just to the senior personnel officer, Department of Defense. Say you assume Bonner was given a leave for some reason or other. Ask, in the event we *do* need any assistance, who we should reach in Washington. But make the whole thing sound like an afterthought, do you know what I mean?"

"Sure. We just happened to notice he was missing. Probably wouldn't have, except that he was to have dinner with us or something."

"Exactly. They'll expect some reaction from us."

"If they know he's not here."

Mario de Spadante sat at the kitchen table in shirt-sleeves. His obese wife was in the process of removing dishes; his daughter, equally obese, dutifully placed a bottle of Strega in front of her father. Mario's younger brother, in a J. Press suit and a wide regimental tie, sat opposite De Spadante, drinking coffee.

Mario waved his wife and daughter out of the room. Alone with his brother, he poured the yellow liquid into a brandy glass and looked up.

"Go on. Be clear, be accurate."

"There's not much more to tell you. The questions seemed phony: Where was Mr. de Spadante? . . . We can only speak with Mr. de Spadante. . . . It seemed like someone just wanted to know where you were. Then, when I heard they came from Torrington Metals—that's Gino's brother's place—we leaned. This guy Pace, Trevayne's partner, was the one who wanted the information."

"And you told him I was in Miami."

"Even gave him the hotel, the one that always says you just checked out."

"Good. Now Trevayne's back east?"

"That's the word. They took his wife to a hospital in Darien. Cancer tests."

"Better they should run a few on him. Trevayne's a sick man; he doesn't know how sick he is."

"What do you want me to do, Mario?"

"Find out exactly where he is. In Darien. Or whether he's in Greenwich and drives back and forth. Or in a motel or some friend's house—Darien's crawling with his type. . . . When you find him, let me know. Don't bother me before you do. I stopped off in Vegas; I'm drained, Augie, all the way down."

Augie de Spadante rose from the table. "I'll go there myself. I'll call you. . . . Suppose I find him this afternoon? Tonight?"

"Then you call; isn't that what I said?"

"But you're beat."

"I'll revive quickly. . . . There's been too goddamn much cockkissing; too much *alternative* bullshit. It's time for Trevayne to get shook. I'm looking forward to that. It'll help make up for nine years ago. . . . Arrogant prick! Velvet pig!"

Mario de Spadante spat on his own kitchen table.

28

The hospital dinner was not an ordinary hospital dinner, even by Darien standards. John Sprague had sent an ambulance—albeit no siren—to the best restaurant in the area; it had returned with trays of steak and lobster and two bottles of Châteauneuf du Pape. Dr. Sprague also reminded his boyhood friend that the New Year's fund drive would be coming up soon. He looked forward to Andrew's communication.

Phyllis tried to get her husband to talk of other things than his all-consuming subcommittee, but it was impossible. The news of Paul Bonner's disappearance both confused and angered him.

"Couldn't he simply have decided to take a couple of days off? You said he doesn't do much; perhaps he just got fed up, bored. I can easily imagine Paul feeling that way."

"Not after my heartbreaking story the other morning. He was ready to commandeer the entire Army Medical Corps, do whatever I wanted him to do. Those two conferences—to recall his words—were the least he could do."

"Darling." Phyllis put the wineglass on the table-cart

and curled her feet under her in the chair. She was
suddenly concerned by Andrew's words. "I like Paul. Oh,
I know his opinions are extreme, and you two argue a lot,
but I know why I like him. . . . I've never heard him
angry. He always seems so kind, so willing to laugh and
have a good time. He's been very nice to us, when you
think about it."

"What's your point? I agree with you."

"Yet there must be a great deal of anger in him. To
do what he's done, be what he is."

"I'll vouch for it. What else?"

"You didn't tell me before that you had given him
such a . . . heartbreaking story. You said you'd just told
him I was going in for tests."

"I didn't elaborate, because I'm not very proud of
myself."

"I'm not either. . . . Which brings me back to Paul. If
you say he accepted your story about me and now he's
disappeared without a word to anyone, I think he's learned
the truth and is trying to find you."

"That's one hell of a leap!"

"Not really. I think Paul trusts you—trusted you. He
disagreed with you, but he trusted you. If there's as much
anger in him as we both believe, he won't settle for
second-hand explanations. Or postponed ones, either."

Trevayne understood his wife's logic. It went to the
essence of a man like Paul Bonner. A man who looked at
people, giving them classifications—labels—only when he
believed those descriptions fit and were not simply popular. Such a man confronted those who mocked his judgment; he wouldn't wait for third parties to do it for him.
Yet Phyllis' assumption was based on Paul's learning the
truth—the truth about her. That was impossible. Only
three people knew. Sam Vicarson, Alan Martin, and Mike
Ryan. Impossible.

"It couldn't be," said Andy. "There's absolutely no
way he could know."

"You're an awful liar, Trevayne." Phyllis smiled.

"I'm getting better. He believed me."

They settled back in their chairs, and Andy turned on
the television set for the seven-o'clock news.

"Maybe we'll find out he left Boise and started a little war somewhere. He'd call it a diversionary tactic," said Trevayne.

"How are you going to get to Green tomorrow? How do you even know he's in the city?"

"I don't. Not yet. . . . But I'll reach him. I'll drive over to Barnegat in an hour or so; Vicarson expects my call at ten. He'll have everything he can get on Green, and between us we'll figure something out. . . . You know, Phyl, I've discovered a very interesting fact of life during the past week."

"I can't wait."

"No, it's true." Andy lifted the glass of wine to his lips. His look was bemused. "All this nonsense about so-called undercover work—intelligence gathering, whatever name you want to give it. It's really very simple; I mean, it's childish. It's like a game." He drank the wine and put the glass back on the table-cart. He looked over at his wife—his so goddamned lovely, understanding wife—and added sadly, "If only the people playing it were children."

Mario de Spadante was in bed watching the seven-o'clock news. He'd called his wife into his bedroom twice. The first time to bring him an ice-cold Coca-Cola, the second to wheel the portable color set several feet to the left so the reflection of the gold crucifix above his pillow wouldn't interfere with the picture.

Then he told her he was going to sleep soon. She shrugged; she and Mario had had separate bedrooms for years. Separate worlds, really. They barely spoke except at weddings and funerals and when their infant grand-children were over. But she had a big, beautiful house now. And a big garden and a big kitchen; even a big car and someone to drive her.

She would go back down to the big kitchen and cook something and watch her own television. Maybe call a friend on the fancy French telephone on the marble counter.

There was nothing of consequence within the first three minutes of the news program, and Mario knew the rest would be twenty-five minutes of "fill" interspersed with commercials. He reached for the remote control and turned the set off. He was tired, but not for the reasons he gave his brother. He had stopped off in Las Vegas, but his whoring had been confined to one quick ball, and even then he had to tell the girl to leave immediately; there were too many phone calls coming in. He hadn't gone near the tables, because one of the phone calls had been from the White House contact, Webster. He had to leave Vegas Wednesday, midnight flight.

For Washington.

Even the cool Webster was beginning to lose his grip. Mario realized that everybody was sitting around making plans. Contingency this, contingency that.

Crap!

There was a time for talk and a time to carve flesh. He was finished bugging the electrical system at Barnegat.

Trevayne was for cutting. Now.

A quiet report from another wound-down subcommittee, quietly, respectfully received by those requesting it—buried and forgotten.

That's the way it was going to be.

The telephone rang, and De Spadante was annoyed. Then his annoyance left him; he saw that the lighted button was his private line, not the house phone. Everyone understood that his private line was used only for important business.

"Yes?"

"Mario? Augie." It was his brother. "He's here."

"Where?"

"In the hospital."

"You sure?"

"Positive. There's a rented car in the parking lot with a Westchester Airport sticker. We checked. It was taken out at three-thirty this afternoon. In his own name, too."

"Where are you calling from?"

De Spadante's brother told him. "I've got Joey watching the lot."

"Stay where you are. Tell Joey to follow him if he leaves; don't lose him! Give Joey the number there. I'll meet you as soon as I can."

"Listen, Mario. There're two guys at the hospital.

One's outside the front entrance, the other's inside somewhere. He comes out every now and then—"

"I know. I know who they are. They'll be out of there
in a half-hour. Tell Joey to stay out of sight."

De Spadante held his finger down on the telephone
button, then released it. He dialed Robert Webster's private number at the White House. Webster was about to
leave for home and was upset that De Spadante had used
that number.

"I told you, Mario—"

"*I'm* doing the telling now. Unless you want a couple
of unexplained sacks in your files!"

And with unsubtle, barely coded phrases, De Spadante
gave his orders. He didn't care how Bobby Webster did it,
but he wanted the 1600 Patrol removed immediately.

Mario replaced the telephone and got out of bed. He
dressed quickly and after combing his sparse hair opened
the top drawer of his bureau. He removed two items.

One was a .38-caliber magazine-clip pistol. The other,
an ominous-looking object of black metal with four rings
attached to one another above a flat base of ridged iron.

With a clenched fist it would break off a man's jaw
from the neck joints. With an open hand it would rip a
man's flesh to the bone.

The F-40 jet was given a priority clearance from its
holding pattern and landed on runway five at Andrews Air
Force Base. At the end of the strip the aircraft made its
turn and stopped. The Major climbed out, waved to the
pilot, and walked rapidly to a waiting jeep.

Paul Bonner ordered the driver to take him immediately
to Operations. The driver pressed the accelerator without
greeting or comment. The Major looked like a tight-ass;
you didn't try to be friendly with that type.

Bonner walked rapidly into Operations and requested
a private office for ten or fifteen minutes. The Operations
duty officer, a lieutenant colonel who only minutes ago
had called Defense to find out "What kind of frigging
priority this clown Bonner had," offered the Major his
own office. The Lieutenant Colonel had been told what

kind of priority was due Major Bonner. By an aide to Brigadier General Lester Cooper.

Paul thanked the Lieutenant Colonel as the latter closed his office door, leaving Bonner alone. The Major instantly reached for the telephone and dialed Cooper's private number. He looked at his watch. It read two-forty, which meant that it was twenty to six, eastern time. He cupped the telephone under his chin and began to set the correct time on his watch, but before he was able to do so, Cooper answered.

The General was furious; the Pentagon's Young Turk had no right making decisions that transported him three-quarters across the country without prior consultation, without *permission*, really.

"Major, I think we deserve an explanation," said the General tersely, knowing Bonner would expect the reprimand.

"I'm not sure there's time, General—"

"*I'm sure there is!* We've covered your request from Billings to Andrews. Now, I think you'd better explain. . . . Has it occurred to you that even *I* might have to explain?"

"No, it hadn't," lied Bonner. "I don't want to argue, General; I'm trying to help, help all of us. I think I can, if I'm able to reach Trevayne."

"Why? What happened?"

"He's being fed information by a psychopath."

"*What?* Who?"

"One of Goddard's men. The same one who dealt with us."

"Oh, Christ!"

"Which means whatever we've learned could be all fouled-up crap. . . . He's a sick one, General. He's not after money; I should have spotted that when he negotiated so low. If what he gave us was on target, he could have asked three times the amount and we wouldn't have blinked."

"What he gave *you*, Major. Not *us*." What Cooper implied put Paul Bonner on notice. The first of its kind he'd ever received.

"All right, General. What he gave *me*. . . . And whatever he gave me I passed on to you, and you acted on it. I don't move in those circles."

Lester Cooper controlled his anger. The Young Turk was actually threatening him. There'd been too many threats; the General was wearying of them. He wasn't capable of dealing with these constant assaults of subtlety. "There's no cause for insubordination, Major. I'm merely defining lines of intelligence. We're in this together."

"In what, General?"

"You know perfectly well! The erosion of military influence; the accelerated lessening of defense necessities. We're paid to uphold this country's state of preparedness, not watch it disintegrate!"

"I read you, General." And Bonner did. Except he suddenly had grave doubts about his superior's ability to cope with the situation. Cooper was spewing out Pentagon clichés as though they were biblical revelations. He was not thoroughly in control of himself, and the circumstances called for absolute stability. And at this moment of doubt, Bonner made a decision he knew was not his to make. He would withhold the detailed specifics of why he came to Washington from Cooper. At least for the time being, until he spoke to Trevayne.

". . . since you condescend to agree with me, Major, I'll expect you in my office by nineteen hundred. That's an hour and fifteen minutes." Cooper had been talking, but Paul was barely aware of it. In some unconscious way he had dismissed his superior officer.

"General, if that's an order, I'll obey, of course. But I submit, sir, that every minute I spend *not* trying to reach Trevayne could have serious consequences. . . . He'll *listen* to me."

There was a pause on the other end of the line, and Bonner knew he'd win. "What will you tell him?"

"The truth—as I see it. He's been talking to the wrong person. A maladjusted psychopath. Perhaps more than one; it's happened before. And if this source is symptomatic of his other contacts—and it probably is, they all know each other—he should be told that he's getting biased data."

"Where is he now?" Bonner could sense the slight relief in the General's voice.

"All I know is that he's in Washington. I think I can find him."

Paul could hear Cooper inhale over the wire. The brigadier was struggling to make his decision seem wise and strong and well-thought-out, when in reality it was the only decision that could be made. "I'll expect you to phone me with a progress report by twenty-three hundred. I'll be at home."

Bonner was tempted to dispute the order; he had no intention of calling the General at twenty-three hundred. Unless he was doing absolutely nothing.

After lighting one of his infrequent cigarettes, Bonner again picked up the phone and called a friend he knew was on a twelve-to-eight post at Army G-2. A minute later he had the telephone number of Senator Mitchell Armbruster's office and home.

He found him at home.

"Senator, I have to locate Andrew Trevayne."

"Why call me?" The total lack of expression in Armbruster's voice betrayed him. And like the tumblers in a lock falling into place, Bonner suddenly understood the meaning of Sam Vicarson's notation: "10:00-11:30 S.A. Qu."

Senator Armbruster had been in a quorum call on the Senate floor; the call was scheduled between those times, and Trevayne had to know it if he wanted to intercept the man.

"I don't have time for explanations, Senator. I assume you met with Trevayne around noon. . . ." Bonner paused to hear a denial or a confirmation. There was none, which was the same as the latter. "It's imperative I find him. In quick words, he's been given highly misleading information; information that compromises a great many people who are completely above reproach—you among them, sir."

"I have no idea what you're talking about, Major . . . Bonner, was it?"

"Senator! There's a hundred and seventy-eight million dollars that Defense can substantiate as a long-standing priority request. Does that give you some idea?"

"I have nothing to say. . . ."

"You may have if I don't find Trevayne and tell him he's been dealing with enemies of this country! I can't put it any plainer."

Silence.

"Senator Armbruster!"

"He instructed the cab to take him to Dulles Airport." The same expressionless voice.

"Thank you, *sir*."

Bonner slammed down the phone. He leaned back in the Lieutenant Colonel's chair and brought his hand to his forehead. Oh Christ! he thought, the age of instant mobility! He reached for the telephone once again and called Traffic Control, Dulles.

The Lear jet under charter to Douglas Pace had left the airport at two-seventeen in the afternoon. Destination: Westchester, New York. Arrival time: three-twenty-four.

So Trevayne had gone home—or near home. And if that was so, he would see his wife—especially under the strained circumstances. Of course, he'd go to his wife! It was inconceivable that he wouldn't. Andy had that rare thing, a wife he *liked*—beyond the love, thought Bonner. Trevayne would travel miles, take hours, to be in her company, even for short periods of time. Most married men he knew would travel miles and take hours to avoid theirs.

Paul walked to the door, opened it, and looked for the Lieutenant Colonel. He was standing by a complex panel of instruments studying some pages on a clipboard.

"Colonel, I need a pilot. Would you have my plane refueled and checked out as soon as possible?"

"Hey, wait a minute, Major. We don't run Andrews Field for your personal convenience!"

"I need a pilot, Colonel. Mine's been on call for over twenty-four hours."

"That could just be *your* problem."

"Colonel, do you want General Cooper's private telephone number and *you* tell *him* it's my problem? I'll be happy to give it to you."

The Lieutenant Colonel lowered the clipboard and searched the face of the Major. "You're with counter-intelligence, aren't you?"

Bonner waited a few seconds before making his reply. "You know I can't answer that."

"Which gives me my answer."

"Do you want the General's private number?"

"You'll have your pilot. . . . When do you want to be airborne?"

Paul looked up at the numerous dials on the wall. It was just seven o'clock, eastern time.

"An hour ago, Colonel."

29

Bonner had gotten the name of the private hospital from 1600 Security. He then processed a driving route from Andrews Transport, secured a vehicle to be at his disposal once he arrived at Westchester, and thanked the Lieutenant Colonel with as much sincerity as he could muster.

The vehicle turned out to be a motor-pool sedan which an Army corporal from some totally obscure post in Nyack, New York, had driven over to the Westchester airport.

Since the Corporal expected he would be the Major's driver, Bonner gave him twenty dollars to find his way back to his unmapped base in Nyack. The Major also informed the Corporal that there was no point in his returning before noon on the following day, and gave him a note so specifying. The Corporal was delighted.

Bonner drove up to the open iron gates of the hospital and entered the circular drive. The clock on the dashboard read nine-thirty-five. There were no automobiles in the circle; two illuminated signs directed cars to a parking lot on the far side of the building. Bonner was not about to be so directed. Instead, he clung to the right of the driveway—so as to let other cars pass—and parked half on the grass. There were flurries of snow descending; wet, not sticking to the ground for long before melting. He got out of the car and automatically expected the 1600 Patrol to approach. It was, after all, an Army vehicle. He was prepared to deal with them. Explain, if necessary; which, of course, it would be.

No one came into view.

Bonner was confused. He'd read the rigid instructions the 1600 Patrol were to follow. With such buildings as the private hospital, housing a singular vehicular entrance and no more than three stories in height, one man was to remain outside, the other within, both in instant radio contact. The men from 1600 were the best in matters of security. They would not deviate except in an emergency.

To make certain it was not simply a case of observance without contact, Bonner walked slowly around the car and spoke clearly, projecting his voice slightly, not shouting.

"Bonner, Paul. Major, D.O.D. 'Sixteen hundred,' please respond. . . . Repeat. 'Sixteen hundred,' please reply."

Nothing. Only the silent tone of the night, the muted hum of the peaceful building.

Paul Bonner reached under his tunic to his belt. He withdrew his "civilian" pistol—a custom-tooled, short-barreled, heavy .44. It would blow a human being into a jack-knifed, flying corpse.

He raced across the drive to the front entrance of the private hospital. He couldn't know what was happening inside. His uniform might be a deterrent or a provocation—it was certainly a target. He put the pistol in his tunic pocket and kept his hand on the stock, his finger curled in the trigger housing; with his thumb he released the safety and held the weapon in a horizontal position. He was prepared to fire through the cloth.

He turned the large brass knob quietly, and swiftly opened the white colonial door, startling an attractive, intelligent-looking nurse behind an admissions counter. She'd been reading at the desk; there was no panic within. He approached and spoke calmly.

"Miss, my name is Bonner. I understand Mrs. Andrew Trevayne is a patient here."

"Yes . . . Colonel."

" 'Major' is fine."

"I can never get those insignias straight," said the girl pleasantly, getting out of the chair.

"I have trouble myself; the Navy stripes always confuse me." Bonner looked around for the 1600 Patrol.

No one.

"Yes, Mrs. Trevayne's a patient. Is she expecting you? It's somewhat after the usual visiting hours, Major."

"Actually, I'm looking for *Mr.* Trevayne. I was told I'd find him here."

"I'm afraid you missed him. He left about an hour ago."

"Oh? Then I wonder . . . perhaps I might speak with Mrs. Trevayne's driver. I believe arrangements were made for a driver and a secretary; I think . . ."

"It's all right, Major," said the nurse, smiling. "Our registration book is filled with 'captains and kings,' and people who keep them from being bothered by other people. I gather you're referring to the two gentlemen who arrived with Mrs. Trevayne. Nice guys."

"That's who I'm referring to. Where are they?"

"It's not your night, Major. *They* left before Mr. Trevayne."

"Did they say where they were going? It's really quite urgent that I talk to them."

"No. . . . Mr. Callahan, the one in the corridor, got a phone call around seven-thirty. All he said was that he and his friend had the night off. I think he liked the idea."

"Who took the call? I mean, do you know where it came from?" Bonner tried to conceal his anxiety, none too successfully.

"The switchboard." The nurse understood the look in Paul's eyes. "Shall I ask the operator if she can recall?"

"Please."

The girl crossed rapidly to a white, paneled door to the right, behind the counter, and opened it. Bonner could see a small switchboard and a middle-aged woman seated in front of it. He thought how different things were in a private hospital; even a switchboard was kept from public scrutiny. No large glass walls with impersonal robots plugging in wires; no starched, hard mannequins announcing institutional names over the hectic drone of mechanized activity. Everything secreted gracefully, everything personal, so nonpublic; elegant, somehow.

The nurse returned. "The call was long-distance; a

Washingon, D.C., operator. Person-to-person for Mr. Callahan, Mrs. Trevayne's party."

"And then he left?" Paul's anxiety turned to concrete fear. On several levels; for a number of reasons. There had to be an explanation, and he had to know what it was.

"That's right," answered the girl. "Major? Would you like to use the telephone?"

Bonner felt relief at the nurse's perception. "I would very much. Is there—"

"There's a phone in the waiting room. Right through there." She pointed at an open door across the hall. "On the table next to the window. Just tell the operator to bill it to room . . . two-twelve. You'll have privacy."

"You're very kind."

"You're very uptight."

The "waiting room" was a living room, gracefully secreted, warmly appointed, rugs on the floor. So different from the plastic couches and the confusing array of magazine racks usually found in hospitals.

Paul gave the Washington number to the operator, and before the first ring was completed, 1600 Security answered.

"It's Major Bonner again. Is this the same—"

"Right, Major. Four-to-twelve shift. Did you find the place?"

"Yes, I'm calling from there. What happened?"

"What happened where?"

"Here. Darien. Who relieved the men?"

"Relieved? What are you talking about?"

"The men were relieved. They were released at seven-thirty, or around then. Why?"

"No one released anybody, Bonner. What the hell are you talking about?"

"The men aren't *here*."

"Look around, Major. They're there. They may not want you to know it, but—"

"I'm telling you, they *left*. Do you have a man named Callahan?"

"Hold it. I'll get the route sheet; it's right over here. . . . Yes, Callahan and Ellis. They're on till two A.M."

"They're *not* on, goddamn it! Callahan got a phone

call from Washington. At seven-thirty. He left; he told the nurse he and his partner had the night off."

"That's crazy! No release went out. If it did, I'd know about it; it'd be listed on the route sheet. Damn it, Bonner, I'd be the one to make contact."

"Are you telling me Callahan lied? He's not here; take my word for it. Neither of them is."

"There'd be no reason for Callahan to lie. On the other hand, he couldn't have been released unless the call came from here. He *couldn't* have—"

"Why not?"

"Well, routine procedures . . . you know. I.D. codes change every twenty-four hours. Those words are locked tight. He'd have to be given a code phrase before he accepted any instructions. *You* know . . ."

"Then somebody's got your words, buddy, 'cause the boys have gone."

"That's just *crazy!*"

"Look, I don't want to argue; get the next team over."

"They're due at two—"

"Now!"

"They'll be pissed off; I may have trouble finding—"

"Then use locals! Get this post covered within fifteen minutes! I don't care if you have to use the Darien Boy Scouts! And find out who called Callahan."

"Take it easy, Major. You're not running this office."

"You may not be either if a foul-up like this can happen!"

"Hey, wait a minute! You know who could have released them?"

"Who?"

"Trevayne."

"He was upstairs with his wife when the call came."

"He could have told them *before,* you know. I mean Callahan's call could have been personal. Those guys *do* have wives and families, you know. People don't think of that. *I* have to."

"You sound just dandy, buddy. Do as I tell you; I'll have D.O.D. Security check up on you." Bonner replaced the phone with irritation. And then he thought about 1600's suggestion. *If* Andy had spoken to the Patrol, it was conceivable that he wasn't giving them time off but, instead, sending them somewhere else. It was remote but possible. And if it was possible, it meant that Andy expected an emergency somewhere else. Otherwise he wouldn't leave Phyllis exposed for even a short period.

But if he hadn't released the Patrol, it meant someone else had. Without authorization.

Andrew Trevayne was either setting a trap or the object of one.

Paul walked back through the door to the admissions desk. The nurse greeted him.

"Hi. Everything okay?"

"I think so. You've been a great help, and I'm going to have to burden you further. . . . We're security people, and we always make errors on the side of caution. Do you have a night watchman or a guard?"

"Yes. Two."

Bonner calmly requested that the men be stationed, one outside Phyllis' door, the other in the lobby, which, he presumed, would cover the man's normal duties. He explained that a simple scheduling mistake had taken place, and it was necessary—formally, if for no other reason— that men be posted. Others would be sent shortly to relieve them.

"I understand, Major," said the girl, with equal calm. And Bonner believed she did.

"You said room two-twelve. I assume that's the second floor? I'd like to see Mrs. Trevayne. May I?"

"Of course. Up the stairs to the left. It's the room at the end of the corridor. Shall I ring through?"

"If you have to, by all means. I'd rather you didn't."

"I don't."

"Thank you. . . . You're very kind. But I said that, didn't I?" As Paul Bonner looked at the assured, lovely face of the girl, he recognized a professional; as he was a professional. He felt that she knew it, too. It happened so seldom these days.

"I'd better go up," he said.

Bonner raced up the stairs and into the second floor corridor. He ran to the end. Room two-twelve was closed;

most of the others were open. He knocked rapidly, and the instant he heard Phyllis' voice, he opened it.

"Paul! My God!" She was sitting in the chair reading a book.

"Phyllis, where's Andy?"

"Just calm down, Paul!" Phyllis was obviously afraid for her husband. Paul Bonner had a wild look about him. She hadn't seen that look before. "I *knew* it; but you don't understand. Now, close the door, and let me talk to you."

"*You* don't understand, and *I* don't have time. Where did he go?" The Major saw that Phyllis was going to stall him, stall for her husband. He didn't want to tell her about the removal of the patrol, but he had to get his message across. He closed the door and approached the chair. "Listen to me, Phyllis. I want to help Andy. . . . Sure, I'm mad as hell about this whole hospital bull, but that can wait. Right now I've got to *find* him!"

"Something's happened." Phyllis' fear took another turn. "Is he in trouble?"

"I'm not sure, but he could be."

"You didn't follow him all the way from Boise or Denver unless you *were* sure. What is it?"

"*Please*, Phyl! Just tell me where he is."

"He drove back to Barnegat. . . ."

"I don't know the area. Which road would he take?"

"Merritt Parkway. It's about a half-mile away to your left as you leave the hospital. On Calibar Lane."

"What exit on the parkway?"

"First Greenwich toll. You turn right out of the ramp and get on Shore Road. Stay on it for about six miles. There's a fork; the left is Shore Road, Northwest. . . ."

"That's the one that becomes dirt?"

"It's our property line. . . . Paul, what *is* it?"

"I . . . I just have to talk to him. Good-bye, Phyl." Bonner opened the door and closed it rapidly behind him. He didn't want Phyllis to see him running down the corridor.

The exit ramp at the first Greenwich toll station had a speed limit of twenty-five miles an hour. Paul Bonner was going over forty, although making sure the tires gripped the wet pavement. On Shore Road he passed car after car, scrutinizing each one as best he could while the speedometer crept toward seventy.

He reached the fork, traveled about a mile and a half, and the road became dirt. He had entered the property of High Barnegat.

He slowed down; the snow was falling heavier now, the reflection of the headlights creating thousands of dancing white spots. He had driven the road perhaps three or four times during the weekend he'd spent with the Trevaynes, but he wasn't sure of the turns.

Suddenly he had to stop. A flashlight was waving in small circles about a hundred yards ahead. A man came running toward the car. Bonner's window was open.

"Mario. Mario. . . . It's Joey." The voice was urgent but not loud.

Bonner waited in the seat, his hand gripping his pistol. The stranger stopped. The car was not the car he expected. The night, the wet snow, the glare of the headlights on the private back road, had caused the man to see what he anticipated, not what was there. An Army vehicle with its unmistakable dull-brown finish. He reached into his jacket—to a holster, for a weapon, thought Paul.

"Hold it! Stay where you are! You move, you're dead!" The Major opened his door and crouched.

Four shots, muffled by a silencer, was the stranger's reply. Three bullets embedded themselves in the metal of the door; one shattered the windshield above the steering wheel, leaving a tiny hole in the center of the cracked glass. Bonner could hear the man begin to back away on the soft, snow-covered road. He raised his head; another puff of the silencer was heard, and a bullet whistled through the air above him.

Paul whipped to the rear of the car, protected by the open door, and flung himself on the ground. Underneath, between the two front tires, he could see the man running toward the woods, looking back, shielding his eyes against the glare of the lights. The man stopped at the edge of the trees, his body in shadows about forty yards down the road. It was obvious to Bonner that the man wanted to come back to the Army car, to see if he'd hit Paul with his last shot. But he was afraid. Yet for some reason he couldn't leave the scene; couldn't run away. Then the man disappeared into the woods.

Bonner understood. The man with the gun had first come out with his flashlight to stop a car he was expecting. Now he had to get around the Army vehicle—with its alive or dead driver—and intercept the automobile he'd been waiting for.

That meant he'd make his way west through the dense forest of High Barnegat to a point behind Paul on Shore Road.

Major Paul Bonner felt a surge of confidence. He had learned his lessons in the Special Forces, in the scores of remote fire bases in Laos and Cambodia where his life and the lives of his team depended upon the swift, silent killing of enemy scouts. He knew the man with the gun who shielded his eyes from the headlights was no match.

Paul quickly estimated the man's distance—the distance to the point at which he'd entered the woods. No more than a hundred and twenty-five feet. Bonner knew he had the time. If he was fast—and quiet.

He dashed from the car to the woods and bent his elbows to fend the branches in front of him—never letting them slap back, never letting them break. He assumed a semicrouch, his legs thrust forward, his feet nearly balletic as he tested the dark earth beneath him. Once or twice his foot touched a hard object—a rock or a fallen tree limb—and like a trained tentacle, it dodged or went above the object without interrupting the body's motion. In this manner Bonner silently, rapidly made his way thirty feet into the wet, dense foliage. He angled his incursion line on an oblique left course so that when he had penetrated as far as he wished, he was directly parallel to the beams of the headlights out on Shore Road. He found a wide tree trunk and stood up, positioning himself so that whoever crossed between the trunk of the tree and the lights on the road would be silhouetted; Paul would see the man without any chance of being seen.

As he pressed himself against the bark and waited, Bonner recalled how often he had employed this tactic—

using the light of the sun at dawn or a low moon at night—to singularly ambush a scout or an infiltrator.

He was good. He knew the jungles.

What did the beavers know?

The man came into view. He was awkwardly sidestepping his way through the woods, shouldering the branches, his eyes on the road, his pistol raised, prepared to fire at any moving thing. He was about fifteen feet from Paul, concentrating on the obscured outline of the Army vehicle.

Paul picked the least obstructed path between himself and the man with the gun and prejudged the timing. He would have to divert the stranger for a second or two; do it in such a way as to cause him to stop at precisely that spot where their paths would meet. He reached down and felt the ground for a rock, a stone. He found one, rose to his feet, and silently counted off the man's steps.

He threw the rock with all his strength just above the heavy ground cover toward the car on the road. The sound of the rock's impact on the automobile's hood caused the man to freeze, to fire his reloaded pistol repeatedly. There were five puffs from the silencer, and by the time the man crouched instinctively for protection, Bonner was on him.

He simultaneously grabbed the man's hair and right wrist, crashing his left knee into the gunman's rib cage with enormous force. Paul could hear the crack of the bone tissue as the man screamed in anguish. The pistol dropped, the neck wrenched back, blood matted the scalp where the hair was torn from the flesh.

It was over in less than ten seconds.

The man with the gun was immobilized, pain wracking his entire body—but, as Bonner had planned, not unconscious.

He pulled the man out of the woods to the car and threw him into the front. He ran around, got in the driver's seat, and sped down the remaining dirt road to the Trevayne driveway.

The immobilized gunman wept and groaned and pleaded for aid.

Paul remembered that the drive in front of Trevayne's house had an offshoot that led to a large, four-car garage to the left of the main building. He drove into it and pulled the Army vehicle up to an open garage door. There was no automobile inside, so he entered, and as he did so, the man beside him began moaning again in pain. Bonner parked the car, grabbed the man's coat so that the head fell forward, and clenched his fist as tightly as he could. He then punched the anguished man just below the chin line so the blow would render him instantly unconscious, but with no danger of death.

In a way, the Major reflected, it was a humanitarian gesture; there was nothing quite so painful as broken ribs. He turned off the lights and got out of the car.

Running back toward the front entrance, he saw that the door was open. The maid, Lillian, was standing in the light.

"Oh, Major Bonner. I thought I heard a car. How are you, sir?"

"Fine, Lillian. Where's Mr. Trevayne?"

"He's downstairs in his study. He's been on the phone since he arrived. I'll ring down and tell him you're here."

Paul remembered Andy's soundproof study that overlooked the water. He wouldn't have heard the car. Or anything else, for that matter. "Lillian, I don't want to alarm you, but we've got to turn off all the lights. We've got to do it quickly."

"I beg your pardon." Lillian was a modern servant but retained the old traditions. She accepted orders from her employers, not from guests.

"Where is the phone to Mr. Trevayne's study?" asked Bonner as he stepped into the hallway. There was no time to convince Lillian.

"Right there, sir," answered the maid, pointing to a telephone by the staircase. "Third button, and press 'Signal.'"

"Paul! What are you doing *here?*"

"We can discuss that—argue it, if you like—later. Right now I want you to tell Lillian to do as I say. I want all the lights off. . . . I'm *serious*, Andy."

Trevayne didn't hesitate. "Put her on."

Lillian uttered four words. "Right away, Mr. Trevayne."

If she hurried, thought Bonner as he looked through to the living room and recalled the few lights on upstairs, it shouldn't take her long. He couldn't take time to help her; he had to talk to Trevayne.

"Lillian, when you've finished, come downstairs to Mr. Trevayne's study. There's nothing to worry about. I just want to make sure he doesn't have to meet with someone . . . he doesn't wish to see. It would be embarrassing for both of them."

The explanation worked. Lillian sighed, half-humorously. She would be calm now; Paul had eliminated the essential fear. He started for the lower-level staircase, which was at the rear of the hallway, careful to keep his walk relaxed. Once on the stairs, he took them three at a time.

Trevayne was standing by his desk, its surface covered with torn-off pages of a yellow pad. "For God's sake, what is it? What *are* you doing here?"

"You mean, neither Sam nor Alan called you?"

"Sam did. You left in a hurry. Is this . . . current tactic so you can take me apart? The Army way. You could probably do it."

"Oh, shut up! Not that you haven't given me reason." Bonner crossed to the single large window.

"You're right. I'm sorry. I thought it was necessary."

"Don't you have curtains or a shade here?"

"They're electric. Buttons on either side. Here, I'll show—"

"Stay back there!" Bonner barked his order sharply as he found the button and two slatted, vertical blinds came out of each side of the window. "Jesus! Electronic shades."

"My brother-in-law; he's obsessed with gadgets."

"One Douglas Pace. Two Lear jets. Chartered between such diverse locations as San Francisco, San Bernardino, Houston, Boise, Tacoma, and Dulles Airport." The blind closed, and Bonner turned to face Trevayne. For several moments neither spoke.

"You've put your well-known resourcefulness to work, haven't you, Paul?"

"It wasn't difficult."

"I don't imagine it was. I've been engaged in a little behind-the-lines work myself. It's overrated."

"You're understaffed. You don't know what you've left

back there. . . . Someone's after you, Andy. I judge no more than a couple of miles—if we're lucky."

"What are you talking about?"

Bonner told him as rapidly as possible, before the maid came downstairs. Trevayne's reaction to the patrols at the hospital was immediate, panicked concern for Phyllis. Paul reduced the issue by explaining the precautions he'd taken. He minimized the encounter in the Barnegat woods, saying only that the injured man was unconscious in Trevayne's garage.

"Do you know anyone named Mario?"

"De Spadante," answered Andy without a pause.

"The Mafia boss?"

"Yes. He lives in New Haven. He was in San Francisco a couple of days ago. His people tried to cover for him, but we assume it was him."

"He's the one on his way here."

"Then we'll see him."

"All right, but on our terms. Remember, he was able to remove the patrol. That connects him with someone—someone very important—in Washington. His man tried to kill me."

"You didn't put it that way." Andrew replied in a monotone, as if he didn't quite believe Paul.

"Details are time-consuming." Bonner reached into his tunic and withdrew a gun, handing it to Andy. "Here's a weapon; I reloaded it. There's a full magazine." He crossed to Trevayne's desk and took out bullets from his trousers pocket. He put them on the blotter; there were eleven. "Here are extra shells. Put the gun in your belt; it'll frighten what's-her-name. Lillian. . . . Is there a door down here, or back here, that can get me to the garage without going out front?"

"Over there." Trevayne pointed to a heavy oak door that once had been a ship's hatch. "It goes out to the terrace. There's a flagstone path to the left, past that window—"

"It leads to a side door at the garage," interrupted Paul, remembering.

"That's right."

The sound of the maid's footsteps could be heard on the stairs.

"Does Lillian scare easily?" asked Bonner.

"Obviously not. She stays here alone, often for weeks at a time. We've offered to get her a companion; she's always refused. Her husband—he's dead—was a New York cop. What about Phyllis? The hospital. You said you'd check." Andrew watched Bonner closely.

"Will do." Paul reached down on the desk for the telephone as Lillian opened the door. Before closing it, she snapped the wall switch in the lower-level hallway, and the lights went out. Trevayne took her aside and spoke softly while Bonner put through a call to 1600 Security.

The Major suffered through the whining discourse of 1600's problems but was satisfied that the relief men were on their way to the hospital, if they weren't there already. His memory temporarily wandered back to the nurse. . . . Phyllis was in good hands. Bonner hung up as Trevayne spoke from across the room.

"I've told Lillian the truth. As you've told it to me."

Paul turned and looked at the maid. There was only the single light of the desk lamp, and it was difficult for him to see her eyes. Always the eyes. But he did see that the strong, middle-aged face was calm, the head firm.

"Good." Bonner crossed to the hatch door. "I'm going to bring in our friend from the garage. If I hear or see anything, I'll get back here fast, with or without him."

"Don't you want me to help?" asked Trevayne.

"I don't want you to leave this room! Lock the door behind me."

30

The man named Joey was slumped forward in the front seat of the Army vehicle, his forehead resting on the dashboard, the blood from his scalp partially congealed in splotches. Bonner pulled him out the door and lifted the gunman's midsection so he could slide his shoulder underneath and carry him fireman-style.

He returned to the side door of the garage and started back toward the terrace. Outside the door he walked along the side of the garage to where the driveway veered to the right, the flagstone path straight ahead toward the rear of the house.

He stopped. There was a dim reflection of light far off on the approach road. If he judged correctly, it was several hundred yards away, near where the man now slumped over his shoulder had tried to kill him. The light moved up and down, the motion emphasized by the falling snow. It was an automobile going over the bumps in the dirt road, the driver traveling slowly. Perhaps looking for a gunman.

Paul ran with his charge back to the study door and knocked. "Hurry up!"

The door opened, and Bonner raced in, throwing the gunman down on the couch.

"Good Lord, he's a mess!" said Andy.

"Better him than me," replied the Major. "Now, listen. There's a car up the road. . . . I'm going to let it be your decision, but I want to present my case before you choose an alternative."

"You sound very military. Is this Fifth Avenue? Sunset Boulevard again? Are *you* bringing out coffins?"

"Cut it out, Andy!"

"Was *that* necessary?" Trevayne spoke angrily, pointing to the unconscious, brutalized man on the couch.

"*Yes!* Do you want to call the police?"

"I certainly do, and I will." Trevayne started for the desk. Bonner overtook him and leaned across the top, between Andrew and the telephone.

"Will you *listen* to me?"

"This is no private mock battlefield, Major! I don't know what you people are trying to do, but you won't do it *here*. These tactics don't frighten me, soldier-boy."

"Oh, *Jesus*, you're not reading me."

"I'm just *beginning* to!"

"Hear me out, Andy. You think I'm part of something that's against you; in a way, maybe I am, but not *this*."

"You have a remarkable ability for tracing itineraries. Doug Pace, two Lear jets . . ."

"Okay. But not this! Whoever's in that car was able to reach right up into 'sixteen hundred.' That's out of line!"

"We both know how, though, don't we Major? Genessee Industries!"

"*No*. Not *this* way. Not a Mario whatever-his-name-is."

"What *are* you people—"

"Give me a chance to find out. Please! If you call in the police, we never will."

"Why not?"

"Police matters mean courts and lawyers and horse-shit! Give me ten, fifteen minutes."

Trevayne searched Bonner's face. The Major wasn't lying; the Major was too angry, too bewildered to lie.

"Ten minutes."

It was Laos again for Paul. He recognized the weakness of his exhilaration but rationalized it by telling himself that a man was cheated if he couldn't practice what he was trained for; and no one was trained better than he. He ran to the end of the terrace, and by instinct, looked down the slope at the stone steps leading to the dock and the boathouse. Always know your environs, commit them to memory; you might use them.

He crept up the lawn, staying close to the side of the house, until he reached the front. There were no headlights in the distance now, no sound but that of the falling snow. He had to assume that whoever was in the car up the road had stopped, shut off the engine, and was on foot.

Good. He knew the area. Not well, but probably better than the intruders.

He saw that the snow was holding to the ground a bit better than it had been, so he removed his tunic in the shadows. A light khaki shirt was less obvious than the dark cloth of a uniform. A little thing, but then, there were no little things—not when patrols were removed without authorization and murder attempted. He dashed across the open lawn to the outer perimeter of the drive and began making his way silently through the bordering woods, toward the dirt road.

Two minutes later he had reached the end of the straight approach to the driveway. He could see the out-

line of an automobile several hundred feet down the road.
And then he saw the glare of a cigarette within.

Suddenly there was the beam of a flashlight pointed
downward on the side of the road, his side. It had come
from the woods. Then there were voices, agitated, rising
and falling, but never loud. Quietly shrill.

Bonner instantly knew what provoked the excitement.
The flashlight on the side had come out of the woods
precisely where he had pulled the bleeding gunman to the
Army car. The snow, still thin, still wet, had not yet
covered the blood on the road. The footprints.

A second beam of light emerged from the opposite
side. There were three men. The man inside the car got
out and threw away his cigarette. Bonner crept forward,
every nerve taut, every reflex ready to spring into motion.

He was within a hundred feet now, and began to
discern the spoken words. The man who had come out of
the automobile was issuing orders.

He instructed the one on his right to go down the
road to the house and cut the telephone wires. The "lieutenant" seemed to understand, which told Bonner something about the man. The second, addressed as "Augie,"
was told to walk back behind the car and watch for anyone
driving up the road. If he saw anything, he was to shout.

The man called Augie said, "Okay, Mario. I can't think
what happened!"

"You can't *think*, fratello!"

So Mario de Spadante was protecting his flanks.

Good, thought Bonner. He'd remove the artillery,
expose the flanks.

The first man was really quite simple. He never knew
what happened. Paul followed the telephone cables as he was
sure the "lieutenant" would do, and waited in the darkness
by a tree. As the man reached into his pocket for a knife,
Bonner came forward and crashed a karate hand into the base
of his neck. The man fell, urinating through his trousers.
The Major removed the knife from the immobile hand.

Since he was a short distance from the study, Paul ran
down the slope to the terrace and knocked quietly on the
door. It was a time for instilling calm. In others. Andrew
spoke through the thick wood.

"Paul?"

"Yes." The door opened. "Everything's going to be fine. This De Spadante's alone," he lied. "He's waiting in the car; probably for his friend. I'm going to talk to him."

"Bring him here, Paul. I insist on that. Whatever he's got to say, I want to hear it."

"My word. It may take a little more time. He backed his car up, and I want to approach him from the rear. So there won't be any trouble. I just wanted you to know. No sweat. I'll have him here in ten, fifteen minutes." Bonner left quickly, before Trevayne could speak.

It took Bonner less than five minutes to pass De Spadante's car in the woods. As he came parallel, he could see the huge Italian standing by the hood, lighting a cigarette, cupping the flame. He seemed to be kneading something in his hand. He removed the cigarette with his left and then did a strange thing; he placed his right hand on the car and scraped the hood. It was a harsh, grating sound, and incomprehensible to Bonner. It was some kind of furious, destructive gesture with metal against metal.

The man called Augie was sitting on a large white-washed rock in a bend on the road. He held an unlit flashlight in his left hand, a pistol in his right. He was staring straight ahead, shoulders hunched against the cold wetness. He was also on the opposite side of the road from Paul.

Bonner swore to himself in irritation and backtracked swiftly, to cross the road unseen into the opposite woods. Once there, he edged his way west until he was within ten feet of his target. The man had not moved, and Paul realized he was faced with a problem. It would be so easy for the pistol to be fired in surprise, and even if it was silenced, as had been the weapon fired by his assailant, De Spadante would distinguish the sound. If there was no silencer, the report might be heard by Trevayne back in the study. Even soundproof rooms weren't guaranteed against gunfire. Trevayne would telephone the police.

The Major did not want the police. Not yet.

Bonner knew he would have to risk murder.

He withdrew the knife he'd taken from the man at the telephone wires and inched his way forward. The knife was a large utility knife that locked into position. Its point was sharp, its edge like a razor. He knew that if he inserted the blade in the lower-right midsection of a body, the reaction would be spastic: appendages, fingers, would fly out, open, rather than be clutched. The neck would arch back, again spastically, and there would be a brief instant before the windpipe had enough air to emit sound. During that instant he would have to yank the man's mouth nearly out of his head in order to keep him silent, and simultaneously crack the pistol out of his wrist.

The man's life was dependent upon three problems of the assault: the length of blade penetration—internal bleeding; shock, coupled with the temporary cutting off of air, which could cause a death paralysis; and the possibility that the knife would sever vital organs.

There was no alternative; a weapon had been fired at him. The intent was to kill. This man, this mafioso of Mario de Spadante, would not weep for him.

Bonner lunged at the sitting figure and executed the attack. There was no sound but the quick retch of air as the body went limp.

And Major Paul Bonner knew his execution had not been perfect, but, nevertheless, complete. The man called "Augie" was dead.

He pulled the body off the road, into the woods, and began making his way back toward De Spadante's car. The snow was heavier, wetter now. The juxtaposition of ocean and land created a moisture inhospitable to clean, dry snow. The earth beneath him was getting soft, almost muddy.

He reached a position parallel to the automobile. Mario de Spadante wasn't there. He bent down and crept to the edge of the road.

No one.

And then he saw the outline of the footsteps in the snow. De Spadante had gone toward the house. As he looked closer, he realized that the first few imprints were separated only by inches, then immediately by over a foot or two. The track signs of a man who'd started to run. Something had caused De Spadante to race toward the house.

Bonner tried to imagine why. The "lieutenant" by the telephone wires would remain unconscious for at least three or four hours; Paul had made sure of that. He'd moved the body out of sight and used the man's belt to tie his legs. It hadn't been pleasant. He'd had trouble with the belt, and the man's trousers had been drenched with urine; he'd rubbed his hands in the snow to try to cleanse them.

Why had De Spadante suddenly, in such a hurry, run to Trevayne's house?

There was no time to speculate. Trevayne's safety was uppermost, and if De Spadante was near the house, that safety was in jeopardy.

Time couldn't be wasted using the woods, either. Bonner started down the road, keeping the footsteps in view. They became clearer, newer, as he approached the drive. Once in sight of the house, his instincts told him to take cover, not expose himself on the open driveway, assess the area before entering it. But his concern for Trevayne overrode his alarms. The footsteps led to the telephone cables, and then sharply angled away onto the driveway, toward the front of the house.

De Spadante was searching, obviously for the man he'd sent to cut the wires. He had to know there'd been a fight, thought Paul. The ground around the telephone housing was disturbed, the snow parted by his dragging the body to the woods.

It was then that Bonner knew he'd been taken—or was about to be taken if he wasn't careful. Of course, De Spadante had seen the ground and the interrupted patterns in the newly fallen snow. Of course, he saw the path created by the immobile body pulled into the tall grass. And he'd done what any man used to the hunt would do; he'd faked out the hunter. He'd tracked away from the area and then doubled back somewhere, somehow, and was waiting; perhaps watching.

Paul rushed to the steps of the front entrance, where the footprints stopped. Where? How?

And then he saw what De Spadante had done, and a grudging respect surfaced for the mafioso. Along the base of the building, behind the shrubbery, the earth was simply damp, black with dirt and peat moss; the snow deflected from above. There was a straight, clear border nearly two feet wide heading straight to the end of the house, to the corner where the telephone wires descended. Bonner bent down and could see the fresh print of a man's shoe.

De Spadante had doubled back, hugging the side of the house. The next logical thing for him to do would be to wait in the shadows. Wait until he found the man who'd attacked his "lieutenant."

De Spadante had seen him on the road approaching the drive, had waited, perhaps yards away, for him to run toward the front steps from the telephone wires. Only seconds ago.

But where was he now?

Again the logic of the hunter—or the hunted: De Spadante would use the existing tracks in the wet snow and follow them into the woods.

The Major could not underestimate his opponent. They both were quarry, both hunters now.

He quickly slipped around the front steps to the other side of the raised entrance, dashed to the end of the house, and entered the offshoot drive toward the garage. Once near the garage, he turned right onto the flagstone path that led to the terrace and the stone steps above the dock and the boathouse. Instead of crossing onto the terrace, Bonner jumped over the brick wall and steadied himself on the rocky slope beneath. He made his way around to the stone steps and continued beyond, to a point directly above the boathouse. He crept to the top of the promontory and was at the edge of the ocean side of the Barnegat woods.

He remained on his hands and knees and crawled in the direction of the spot where he'd left the first man. He shut his eyes several times for periods of five seconds so as to make them more sensitive to the darkness. It was a theory doctors disputed, but sworn to by Special Forces infiltrators.

Thirty to forty feet inside the small section of the forest he saw him.

Mario de Spadante squatted by a large fallen tree

limb. He was facing the house, a gun in his left hand, his right gripping a low branch to steady his hulking weight. The Italian had positioned himself quite far from his "lieutenant." Mario de Spadante wanted to be able to reach the driveway quickly if alerted by the man up the road—the man who lay dead, the result of an imperfect assault.

Bonner rose silently to his feet. He withdrew his forty-four and held it straight out. He stood beside a wide tree, knowing he could dodge behind it at the first sign of hostility.

"The back of your head is my target. I won't miss."

De Spadante froze, then tried to turn around. Bonner shouted. "Don't move. You do, and I'll blow your head off. . . . Open your fingers in front of you. *Open* them! . . . Now, shake the gun off."

The Italian complied. "Who the hell are you?"

"Someone you missed taking out at the hospital, you fat bastard."

"What hospital? I don't know any hospital."

"Of course you don't. You're just here making a survey. You don't know anyone named *Joey;* no one named Joey followed Trevayne, set him up for your personal attention."

De Spadante was furious and unable to conceal it. "Who sent you?" he asked Bonner in his rasping voice. "Where are you from?"

"Get up. Slowly!"

De Spadante did so with difficulty. "Okay. . . . Okay. What do you want from me? You know who I am?"

"I know you sent a man down here to cut the telephone wires. That you posted another up the road. Are you expecting someone?"

"Maybe. . . . I asked you a question."

"You asked me several. Start walking out to the drive. And be careful, De Spadante. It wouldn't bother me one bit to kill you."

"You *know* me!" De Spadante turned.

"Keep walking."

"You touch me, an army comes after you."

"Really? I may have one of my own to hold them off."

De Spadante, now only feet ahead of Bonner, turned

while walking, his hands angled in front of him to ward off the branches. In the very dim light he squinted the large eyes in his huge head. "Yeah. . . . Yeah, that shirt; that shiny buckle. I saw. You're a soldier."

"Not one of yours. No family; just colonels and generals. Turn around. Keep moving."

They reached the edge of the woods and walked onto the driveway.

"Listen, soldier. You're making a mistake. I do a lot of work for you people. You know me, you should know that."

"You can tell us all about it. Go down the side of the house. Straight ahead. Down to that terrace."

"Then he *is* here. . . . Where's that little prick, Joey?"

"You tell me why you left the car in such a hurry to get down here, I'll tell you about Joey."

"I told that son-of-a-bitch to cut the wires and signal with his flashlight. Cutting a couple of wires don't take no ten minutes."

"Check. Your friend Joey's inside. He's not well."

They walked down the sloping lawn on the right side of the house. De Spadante stopped midway to the terrace.

"Move it!"

"Wait a minute. Talk. . . . What can a little talk do? Two minutes."

"Let's say I've got a time problem." Bonner had checked his watch. Actually, he had probably five minutes before Trevayne would telephone the police. And then he wondered. Perhaps De Spadante might tell him something he wouldn't say in front of Trevayne. "Go ahead."

"What are you? A captain, maybe? You talk too good for a sergeant-type."

"I've got rank."

"Good. Very good. Rank. Very military. Tell you what; this rank of yours. I'll up it one, maybe two. How about that?"

"You'll do *what?*"

"Like I say, maybe you're a captain. What's next? A major? Then a colonel, right? Okay, I guarantee the major. But I can probably get you the colonel."

"That's horseshit."

"Come on, soldier. You and me, we have no argument. Put down that gun. We got the same fight; we're on the same side."

"I'm not on any side of yours."

"What do you want? Proof? Take me to a phone; I'll give you proof."

Bonner was stunned. De Spadante was lying, of course; but his arrogance was convincing. "Who would you call?"

"That's my business. Two-oh-two's the area code. You recognize it, soldier?"

"Washington."

"I'll go further. The first two numbers of the exchange are eight-eight."

Christ! Eight-eight-six, thought Bonner. *Defense Department.* "You're lying."

"I repeat. Take me to a phone. Before we see Trevayne. You'll never regret it, soldier. . . . Never."

De Spadante saw the astonishment on Bonner's face. He also saw the military man's disbelief turning into unwanted reality. Unacceptable reality. And that left him no choice.

De Spadante's foot slid on the snow-covered slope. Not much, just a few inches. Enough to establish the possibility of falling on the wet lawn. He steadied himself.

"Who at Defense would you call?"

"Oh, no. If he wants to talk to you, let *him* tell you. Are you going to take me to a phone?"

"Maybe."

De Spadante knew the soldier was lying. His other foot slipped, and once more he steadied himself. "Fucking hill's like ice. . . . Come on, soldier. Don't be dumb."

For a third time De Spadante seemed to lose his balance.

Suddenly, instead of regaining his posture, the Italian's left hand lashed out at Bonner's wrist. With his right he slapped the flat of his palm across Bonner's forearm. The flesh tore open, the sleeve of the shirt instantly saturated with blood. De Spadante whipped his hand up into Bonner's neck; again the flesh ripped open in serrated lacerations.

Paul recoiled, aware that blood was pouring out of

him, seeing strips of his own flesh beneath his eyes. Still he held on to the gun, which De Spadante tried to pry loose. He brought his knee into the soft flesh of the Italian's groin, but it had no effect. De Spadante pummeled the other side of Bonner's head with slaps, drawing more blood with each contact. Paul realized that De Spadante's weapon was some kind of razor-sharp implement fitted into his right fist. He had to grab that first and hold it, keep it away.

De Spadante was beneath him, then above him. They rolled, twisted; slipped on the white, wet earth. Two animals in a death struggle. Still De Spadante locked his immensely strong fingers over the chamber of the forty-four in Bonner's hand; still Bonner held the razor-sharp iron knuckles away from his bleeding wounds.

Bonner kept bringing his knee up with crushing assaults into the Italian's testicles. The repeated hammering began to have an effect. De Spadante's grip lessened. Minutely so, but nevertheless he was weakening. Bonner exploded with his last—he believed it was his last—surge of strength.

The sound of the forty-four was thunderous. It echoed throughout the quiet, white stillness, and within seconds Trevayne came out on the terrace, pistol raised, ready to fire.

Paul Bonner, covered with blood, weaved as he stood up. Mario de Spadante lay in the snow, curled up, his hands clutched over his huge stomach.

Paul's senses were numbed. The images in front of his eyes blurred; his hearing was sporadic—words audible and then indistinguishable. He felt hands over his body. Flesh, his flesh, was being touched. But gently.

And then he heard Trevayne speak. Or, to be more accurate, he was able to make out the words of a single sentence.

"We'll need a tourniquet."

The blackness enveloped Bonner. He knew he was falling. He wondered what a man like Trevayne knew about tourniquets.

31

Paul Bonner felt the moisture on his neck before he opened his eyes. And then he heard a man's voice quietly making pronouncements. He wanted to stretch, but when he tried, there was a terrible pain in his right arm.

The people came into focus first, then the room. It was a hospital room.

There was a doctor—he had to be a doctor, he was in a white cloth jacket—at his side. Andy and Phyllis were at the foot of the bed.

"Welcome, Major," said the doctor. "You've had quite an evening."

"I'm in Darien?"

"Yes," answered Trevayne.

"How do you feel, Paul?" Phyllis' eyes couldn't hide the anxiety she felt at the sight of Bonner's dressed wounds.

"Stiff, I guess."

"You're liable to have a few scars on your neck," said the doctor. "He missed your face, fortunately."

"Is he dead? De Spadante?" Paul found it difficult to speak. Not painful, just exhausting.

"They're operating now. In Greenwich. They give him sixty-forty—against him," replied the doctor.

"We brought you up here. This is John Sprague, Paul. Our doctor." Trevayne gestured with his head in Sprague's direction.

"Thank you, doctor."

"Oh, I didn't do a hell of a lot. A few stitches. Luckily our benefactor here had you squeezed up in a couple of places. And Lillian held your neck in iced compresses for damn near forty-five minutes."

"You give her a raise, Andy." Bonner smiled weakly.

"She's got it," answered Phyllis.

"How long will I be wrapped up like this? When can I get out of here?"

"A few days, perhaps a week. It depends on you.

276

Those stitches have got to set. The right forearm and both sides of your neck are cut up pretty badly."

"Those are controllable areas, doctor." Bonner looked up at Sprague. "An air-flow brace and a simple gauze casing on my arm would work fine."

"Are you telling me?" Sprague smiled.

"I'm consulting. . . . I really have to get out of here. No offense, please."

"Now, just a minute." Phyllis walked around the bed to Paul's right side. "As far as I'm concerned, you saved Andy's life. That makes you special material, Major Bonner. I won't have you abused. By you or anyone else."

"That's sweet, honey, but he also saved—"

"This is getting saccharine," interrupted Trevayne. "You need rest, Paul. We'll talk in the morning. I'll be over early."

"No. Not in the morning. Now." Bonner looked at Andy, his eyes imploring but stern. "A few minutes, please."

"What do you say, John?" Trevayne returned Bonner's look while asking the question.

Sprague watched the interplay between the two men. "A few minutes means just that. More than two, less than five. I assume you want to be alone; I'll take Phyllis back to her room." He looked at Trevayne's wife. "Did your considerate husband think to bring you some Scotch, or should we stop off at my office?"

"I brought it," Phyllis answered as she bent over Paul and kissed him on the cheek. "Thank you more than I can ever say. You're a very brave man . . . and very dear. And we apologize."

John Sprague held the door for Phyllis. As she walked into the hospital corridor, Sprague turned and spoke to Bonner. "You happen to be right, *doctor*. The neck and the forearm are mobility control areas. The medical concern, however, is that the control be exercised by the patient."

The door closed, and the two men were alone.

"I didn't think anything like this would happen," said Bonner.

"If I'd thought it was ever remotely possible, I would have stopped you; I would have phoned the police. A man was killed, Paul."

"I killed him. They had guns out for you."

"Then why did you lie to me?"

"Would you have believed me?"

"I'm not sure. All the more reason to call the police. I never thought they'd go this far. It's unbelievable."

" *'They'* means us, doesn't it?"

"Obviously not *you*. You might have lost your life; you nearly did. . . . Genessee Industries."

"You're wrong. That's what I wanted to prove. I wanted to bring that fat bastard to you so you'd know the truth." Bonner was finding it difficult to sustain his speech. "Make him tell you the truth. He's not Genessee; he's not with us."

"You can't believe that, Paul. Not after tonight."

"Yes, I can. Just like the information you paid for in San Francisco. You bought it from a certifiable psychopath. 'L.R.' I know. I paid him, too. Three hundred dollars. . . . Funny, isn't it?"

Trevayne couldn't help but smile. "Actually, it is. . . . You *have* been busy. And resourceful. But for accuracy's sake, it wasn't information, per se. It was confirmation. We had the figures."

"On Armbruster?"

"Yes."

"He's a good man. He thinks like you do."

"He's a very good man. And a sad one. There are a lot of sad men. That's the tragedy of this whole thing."

"In Houston? Pasadena? Tacoma? Or should I say, Seattle?"

"Yes. And right down the line in Greenwich. On an operating table. Only I don't think of him as sad, just filthy. He tried to kill you, Paul. He *is* part of it."

Bonner looked away from Trevayne. For the first time since the beginning of their numerous serious and semi-serious arguments, Andy saw doubt on Paul's face. "You can't be sure of that."

"Yes, I can. He was in San Francisco when we were. He roughed up a congressman from California several weeks ago in Maryland. The Congressman made the mistake of mentioning Genessee when he was drunk. . . . He's part of it."

Bonner was exhausted and began breathing through his mouth. He knew the few minutes were up. He couldn't sustain much more. He could only make one last attempt to convince Trevayne. "Back off, Andy. You're going to raise a lot more problems than you'll solve. We'll get rid of the scum. You'll magnify things out of proportion."

"I've heard that before; I won't buy it, Paul."

"Principles . . . Those goddamn principles your bank account bought for you?"

"Something like that, I guess. I said it at the beginning; I've nothing to gain or lose. I've repeated it several times since . . . for anyone who wants to listen."

"You're going to do a lot of damage."

"And there are a lot of people I'll feel genuinely sorry for. I'll probably end up giving them a hand, if that'll make you feel better."

"Horseshit! I don't give a goddamn about people. I care, care deeply, about this country. . . . There isn't *time* for you. We can't slide back!" Bonner was breathing too hard now, and Andy recognized it.

"Okay, Paul. Okay. I'll see you tomorrow."

Bonner closed his eyes. "Will . . . you listen to me tomorrow? Will you consider letting us clean our own house? . . . Will you stop? . . . We can clean our own house." He opened his eyes and stared at Andy.

Trevayne thought for a moment of the rodentlike Roderick Bruce who wanted to crucify Paul Bonner. How he had refused to be cowed by the newsman's threats. Bonner would never know that. "I respect you, Paul. If the rest were like you, I'd consider the question. But they're not, and the answer is no."

"Then go to hell. . . . Don't come around tomorrow; I don't want to see you."

"All right."

Bonner was falling off to sleep. The sleep of a wounded, hurt man. "I'm going to fight you, Trevayne. . . ."

His eyes closed, and Andy let himself out quietly.

32

Trevayne awoke early, before seven o'clock. Outside the bedroom window the morning looked incredibly peaceful. The snow had reached perhaps three inches; enough to cover, but not so heavy as to warp the perfect designs of nature. Beyond the pines and the thousands of speckled foliage on the ocean slope, the water was calm, slowed down for the winter months; only the waves hitting the rocks were irascible, still fighting for identity. This was, after all, the sea.

Andrew decided to make his own breakfast. He didn't want to ring Lillian. She had been through so much.

He spread the yellow pages he'd gathered up from his study desk over the kitchen table. The writing was large, hastily scribbled. It consisted of half-sentences and brief notations, proper nouns and corporate titles. It was the information Vicarson had compiled on Aaron Green: much of it extracted from *Who's Who;* some from public Securities Exchange prospectus files; the remainder—the specifics on personal habits—from a creative director of the Green Agency in New York. The creative head was under the impression that Sam represented a television documentary firm contemplating a feature on Green.

So simple. . . . Games. But not for children.

Green was not from Birmingham's *Our Crowd,* as Alan Martin had suggested. There were no Lehmans or Strauses in his family background, no old German-Jewish money giving him entree into the hallowed houses of Seligman or Manfried. Instead, Aaron Green was an immigrant refugee from Stuttgart who arrived in the United States in 1939 at the age of forty. Very little was listed about his life in Germany other than the fact that he'd been a sales representative for a large printing company, Schreibwaren, with branch offices in Berlin and Hamburg. Apparently he'd been married in the late twenties, but the marriage ended before he left Germany just ahead of the

Nazi boot. In America, Aaron Green's success was quiet but meteoric. Together with several other older refugees he formed a small printing company in lower Manhattan. Using the advanced plate techniques developed at Schreibwaren—soon to become Hitler's (Goebbels') propaganda printing base—the small firm's ability to outproduce larger competitors soon became apparent to New York's diverse publishing needs. In a matter of two years the firm had expanded its quarters fourfold; Green, as spokesman, had obtained temporary patents of the Schreibwaren process in his own name; the rest was publishing-printing history.

With America's formal entry into the war and the resultant restrictions on paper and print, only the most efficient survived. And in an industry notorious for trial-and-error waste, Green's operation had a decided advantage. The Schreibwaren process reduced the waste factor to an unheard-of degree, and consequently the production speed was accelerated beyond competitors' imaginations.

Aaron Green's company was awarded huge government printing contracts.

War contracts.

"My old associates speak for Nazi *Schlange*; I, for the lady with the torch. I ask you, who is on the side of the angels?"

At this juncture, Aaron Green made several decisions which ensured his future. He bought out his partners, moved his plant out of Manhattan into inexpensive acreage in southern New Jersey, scoured the immigration rolls for grateful employees, and literally repopulated a dying town with European transplants.

The price of the New Jersey land was negligible, but wouldn't always remain so; the expanding payrolls were peopled with men and women who looked upon their employer as a savior—the concept of organized labor, unionism, was unthinkable; and once the initial shock of "all those Jews" moving into the area was overcome and a temple built, Aaron Green's millions were secure. For as his profits accumulated, he purchased additional land for postwar growth and diversification.

A ride down New Jersey's Garden State Parkway to

this day bore witness to Green's financial acumen, thought
Trevayne as he turned over a yellow page.

After the war, Aaron Green found new interests. He
foresaw the enormous profits intrinsic to the rapidly de-
veloping television industry, and chose to reach them
through advertising. The creativity of the written, spoken,
and visualized word.

It was as if the postwar era was waiting for his combined talents. Aaron Green formed the Green Agency and
staffed it with the brightest minds he could find. His
millions allowed him to raid the best men in existing
agencies; his printing facilities afforded him the capability
of luring away accounts from others with contracts competitors couldn't match; his contacts within government
circles kept antitrust suits at bay, and by the time the
television revenue schedules were set, Green's sudden
supremacy in magazines, newspapers, and print promo-
tions made the Green Agency the most sought-after advertising firm in New York.

The personal life of Aaron Green was clouded. He
had remarried; had two sons and a daughter; lived on
Long Island in a mansion that had twenty-odd rooms and
gardens rivaling the Tuileries; gave with extraordinary
generosity to many charities; published quality literature
with no thoughts of profit; and was an espouser of liberal
causes. He contributed to political campaigns without much
concern for parties, but with a sharp eye for social reform.
He had, however, a quirk which ultimately caused him to
be brought into court by the American Civil Liberties
Union, joined, reluctantly, by the U.S. Employment Service. He refused to hire employees of German extraction.
A non-Jewish German name was sufficient to disqualify an
applicant.

Aaron Green paid the fines and quietly continued the
practice.

Trevayne finished his breakfast and tried to form a
picture of Green.

Why Genessee Industries? Why the covert support of
the same type of militaristic purpose he'd escaped from
and obviously still held in contempt. A man who succored

the dispossessed and championed liberal reforms was not a logical advocate of the Pentagon.

At the Westchester airport he returned the rented car, made arrangements for the jet to be flown to La Guardia, later in the day, and hired a helicopter to fly him to Hampton Bays in central Long Island.

At Hampton Bays he rented another car and drove south to the town of Sail Harbor. To Aaron Green's home.

He arrived at the gates at eleven o'clock, and when a startled Green greeted him in the living room, the look in Green's eyes told him that the old gentleman had been alerted.

Aaron Green's handsome Semitic features were creased; there was both sorrow and anger in his countenance. His voice—deep, vibrant, still possessed of an accent after more than thirty years—emerged like the gentle roll of kettle drums.

"It is the Hebrew Sabbath, Mr. Trevayne. I might have thought you'd consider that; at least to the extent of a telephone call. This house is Orthodox."

"My apologies; I didn't know. My schedule is very tight, the decision to drive over here a last minute one. I was visiting friends nearby. . . . I can return at another time. . . ."

"Do not compound your offense. East Hampton is not Boise, Idaho. Come out to the porch." Green led Trevayne to a large glass-enclosed room that looked out over the side and back lawns. There were plants everywhere, the furniture white wrought iron with dozens of printed cushions. It was like a summer garden set down in the middle of a winter snowfall.

It was completely charming.

"Would you care for coffee? Perhaps some sweet buns?" asked Green as Andrew sat down.

"No, thank you."

"Come, don't let my short temper deprive you of excellent cakes. I can't speak that well of the coffee, but our cook is a superb baker." Aaron Green, lips tight, smiled warmly.

"I deserved the short temper. I don't deserve your hospitality."

"Good! Then you'll have some. . . . To tell you the truth, I'd like a little *nosh* myself. They won't let me indulge; company is the only way I get around them." Green walked to a glass-topped iron table by the wall and pressed a button on a white intercom. He spoke in his deep, resonant voice. "Shirley, darling. Our guest would like coffee and some of your cakes which I have positively advertised. Bring enough for two, and it would be pointless to tell Mrs. Green. Thank you, darling." He returned to the chair opposite Trevayne.

"You're too kind."

"No. I have merely changed attitudes—from irritation to common sense. That makes me *appear* kind. Don't be fooled. . . . I was expecting you to call upon me. One day; I wasn't sure when, and certainly did not think it would be so soon."

"I understand the Defense Department is . . . upset. I assume they've contacted you."

"Most definitely. A number of others as well. You are causing excited reactions in many quarters, Mr. Trevayne. You breed fear in men who are paid to be unafraid. I have told several they would not draw an additional week's salary from me. Unfortunately—and I use the word well— they are not in my hire."

"Then I don't have to beat around the bush, do I?"

"Beating bushes was always a questionable method of hunting, used by the poor because they couldn't afford bait. It had two adverse possibilities. One: the game always had the advantage due to its smell detectors and could choose its avenue of escape. And two: if aroused, it could turn on the hunter and attack without warning. Unseen, as it were. . . . You can do better, Mr. Trevayne. You're neither poor nor unintelligent."

"On the other hand, I find the idea of placing bait a little distasteful."

"Excellent! You're very quick; I like you."

"And I understand why you have such a loyal following."

"Ahh! Fooled again, my friend. My following—if I *really* have one—has been purchased. We both have money,

Mr. Trevayne. Surely you've learned, even at your young age, that money begets followers. By itself, isolated, money is useless, merely a by-product. But it can be a bridge. Used correctly, it promulgates the idea. The *idea*, Mr. Trevayne. The idea is a greater monument than a temple. . . . Certainly I have followers. What's more important is that they transport and convey my *ideas*."

A uniformed servant came through the porch door carrying a silver tray. Green introduced Shirley, and Trevayne stood up—to Green's obvious approval—and helped place the tray on the exquisite wrought-iron coffee table.

Shirley departed quickly, hoping Mr. Trevayne would enjoy the cakes.

"A gem! An absolute gem," said Green. "I found her at the Israeli Pavilion at the Montreal Exposition. She was American, you know. I had to endow a half a dozen orange groves in Haifa to convince her to come back and work for us. . . . The cakes, the cakes. Eat!"

The cakes *were* delicious.

"These are marvelous."

"I told you. Falsehoods may pass in this room with our ensuing conversation, but not about the cakes. . . . Come, let us enjoy them."

Both men warily, with some humor, bandied about trivialities until the cakes were finished. Each sized up the other, each found himself confident but apprehensive, as two extremely good tennis players approaching a play-off match.

Green put down his coffee and sighed audibly. "The *nosh* is finished. We talk. . . . What are your concerns, Mr. Subcommittee Chairman? What brings you to this house under such unusual circumstances?"

"Genessee Industries. You dispense, partially through your agency, an acknowledged seven million a year—we estimate closer to twelve, possibly more—for the purposes of convincing the country that Genessee is intrinsic to our survival. We know you've been doing this for at least ten years. That totals anywhere between seventy and a hundred and twenty million dollars. Again, possibly more."

"And those figures frighten you?"

"I didn't say that. You were right the first time. They concern me."

"Why? Even the disparity between the figures can be accounted for; and you *were* right. It is the higher amount."

"Perhaps accounted for; can they be justified?"

"That would depend on who seeks justification. . . . Yes, they can be justified. *I* justify them."

"How?"

Green pressed his back into the chair. The patriarch about to dispense wisdom, thought Trevayne. "To begin with, a million dollars in today's purchase market is not what the average citizen thinks it is. General Motors alone bills twenty-two million annually in advertising. The new Post Office Utility, seventeen."

"And they happen to be the two largest consumer corporations on earth. Try again."

"They're infinitesimal compared to the government. And since the government is the predominant client—consumer—of Genessee Industries, certain scholastic logic might be applicable."

"But it isn't. Unless the client is, in fact, his own company. Its own source. Even I don't believe that."

"Every viewpoint has its own visual frame, Mr. Trevayne. You look at a tree, you may see the sun reflected off its leaves. I look at it, I see the sunlight filtering through. Two different trees if we described them, wouldn't you say?"

"I fail to see the analogy."

"Oh, you're capable of seeing it; you simply refuse to. You see only the reflection, not what's underneath."

"Riddles are annoying, Mr. Green, set-up riddles, insulting. For your edification, sir, I've gotten a glimpse of what's underneath, and that's why I'm here under these unusual circumstances."

"I see." Green nodded his head. The patriarch again, thought Trevayne; this time tolerantly accepting the inconsequential judgment of an inferior. "I see. You're a tough fellow. A very hard man. . . . You have chutzpah."

"I'm not selling anything. I don't need chutzpah."

Suddenly Aaron Green slapped the flat of his hand against the hard metal of his chair. The slap was loud, ugly. "Of course, you're selling!" The old Jew shouted, his deep voice seemed to echo, his eyes glared at Trevayne.

"You're selling the most despicable merchandise a man can peddle. The narcotic of complacency. Weakness! You should know better."

"Not guilty. If I'm selling anything, it's the proposition that the country has the right to know how its money is spent. Whether those expenditures are the result of necessity or because an industrial monster has been spawned and become insatiable. Controlled by a small group of men who arbitrarily decide where the millions will be allocated."

"Schoolboy! You are a schoolboy. You soil your pants. . . . What is this 'arbitrary'? Who is arbitrary? You set yourself up as a judge of necessity? You imply that from-sea-to-shining-sea there is some great intelligence that is all-knowing? Tell me, Wise Rabbi, where was this mass intellect in nineteen seventeen? In nineteen forty-one? Yes, even in nineteen fifty and sixty-five? I'll tell you where. Standing in weakness, in complacency. And this weakness, this complacency, was paid for. With the blood of hundreds of thousands of beautiful young men." Green suddenly lowered his voice. "With the lives of millions of innocent children and their mothers and fathers, marching, straggling naked into the cement walls of death. Do not speak to me of 'arbitrary'; you are a fool."

Trevayne waited until Aaron Green calmed himself. "I submit, Mr. Green, and I say it with respect, that you're applying solutions to problems that belong in another time. We're faced with different problems now. Different priorities."

"Fancy talk. The reasoning of cowards."

"The thermonuclear age doesn't have very much room for heroes."

"More garbage!" Green laughed derisively. He put his two hands together, his elbows at his side. The patriarch toying with an unenlightened adversary, thought Trevayne. "Tell me, Mr. Subcommittee Chairman, what is my crime? You haven't made that clear."

"You know as well as I do. Using funds inappropriately—"

"Inappropriately or illegally?" Green interrupted, separating his hands, holding them out with their palms up, his deep voice trailing off.

Trevayne paused before answering. By doing so he made clear his distaste. "The courts decide those questions, when they're capable of it. . . . We find out what we can and make recommendations."

"Just how are these funds used . . . inappropriately?"

"For purposes of persuasion. I suspect an enormous barrel of pork that's distributed to retain support or eliminate opposition to Genessee contracts. In a dozen areas. Labor, talent, Congress, to mention three."

"You *suspect?* You make charges on what you *suspect?*"

"I've seen enough. I chose those three on the basis of what I've seen."

"And what *have* you seen? Men growing wealthy beyond their abilities to earn? Worthless endeavors paid for by Genessee Industries? Come, Mr. Subcommittee, where is this moral decay? Who, may I ask you, has been so hurt, so corrupted?"

Andrew watched the calm but nearly triumphant expression on Aaron Green's face. And understood the pure genius behind Genessee's use of the bribe. At least with regard to the enormous sums dispensed by Green, the most important commitments. Nothing was paid out that couldn't legally, logically, or at least emotionally be justified. There was Ernest Manolo, the infant labor baron of southern California. What could be more logical than to contain the spiraling national union demands with pettycash vouchers and jurisdictional guarantees for certain geographical areas? And the brilliant scientist, Ralph Jamison, Ph.D. Should such a mind stop functioning, stop contributing, because it was troubled with real or imaginary problems? And Mitchell Armbruster. Perhaps the saddest of all. The fiery, liberal Senator pushed into line. But who could argue the benefits of the Armbruster Cancer Clinic? The mobile medical units traveling throughout the California ghettos? Who could term such contributions corrupt? What manner of cruel inquisitor would manufacture connectives that surely would cause the generosity to cease?

Inquisitor.

We don't want an inquisitor. Big Billy Hill.

There was Joshua Studebaker, too, plaintively searching for a way to make permanent his past emancipations.

But that wasn't Aaron Green's domain. Studebaker belonged somewhere else. Yet if Sam Vicarson spoke the truth, Studebaker and Green were alike. In so many ways; both brilliant, complex; both hurt yet giantlike.

"So?" Green was leaning forward on the chair. "You find it difficult to be specific about this mass depravity you've uncovered? Come, Mr. Subcommittee. At least a for-instance."

"You're incredible, aren't you?"

"So?" Green was perplexed by Andrew's abruptly inserted question. "What's incredible?"

"You must have volumes. Each case a history, every expenditure balanced. If I picked an isolated 'for-instance,' you'd have a story."

Green understood. He smiled and once again sat back in his chair. "I have learned the lesson of Sholom Aleichem. I do not buy a billy goat with no testicles. Select, Mr. Subcommittee. Give me an example of this degeneracy and I will make a telephone call. Within minutes you will learn the truth."

"Your truth."

"The tree, Mr. Trevayne. Remember the tree. Which tree are we describing? Yours or mine?"

Andrew pictured in his mind some steel-encased vault with thousands of carefully annotated insertions, a massive directory of corruption. Corruption for him; justification for Aaron Green. It had to be something like that.

To even begin to unravel such an encyclopedia—if he could find it—would take years. And each case a complication in itself.

"Why, Mr. Green? Why?" asked Trevayne softly.

"Are we talking, as they say, not on the record?"

"I can't promise that. On the other hand, I don't expect to spend the rest of my life on this subcommittee. If I brought you in, brought in this extraordinary source material of yours, I have an idea that we'd become a permanent fixture in Washington. I'm not prepared for that, and I think you know it."

"Come with me." Green got up from his chair; it was the effort of an old man, a tired man. He walked to a glass-louvered door that led to the back lawn. On the wall by the door were several ornate coat hooks, a woolen muffler hanging from one of them. He reached for it and wrapped it around his neck. "I am an old woman; I need my shawl. You are young; the cold air will be invigorating. The snow beneath your feet won't hurt good leather. I know. When I was a child in the Stuttgart winters, my shoe leather was ersatz. My feet were always cold."

He opened the door and led Trevayne out on the snow-covered grass. They walked to the far end of the lawn, past burlap-covered bushes and a marble table which stood in front of a white latticed arbor. Summer tea, thought Trevayne. They went just beyond the arbor to the edge of a tall Japanese maple and turned right. This section of the lawn was narrow, bordered by the maple and a row of evergreens on the other side. It was actually a wide path.

The flickering immediately caught Trevayne's eye.

At the end of the wooded corridor was a bronze Star of David raised perhaps a foot above the ground. It measured no larger than twenty or twenty-five inches, and on each side there was a small recessed casing in which a flame burned steadily. It was like a miniature altar protected by fire, the two jets of flame somehow strong and fierce. And very sad.

"No tears, Mr. Trevayne. No wringing of hands or mournful wails. It's been nearly half a century now; there's some comfort in that. Or adjustment, as the Viennese doctors say. . . . This is in memory of my wife. My first wife, Mr. Trevayne; and my first child. A little daughter. We last saw each other through a fence. An ugly, rust-covered fence that tore the flesh off my hands as I tried to rip it apart. . . ."

Aaron Green stopped and looked up at Trevayne. He was perfectly calm; if it pained him to remember, the hurt was recessed far inside him. But the memory of horror was in his voice. Its quiet, utter violence was unmistakable.

"Never, *ever* again, Mr. Trevayne."

33

Paul Bonner adjusted the brace so the metal collar was less irritating. The flight from Westchester airport, in the cramped quarters of the plane's bucket seat, had caused considerable chafing on his neck. He'd told his fellow officers in the adjacent Pentagon rooms that he'd jumped the skiing season in Idaho and regretted it.

It wasn't what he was going to tell Brigadier General Lester Cooper. He would tell Cooper the truth.

And demand answers.

He got out of the elevator on the fifth floor—Brasswares—and walked to his left. To the last office in the corridor.

The Brigadier General stared at Paul's bandaged arm and neck and tried his best to hold his reaction in check. Violence, physical violence, was the *last* thing he wanted. *They* wanted. The Young Turk—accustomed to violence, so prone to seek it out—had taken action without authorization.

What, in God's name, had he done?

Who had he involved?

"What happened to you?" asked the Brigadier coldly. "How seriously are you hurt?"

"I'm fine. . . . As to what happened, sir, I'll need your help."

"You're insubordinate, Major."

"Sorry. My neck hurts."

"I don't even know where you've been. How could I help you?"

"By first telling me why Trevayne's Patrols were removed by untraceable orders so Trevayne could be led into a trap."

Cooper shot up from the desk. His face was suddenly white with shock. At first he couldn't find the words; he began to stutter, and once again Bonner found the impediment astonishing. Finally: "What are you saying?"

291

"My apologies, General. I wanted to know if you'd been informed. . . . You haven't been."

"Answer me!"

"I told you. Both sixteen hundreds. White House security men. Someone who knew the I.D. codes ordered them out of the area. Trevayne was subsequently followed and set up for execution. At least, I think that was the objective."

"How do you know this?"

"I was there, General."

"Oh, my God." Cooper sat down at his desk, his voice trailing off inaudibly. When he looked up at Paul, his expression was that of a bewildered noncom, not that of a brigadier who had acquitted himself superbly in three wars; a man Bonner had held—until three months ago—in his highest esteem. A *commander*, with all that the name implied.

This was not that man. This was a disintegrating, frail human being.

"It's true, General."

"How did it happen? Tell me what you can."

So Bonner told him.

Everything.

Cooper simply stared at a picture on the wall as Paul related the events of the previous night. The picture was an oil painting of a remodeled eighteenth-century farmhouse with mountains in the distance: the General's home in Rutland, Vermont. He'd soon be there . . . permanently, thought the Major.

"No doubt you saved Trevayne's life," said Cooper when Paul had finished.

"I operated on that basis. The fact that I was fired upon convinced me. However, we can't be sure they were there to kill him. If De Spadante lives, maybe we'll find out. . . . What I have to know, General, is why De Spadante was there in the first place. What has he got to do with Trevayne? . . . With us?"

"How would I know?" Cooper's attention was back on the oil painting.

"No Twenty Questions, General. My tour of duty's been too inclusive for that. I'm entitled to something more."

"You watch your mouth, soldier." Cooper pulled his eyes off the painting, back to Bonner. "Nobody ordered you to follow that man to the state of Connecticut. You did that on your own."

"You authorized the plane. You gave me your consent by not countermanding my proposed intentions."

"I also ordered you to phone in a progress report by twenty-one hundred hours. You failed to do that. In the absence of that report, any decisions you made were of your own doing. If a superior officer is not apprised of a subordinate's progress—"

"Horseshit!"

Brigadier General Lester Cooper once more stood up, this time not in shock but in anger. "This is not the barracks, *soldier,* and I'm not your company sergeant. You will apologize forthwith. Consider yourself fortunate that I don't charge you with gross insubordination."

"I'm glad you can still fight, General. I was beginning to worry. . . . I apologize for my expletive, *sir,* I'm sorry if I offended the General, *sir.* But I'm afraid I will *not* withdraw the question . . . *sir!* What has Mario de Spadante got to do with Trevayne's investigation of us? And if you won't tell me, *sir,* I'll go higher up to find out!"

"*Stop it!*" Cooper was breathing hard; his forehead had small rivulets of perspiration at the hairline. He lowered his voice and lost much of his posture. His shoulders came forward, his stomach loose. For Bonner, it was a pathetic sight. "Stop it, Major. You're beyond your depth. Beyond *my* depth."

"I can't accept that, General. Don't ask me to. De Spadante is garbage. Yet he told me he could make just one phone call to this building and I'd be a colonel. How could he *say* that? Who was he calling? How? *Why,* General?"

"And who." Cooper quietly interjected the statement as he sat down in his chair. "Shall I tell you *who* he was calling?"

"Oh, Christ." Bonner felt sick.

"Yes, Major. His call would have come to me."

"I don't believe it."

"You don't *want* to believe it, you mean. . . . Don't

make hasty assumptions, soldier. I would have taken the call; it doesn't mean I would have complied."

"The fact that he was able to reach you is bad enough."

"Is it? Is it any worse than the hundreds of contacts you've made? From Vientiane to the Mekong Delta to . . . the last, I believe, was San Francisco? Is De Spadante so much less reputable than the 'garbage' you've dealt with?"

"Entirely different. Those were intelligence runs, usually in hostile territory. You know that."

"Bought and paid for. Thus bringing us nearer whatever our objectives were at the given times. No different, Major. Mister de Spadante also serves a purpose. And we're in hostile territory, in case you hadn't noticed."

"What purpose?"

"I can't give you a complete answer; I don't have all the facts; and even if I did, I'm not sure you'd be cleared. I *can* tell you that De Spadante's influence is considerable in a number of vital areas. Transportation is one of them."

"I thought he was in construction."

"I'm sure he is. He's also in trucking and waterfront operations. Shipping lines listen to him. Trucking firms give him priority. He gets cooperation when it's necessary."

"You're implying we *need* him," said Bonner incredulously.

"We need every*thing* and every*body* we can get, Major. I don't have to tell you that, do I? Go up on the Hill and look around. Every appropriation we ask for gets put through a wringer. We're the politicians' whipping boys; they can't live without us, and they'll be goddamned if they'll live *with* us. The only supporters we have belong in fruitcake farms. Or in the movies, charging up some goddamn San Juan Hill with Teddy Roosevelt. . . . We've got *problems*, Major Bonner."

"And we solve them by using criminals, gunmen? We enlist the support of the Mafia—or aren't we allowed to use the term anymore?"

"We solve them any way we can. I'm surprised at you, Bonner. You amaze me. Since when did someone's way of making a living stop you from using them in the field?"

"Probably never. Because I knew *I* was using *them*,

not the other way around. And whatever I did was pretty far down the line. Dog territory. You live differently down there. I had the mistaken idea that you people up here were better than we were. That's right, General, *better.*"

"So you found out we're not, and you're shocked. . . . Where the hell did you people in 'dog territory' think you got your hardware, soldier? From little old ladies in tennis shoes who shouted, 'Support our boys' and presto, there were ships full of jet fuel and cargoes of ammunition? Come off it. Major! The weapons you used in the Plain of Jars may have been loaded out of the San Diego waterfront courtesy of Mario de Spadante. The copter that picked you up ten miles south of Haiphong might just be the 'snake' we squeezed off a production line somewhere because De Spadante's friends called off a strike. Don't be so particular, Bonner. It doesn't become the 'killer from Saigon.' "

Deals were made on the waterfront, in the factories. Paul knew that. But that was different. That was as far down the line as "dog territory" was for him. De Spadante and his gunmen weren't on the waterfront or at a factory last night. They were at Trevayne's *house*. Couldn't the brigadier *see?*

"General." Bonner spoke slowly but with intensity. "What I made contact with eighteen hours ago, on the property of the chairman of a subcommittee appointed by the President and the Senate, were two hired killers and a Mafia boss who wore iron spikes on his fist and took a lot of skin off my arm and my neck. For me that's different from stealing files and trying to louse up or outsmart some congressional committee that's determined to knock us out of the box."

"Why? Because the fight's physical? Not on paper but in the flesh?"

"Maybe. . . . Maybe it's as simple as that. Or maybe I'm just worried that the next step will be for the De Spadantes to be appointed to the Chiefs of Staff. Or made part of the faculty at the War College. . . . If they're not on both already."

"Is he dead?" asked Robert Webster into the telephone, holding his briefcase between his knees in the booth on Michigan Avenue.

"No. He's a tough old guinea. They think he'll pull through now," said the doctor at the other end of the line in another public phone booth in Greenwich, Connecticut.

"That's not particularly good news."

"They worked on him for three hours. Tied up a dozen veins, spliced twice as many and patched walls all over. He'll be on critical for a few days, but the odds are he'll make it."

"We don't want that, doctor. That's unacceptable to us. . . . There's got to be a miscalculation somewhere."

"Forget it, Bobby. This place is swarming with guns. Every entrance, the elevators, even the roof. The nurses aren't even ours, they're his. Four priests rotate the last rites watch inside his room; if they're priests, I'm Mother Cabrini."

"I repeat, *some way* has *got* to be found."

"Then you find it, but not here. If anything happened to him now, they'd burn the hospital to the ground with all of us in it. And *that's* unacceptable to me."

"All right, all right. No medical accidents."

"You bet your ass! . . . Why the elimination?"

"He asked too many favors; he got them. He's become too much of a liability."

The doctor paused. "Not here, Bobby."

"All right. We'll think of something else."

"By the way, the discharge papers came through. I'm clean. Thanks a lot. You didn't have to add the citation, but it was a nice touch."

"Better than dishonorable. You must have made a killing."

"I did." The doctor laughed. "If you're strapped for a buck, let me know."

"Be in touch." Webster hung up and awkwardly manipulated his briefcase and the phone-booth door. He had to figure out what to do about De Spadante. The situation could become dangerous. Somehow he'd use the doctor in Greenwich. Why not? The doctor's debt wasn't nearly paid off. The doctor had run a series of abortion mills, in one Army hospital after another. He'd used government equipment and goddamned near advertised in base newspapers. The doctor had made a fortune two years after he'd finished internship.

Webster hailed a taxi and was about to give the driver the White House destination. Then he changed his mind.

"Twelve-twenty-two Louisiana."

It was the address of the Gallabretto Construction Company. Mario de Spadante's Washington firm.

The nurse opened the door solemnly, silently. The priest removed his hand from his jacket, and the gold chain with the cross attached rattled slightly. He got out of the chair and whispered to the visitor.

"His eyes are closed, but he hears every fuckin' word."

"Leave us," said the weak, rasping voice from the bed. "Come back when William's gone, Rocco."

"Sure, boss."

The priest put his finger between the clerical collar and his skin and stretched his neck. He picked up his small leather missa solemnis and opened the door, slightly embarrassed.

The visitor and Mario de Spadante were alone.

"I can't stay more than a few minutes, Mario. The doctors won't let me. You're going to be all right, you know that, don't you?"

"Hey, you look good, William. Big West Coast lawyer now, huh? You dress *good*. You make me proud, little cousin. Real proud."

"Don't waste breath, Mario. We've got several things to go over, and I want you cognizant."

"Listen to the word. 'Cognizant.' " De Spadante smiled lamely. It took strength to smile, and he was pitifully weak. "They sent *you* in from the Coast. Imagine that."

"Let me do the talking, Mario. . . . First of all, you went to Trevayne's place in hopes that he might be home. You didn't have his unlisted number; you were in Greenwich on business—you're doing some work down here—and you'd heard his wife was in a hospital. You knew him in New Haven, reacquainted yourselves on the plane to Washington. You were simply concerned. That's all. It was purely a social call. Perhaps a bit presumptuous on your part, but that's not contradictory to your . . . expansiveness."

De Spadante nodded, his eyes half-closed. "Little Willie Gallabretto," he said with his faint smile. "You talk good, William. I'm real proud." De Spadante kept nodding his frail affirmation. "You talk so good. So quick, William."

"Thank you." The lawyer looked at his gold Rolex watch and continued. "This is most important, Mario. At Trevayne's house your car got stuck in the snow. The *mud* and the snow. We've got confirmation from the police. Incidentally, it cost a thousand with a man named Fowler, and the tracks have been erased. But remember, the mud and the snow. That's all you remember until you were attacked. Have you got that?"

"Yes, *consigliori,* I've got that."

"Good. . . . Now, I should go. My associates in Los Angeles send you their best. You'll be fine, Uncle Mario."

"Fine. . . . Fine." De Spadante raised his hand an inch or two off the blanket. The lawyer halted. "Now you finished?"

"Yes."

"Fine. Now, stop talking the fancy talk and hear me. Hear me good. . . . You put out a contract on this soldier boy. I want it *tormento lento.* You put it out tonight."

"No, Mario. No contract. He's Army, federal. No contract."

"You *dispute me?* You a *caporegima* dare to talk back to *capo di tutti capi!* I say a contract. Ten big ones a contract. Put it out."

"Uncle Mario, the days of *The Godfather* are finished." William Gallabretto spoke calmly, sympathetically, to his relative. "We have better ways."

"Better. What's better than *tormento lento?* A slow death for the pig that took my brother! *You* know. *I* know. A knife in the back. *Miole.* A contract. I say no more." De Spadante inhaled deeply and rested his head back on the pillow.

"Listen to me, Uncle Mario. This soldier, this Major Bonner, will be arrested. He'll be indicted for murder—one. He has no defense. It was wanton killing without provocation. He's been in trouble before—"

"A contract." De Spadante interrupted, his voice growing weaker.

"*No*. It's not necessary. There are a lot of people who want to see this Bonner not only finished, but *discredited*. Right up to the top. . . . We even have a newspaperman, a famous columnist. A writer named Roderick Bruce. This Bonner is a psycho. He'll draw life. And *then*—somewhere in a penitentiary—he'll get the knife."

"It's no good. You talk crap. . . . You stay out of the courts. No lawyer shit. That's no good. You put out my contract."

William Gallabretto retreated from the bedside. "All right, Uncle Mario," he lied. "You rest now."

34

Trevayne sat on the hotel bed, fighting to keep his eyes open, to keep his attention on the neatly typed pages in front of him. He knew he was losing the fight, and so he reached for the telephone and requested a call for seven in the morning.

He'd left Aaron Green shortly after one o'clock, much earlier than he'd expected. Green had offered him lunch, but Andy had declined, making a feeble excuse that he had to drive into New York—business undisclosed. The truth was that he couldn't stand being near Green. There was nothing he could say to him. The old Jew had destroyed any argument he might have presented. What words could be found to counter the sight in Green's back lawn or lessen the motive created nearly forty years ago alongside a fence in Auschwitz?

Aaron Green was no anomaly. He was totally consistent by his lights. He *did* believe in all the liberal reforms for which he was noted; he *was* a compassionate man, a generous man, who lavished huge personal sums on causes that strived to better the plights of the unfortunate. And he would spend the last dollar of his fortune, use the last energies of his financial genius to make sure his adopted country would maintain the climate that permitted his philosophy. Such a nation had to be the strongest on earth. Its borders could not be weakened by the necessarily soft flexible interior; the shell had to be impenetrable.

Green was blind to the fact that the more absolute strength permitted the protectors—the shell—the greater the possibility that they would usurp the rights of the protected—the interior. It was the classic manifestation, the *a priori* conclusion, but Green rejected it. If it were possible to build a fortress from the finances of the marketplace, that power would be penultimate, he thought; the ultimate would remain where it was conceived—in the civilian economy. It was a ludicrous assumption, as ludicrous as the Wehrmacht animals counting off numbers to which the naked dead were to march. But the memory of that sight shattered Aaron Green's perception.

And there was absolutely nothing Trevayne could say to alter the old man's thinking.

When the Lear jet had landed at Chicago's O'Hare Airport, Trevayne immediately telephoned Sam Vicarson in Salt Lake City. Vicarson told him the Ian Hamilton dossier was typed and waiting for him at his hotel. It had been a simple one. The American Bar Association was immensely proud of Ian Hamilton, and its professional biography was extensive. Additional information was supplied by Hamilton's son. The choice of the son was another Vicarson touch, thought Andrew. The Hamilton boy—young man—was the "now" generation; the break with the family's long establishment tradition. He was a folk singer with his own group, a graduate of the acid-rock scene who made the transition to the new-new music successfully. He had no hang-ups talking about his father. The son considered—or arrived at the conclusion—that the old man did "his thing" with more intelligence than imagination, but did it well because he was dedicated to the proposition that the elite had to show the way for the unenlightened.

That summation turned out to be the most perceptive analysis of Ian Hamilton that Trevayne would find.

Hamilton came from very old, very secure upstate New York money and traced his ancestry back to the

British Alexander and his antecedents in Ayrshire, Scotland, where the Hamiltons were lairds of Cambuskeith. He had attended the proper schools—Rectory, Groton, Harvard—and been graduated near the top of his class at Harvard Law. A postlaw year at Cambridge in England opened the door for him to spend the war years in London as a Navy legal officer attached to Eisenhower's General Staff. He'd married an English girl from the small social sea of acceptable British fish, and their only child, the son, was born in the Naval Hospital in Surrey.

After the war, Ian Hamilton's credentials—and brains—secured him a series of enviable positions, culminating in a partnership with one of New York's most prestigious firms. Specialty: corporate law with heavy diversification in municipal bonds. His wartime associations, beginning with the Eisenhower administration, brought him frequently to Washington; so often that his firm opened a Washington office. In succeeding administrations Ian Hamilton became more and more identified with the Washington scene. Though nominally a Republican, he was not doctrinaire. His working relationships with a Democratic House and Senate were solid. John Kennedy offered him the London embassy—which was a logical and politically shrewd decision—but Hamilton gracefully declined. Instead, he continued his progress up the Washington law ladder to the rung that allowed him the description of "adviser to presidents." He was experienced enough to warrant attention and yet young enough—in his middle fifties—to be flexible. His friendship was an asset.

And then, two years ago, Ian Hamilton did what no one expected him to do. He quietly resigned from his firm and stated—again quietly, to friends—that he was going to take a "long, I hope deserved, sabbatical." There were the obvious jokes that he'd make more money managing his folk-rock, guitar-playing son, and less pleasant speculation on his health. Hamilton heard them and accepted them, characteristically, in good grace.

Nevertheless, he left Washington and with his wife took a world cruise for twenty-two weeks.

Six months ago Ian Hamilton again did the unexpected and, again, without fanfare or excessive press coverage. Hamilton joined the old Chicago firm of Brandon and Smith. He cut his ties with Washington and New York and moved into a mansion in Evanston on the shores of Lake Michigan. Ian Hamilton had apparently decided on a less hectic life and was welcomed—quietly—into the social confines of the Evanston executive rich.

There was the matter of the bond issue raised by Genessee Industries and given to the firm of Brandon and Smith—the result of Hamilton's breaking silence while a member of the President's Steel Import Commission.

Genessee Industries now had the services of the most esteemed law firm in the Midwest—Brandon, Smith, and Hamilton. Genessee was covered in the highest financial echelons on both coasts: Green in New York; the company plants and Senator Armbruster in California. So it was logical that they establish a seat of influence in Middle America.

If what Trevayne perceived was the emerging pattern was correct.

And with Ian Hamilton that pattern spread into the area of the executive branch of the government. The President of the United States. For Hamilton, adviser to presidents, moved cautiously with quiet but enormous power.

In the morning, Trevayne would drive out to Evanston and surprise Ian Hamilton on the Christian Sabbath, as he'd surprised Aaron Green on the Hebrew Sabbath in Sail Harbor.

Robert Webster kissed his wife good night and swore again at the telephone. When they lived in Akron, Ohio, they never got calls at midnight that required his leaving the house. Of course, when they lived in Akron they could never have afforded such a home for him to leave. And how many Akron boys got calls from the White House? Though, God knew, this call wasn't from there.

Webster backed his car out of the garage and sped off down the street. According to the message, he had to be at the intersection of Nebraska and 21st in ten minutes—eight minutes now.

He spotted the car, a white Chevrolet, with a man's arm out the window.

He pushed the rim of his horn with two short blasts.

The white Chevrolet responded with one long sound of its horn.

Webster continued down Nebraska Avenue as the Chevrolet whipped out of its parking place and followed.

The two cars reached the immense parking lot of the old Carter Baron Amphitheater and came to a stop adjacent to each other.

Robert Webster got out and walked around to meet the man. "Christ! I hope this is worth it! I need a night's sleep!"

"It's worth it," said the dark man in the shadows. "Move against the soldier. Everybody's covered."

"Who says?"

"Willie Gallabretto; that's who says. It's straight. I'm to tell you to go for the mark. Put him away. *Loud*."

"What about De Spadante?"

"He's a corpse as soon as he gets back to New Haven."

Robert Webster sighed and smiled at the same time. "It's worth it," he said as he turned and walked back to his car.

The iron sign with the brass letters read one word: "Lakeside."

Trevayne turned the car into the snow-plowed drive and started down the gentle slope toward the main house. It was a large white Georgian structure that seemed uprooted from some antebellum plantation in the Carolinas. There were tall trees everywhere. Beyond the house and the trees were the mostly frozen waters of Lake Michigan.

As he drove his car into a parking area in front of the three-car garage, Trevayne saw a man in a mackinaw coat and a fur cap walking with a large dog on a path. The sound of the automobile caused the man to turn, and the dog, a beautiful Chesapeake retriever, to start barking.

Andrew recognized Ian Hamilton immediately. Tall, slender, elegant even in his lumberjack clothes. There was a quality about him that reminded Trevayne of Walter Madison, another eastern-establishment corporate lawyer; but Madison—as good as he was—had a slight vulnerability about him. Hamilton had none whatsoever.

"Yes? May I help you?" said Ian Hamilton, holding the retriever by the collar as he approached the car.

Trevayne had rolled down his window. "Mr. Hamilton?"

"Good Lord. You're Trevayne. Andrew Trevayne. What are *you* doing here?" Hamilton looked as though he'd misplaced his senses but would quickly find them again.

Another one alerted, thought Trevayne. Another player had received his warning. It was unmistakable.

"I was visiting friends several miles from here . . ."

Trevayne repeated a variation of the lie, and other than serving as a social buffer to lessen the awkwardness, it was no more believed than his previous lies had been. Hamilton, ever-gracious, pretended to accept it—without enthusiasm—and led Trevayne into the house. There was a roaring fire in the living-room fireplace, the Sunday papers strewn about the sofa and on the floor around a gold velvet-covered reclining chair. On a table in front of a bay window looking over the lakefront was a silver coffee service and the remnants of a single breakfast.

"My wife will be down shortly," said Hamilton, indicating a chair for Trevayne, taking his overcoat. "We've had a twenty-year understanding. Every Sunday she reads and breakfasts in bed while I take my dogs—or dog, as the case is now—for a run. We both find a gratifying hour or so of solitude this way. . . . I imagine it sounds rather old-fashioned." Hamilton removed his mackinaw and fur cap and carried Trevayne's overcoat into the hallway.

"Not at all," answered Andy. "It sounds very civilized."

Hamilton returned from hanging up the coats and looked at Trevayne. Even in a sloppy cardigan sweater, the lawyer had a custom-tailored appearance, thought Andrew. "Yes. It *is* civilized. . . . Actually, I'm the one who formalized the routine. It gave me an excuse not to accept telephone calls . . . or interruptions."

"I stand rebuked."

"I'm sorry." Hamilton walked toward the table by the bay window. "That was unnecessarily rude of me; I *do* apologize. My life these days is really far less strenuous than it's been in decades. I have no right to complain. Have some coffee?"

"Thank you, no."

"Decades . . ." Hamilton chuckled as he poured himself coffee. "I sound like an old man. I'm not really. Fifty-eight next April. Most men my age are in the heavy-thick of it now. . . . Walter Madison, for instance. You're a client of Madison's, aren't you?"

"Yes."

"Give Walter my regards. I've always liked him. . . . Very agile but completely ethical. You have a fine attorney, Mr. Trevayne." Hamilton walked to the sofa opposite Trevayne and sat down, putting his cup and saucer on the solid oak coffee table.

"Yes, I know. He's spoken of you often. He considers you a brilliant man."

"Compared to what? . . . That's a deceptive word, 'brilliant.' Overworked these days. A brief is brilliant, a dancer's brilliant; a book, a hairpiece, eggs benedict, plans, machinery . . . I recall last summer a neighbor up the road called the horse manure for his garden 'brilliant.' "

"I'm sure Walter's more selective."

"Of course he is. And unduly flattering. . . . Enough about me, I'm really semiretired these days, just a name on the stationery. My son is rather prominent, though, wouldn't you say?"

"Extremely. That was a good story in *Life* the other month."

"It was highly fictionalized, to tell you the truth." Hamilton laughed his elegant laugh as he sipped coffee. "You know, that story was intended to be derogatory. Nasty girl writer, up to her eyeballs in women's liberation and convinced my son made sex objects of all females. He found out, I'm told, seduced the poor crusading bitch, and the article turned out fine."

"He's a remarkable talent."

"I like what he's doing now more than I did his previous work. More reflective, less frantic. . . . Certainly you didn't drop by to chat about the Hamilton family's endeavors, Mr. Trevayne."

Andrew was startled by the lawyer's abrupt transition. Then he understood. Hamilton had used the small talk to marshal his thoughts, his defenses, perhaps. He sat

back on the sofa with the expression of a very knowledgeable debater.

"The Hamilton endeavors." Trevayne paused as though
his words were a title. "That's accurate, as a matter of fact.
I dropped in because I find it necessary to discuss your
endeavors, Mr. Hamilton. Relative to Genessee Industries."

"On what possible presumption do you find this
necessity?"

"As chairman of the subcommittee for the Defense
Allocations Commission."

"An *ad hoc* committee, if I'm not mistaken, although
I know very little about it."

"We've been granted power of subpoena."

"Which, if exercised, I'd challenge instantly."

"So far, there's been no need for such challenges."

Hamilton let the point pass. "Genessee Industries is a
client of our firm. A substantial and respected client. I
wouldn't for one second violate the sanctioned relationship
between lawyer and client. You may have dropped in to
no avail, Mr. Trevayne."

"Mr. Hamilton, my interest in your endeavors for
Genessee Industries precedes the lawyer-client relationship. By nearly two years. The subcommittee is trying to
piece together a . . . financial narrative, I guess you'd call
it. How did we get where we are? A harmless variation on
the Pentagon Papers."

"Two years ago I had nothing to do with Genessee
Industries. There *were* no endeavors."

"Perhaps not directly. But there's speculation—"

"Neither directly nor indirectly, Mr. Trevayne," interrupted Hamilton.

"You were a member of the President's Steel Import
Commission."

"I certainly was."

"A month or two prior to the commission's public
ruling on steel quotas, Genessee Industries imported excessive tonnage from Tamishito in Japan, pocketing
enormous savings. Several months afterward, Genessee
floated a bond issue, with Brandon and Smith handling
the legal work. Three months after that, you became a

partner with Brandon and Smith. . . . The diagram would seem apparent."

Ian Hamilton sat rigidly on the couch, his eyes blazing in anger, but icily controlled. "That is the most scurrilous distortion of fact that I've heard in thirty-five years of practice. Out-of-context assumption. Misplaced concretion. And you *know* it, sir."

"I don't know it. Neither do several members of the subcommittee."

Hamilton remained frozen, but Trevayne saw the lawyer's mouth twitch—imperceptibly—at the mention of "several members of the subcommittee."

The ploy was working. It was the public speculation that Hamilton feared.

"To enlighten you . . . and your exceedingly misinformed associates, any damn fool involved with steel two years ago knew a ruling was forthcoming. Japanese, Czechoslovakian . . . yes, even Chinese mills by way of Canada, were surfeited with American orders. They couldn't possibly meet the demands. . . . In the basic rule of production, a single buyer is preferable to many. It's cheaper, Mr. Trevayne. . . . Genessee Industries obviously had the wherewithal—more so than its competitors—and therefore became the major purchaser from Tamishito. . . . They didn't need me to tell them. Or anyone else, for that matter."

"I'm sure that's logical for those who deal in such economics; I'm not sure it would cut ice with the citizen-taxpayer. And he *does* foot the bill."

"Sophistry, Mr. Trevayne. And, again, you know it. A false argument. The American citizen is the most fortunate man on earth. He has the best minds, the most dedicated men watching out for him."

"I agree," said Trevayne, and he did. "However, I prefer the term 'working for,' him, not 'watching out.' After all, they're paid."

"Irrelevant. The definition is interchangeable."

"I hope so. . . . You *did* join Brandon and Smith at a propitious time."

"That will be about enough! If you're suggesting there was reciprocity, I trust you're prepared to substantiate the charge. My integrity is well established, Trevayne. I wouldn't attempt a gutter assault, if I were you."

"I'm aware of your reputation. And the high regard people have for you. . . . It's why I came to warn you, give you time to prepare your answers."

"You came to *warn* me?" Hamilton involuntarily sat forward. He was stunned.

"Yes. The question of impropriety *has* been raised. It will call for a reply from you."

"To whom?" The lawyer couldn't believe what he was hearing.

"To the subcommittee. In open session."

"In *open* . . ." Hamilton's expression was one of complete astonishment. "You can't mean what you're saying."

"I'm afraid I do."

"You have no right to parade whomever you choose in front of an *ad hoc* committee. In open session!"

"The witnesses will be voluntary, Mr. Hamilton, not paraded. That's the way we'd prefer it."

"You'd *prefer?* You've lost your senses. We have laws to protect fundamental rights, Trevayne. You'll not indiscriminately impugn the characters of men *you* see fit to harass."

"No harassments. After all, it won't be a trial—"

"You know perfectly well what I mean."

"Are you telling me you won't accept our invitation?"

Hamilton abruptly frowned and stared at Trevayne. He recognized the trap and wasn't about to be ensnared. "I will privately give you the information you seek relative to my professional association with the firm of Brandon and Smith. It will answer the question you raised and remove any grounds for my appearance before your subcommittee."

"How?"

Hamilton didn't like being pressed. He knew the dangers of letting an adversary know too much of one's defense. Nevertheless, he could hardly refuse to answer. "I will make available to you documents which show that in no way do I participate in any profits accruing from the Genessee bond issue. It was legal work obtained before our partnership agreement; I'm not entitled to participation, nor have I sought it."

"Some might say documents like that are easily written. Easily amended at later dates."

"Company audits and moneys due from existing contracts are not. No partnership is entered into without full audit disclosures."

"I see." Trevayne smiled and spoke pleasantly. "Then it should be a simple matter for you to submit the papers and refute the allegation; over in two minutes."

"I said I would make the documents available to *you*. I did not say I would submit to questioning. I will not dignify such allegations; no one in my position would."

"You flatter me, Mr. Hamilton. You're assuming me to be some kind of grand jury."

"I assume you establish the ground rules for your subcommittee's procedures. Unless you're misrepresenting yourself."

"Not intentionally. Or should I put it this way? Those kinds of documents—accounts, audits, whatever you call them—don't impress me very much. I'm afraid I must insist on your appearance."

It took all of Hamilton's control not to lash out at Trevayne. "Mr. Trevayne, I've spent the better part of two decades in Washington. I left it by choice, hardly necessity; there was no lack of interest in my capabilities. I still retain very solid relationships there."

"Are you threatening me?"

"Only with enlightenment. I have personal reasons for not wishing to become part of any subcommittee circus maximus. I fully understand that such a road may be the only one for you to follow; by reputation you're not a lean-and-hungry man. But I must insist on my privacy."

"I'm not sure what you're saying."

Hamilton sat back on the sofa. "Should you not accept my personal vindication, should you insist on my appearing before your *ad hoc* committee, I shall use all of my influence—including the Department of Justice—to see you branded for what I think you are. An egomaniac intent on building your reputation by slandering others. If I'm not mistaken, you were warned once before about this unfortunate tendency. The old gentleman was subsequently killed in an automobile accident in Fairfax, Virginia. . . . A number of questions might be raised."

It was Trevayne now who leaned forward in his chair. He thought it was incredible. Ian Hamilton's anger—fear, anger, panic—had caused the lawyer to reveal the connection he was looking for. It was almost laughable, because it was—contradictorily—so naïve on Hamilton's part. As he looked at Hamilton, Andrew reflected that none of them took him at his word. *None of them.* They simply didn't believe him when he repeated over and over again that he had nothing to lose. Or gain.

"Mr. Hamilton, I think it's time we both stopped making threats. Mainly for your sake. . . . Tell me, does your influence also include Mitchell Armbruster, Genessee's senator from California? Joshua Studebaker, Genessee's circuit court judge in Seattle? A labor leader named Manolo—and probably dozens like him—handling jurisdictional contracts all over the country? And a scientist named Jamison—probably hundreds like him, maybe thousands— bought and paid for and blackmailed into unswerving loyalty to the Genessee laboratories? Or Aaron Green? What can anyone say about Green? You've all convinced him that 'never again' means creating the very same climate of military influence that led his wife and child into showers at Auschwitz. What about it, counselor? Do you want to threaten me with these things, these people? Because I'll tell you, frankly, I'm scared to death right *now.*"

Ian Hamilton looked as though he'd just witnessed a swift, brutal hanging, a cruel execution. For several moments he was speechless, and Trevayne would not break the silence. Finally the lawyer spoke, almost inaudibly.

"What have you done?"

Trevayne remembered Green's words. "My homework, Mr. Hamilton. I've attended to my books. But I have an idea I've only just begun. There's also an impeccable fellow, a senator from Maryland, who's done very well. Another senator, this one from Vermont, hasn't done badly, I suspect. And the less respectable boys—on the surface less respectable. Men like Mario de Spadante and his organization of good-fellows, who happen to be experts

with knives and guns. They're doing nicely, thank you. . . .
Oh, Christ, I'm sure I've a long way to go. And you're just
the man who can help me. Because while the rest of them
have spheres of influence, you go right to the seat of
power, don't you?"

"You don't know what you're saying." Hamilton's voice
was flat, almost guttural.

"Yes, I do. And it's why I saved you for last. The last
one on my list. Because we're somewhat alike, Mr. Hamilton. Every one else has an *ax*, or a *need*. Something he
needs or wants in the money area, or something he has to
have rectified or avenged. We don't. At least I can't think
what it might be. If you've got some kind of Rasputin
complex, you picked a hell of a way to exercise it; as you
said, 'semiretired.' Out of Washington. . . . I want answers, and I'll get them from you, or I'll parade you in
front of that subcommittee as though you were the biggest
float in the Tournament of Roses."

"Stop it!" Hamilton sprang up from the couch and
stood rigidly in front of Andrew. "Stop it. . . . You'll do
extraordinary damage, Mr. Trevayne. You have no idea
how dangerous your interfering could be for this country."

The lawyer walked slowly toward the bay window. It
was apparent to Trevayne that Hamilton had nearly reached
the decision to speak plainly.

"How is that? I'm not unreasonable."

Hamilton looked out the window. "I hope that's true.
I've spent years watching dedicated men drive themselves
to unendurable lengths trying to wrench vital decisions
from the bureaucracy. I've seen executives in agencies
throughout the government openly weep, scream at their
subordinates, even destroy their marriages . . . because
they were caught in the political labyrinth, their ability to
act numbed by the counterthrust of indecision. Most tragic,
I've stood helplessly by while this nation very nearly was
plunged into catastrophe because men were too frightened
to take positions, too concerned with their constituencies
to accept the mantles of responsibility." Hamilton turned
from the window and looked at Andrew. "Our government
has reached the point of unmanageability, Mr. Trevayne.
It's across-the-board; it's not restricted to any one area.

We've become a grotesque, awkward, fumbling giant. Instant communications have brought the decision-making processes into the living rooms of two hundred million uninformed households. And in this democratization we've necessarily lowered our standards abysmally. We have settled, *strived* for . . . mediocrity."

"That's a pretty bleak picture, Mr. Hamilton. I'm not sure it's an accurate one; not to the extent you describe."

"Of course it is, and you know it."

"I wish you'd stop saying that. I *don't* know it."

"Then you've lost your powers of observation. Take the past two decades. Forgetting for a minute the extraterritorial problems such as Southeast Asia, Korea, the Middle East, the Bay of Pigs, the Berlin Wall, NATO—all of which could have been handled with infinitely greater wisdom by unencumbered leaders—let's look at the country itself. An inscrutable, totally unreliable economy; terrible recessions, inflation, mass unemployment. The urban crises which threaten revolution, and I mean *armed* revolution, Mr. Trevayne. The abusive riots; the overreactions of police and National Guard; labor and corporate corruption; uncontrolled strikes; utility services lost for weeks; a dissolute military, rife with incompetency and inadequate command. Can you say these are the products of an orderly society, Trevayne?"

"They're the result of a country undergoing a very skeptical self-examination. We have different viewpoints. A lot of it's terrible . . . even tragic; there's a lot that's healthy, too."

"Nonsense. . . . Tell me, you started a business; you made a success of it. Would you have done so if the decisions were allowed to be made by your clerks?"

"We were the specialists. It was our job to make the decisions."

"Then can't you see? The *clerks* are making national and international decisions!"

"The clerks elect the specialists. The voting booth—"

"The voting booth is the answer to mediocrity's prayer! . . . If only restricted to these times."

Trevayne looked up at the elegant lawyer, willing to give Hamilton more rope. "Whatever your motives, the subcommittee has to be convinced there's no gross illegality. We're not . . . inquisitors; we're reasonable."

"There's *no* illegality, Mr. Trevayne," Hamilton went on, more gently. "We are an apolitical group of men who are trying solely to contribute. With no thoughts of self-aggrandizement."

"How does Genessee Industries fit in? I have to know that."

"Merely an instrument. An imperfect one, to be sure; but you've learned that . . ."

What followed frightened Trevayne more than he thought possible. Emphasized by Hamilton's quiet benevolence. The lawyer would not deal in specifics, but what he described in generous abstractions was a government potentially more powerful than the nation in which it was housed.

Genessee Industries was far more than "an instrument." It was—or was intended to become—a council of the elite. Through its mammoth resources those privileged to execute Genessee's policies would be capable of rushing in where national problems were critical—before those problems disintegrated into chaos. This capability was, of course, years off; but in lesser examples Genessee had already proven itself, justified the considered projections of its architects. There were unemployment areas pulled out of the doldrums by Genessee; labor disputes settled reasonably in scores of strike-bound plants; companies saved from bankruptcy, resurrected by Genessee management. These were essentially economic problems; there were other kinds. In science, the Genessee laboratories were working on major socioscientific studies that would be invaluable in the areas of ecology, pollution. Inner-city disease crises had been averted with Genessee medical units, and medical research itself was of primary interest to the company. And the military. It must always be closely watched, controlled, a true servant; but Genessee had made possible certain necessary armaments which had resulted in saving thousands upon thousands of lives. The military was beholden to Genessee. It would remain so.

The key to these successes was in the ability to move

quickly and commit vast sums. Sums not hampered by political considerations.

Sums allocated by the judgment of an elite corps of wise men, good men, men dedicated to the promise of America.

An America for all, not a few.

It was simply the method.

"This country was founded as a republic, Mr. Trevayne," said Hamilton, sitting down on the sofa opposite Andrew. "Democracy is an abstraction. . . . One definition of 'republic' is a state governed by those *entitled* to vote, to shape its policies. Not blanketly franchised. Now, of course, no one would conceive of implementing this definition. But to borrow in principle—if only slightly, temporarily—has historical precedence. . . . The times we live in call for it."

"I see." Trevayne had to ask the question, if only to hear how Hamilton dodged it. "Don't you run the risk of those entitled to shape policy . . . wanting to make sure the trains-run-on-time? Of seeking final solutions?"

"Never." Hamilton answered with quiet sincerity. "Because there's no motive. No such dark ambitions. . . . You said something earlier that impressed me, Trevayne. You said you came to me because—as yourself—I had neither financial need nor vengeance to carry out. . . . Of course, we never know the other fellow's problems, but you happen to be right. My needs are satisfied, my vengeances minor. You and I, no political comets, proven in the marketplace, thinkers who can be decisive, concerned for the less fortunate. We are the aristocracy that must run the republic. The time will shortly be upon us when we either accept the responsibility, or there'll be no republic."

"The rule of benevolent monarchy."

"Oh, no, not monarchy. Aristocracy. And not attained through bloodlines."

"Does the President know about this?"

Hamilton hesitated. "No, he does not. He's not even aware of the hundreds of problems we've solved for him. They just disappear. . . . We are always at his disposal. In the most positive sense, I should add."

Trevayne rose from his chair. It was time to leave,

time to think. "You've been candid, and I appreciate it, Mr. Hamilton."

"I've also been most general. I trust you appreciate that, too. No names, no specifics, only generalizations with examples . . . of corporate responsibility."

"Which means if I allude to this conversation you would . . ."

"What conversation, Mr. Trevayne?"

"Yes, of course."

"You *do* see the good? The extraordinary possibilities?"

"They're remarkable. But you never know the other fellow's problems. Isn't that what you said?"

Trevayne drove down the snow-banked roads out of Evanston. He drove slowly, letting the infrequent Sunday drivers pass him, not thinking of the speed or his destination. Thinking only of the unbelievable information he'd learned.

A council of the elite.

The United States of Genessee Industries.

PART 3

35

Robert Webster walked out the east White House portico toward the staff parking area. He'd excused himself from the press conference briefing, leaving his suggestions—mostly anticipated questions—with one of the other aides. He had no time for protective presidential routines; he had far more important problems to control. To orchestrate, really.

The leak to Roderick Bruce would result in damaging rumors circulated throughout every important office—Senate, House, Justice, Defense—and then exploding into headlines. The sort of headlines that would destroy the effectiveness of any subcommittee chairman and reduce a subcommittee itself to rubble.

Webster was pleased with himself. The solution for Mario de Spadante led directly to the elimination of Trevayne. With amazing clarity. The only extra bonus needed was throwing Paul Bonner to Roderick Bruce.

The rest was already established as much as was necessary. The close working relationship between De Spadante and Trevayne. De Spadante's meeting Trevayne late at night in Connecticut when the subcommittee chairman was supposed to be away on subcommittee business. Trevayne's first trip to Washington with Mario as traveling companion. The limousine ride from Dulles Airport to the Hilton. Trevayne and De Spadante together in Georgetown at the home of a less-than-welcomed attaché of the French government, a man known to be involved with the American underworld.

It was all that was needed.

Andrew Trevayne and Mario de Spadante.

Corruption.

When De Spadante was murdered in New Haven, his death would be attributed to a Mafia war. But it would be in print and on the news programs that Trevayne had been at his hospital bedside a week before the murder.

Corruption.

It was all going to be all right, thought Webster, as he turned left up Pennsylvania Avenue. De Spadante would be eliminated, and Trevayne effectively removed from Washington.

Trevayne *and* De Spadante had become too unpredictable. Trevayne could no longer be trusted to go through him to the President. Trevayne had covered extraordinary ground—from Houston to Seattle—yet the only request he'd made was for information about De Spadante. Nothing else. That was too dangerous. Ultimately Trevayne could be killed, if need be, but that could backfire into a full-scale investigation. They weren't ready for that.

De Spadante, on the other hand, *had* to be killed. He'd gone too far, infiltrated too deeply. Webster had brought the mafioso into the Genessee picture originally— and solely—to solve waterfront problems easily controlled by Mafia commands. Then De Spadante had seen the enormous possibilities of aiding powerful men in high federal places. He didn't let go.

But De Spadante had to be eliminated by his own. Not by elements outside his world; that could prove disastrous. He had to be murdered by other De Spadantes.

Willie Gallabretto understood. The Gallabretto family —both blood and organizational—was getting fed up with the muscle theatrics of its Connecticut relative. The Gallabrettos were the new breed; the slim, conservatively groomed college graduates who had no use either for the Old World tactics of their forebears or the pampered, long-haired dropouts of the "now" generation.

They fell beautifully in between, within the borders of respectability—almost Middle America respectability. If it were not for their names, they'd be farther up a hundred thousand corporate ladders.

Webster turned right on 27th Street and watched the numbers of the buildings. He was looking for 112.

Roderick Bruce's apartment house.

Paul Bonner stared alternately at the letter and at the Captain from the Provost Marshal's office who'd delivered it. The Captain leaned nonchalantly against the door of Bonner's office.

"What the hell is this, Captain? One lousy fucking joke?"

"No joke, Major. You're confined to BOQ, Arlington, until further notice. You're being tried for murder in the first degree."

"I'm *what?*"

"The state of Connecticut filed charges. The prosecution has accepted our responsibility for your detention. That's a break. Whatever the verdict, the Army then faces a five-million-dollar suit from the family of the deceased, one August de Spadante. . . . We'll settle; no one's worth five million bucks."

"Settle? Murder? Those sons-of-bitches were gunning for Trevayne! What was I supposed to do? Let them *kill* him!"

"Major, have you got one shred of evidence that August de Spadante was there to do injury? Even in a hostile frame of mind? . . . Because if you do, you'd better let us have it; we can't find it."

"You're funny. He was armed, ready to fire."

"Your word. It was dark out; no weapon was found."

"Then it was stolen."

"Prove it."

"Two Secret Service men from 'sixteen hundred' were deliberately removed—contrary to orders. In Darien. At the hospital. I was shot at, driving into the Barnegat property. I rendered the man unconscious and took his weapon."

The Captain pushed himself away from the door and approached Bonner's desk. "We read that in your report. The man you say fired at you claims he didn't own a gun. You jumped him."

"*And* took his piece; I can prove *that!* I gave it to Trevayne."

"You gave *a* gun to Trevayne. An unregistered handgun with no other fingerprints on it but his and yours."

"Where the hell did I get it, then?"

"Good question. The injured party says it's not his. I understand you have quite a collection."

"Horseshit!"

"And no Secret Service men were removed from Darien, because they weren't scheduled to be there."

"Double horseshit! Check the rosters!"

"We have. The Trevayne detachment was recalled to the White House for further assignment. Its duties were assumed by local authorities through the office of the County Sheriff, Fairfield, Connecticut."

"That's a lie! I called them in; through 1600." Bonner rose from his chair.

"A mistake at Security Control, maybe. No lie. Take it up with Robert Webster at 1600. Presidential Assistant Webster, I should add. He said he was sure his office advised Trevayne of the switch. Although it wasn't required to."

"Then where *were* the locals?"

"In a patrol car in the parking lot."

"I didn't see them!"

"Did you look?"

Bonner thought for a moment. He remembered the sign in the hospital driveway directing automobiles to the rear parking area. "No, I didn't. . . . If they were there, they were out of position!"

"No question about it. Sloppy work. But then, those cops aren't 1600."

"You're telling me I misinterpreted everything that happened. The patrol, the shots. That hood with a gun . . . Goddamn it, Captain, I don't make mistakes like that!"

"That's the opinion of the prosecution, too. You *don't* make mistakes like that. You tell lies."

"I'd go easy if I were you, Captain. Don't let this brace fool you."

"Get off it, Major! I'm defending you! And one of the tougher aspects of that defense is your reputation for unprovoked assault. A proclivity, in the field, for *un*justifiable homicide. You're not going to do yourself any good if you beat me up."

Bonner took a deep breath. "Trevayne will back me up; he'll straighten it out. He was right there."

"Did he hear any threats? Did he see any gestures— even at a distance—that could be interpreted as hostility?"

Bonner paused. "No."

"What about the housekeeper?"

"No, again. . . . Except she held my neck together; Trevayne put a tourniquet around my arm."

"That's no good. Mario de Spadante claims self-defense. You held a weapon on him. According to him, you pistol-whipped his head."

"After he tore me apart with those iron-spiked knuckles."

"He admits the knuckles. It's a fifty-dollar fine. . . . Did either of the other two, the deceased and the one you 'chopped,' did they initiate any assaults?" The Captain watched Bonner carefully.

"No."

"You're sure we couldn't find anything?"

"No."

"Thanks for that. A lie wouldn't hold up under diagrams. They've got us with the first man. His injuries were caused by an attack from the rear. A lie would finish you."

"I'm not lying."

"Okay, okay."

"Have you talked to Cooper? General Cooper?"

"We've got his deposition. He claims he gave you authorization for a plane in from Boise, Idaho, but had no knowledge of your trip to Connecticut. The operations officer at Andrews said you told him you *had* Cooper's authorization. Conflict there. Cooper also says you failed to phone in a progress report."

"For Christ's sake, I was being ripped apart."

The Captain moved away from Bonner's desk. He spoke with his back to Paul. "Major, I'm going to ask you a question, but before I do, I want you to know that I won't use the answer unless I think it'll do us some good. Even then, you could stop me. Fair enough?"

"Go ahead."

The Captain turned and looked at Bonner. "Did you have some kind of an agreement with Trevayne and De Spadante? Have you been taken? Squeezed out after delivering something you can't admit to?"

"You're way off, Captain."

"Then what *was* De Spadante doing there?"

"I told you. A job on Trevayne. I'm not wrong about that."

"Are you sure? . . . Trevayne was supposed to be in Denver, in conferences. That's an established fact. No reason for anyone to think otherwise—unless he was *told*. What was he doing back in Connecticut, unless it was to meet De Spadante?"

"Seeing his wife at the hospital."

"Now you're way off, Major. We ran confidential interrogations all day long. With every technician at that hospital. There were no tests run on Mrs. Trevayne. It was a setup."

"What's your point?"

"I think Trevayne came back to see De Spadante, and you bungled into the biggest mistake of your career."

Roderick Bruce, watchdog of Washington—once little Roger Brewster of Erie, Pennsylvania—pulled the page out of his typewriter and got out of his specially constructed chair. The messenger from the paper was waiting in the kitchen.

He placed the page at the bottom of several others and leaned back to read.

His quest was about over. Major Paul Bonner wouldn't survive the week.

And that was justice.

Chalk one up for Alex. Dear, gentle Alex.

Bruce read each page slowly, savoring the knifelike words. It was the sort of story every newspaperman dreamed of: the reporting of terrible events he'd forecast; reporting them before anyone else did—substantiating them with irrefutable proof.

Sweet, lonely Alex. Bewildered Alex, who cared only for his precious remnants of antiquity. And him, of course. He cared about Rod Bruce.

Had cared.

He'd always called him Roger, not Rod, or Roderick. Alex always said it made him feel closer to call him by his right name. "Roger," he said, was a beautiful name, soft and sensitive.

Bruce reached the last page of his copy:

. . . and whatever the speculations on August de Spadante's background—and they are *only* speculations—he was a good husband; a father of five innocent children who, today, weep without comprehension over his casket. August de Spadante served with distinction in the armed forces. He carried shrapnel wounds from Korea to his death.

The *tragedy*—there is no other word but "tragedy"—is that too often the citizen soldier, men like August de Spadante, serve in blood-soaked battles *created* (*created*, mind you) by ambitious, rank-conscious, half-crazed military butchers who feed on war, demand war, plunge us into war for their own obsessions.

Such a man, such a butcher, plunged a knife, drove it deeply into the back (*back*, mind you) of August de Spadante, waiting in darkness, on an errand of mercy.

This killer, this Paul Bonner, is no stranger to wanton murder, as readers of this column have surmised. But he's been protected; perhaps he was protecting others.

Are we as citizens going to allow the United States Army to harbor hired killers, killers let loose to make their own decisions as to who will live and who will die?

Bruce smiled as he clipped the pages together. He got up and stretched his five-foot-three-inch body. He went to his desk, took a manila envelope from a drawer, and placed the pages within it. He sealed the envelope and stamped both sides with his usual rubber stamp: "Roderick Bruce Copy—Special: City Desk."

He had started for the kitchen door when his eyes caught sight of the Chinese box in his walled bookcase. He stopped and crossed to it, putting the envelope down and reaching into his pocket for his key chain. He removed the box, inserted a tiny key into its lock and opened the lid.

Alex's letters.

All addressed to Roger Brewster and sent to a special

general-delivery number in the large overburdened downtown Washington Post Office.

He had to be careful. They both had to be careful,
but he had to be more careful than Alex.

Alex, young enough to be his son—his daughter.
Only neither son nor daughter, but lover. Passionate,
understanding, teaching Roger Brewster to vent the pent-up
physical emotions of a lifetime. His first love.

Alex was an ex-graduate student, a young genius whose
expertise in Far East languages and cultures led to scholarship after scholarship, and a doctoral thesis from the
University of Chicago. He had been sent to Washington
on a grant to evaluate Oriental artifacts willed to the
Smithsonian.

But his deferment was ended; Alex was taken into the
Army, and Roderick Bruce dared not interfere—although
the temptation nearly drove him insane. Instead, Alex was
commissioned because Rod Bruce *did* point out to certain
military personnel that Alex's background could be put to
good use in the Pentagon-based Asian Affairs Bureau. It
seemed as though their life would go on—quietly, lovingly.
Then, suddenly, without planning, without prior knowledge, without *warning,* Alex was told he had four hours to
gather his belongings—no more than sixty-five pounds
—straighten out whatever personal affairs he had, and
report to Andrews Air Force Base.

He was being flown across the world to Saigon.

No one would tell him why. And Roderick Bruce,
frightened for himself and his lover, overcame his fears
and tried to find out what had happened.

It was too classified even for him.

And then Alex's letters started to arrive. He was part
of an intelligence team in training for some sort of trip into
the northeastern areas. He had been told that they needed
an American interpreter—they couldn't trust the local agents
and feared ARVN leaks—preferably a man with some knowledge of the religious habits and superstitions of the people. The computers had come up with his name; that's the
way the commander of the unit had put it. A major named
Bonner, who was nothing short of a maniac. Alex knew
this Bonner despised him. "He's a repressed you-know-

what." The Major drove Alex incessantly, was unrelenting in his harassment, brutal in his insults.

Then the letters stopped. For weeks Roderick Bruce made the trips downtown to the post office, sometimes two and three times a day. Nothing.

And then he confirmed the horror, *his* horror.

The name was simply a name on the Pentagon casualty list. One of thirty-eight that week. Discreet inquiry, on the pretext of knowing the parents, uncovered the fact that Alex had been taken prisoner in Chung-Kal in northern Cambodia near the border of Thailand. It had been an intelligence operation under the command of Major Paul Bonner—one of the six men to survive the mission. Alex's body had been found by Cambodian farmers.

He'd been executed.

And several months later the name Paul Bonner came up for another sort of scrutiny, a more public one, and Roderick Bruce knew he'd found the means to avenge his lover. His beautiful, studious, gentle lover who had opened a world of physical ecstasy to him. His lover, led to death by an arrogant major who now was being accused by his own colleagues of being a law unto himself.

The hunt began when Roderick Bruce informed his editors he was going to do a series of columns from Southeast Asia. A general covering, with, perhaps, concentration on the men in the field—a contemporary Ernie Pyle approach; no one had done that very well in Vietnam.

The editors were delighted. Roderick Bruce, reporting from Danang, or Son Toy, or the Mekong Delta, had a sound to it reminiscent of the best of vintage war reporting. It was bound to sell more papers and enhance the already superior reputation of the columnist.

It took Rod Bruce less than a month to file his first story about the Major being held incommunicado, awaiting a military court's decision as to whether it had grounds for charges. Several other columns followed, each more damaging than its predecessor. Six weeks after he left Washington Roderick Bruce unearthed the phrase "killer from Saigon."

He used it unmercifully.

But the military court wasn't listening. It had orders

from some other place, and Major Paul Bonner was quietly released and sent back to the States for obscure duty in the Pentagon.

The military would listen now. Three years and four months after the death of Alex, his Alex, they'd listen. And they'd comply with his demands.

36

Trevayne was annoyed that Walter Madison hesitated. He curled the telephone cord around his finger, his eyes on the folded newspaper in front of him. He kept looking at the three-column story in the lower-left corner of the front page. Its caption was simple, understated: "Army Officer Held in Slaying."

The subheading was less restrained: "Ex-Special Forces Major Accused of Murders in Indochina Three Years Ago Charged with Brutal Killing in Connecticut."

Madison was now muttering legalistic platitudes about caution.

"Walter, he's being railroaded! Let's not argue the merits; you'll see I'm right. I just want you to say you'll defend him, be his civilian attorney."

"That's a tall order, Andy. There are several preliminaries we might not overcome; have you thought of that?"

"What preliminaries?"

"To begin with, he might not want us to represent him. And, frankly, I'm not sure I'd care to. My partners would object strenuously."

"What the hell are you talking about?" Andrew found himself angry; Madison was going to refuse him. For convenience. "I haven't noticed any strenuous objecting when I've brought you people a few hundred contract situations which were a damn sight more offensive than defending an innocent man. A man, incidentally, who saved my life, thus allowing me to continue to provide you with retainers. Do I make myself clear?"

"In your usual forthright manner. . . . Calm down,

Andy. You were on the scene; you're too close to it. I'm thinking of you. If we jump into the defense, we're tying you to Bonner and—*not* incidentally—to De Spadante. I don't think that's wise. You *do* retain me to make such judgments. You may not always like them, but—"

"I don't care about that," interrupted Trevayne. "I know what you're saying, and I appreciate it; but it doesn't matter. I want him to have the best."

"Have you read Roderick Bruce's stuff? It's very unpleasant. So far he's left you on the sidelines; that's not going to be possible much longer. Even so, I'd like to keep him neutral where you're concerned. We can't accomplish that if we're Bonner's attorney."

"For Christ's sake, Walter. What words do I have to use? I don't give a goddamn on that level. I really don't; I wish you'd believe that. Bruce is a nasty little bastard with a lot of venom and a nose for blood. Bonner's a perfect target. *Nobody* likes him."

"Apparently with reason. He seems to have a capacity for implementing his own rather violent solutions. Andy, it's not a question of likes and dislikes. It's justified disapproval. The man's a psychopath."

"That's not true. He's been ordered into terribly violent situations. He didn't create them. . . . Look, Walter, I don't want to hire a military crusader. I want a solid firm who's anxious to handle the job because it publicly thinks it can win an acquittal."

"That could very well disqualify us."

"I said 'publicly'; I don't give a damn what you think personally. You'll change your mind when you've got the facts; I'm sure of that."

There was a pause. Madison exhaled audibly into the telephone. "What facts, Andy? Are there really any supportable *facts* that disprove the charge that Bonner stabbed the man without so much as determining who he was or what he was doing there? I've read the newspaper accounts *and* Bruce's columns. Bonner admits to the accusations. The only mitigating circumstance is his claim that he was protecting you. But from what?"

"He was shot at! There's an Army car with bulletholes in the door and through the glass."

"Then you haven't read Bruce's follow-ups. That car had one bullet mark in the windshield and three in the door pane. They very well could have been put there with a revolver owned by Bonner. The man denies he had a gun."

"That's a lie!"

"I'm not a fan of Bruce, but I'd be reluctant to call him a liar. His facts are too specific. You know, of course, he ridicules Bonner's statement that the guards were removed."

"Also a lie. . . . Wait a minute. . . . Walter, is all that stuff—Paul's statements, the car, the patrols—is that public?"

"How do you mean?"

"Is it public information?"

"It's easily pieced together from charges and defense statements. Certainly no problem for an experienced reporter. Especially someone like Bruce."

"But Paul's Army counsel hasn't held any press conferences."

"He wouldn't have to. Bruce wouldn't need them."

Trevayne forgot for a moment his argument with Walter Madison. He was suddenly concerned with Roderick Bruce. With an aspect of the diminutive columnist that he hadn't thoroughly considered before. Trevayne had thought Bruce was after Paul Bonner for some mythical conspiratorial theory associated with right-wing politics, Paul being the symbol of the military fascist. But Bruce hadn't pursued that line of attack. Instead, he'd isolated Bonner, concentrated on the specifics related to the Connecticut incident alone. There were allusions to Indochina, to the murders in the field; but that was all, just allusions. No conspiracy, no Pentagon guilt, no philosophical implications. Just Major Paul Bonner, the "killer from Saigon," let loose in Connecticut.

It wasn't logical, thought Trevayne as his mind raced, knowing Madison expected him to speak. Bruce had the ammunition to go after the Pentagon hard-liners, the men who ostensibly issued orders to someone like Paul Bonner. But he hadn't; he hadn't even speculated on Bonner's superiors.

Again, just Bonner.

It was a subtle omission. But it was there.

"Walter, I know your position, and I won't play dirty games. No threats—"

"I should hope not, Andy." It was Madison's turn to interrupt, and he recognized it. "We've been through too many productive years to see them buried by an Army officer who, I gather, hasn't much use for you."

"You're right." Trevayne momentarily lowered his eyes to the telephone. Madison's statement confused him, but he didn't have the time to go into it. "Think it over; talk to your partners. Let me know in a couple of hours. If the answer's negative, I *will* want to be apprised of your reasons; I think I deserve that. If it's yes, I'll expect a whopping bill."

"I'll get back to you this afternoon or early evening. Will you be at your office?"

"If I'm not, Sam Vicarson will know where to reach me. I'll be home later, Tawning Spring number. I'll expect your call."

Trevayne hung up and made a decision. Sam Vicarson had a new research project.

By early afternoon Sam had gathered together every column Roderick Bruce had written that had any mention of Paul Bonner, the "killer from Saigon."

The writings revealed only that Bruce had latched onto a volatile story made more explosive by the government's insistence on keeping it classified three years ago. It was difficult to tell whether the extraordinary invective used against Paul Bonner was directed at him or at those in command who were protecting the Special Forces Major. The columns were semibalanced in this respect. But sporadically this posture appeared as an excuse, a springboard, to remount an attack on one man—the symbol of monstrosity that was Paul Bonner.

The attacks were superbly written exercises in character assassination. Bonner was both the creator and product of a brutal system of armed exploitation. He was to be scorned and pitied; the pity very much an afterthought and only to be employed as one pities a barbarian who impales the bodies of children because he believes they stem from evil ancestors. Pity the primitive motive, but first destroy the Hun.

And then—as Trevayne had accurately assessed—the current writings shifted. No longer was there any attempt to lock in Bonner with a system. No product now, only a creator.

An isolated monster who betrayed his uniform.

There *was* a difference.

"Man, he's out for a firing squad!" Vicarson whistled before making the pronouncement.

"He certainly is, and I want to know why."

"I think it's there. Underneath the Savile Row clothes and expensive restaurants, Rod Bruce is the freaked-out new left."

"Then why isn't he asking for more than one execution? . . . Find out where they've got Bonner. I want to see him."

Paul removed the irritating neck brace and leaned his back against the wall while sitting on the regulation Army bed. Andrew remained standing; the first few minutes of their meeting had been awkward. The BOQ room was small; there was an Army guard stationed in the corridor, and Trevayne had been startled at Bonner's explanation that he was not permitted outside the room except for exercise periods.

"It's better than a cell, I suppose," said Andy.

"Not a hell of a lot."

Trevayne began the questioning cautiously. "I know you can't, or won't, discuss these things, but I want to help. I hope I don't have to convince you of that."

"No. I'll buy it. But I don't think I'm going to need any."

"You sound confident."

"Cooper's expected back in a few days. I've gone through this before, remember? There's a lot of yelling, a lot of formalities; then somehow it all rides out and I'm quietly transferred somewhere else."

"You *believe* that?"

Bonner looked reflective. "Yes, I do. . . . For a lot of

reasons. If I were in Cooper's place—or in the shoes of the other guys up there in Brasswares—I'd do just what they're doing. Let the flap settle. . . . I've thought about it." Paul smiled and gave a short laugh. "The Army moves in mysterious ways."

"Have you seen the newspapers?"

"Sure. I saw them three years ago, too. Back when I rated ten minutes on the seven-o'clock news. Now, it's barely a couple of seconds. . . . But I appreciate your concern. Especially since I told you to go to hell the last time we talked."

"I gather you won't give me a return-trip ticket."

"No, I won't, Andy. You're doing a lot of damage. I'm only a minor—and temporary—casualty."

"I hope you haven't lulled yourself into a false sense of security."

"That's civilian talk. We have a different meaning for security. What is it you want to discuss that I won't, or can't?"

"Why you're the all-time pariah for Roderick Bruce."

"I've often wondered. An Army psychiatrist told me that I'm sort of everything Bruce wishes he was but can't be; that he takes *his* aggression out on a typewriter. . . . The simpler explanation is that I stand for large D.O.D. appropriations, and that's grist for his mill."

"I can't accept either. You never met him?"

"Nope."

"You never quashed any stories he might have written from Indochina? For security—your version of it."

"How could I? I was never in that position. And I don't think he was there when I was operating in the field."

"That's right. . . ." Trevayne walked to the single chair in the small room and sat down. "He went gunning for you after our embassy in Saigon demanded that charges be brought against you. . . . Paul, please answer this; I can get the information, take my word for it. Bruce's articles said you were charged with killing three to five men; that the CIA denied having given you the license by using the term 'extreme dispatch' or 'prejudice' or whatever the hell it's called. Bruce has friends in every section of the government. By implicating CIA, could you have caused the Agency to dismiss anyone? Someone he might have known?"

Bonner stared at Trevayne without answering for several moments. He raised his hand to touch the tender skin around his neck and spoke slowly. "Okay. . . . I'll tell you what happened. . . . If only to get you off the CIA's butt; they've got enough trouble. There were five slants, double agents. I killed all five. Three because they surrounded my bivouac and let loose with enough firepower to blow up an airstrip. I wasn't inside, thanks to the CIA boys who'd alerted me. I dropped the last two at the Thai border when I caught them with North Vietnamese pouches. They were using our contact sheets and buying off the tribe leaders I'd busted my ass cultivating. . . . To tell you the truth, the Agency quietly got me out of the whole mess. Any implications were the result of hotheaded Army lawyers; we told them all to go to hell."

"Then why were charges brought in the first place?"

"You don't know Saigon politics. There was never—in history—any corruption like Saigon corruption. Two of those double agents had brothers in the Cabinet. . . . At any rate, you can forget CIA."

Trevayne had removed a thin notebook from his pocket and flipped through the pages. "The charges against you were made public in February. By March twenty-first, Bruce was on your back. He traveled from Danang to the Mekong Delta interviewing anyone who had business with you."

"He talked to the wrong people. I operated in Laos, Thailand, and northern Cambodia mostly. Usually with teams of six to eight, and they were almost exclusively Asian nonmilitary."

Trevayne looked up from his notebook. "I thought Special Forces traveled in units; their own units."

"Some do. Mostly I didn't. I have a working knowledge of the Thai and Laotian languages—enough tonal understanding to get by—not Cambodian, though. Whenever I went into Cambodia I recruited, when we felt the security was tight enough. It usually wasn't. Once or twice we had to scour our own people to come up with someone we could train in a hurry."

"Train for what?"

"To stay alive. We weren't always successful. A case in point was Chung Kal. . . ."

They talked for fifteen minutes longer, and Trevayne knew he had found what he was looking for.

Sam Vicarson could put the pieces together.

Sam Vicarson rang the door chimes at Trevayne's rented home in Tawning Spring. Phyllis answered and greeted Sam with a firm handshake.

"Glad you're out of the hospital, Mrs. Trevayne."

"If that's meant to be funny, I won't get you a drink." Phyllis laughed. "Andy's downstairs, he's expecting you."

"Thanks. I really am glad you're out."

"I never should have gone in. Hurry up; your chairman's anxious."

Downstairs in the recreation-room-turned-office, Trevayne was on the telephone, sitting in a chair, listening impatiently. At the sight of Vicarson, his impatience heightened. In words bordering on rudeness, he extricated himself from the conversation.

"That was Walter Madison. I wish I hadn't promised to play fair. His partners don't want the Bonner case, even if it means losing me as a client; which Walter told them, of course, it wouldn't."

"There's such a thing as changing your mind."

"I might do that. Their reasoning's fatuous. They respect the prosecution's case and have none for the defendant."

"Why is that fatuous?"

"They haven't heard, nor do they wish to hear, the defendant's story. They don't want to get involved; clients to protect, including me."

"That's fatuous. . . . However, I think we can turn the hysterical newshound into an enthusiastic character witness for the maligned Major; that is, if we want to. The least we can do is shut him up."

"Bruce?"

"In lavender spades."

Vicarson's research had been accomplished with comparative ease. The man's name was Alexander Coffey. The Asian Affairs Bureau at the Pentagon—that is, the officer in charge at A.A.B.—recalled that Roderick Bruce *had* brought to his attention Coffey's background. And A.A.B. had been happy to catch the Ph.D. Far East scholars were hard to come by. The officer was, of course, saddened about the Chung Kal operation, but apparently some good had come out of it. At least, that's what he'd been told. It was always dangerous to put a research analyst into a combat situation. . . . He gave Coffey's file to Sam.

Vicarson had then gone to the Smithsonian Far East Archives. The head archivist there remembered Coffey clearly. The young man was a brilliant scholar but an obvious homosexual. It had surprised the archivist that Coffey hadn't used his deviation to avoid being drafted, but since his future would be involved with foundations, and foundations were conservative organizations, by and large, the Smithsonian assumed Coffey didn't want the proof on record. Also, the archivist had the suspicion that Coffey knew someone who could steer him into a pleasant military assignment. The man had heard that Coffey was stationed in Washington, and so presumed his suspicions were correct. He obviously didn't know about Coffey's death at Chung Kal, and Vicarson did not bother to tell him. The archivist showed him Coffey's identification card. On it was an address on 21st Street, Northwest, and the name of a roommate.

As Vicarson learned, a former roommate.

The roommate still blamed the "rich-bitch" Coffey had moved in with for Alex's death. Alex never told him who it was, but "he came around often enough—to get away from that awful glutton." Alexander Coffey "came around" in new clothes, a new car, and new jewelry. He also came with news that his benefactor had arranged the perfect "situation" in the Army that wouldn't require even one day of barracks, one day out of Washington. A simple exchange of clothes for the daytime, and the uniform would be custom-made in soft flannel. It was, according to Alex, the "perfect solution" for his career. Even an Army commission thrown into the bargain. What foundation could refuse him? And then he was "hijacked," probably "betrayed" by the "rich-bitch."

Vicarson had heard enough. He drove out to Arlington and saw Paul Bonner.

Bonner remembered Coffey. He had respected him; liked him, actually. The young man had an extraordinary knowledge of the north Cambodian tribes and came up with ingenious suggestions as to how to implement religious symbols in initial contacts. A bold method of operation never considered before.

One aspect of Coffey's joining the unit stood out in Bonner's memory. The man was totally soft, completely alien to the demands that would be made upon him in the hills. Probably a faggot, too. As a result of this knowledge, Bonner drove him hard, relentlessly. Not that six weeks would make up for a lifetime, but perhaps enough could be instilled to help him in a pinch.

But it hadn't been enough, and Coffey was captured in a "scramble." Bonner blamed himself for not having been tougher with the scholar; but as a professional, he couldn't dwell on it. He could only learn from it. If the situation ever arose again, where such a man was assigned to him, he'd be unmerciful. Then, perhaps, the man might survive.

"There it is, Mr. Trevayne. Lover-didn't-come-back-to-me."

Trevayne winced. "Really, Sam. It's very sad."

"Sure as hell is. But it's also enough to throw Bruce out of the box. I happen to *like* Paul Bonner; I don't give a shit for that cocksucker. I use the word with legal expertise, sir."

"I'm sure you do. Now, just hold it on a front burner and we'll consider all our options."

"Look, if you're reluctant to get into this gutter, Mr. Trevayne, I'm *not*. I mean, it's not very nice for someone like you, but I'm just a wandering legal genius who has no roots. Just influential employers who, I trust, will not forget my contributions. . . . Let me kick him in the balls; I'd love it."

"You're impossible, Sam."

"Your wife once told me I reminded her of you. Best

compliment I ever had. . . . You shouldn't do it. It's my job."

"My wife is an incurable romantic when it comes to energetic young men. And it's not your job. It's nobody's at the moment."

"Why not?"

"Because Roderick Bruce isn't acting alone. He's being fed. He's not flying solo, Sam. He's got confederates; right among the people Paul Bonner thinks are his enthusiastic supporters."

Vicarson lifted his glass as Phyllis Trevayne walked down the stairs and entered the room. "Wow, that's a wrinkle."

"You keep that up, Sam, you won't be invited to a candlelight dinner when Andy's away."

"Which is tomorrow," added Trevayne. "Webster implied that the President thinks I should hear what De Spadante has to say in the morning . . . in Bonner's behalf. Which means I listen to Mario de Spadante tomorrow morning 'up in Greenwich.'"

"You'll be back by the afternoon. There goes our candlelight dinner, Mrs. Trevayne."

"Not at all," said Andy. "I want you and Alan here by five-thirty. Light the candles, Phyl. We may need them."

37

Mario De Spadante was annoyed that the nurse insisted the shades be raised so as to let in the morning sunlight. But she was a good nurse—not one of his, the hospital's— and Mario was a polite man to those not in his employ. He let the shades stay up.

Andrew Trevayne had just arrived; he was downstairs being met at a side entrance. He had driven into the parking lot two minutes ago and soon would be coming through the door. Mario had arranged the room as he felt it should look. He was raised in the bed as high as possible, the chair beside him low. The young, well-dressed guard on duty across the room smiled as De Spadante instructed him to crank the bed handle and move the furniture.

The young man was one of William Gallabretto's assistants from California. He realized that De Spadante might soon order him out of the room, and that meant he had very little time to accomplish his task.

For attached to his lapel in the form of a jeweled American flag was a miniature camera with a shutter-release wire threaded down to his left jacket pocket.

The door opened, and Andrew Trevayne walked into the room. The corridor guard closed the door, making a last-instant check that the third man was inside.

"Sit, sit, Mr. Trevayne." De Spadante held out his hand, and Andy had no choice but to take it.

The young man by the wall had his hand in his pocket, and, unseen by both men, his thumb made rapid compressions against a small flat metal plunger.

Trevayne sat in the chair, releasing the Italian's grip as swiftly as possible. "I won't pretend that I looked forward to this visit, Mr. de Spadante. I'm not sure we have anything to say to each other."

That's right, thought the young man by the wall. *Move in a bit and look thoughtful, perhaps a little wary, Trevayne. It'll come out as fear.*

"We got a lot to say, *amico*. I got nothing against you. This soldier, yes. Him I owe for the death of my little brother. Not you."

"That soldier was attacked, and you know it. I'm sorry about your brother, but he was armed and prowling around on my property. If you were responsible for his being there, look to yourself."

"What is *this*? I walked in my neighbor's field, and he takes my *life*? What kind of world have we come to?"

"The analogy doesn't fit. Walking in a field is hardly the same as stalking at night with pistols, knives and . . . what was it? Oh, yes, iron spikes wrapped around your fingers."

Perfect, Trevayne, thought the man by the wall. *That slight gesture with your palm up. Just right. You, the "capo regime," explaining to your "capo di tutti capi."*

"I grew up having to defend myself, *amico*. My fancy schools were the streets, my teachers the big niggers who liked to hammer wop heads. A bad habit, I confess, but an understandable one that I often carry my fist in my pocket. But no guns; never guns!"

"Apparently you have no need for one." Trevayne looked over at the young man by the wall with his left hand ominously in his jacket pocket. "He looks like a cartoon."

You're very funny, too, Trevayne, thought the man by the wall.

"You! Out! . . . A friend of a cousin; they're young, what can I do? They have great affection. . . . Out! Leave us."

"Sure, Mr. de Spadante. Whatever you say." The young man removed his hand from his jacket pocket. In it he held a box of jujubes. "Care for a candy, Mr. Trevayne?"

"No, thank you."

"Get out! . . . Christ, penny candy they got!"

The door closed, and De Spadante shifted his huge bulk in the pillows. "Now, we do some talking, okay?"

"It's why I flew up. I'd like to make it as short as possible. I want to hear what you have to say; I want you to hear me."

"You shouldn't be so arrogant. You know, a lot of people say you're arrogant, but I tell them that my good *amico*, Trevayne, he's not like that. He's just practical; he doesn't waste words."

"I don't need your defending me—"

"You need something," interrupted De Spadante. "Christ, you need *help*."

"I'm here for one reason only. To tell you to back off from Paul Bonner. You may control your own hoods, De Spadante; get them to swear to whatever you say. But you won't stand up to the cross-examination we throw at you personally. . . . You're right, I don't waste words. You were seen mauling and threatening a congressman one night on the golf course in Chevy Chase. You were seen by a man who reported the incident to me and Major Bonner. That was an act of physical violence; knowledge of it was all the motive Bonner needed to be on guard. Later you were observed thirty-five hundred miles away, following me to San Francisco. We have sworn testimony to that. Major Bonner had every reason to fear for my life. . . . Beyond these irrefutable facts and subsequent reasonable concerns, there are other speculations. How does a man like you get off physically abusing a United States congressman? Because he had the temerity to mention an aircraft company? Why did you follow me to California? Were you trying to corner an assistant of mine down at Fisherman's Wharf? Attack him too? Why? What have you got to do with Genessee Industries, De Spadante? The court's going to be concerned with these questions. I'll make sure of it, because I'll tie them to your assault on Paul Bonner last Saturday night. . . . I know a little more than I did on that shuttle flight to Dulles. You're finished . . . because you're too obvious. You're just not desirable."

Mario de Spadante, through heavy-lidded eyes, looked at Trevayne with hatred. His voice, however, remained calm, only the rasp slightly more pronounced. "That's a favorite word of your kind, isn't it? 'Desirable.' We're . . . 'just not desirable.' "

"Don't make a sociological case out of it. You're not an appropriate spokesman."

De Spadante shrugged. "Even your insults don't bother me, my good *amico*. You know why? . . . Because you're a troubled man, and a man with troubles has a bad tongue. . . . No, I'm still going to help you."

"You may, but I doubt that it'll be voluntary. . . ."

"But first this soldier," continued the Italian, as if Trevayne had not spoken. "This soldier, you forget. There's not going to be any trial. This soldier is a dead man; believe me when I tell you this information. He may be breathing now, but he's a dead man. You forget him. . . . Now, for your good news. . . . Like I said, you got troubles; but your friend Mario is going to make sure that nobody takes advantage of you because of them."

"What are you talking about?"

"You work hard, Trevayne; you spend a lot of time away from home. . . ."

Andrew sat bolt upright in his chair. "You make one

lousy, rotten threat against my family, you filthy son-of-a-bitch, and I'll see you put away for the rest of your life! You'd better not even *think* in those terms, you *animal*. That's one area where the President has given me all the assurances I need! I'll make one telephone call, and you're locked up so far out of sight—"

"*Basta!* You got no right! You shut up!" De Spadante roared as loud as was possible for him, simultaneously clutching his stomach. Then, just as quickly as he had matched Trevayne's intensity, his voice descended to its raspy, quiet norm. "That kind of talk doesn't belong in this room. I got respect for a man's house . . . his children, his brothers. That soldier, *he's* the animal, not me; not De Spadante."

"You were the one who brought it up. I just want to make sure you know where you stand. That's out of bounds, and the man on Pennsylvania Avenue has guaranteed it. He's out of your league, hoodlum."

Mario swallowed, his fury hidden poorly under his rasp. "He doesn't guarantee an Augie de Spadante, does he? Not Augie; he's not desirable."

Trevayne looked at his wristwatch. "You have something to say, say it."

"Sure. Sure, I'll say it. And the only guarantee you got is me. Like I said, you spent a lot of time away from home, picking up your chips. Maybe you don't have enough time left to give proper guidance to your loved ones. You got problems. You got a wild boy who drinks too much and draws blanks after a bad night. Now, that's not too terrible, but he also hits pedestrians. For instance, I got an old man in Cos Cob who was hurt pretty bad by your kid."

"That's a lie."

"We got photographs. We got at least a dozen photographs of a half-crazy kid by his car at night. The car and the kid, a mess. So, this old man who was hit; we paid him to be nice and not hurt a wild kid who didn't mean any harm. I've got the canceled checks—and, of course, a statement. But that's not such a bad thing; millionaires' kids have different values. People understand that. . . . We had a little more trouble with your girl. Yes, *that* was a bad thing; it was very touch-and-go for a while. Your friend Mario spared no expense to protect her . . . and you."

Trevayne sat back in his chair; there was no anger in his expression, only disgust coupled with faint amusement. "The heroin. That was you," he said simply.

"Me? You don't hear good. . . . A little girl, maybe bored, maybe just for kicks, gets hold of a bag of the best Turkish—"

"You *conceivably* think you can prove that?"

"The *best* Turkish; over two hundred thousand worth. Maybe she's got a little network of her own. Those fancy girls' schools are a big part of the scene today. You know that, don't you? There was a diplomat's daughter caught a few months ago; you saw that in the papers, no? He didn't have a friend like your friend Mario."

"I asked you a question. Do you really think you could prove anything?"

"You think I couldn't?" De Spadante suddenly turned on Trevayne and spat out the words. "Don't be so dumb. You're dumb, Mr. Arrogance! You think you know everyone your little girl has been seen with? You think I can't give Lieutenant Fowler of the Greenwich Police Department a list of names and places? Who checks? Seventeen isn't that young these days, *amico*. Maybe you read about those rich kids with the nigger organizations, blowing up buildings, making riots. . . . Now, I don't say your kid is *one* of them; but people got to *think*. They see it every day. And two hundred thousand . . ."

Trevayne stood up, his patience at an end. "You're wasting my time, De Spadante. You're cruder—and denser —than I thought. What you're telling me is that you've engineered potential blackmail situations; I'm sure they're well-thought-out. But you've made a serious mistake. Two mistakes. You're out of date, and you don't know your subjects. You know, you're right. Seventeen and nineteen *aren't* that young these days. Think about it. You're part of what the kids can't stand anymore. Now, whether you'll excuse me or not—"

"What about forty-two?"

"What?"

"Forty-two isn't a kid. You got a pretty wife. A well-stacked lady in her forties with plenty of money and maybe a hunger or two she don't get satisfied inside her big ranch house . . . or maybe in her fancy castle on the ocean. A lady who had a big drinking problem a few years ago?"

"You're on dangerous ground, De Spadante."

"You listen, and you listen good! . . . Some of these classy ladies come into town and hang around the East Side saloons, the ones with French or Spanish names. Others head for the artsy-fartsy places in the Village where the rich fags go, too. Lots of studs down there who'll swing both ways for a buck. . . . And then a few of the real genuine articles go to hotels like the Plaza—"

"I warn you!"

"Before they get to the Plaza—where naturally they got reservations—they make a telephone call to a certain number, these ladies do; these genuine articles. No fuss; no bother, no worries at all. Everything very discreet; satisfaction guaranteed. . . . And the games they play! I tell you, *amico*, you wouldn't believe it!"

Trevayne abruptly swung around and started for the door. De Spadante's voice—louder but not loud—stopped him. "I got a sworn affidavit from a very respected hotel security man. He's been around for a long time; he's seen them all. He can spot the genuine articles; he spotted yours. It's a very ugly statement. And it's true. What he saw."

"You're filth, De Spadante." It was all he could think to say.

"I like that better than 'not desirable,' *amico*. It's stronger, more positive, you know what I mean?"

"Have you finished?"

"Just about. I want you to know that the private troubles you got are going to stay very confidential. Your burdens are safe with me. No newspapers, no television or radio broadcasts; everything quiet. You want to know why?"

"I might be able to guess."

"Yeah, sure you can. . . . Because you're going to go back to Washington and wrap up your little subcommittee. Write a nice report that slaps a few wrists and makes a couple of people get fired—we'll tell you who—and call it a day. You got that?"

"And if I refuse?"

"Oh, Christ, *amico*. You want to put your loved ones through all this *rifiuti*. I mean, what the hell, a little old man in Cos Cob and all those pictures of the drunken kid. They'd look terrible in the newspapers. And a matter of two hundred thousand dollars' worth of uncut Turkish— the cops *found* it, you know what I mean? They couldn't say they didn't. Last, your pretty lady at the Plaza; that hotel security—he's a very respected retired police officer —he wrote up exactly what he saw. You don't even want to see it privately. It'd bring back all kinds of things; like the lady's big drinking problem. That was very real; we got a doctor who helped her a few years back. You know how people think. They never really trust an ex-drunk. There's always that possibility that she's not so ex. Or maybe she just substituted another hangup. You know how people think."

"Everything you say would be exposed for what it is. Lies."

"Of course, you deny! . . . But enough of those items are solid, Trevayne. Real *solid*, you know what I mean? . . . And I read in a book once: accusations—especially with a little foundation, some background, a few photographs, they hit page one. Denials, they come later—on page fifty—between salami ads. . . . Take your choice, Mr. Trevayne. But think it over good."

Trevayne watched the slow smile emerge on the fat Sicilian lips; the satisfied hatred in the tiny eyes, surrounded by rolls of flesh.

"I get the idea you've waited a long time for this, De Spadante."

"All my life, you snot-nosed, velvet pig. Now get out of here and do what I tell you. You're just like all the rest."

38

Robert Webster received the telephone call in his White House office and knew it had to be an emergency. The caller said he had a message from Aaron Green and was instructed to deliver it personally. It couldn't wait; Webster was to meet him within the hour. By three o'clock.

The two men agreed on the Villa d'Este restaurant in Georgetown; second floor, cocktail lounge. The Villa d'Este was an insane conglomeration of Victorian pastiche and Italian Renaissance, had six floors, and catered to a tourist luncheon crowd. No one of consequence in Washington arrived at the Villa d'Este until the late-evening hours, when a tourist couldn't get a reservation unless he had a personal introduction from his senator.

Webster arrived first, in itself a bad omen. Bobby Webster made it a point never to be the one waiting. The advantage of immediate control was too often lost while listening to low-keyed but impressive explanations of tardiness.

And so it was when Aaron Green's man finally showed up, fifteen minutes late. He spoke in rapid, short sentences, making his points apologetically but with an unmistakable air of condescension. He'd had a number of other calls to finish; Aaron Green expected him to accomplish one hell of a lot for a single day in Washington.

And now he could allocate the proper time to their immediate concerns.

Webster watched the man, listened to the understated but confident words, and suddenly realized why he felt uncomfortable, anxious. The man from Green was an operator, as he was an operator. He was comparatively young, as he was young. He was on his way up in the labyrinth world of conglomerate economics, as he was on his way up in the contradictory world of power politics. They both spoke well, carried themselves with assurance, had bearings that were at once strong and yet obedient to those to whom obedience was due.

But there was one profound difference between them, and both men knew it; it needed no elaboration. Green's man was dealing from the position of strength; Robert Webster was not and could not.

Something had happened. Something that directly affected Webster's value, his position of influence. A decision had been made somewhere, in some conference or over some very private dinner, that would alter the course of his immediate existence.

The emissary from Green was his first warning and the cause of Bobby Webster's profound sense of anxiety. For he recognized the preliminary stay of his own symbolic execution.

Webster knew he was on the way out. He'd failed to control the necessities; the best he might hope for was to retreat and salvage what he could.

"Mr. Green is very concerned, Bobby. He understands that solutions have been agreed to without his having been consulted. It's not that he expects to be called every time a decision is made, but Trevayne is a sensitive area."

"We're simply discrediting him. Linking him to De Spadante, that's all. Deballing his subcommittee. It's no big deal."

"Perhaps not. But Mr. Green thinks Trevayne might react differently than the way you've anticipated. He might make it a . . . big deal."

"Then Mr. Green hasn't been given an accurate picture. It doesn't make any difference how Trevayne reacts, because there won't be any charges leveled. Only speculations. And none of us will be involved. . . . As we see it, he'll be compromised to the point of ineffectiveness."

"By associating him with De Spadante?"

"More than verbal association. We have photographs—they came out beautifully. They place him unquestionably at the hospital in Greenwich. They're candids, and more damaging the longer they're looked at. . . . Roderick Bruce will release the first of them in two days."

"After De Spadante is taken to New Haven?" Green's

man was staring hard at Webster, his voice skirting the edge of insult.

"That's right."

"De Spadante will be very much in the news then, won't he? Mr. Green understands he's to be removed from the chessboard."

"That decision emanated from his own associates; they consider it imperative. It has nothing to do with us, except that it happens to be advantageous to our objectives."

"Mr. Green isn't convinced of that."

"It's an underworld action. We couldn't stop it if we wanted to. And with those photographs, properly documented by a couple of Greenwich doctors, Trevayne becomes implicated in the entire mess. He's finished."

"Mr. Green thinks that's oversimplified."

"It's not, because no one's going to claim anything. Can't you *see* that?" Webster now utilized the tone of impatient explanation. It was useless.

The conversation was no more than a ritual dance. The best Webster could expect was that Green's man—for his own protection—might carry back the total strategy to Green; that the old Jew would see the benefits and change his mind.

"I'm only an assistant, Bobby. A messenger."

"But you *do* see the advantages." It wasn't a question, but a statement.

"I'm not sure. This Trevayne is a determined man. He might not accept . . . implications and quietly go away."

"Have you ever seen anyone *turned off* in Washington? It's a hell of a sight. He can yell all he cares to, but somehow no one wants to listen. No one wants to get touched by the leper. . . . Even the President."

"What about him? The President."

"The simplest part of the exercise. I'll hold a group session with the aides, and together we'll present a strong case for the President to extricate himself from Trevayne. He'll listen to us; he's got too goddamned many other problems. We'll give him the options of doing it gracefully or with acid. He'll choose the former, of course. There's an election in eighteen months. He'll see the logic. No one'll have to draw pictures."

Green's man looked sympathetically at Webster as he spoke. "Bobby, I'm here to instruct you to call it all off. That was the exact way Mr. Green put it. 'Instruct him to call everything off.' He doesn't care about De Spadante; you say you can't control that anyway. But Trevayne isn't to be touched. . . . That's the word. It's final."

"It's *wrong*. I've thought this out to the last detail. I've spent weeks making sure every goddamn piece falls into place. It's *perfect*."

"*It's out*. There's a whole new set of circumstances now. Mr. Green is meeting with three or four others to clarify everything. . . . I'm sure you'll be apprised."

Webster understood the throw-away quality of the man's last sentence. He wouldn't be apprised of a damn thing unless they wanted something. Nor could he force his way into the newly formed circle. Alliances were being altered, or, conversely, made more interdependent, consolidated. Whichever, he was excluded.

Webster probed for survival clues. "If there are to be any substantial changes of policy, I think I'd better be informed immediately. I don't like to use the bromide, but the White House *is*, after all, where it's *at*."

"Yes. . . . Yes, of course." Green's man looked at his watch.

"A number of questions will be directed at me. From a wide spectrum of influential people. I should have answers."

"I'll tell Mr. Green."

"He should *know* it." Webster watched himself; he didn't want to appear desperate.

"I'll remind him."

He *was* being excluded, and in a manner that was far too cavalier, thought Webster. The White House was being excluded. It was a moment for audacity.

"Do more than 'remind' him. Make it clear that there are a few of us down here who wield pretty big sticks. There are some areas of Genessee Industries that we're more knowledgeable about than anyone else. We like to think of them as our insurance policies."

The man from Green abruptly looked up from the

table and locked his eyes with Webster's. "I'm not sure that's an apt term, Bobby. 'Insurance policies,' I mean. Unless you're thinking about double indemnity; that's expensive."

The moment sustained itself. Green's man was telling Robert Webster of the White House that he, too, could be removed from the chessboard. Webster knew it was time to initiate the beginning of his retreat. "Let's clarify; since there seems to be a lot of that going around. I'm not so concerned for myself; my credentials couldn't be much better. I can go back to Akron and pick and choose. My wife would like that best. And I wouldn't mind one bit. . . . But there are others; they might not be *able* to pick and choose. None of them *has* the White House on his résumé. They could be troublesome."

"I'm sure everything will work out. For all of you. You're experienced people."

"Well, there aren't that many—"

"We know," interrupted the emissary from Aaron Green. The statement implied far more than the understated way it was phrased. "It's time for me to go. I've still got a lot to do today."

"Sure. I'll pay for the drinks."

"Thanks very much." Green's man got up from the table. "You'll get those photographs back from Ród Bruce? Kill any story?"

"He won't like it, but I will."

"Good. We'll be in touch. . . . And, Bobby. About Akron. Why don't you start preparing that résumé."

39

The servants had turned on the table lamps in Aaron Green's glass-enclosed porch with the potted plants everywhere. Outside, toward the rear, two yellowish floodlights lit up the snow-covered lawn—the burlapped shrubbery and the far-off, ghostlike white arbor in the distance. A silver coffee service was on the glass-topped round table between the white wrought-iron furniture, cups and saucers in their places. Several yards away on still another glass-topped table—this one a rectangle, longer, higher, and against the wall—was a selection of liqueurs with crystal brandy glasses off to the side.

The servants had been excused. Mrs. Green had retired to her sewing room upstairs; the lights in the rest of the house, except for the front hall and entrance, were extinguished.

Aaron Green was about to hold a meeting. A meeting with three men, but only one had been a guest for dinner. A Mr. Ian Hamilton.

The other two were driving out to Sail Harbor together. Walter Madison would stop by Kennedy Airport and pick up Senator Alan Knapp, who was flying in from Washington; together they would drive to Sail Harbor. They would arrive around ten o'clock.

They did. Precisely at ten o'clock.

At six minutes past ten the four men entered the glass-enclosed porch.

"I shall pour coffee, gentlemen. The drinks—the brandies—are over there. I do not trust these old hands to tip a bottle into those tiny glasses. I also find it difficult to read the labels; consequently, I do not indulge. . . . Perhaps it's fortunate I can find my chair."

"Absolutely nothing wrong with you but sheer laziness, Aaron." Ian Hamilton laughed, going to the brandy table. "I'll pour."

Walter Madison accepted his brandy and sat at Green's left. Hamilton brought Knapp's drink to the round table and placed it at Green's right; the Senator sat down promptly. Hamilton then pulled back the chair opposite Aaron Green and did the same, not too promptly.

"We could be sitting down for a hand of bridge," said Madison.

"Or a rough game of poker," added Senator Knapp.

"Perhaps baccarat unlimited might be more appropriate." Ian Hamilton raised his glass to Green. "Your health, Aaron. . . . All our healths."

"Also appropriate, my friend," replied Green in his

low voice. "These are times that require the best of health. Health of body and mind. Especially the mind."

They drank, and Knapp was the first to replace his glass on the table. He was impatient but knew that patience was a valued commodity at this table. Still, he was a respected senator, a man this table needed. There was no point in feigning a composure he did not feel. He was not famous for his tact; tact was irrelevant to him.

"I'll put my first card face-up on the table, Mr. Hamilton, Mr. Green. I'm not leaving you out, Walter, but I think your position here is somewhat the same as mine. All we've heard is that Andrew Trevayne is not to be . . . 'taken advantage of' is the best way to put it. Walter and I discussed it in the car. There's no point obscuring that fact. To be frank, I'll be damned if I can understand. Bobby Webster's strategy seemed to me a beautiful piece of work."

Ian Hamilton looked over at Green, and after several seconds he nodded his head. It was a very slight motion; he was giving the old Jew permission to speak.

"Mr. Webster's strategy *was* a beautiful piece of work, Senator," said Green. "As the General's brilliant maneuver might win a battle—to the great rejoicing of his command post—while in another section of the terrain the enemy mounts a blitzkrieg that will win the war."

"You think," asked Walter Madison, "that rendering Andrew completely ineffective . . . isn't sufficient? Who else is fighting us?"

Ian Hamilton spoke. "Trevayne is in a unique position, Walter. He fully understands what we've done and why we've done it. What he may lack in hard evidence he's more than compensated for by his perception of our larger goals."

"I don't understand that," interrupted Knapp quietly.

"I'll answer," said Green, smiling at Hamilton. "We two are not lawyers, Knapp. If we were—I were—I think I'd say that our Mr. Trevayne has only bits and pieces of directly damaging testimony, but volumes of circumstantial evidence. Is that correctly put, Counselor Hamilton?"

"You may go to the head of the class, Aaron. . . . What Trevayne has done is something no one expected he would do. He threw away the book, the legal book. I suspect he threw it away very early in his research. . . . While we were concerned with a thousand legalities, ten thousand items of cost and processing and allocations, Trevayne was going after something else. Individuals. Men in key positions he correctly assumed were representative. Remember, he's a superb administrator; even those who despise him grant him that. He knew there had to be a pattern, a control process. A company as large and diverse as Genessee couldn't function on the executive-board level if one didn't exist. Especially under the circumstances. Strangely enough, Mario de Spadante's people first perceived it. They purposely sent in contradictory information and waited to be called up on it. They weren't. Of course, they didn't know what to do with what they'd discovered. De Spadante crudely began making threats, upsetting everyone he came in contact with. . . . So much for De Spadante."

"I'm sorry, Mr. Hamilton." Knapp leaned forward on the white wrought-iron chair with its floral-print cushions. "Everything you say leads me right back to Bobby Webster's solution. . . . You imply that Trevayne has pieced together information that endangers everything we've worked for; what better moment to discredit him? Discredit him, we discredit his evidence. At least, sufficiently so for our purposes."

"Why not *kill* him?" Aaron Green's deep voice thundered across the table. It was an angry question and stunned Madison and Knapp. Hamilton had no visible reaction. "That shakes you, eh? Why? It is the unspoken thought, perhaps. . . . I've seen death closer than anyone at this table, so it does not shock *me*. But I will tell you why it is not plausible, just as this peddler Webster's solution is not plausible. . . . Such men as Trevayne are more dangerous in death and forced retirement than they are in active life."

"Why?" asked Walter Madison.

"Because they leave *legacies*," answered Green. "They become rallying points for crusaders. They are the martyrs, the symbols. They cause the breeding of discontented rats that multiply and nibble away at your foundations! We have no time to spend stamping out their nests."

Aaron Green's anger so upset him that his old hands shook. Ian Hamilton's voice was calm but nevertheless commanding. "Don't excite yourself, Aaron. Nothing will be accomplished by it. . . . He's right, you know. We haven't the time for such endeavors. Not only are they distracting, they can't succeed. Men like Trevayne keep extensive records. . . . Instead, one must face a fundamental issue. We can neither obscure it nor sidestep it. We must understand and accept our own motives. . . . In light of the record, I primarily address myself to the Senator and Aaron. You arrived late on the scene, Walter; your participation, though immensely valuable, has not been one of long standing."

"I know that," said Madison softly.

"There are many who could call us power brokers, and they would be right. We dispense authority within the body politic. And though there are ego compensations in what we do, we are not driven by our egos to do it. We, of course, believe in ourselves; but only as instruments to gain our objectives. I explained this—abstractly, to be sure—to Trevayne, and I believe he can be convinced of our sincerity."

Knapp had been staring down at the glass tabletop, listening. Suddenly he whipped his head up and looked at Hamilton in disbelief. "You what?"

"Yes, Senator, that's what it came down to between us. Are you shocked?"

"I think you've lost your mind!"

"Why?" asked Aaron Green sharply. "Have you ultimately done something for which you are ashamed, Senator? Are you more concerned for yourself than for our aims? Are you one of us, or are you something else?" Green leaned forward, his hand trembling on the handle of the coffee cup.

"It's not a question of being ashamed. It's simply one of being misjudged, Mr. Green. You act as a private individual; I am an elected representative. Before I'm held accountable, I want the results to be apparent. We haven't reached that point yet."

"We're nearer than you think," said Hamilton quietly, in counterpoint to both Green and Knapp.

"I fail to see any evidence of that," replied the Senator.

"Then you haven't looked around you." Hamilton raised his brandy glass and drank sparingly. "Everything we've touched, every area we've managed, has been the better for our attentions. There can be no denying it. What we've done, in essence, is to build a financial base of such dimensions that it influences whole sections of the country. And wherever that influence has been felt, we've improved the status quo. Minorities—and majorities—are heeded; employment risen; welfare declined; production continued without interruption. As a result, segments of national interest have benefited. Our military posture has been strengthened unquestionably; geographical areas of the economy remain at high-gross-product levels; social reforms in housing, education, and medicine have been promoted painlessly wherever Genessee's imprimatur is found. . . . What we've proved is that we can bring about social stability. . . . Would you deny this summation, Senator? It's what we've worked for."

Knapp was startled. Hamilton's rapid enumeration of points astonished him; gave him a sense of confidence—identification, perhaps—he had not felt before. "I've been too close to the Washington machinery; obviously you have a better view."

"Granted. I'd still like you to answer the question. Would you deny the facts . . . from what you *have* discovered?"

"No, I imagine I wouldn't . . ."

"You *couldn't*."

"All right, 'couldn't.' "

"Then don't you see the corollary? . . . Don't you realize what we've done?"

"You've outlined the accomplishments; I accept them."

"Not just accomplishments, Senator. I've outlined the leadership functions of the executive branch of the government. . . . With *our* help. Which is why, after painstaking consideration and swift but exhaustive analysis, we are going to offer Andrew Trevayne the presidency of the United States."

*   *   *

No one spoke for several minutes. Ian Hamilton and
Aaron Green sat back in their chairs and let the newcomers absorb the information. Finally, Knapp spoke in a
voice laced with incredulity.

"That's the most preposterous statement I've ever
heard. You've got to be joking."

"And you, Walter?" Hamilton turned to Madison, who
sat staring at his glass. "What's your reaction?"

"I don't know," answered the attorney slowly. "I'm
still trying to digest it. . . . I've been close to Andrew for
many years. I think he's an extraordinarily talented
man. . . . But this? I just don't know."

"But you are *thinking*," said Aaron Green, looking
not at Madison but at Knapp. "You are using your imagination. Our 'elected representative' reacts only to 'preposterous.'"

"For good and sufficient reasons!" snapped Alan Knapp.
"He has no political experience; he's not even a registered
member of either party!"

"Eisenhower had no experience," replied Green. "And
both parties tried to recruit him."

"He has no stature."

"Who had less at the beginning than Harry Truman?"
rejoined the Jew.

"Eisenhower had worldwide exposure, popularity. Truman grew in the job he inherited. Irrelevant examples."

"Exposure's no problem today, Senator," interjected
Hamilton with his prepossessing calm. "There are thirteen
months before the national conventions, eighteen before
the election. Within that period of time, I daresay, Andrew Trevayne could be merchandised with extraordinary
effect. He has all the qualifications for maximum results.
. . . The key is not political experience or affiliation—actually, their absence could be an advantage; nor is it his
current stature—which, incidentally, may be more than
you think, Senator. Neither is it that abstraction, popularity. . . . It's voting blocs. Before and after whatever convention we decide to enter. And Genessee Industries will
deliver those blocs."

Knapp started to speak several times but stopped, as

though rethinking his thoughts, trying to find the words to convey his bewilderment. At last he spread his hands down on the glass-topped table; it was a gesture of superimposing control on himself. "Why? Why in God's name would you do it, even consider it?"

"Now you are *thinking*, 'elected representative.'" Aaron Green patted the back of Knapp's left hand. The Senator drew it off the table quickly.

"Put simply, Senator, it's our judgment that Trevayne would make an extremely competent President. Perhaps even a brilliant one. He would, after all, have the time to pursue those aspects of the office few presidents in this century have been afforded. Time to reflect, concentrate on the nation's foreign relationships, its negotiations and long-range policies. . . . Has it ever occurred to you why we are constantly being outflanked by our global adversaries? It's quite simple, you know. We expect *far* too much of the single man sitting in the Oval Office. He's torn in a thousand directions. He has no time to think. The Frenchman Pierre Larousse, I believe, said it best in the nineteenth century. . . . Our form of government is superb, with one significant imperfection. Every four years we must elect God as our President."

Walter Madison watched Hamilton closely. As a good attorney he had spotted the quantum jump, and it wasn't in his training to let it slide by. "Ian, do you think for one minute Trevayne would accept the condition that the majority of domestic problems be handled outside the decision sphere of the presidency?"

"Certainly not." Hamilton smiled. He accepted the forensic challenge. "Because the majority wouldn't be problems. Put another way, major problems wouldn't be allowed to develop, to the degree heretofore experienced. Questions of domestic irritation are something else again. Every President delegates them and makes the proper palliative statements. They're not time-consuming, and they allow for leadership exposure."

"You know you haven't really answered my question, Mr. Hamilton." Knapp got up from his chair and went to the brandy. "It's one thing to say a man will make a President. Good, bad, or brilliant, it's the making that counts first . . . It's something else again to select this or that specific individual as your chosen candidate. That choice has to reflect something other than idealistic appraisal. Under the circumstances, given someone who's displayed such determination to be his own man, I still want to know why it's Trevayne. . . . Yes, Mr. Green, I think it's preposterous!"

"Because when all the fancy talk is finished, Mr. Elected Representative, we have no choice." Green turned in his chair and looked up at Knapp. "You'd like better so preposterous an idea that you're run out of office for a thief."

"My record is spotless."

"Your associations aren't so clean. Take my word." Green turned back to the table and with his trembling hand reached for his cold coffee.

"Such talk is pointless," said Hamilton, for the first time showing anger. "Trevayne would not have been chosen—and you know this, Aaron—if we felt he wasn't qualified. It's been established that he's an extraordinary executive; that's exactly what the presidency requires."

Knapp returned to the table as Aaron Green looked at Hamilton and spoke softly, with immense feeling. "You know what I require. Nothing else concerns me, or will ever concern me. I want no peddlers to interfere with that. *Strength*. That's all."

Walter Madison watched the old man and thought he understood. He'd heard rumors that Green had quietly financed training camps for the Jewish Defense League. He knew now they weren't just rumors. But Madison was disturbed. He turned to Hamilton, cutting off Knapp, who was about to speak.

"Obviously Andrew hasn't been approached. What makes you think he'll accept? Personally, I don't think he will."

"No man of talent and vanity turns his back on the presidency. Trevayne has both. And he should have. If the talent's authentic, the vanity must follow." Hamilton answered Madison but included Knapp. "At first, his reaction will be no different from the Senator's. Preposterous. We'll expect that. But within a matter of days he will be

shown graphically, *professionally*, that it is a feasible concept, that it's really within his grasp. . . . Spokesmen for
labor, the business community, the sciences, will be brought
to him. Leading political figures from all sections of the
country will telephone him, letting him know that they
are most interested—not committed, but interested—in
the possibility of his candidacy. From these exploratory
confrontations will emerge a practical campaign strategy.
Aaron's agency will assume responsibility."

"*Have* assumed it," said Green. "Already three of my
most trusted people are working behind tight-shut doors.
All are the very best, and each knows if there's a leak, he'll
never work again except maybe in a ditch."

Knapp's astonishment grew in proportion to the extraordinary information. "You've actually begun all this?"

"It is our function to stay well ahead of tomorrow,
Senator," answered Hamilton.

"You can't possibly guarantee that labor, business,
political leaders . . . will agree."

"We can, and those we've reached *have*. They've been
contacted in utter sincerity; they've been sworn to confidence until told otherwise. They are part of a grass-roots
groundswell. In many instances, they're most enthusiastic."

"It's . . . it's . . ."

"We know, preposterous." Green completed Knapp's
exclamation. "You think Genessee Industries is managed
by Washington bureaucrats? By idiots? We're talking about
two or three hundred people, maybe a few mayors, governors; our payrolls are several thousand times that."

"What about the House, the Senate? Those are—"

"The House is under control," interrupted Hamilton.
"The Senate? . . . That's why you're here tonight."

"*Me?*" Knapp's hands were once more back on the
glass-topped table in front of him.

"Yes, Senator." Hamilton spoke with calm conviction.
"You're a dedicated member of the Club. You've also got
the reputation of a skeptic. I've seen in print where you've
been called the 'unpredictable skeptic of the Senate.' You're
going to be our key man in the cloakroom."

"Otherwise," added Aaron Green with a gesture,
"poof!"

Senator Knapp did not pursue the subject.

Walter Madison couldn't help but smile at the old Jew, but his smile faded quickly as he spoke. "Let's grant, hypothetically, that everything you say is possible. Even probable. How do you propose to handle the current President? It's my impression that he intends to run for a second term."

"By no means conclusive. His wife and family are very much against it. And remember, Genessee Industries has removed scores of major problems from his concerns. We can easily re-create them. Finally, if it comes to it, we have medical reports that could finish him a month before the election."

"Are they true?"

Hamilton lowered his eyes. "Partially. But I'm afraid that's irrelevant. We have them; that's relevant."

"Second question. If Andrew is elected, how do you control him? How can you stop him from throwing all of you out?"

"Any man who sits in the President's chair learns one supreme lesson instantly," replied Hamilton. "That it's the most pragmatic of all jobs. He needs every bit of help he can get. Instead of throwing us out, he'll come running for assistance, try to convince us to come out of retirement."

"Retirement?" Knapp's confusion was paramount, but Walter Madison's expression conveyed his understanding.

"Yes. Retirement, Senator. Walter knows. You must try to grasp the subtlety. Trevayne would never accept the proposition if he thought it was engineered by Genessee. Our position will be made clear. We'll be reluctant, but ultimately he has our backing, our endorsement; he's one of us. He's a product of the marketplace. Once he's elected, we have every intention of leaving the scene, living out the remainder of our lives in the comforts we've earned. We'll convince him of this. . . . If he needs us, we're there, but we'd rather not be called. . . . Of course, we have no intention of leaving at all."

"And when he learns this," summed up Walter Madison, attorney-at-law, "it's too late. It's the ultimate compromise."

"Exactly," agreed Ian Hamilton.

"My people behind the tight-shut doors have created a very effective campaign phrase. . . . 'Andrew Trevayne, the Mark of Excellence.' "

"I think they stole it, Aaron," said Hamilton.

40

Trevayne read the newspaper story as a wave of relief swept over him. He never imagined that he could be so filled with joy—there was no other word but "joy"—over a man's death, a man's brutal murder. But there it was, and he was consumed with a sense of deliverance.

"Underworld Chief Slain in Ambush Outside New Haven Home."

The story went on to say how Mario de Spadante, while being transferred from an ambulance into his home on Hamden Terrace, was dropped to the ground and fired upon by six men who had been waiting on both sides of De Spadante's house. None of those carrying the stretcher or the others at the scene, presumably the gangster's personal guards, were injured. Thus the police authorities speculated that the killing was a multiple "contract" issued by "bosses" unhappy over De Spadante's expanding associations outside the Connecticut area. It was no secret that De Spadante, whose brother allegedly was killed by an Army officer—a Major Paul Bonner—had displeased Mafia chieftains with his involvement in government construction projects. There seemed to be a general agreement among underworld powers that De Spadante was exceeding his authority and courting widespread danger for organized crime with his Washington endeavors.

As a side issue, the daylight slaying lent considerable credence to Major Paul Bonner's claim that he was assaulted prior to having killed August de Spadante, the brother of the above. Reached in Arlington, Bonner's military defense attorney stated that the New Haven murder was further evidence that his client was caught in the crossfire of a gangland war; that Major Bonner performed outstandingly to protect Andrew Trevayne from attack. Mr. Trevayne, the article pointed out, was chairman of a subcommittee investigating corporate relationships with the Defense Department; the De Spadantes were known to have profited from several Pentagon contracts.

There followed four photographs showing Mario de Spadante in various stages of his career. Two were police identification shots separated by fifteen years; another on a nightclub floor in the early fifties; and one with his brother, August, in which both were standing in front of a construction crane, grinning the grins of Caesars.

It was so tidy, thought Trevayne. The snuffing out of one life removed so much evil. He had not slept—or if he had, it didn't seem so—since leaving De Spadante's hospital bed. He had asked himself over and over again if it was all worth it. And the answer progressively became a louder and louder negative.

He finally had to admit to himself that De Spadante *had* reached him; *had* compromised him. The Italian succeeded because he had forced him to weigh the values, consider the terrible price. The *rifiuti*, as De Spadante had called it. The garbage that would have buried his wife and children, the stench of its conjecture lingering for years.

It wasn't worth it to him. He would not pay that price for a subcommittee he hadn't sought, for the benefit of a President he owed no debt to, for a Congress that allowed such men as De Spadante to buy and sell its influence. Why should he?

Let someone else pay the price.

And now that part of it was finished. De Spadante was finished. He could put his mind back to the subcommittee report he had attacked with such energy after he'd left Chicago. After he'd left Ian Hamilton.

Three days ago nothing else had seemed so necessary, so vital. He had been distracted by Paul Bonner's murder charge, but every minute away from that concern found him back at the report. He'd had the feeling then—three days ago—that time was the most important thing on earth; the report had to be completed and its summary made known to the highest levels of the government as soon as was humanly possible.

Yet now, as he stared down at the Genessee notebooks piled beside the folded newspaper, he found himself strangely reluctant to plunge back into the work he'd set aside three days ago. He'd traveled to and from his River Styx. Like Charon, he'd carried the souls of the dead across the turbulent waters, and now he needed rest, peace. He had to get out from the lower world for a while.

And Genessee Industries was the lower world.

Or was it? Or was it, instead, only the maximum efforts of misguided men seeking reasonable solutions in unreasonable times?

It was only nine-fifteen in the morning, but Trevayne decided to take the rest of the day off. Perhaps one carefree day—one *free* of *care*—with Phyllis was what he needed.

To get the battery charged again.

Roderick Bruce threw the newspaper across the room and swore at the blue velour walls. That hard-on son-of-a-bitch had betrayed him! That Corn Belt butcher had waltzed him, and when the music stopped, kicked him in the balls and run back to the White House!

. . . the slaying lent considerable credence to Major Paul Bonner's claim . . . assaulted prior to allegedly killing . . . caught in the crossfire of a gangland war . . . performed outstandingly . . .

Bruce swept his tiny arm across the breakfast tray, sending the dishes crashing to the floor. He kicked the blankets off the bed—his and Alex's bed—and leaped onto the lime flotaki rug. He could hear the sound of the maid's footsteps; she was running down the outside corridor toward his room, and he shouted at the top of his lungs.

"Stay *out* of here, you black cunt!"

He ripped his Angkor Wat night shirt—the silk sleeping gown given him by Alex—as he pulled it over his head. Naked on the soft rug, his foot touched the upturned coffee cup; he reached down, picked it up, and slammed it against the onyx bedside table.

He sat down at his desk and purposely straightened his bare back so that it was flat, hard against the chair. He kept his muscles taut, his posture rigid. It was an exercise he used often to discipline himself. To gain control of excessive feelings.

He'd shown Alex one night; a rare evening when they'd fought. Over some silly thing that was inconsequential . . . the roommate, that was it. The dirty roommate from Alex's old apartment on 21st Street. The dirty, filthy roommate who wanted Alex to drive him up to Baltimore because he had too much luggage for the train.

They'd fought that night. But Alex finally understood how the dirty, filthy roommate was taking advantage of him, and so he called him up and told him absolutely *no*. After the telephone call, Alex was still upset, so Rod— Roger—showed him his bedroom desk exercise, and Alex began to laugh. It was a happy laugh; Alex was actually giddy. He told Roger that his exercise in discipline was almost pure Hindu Kantamani, an ancient religious punishment for young boys the priests found masturbating.

Bruce pressed his naked back harder into the chair. He could feel the buttons of the blue-velvet upholstery cutting into his flesh. But it was working; he was thinking clearly now.

Bobby Webster had given him two photographs of Trevayne and De Spadante together in De Spadante's hospital room in Greenwich. The first photograph depicted Trevayne seemingly explaining something to the bedridden gangster. The second showed Trevayne looking angry—"disgruntled" was perhaps more accurate—at something De Spadante had just said. Webster had told him to hold them for seventy-two hours. That was important. Three days. Bruce would understand.

Then the following afternoon Webster had called him all over town, trying to find him. The White House aide was in a panic—as much of a panic as he allowed himself. He demanded the photographs back, and before he even heard the agreeable reply, began threatening White House retaliation.

And Webster had sworn to impose executive isolation if *one word* about Trevayne's visit to De Spadante was even *hinted* at in print.

Roderick Bruce relaxed his posture, let his back fall away from the chair. He recalled Webster's exact words when he asked the White House aide if Trevayne or De Spadante or the photographs would have any bearing on Paul Bonner's murder charge.

"None whatsoever. There's no connection; that stands as is. We're controlling that on all sides."

But he hadn't controlled it. He hadn't even been able to manage the Army lawyer defending Bonner. A Pentagon lawyer!

Bobby Webster hadn't lied; he'd lost his clout. He was helpless. He used strong threats, but he hadn't the muscle to carry them out.

And if there was one thing Roger Brewster of Erie, Pennsylvania, had learned in the cosmopolitan world of the Washington orbit, it was to take advantage of a helpless man, especially one who'd recently lost his muscle. Specifically, one who was helpless and had lost his muscle and was close to power and closer still to panic.

Behind such a man was usually a hell of a story. And Bruce knew how to get it. He'd made copies of the photographs.

Brigadier General Lester Cooper watched the man with the attaché case walk down the path to his car. The Vermont snow was deep and the path not shoveled well. But the driveway was fine. The snow plow had done a fine job all the way out to the road. And the man's car was a heavy automobile with huge snow tires. He'd be all right.

Such men were always all right. Men who worked in skyscrapers for other men like Aaron Green. They moved in cloud-high offices with soft carpeting and softer lights. They spoke quietly into telephones and referred to complex figures—most often with decimal points and percentages within those decimals.

They dealt in the subtleties Brigadier General Lester Cooper abhorred.

He watched the large automobile turn around in the

small parking area and start off down the drive. The man waved, but there was no smile, no sense of friendliness. No thanks for having been treated hospitably in spite of the fact that he had arrived without warning, without announcement.

The subtleties.

And the news he brought to the Rutland farmhouse was a subtlety Lester Cooper felt he would never understand. But then, they didn't ask him to understand, just be aware of, follow instructions. For the good of everyone. The Pentagon would benefit more than any other area of the government; he was assured of that.

Andrew Trevayne, President of the United States.

It was incredible.

It was preposterous.

But if the man from Aaron Green said it was a realistic consideration, Andrew Trevayne was halfway to his inauguration.

Lester Cooper turned away from the path and started back toward the house. As he approached the thick Dutch door he changed his mind and veered off to the left. The powdered snow was lying loose above a hard base, and his feet sank in up to his ankles. He had no boots or galoshes on, but the cold wetness didn't bother him. There was the winter of forty-four, when he hopped off tanks into the snow-cold mud, and it hadn't bothered him then either. Patton, George Patton, kept yelling at him: " . . . Cooper, you stupid son-of-a-bitch! Get the goddamn regulation boots on! We're barrel-assing into a Kraut winter, and you act like it was springtime in Georgia! Take that shit-eating grin off your face!"

He'd yelled right back at George; always smiling, of course. Boots inhibited his tank driving. Shoes were fine.

Patton.

This would have been beyond him, too.

Cooper reached the end of the backyard lawn, fully covered with virgin snow. The sky was dull; one could hardly see the mountains in the distance. But they were there, and not treacherous, and he would look at them every day for the rest of his life—in a very short time.

As soon as he organized the logistics of Aaron Green's

strategy—his part of it, the military end. It wouldn't be difficult; the combined services were all aware of the enormous contributions of Genessee Industries. They were also aware that the future held the greatest military promise in history if Genessee became—as they wanted it to become—the true civilian spokesman for all of them. And if Andrew Trevayne was Genessee's candidate, that was all that mattered.

The word would be passed throughout every post, airfield, training center, and naval station in the world. No identification yet, only the alert. The advance cue that a name would be forthcoming, and that name was the man Genessee Industries and the Pentagon wanted as President. Schedules with proper allocations of space and time should be prepared, allowing for indoctrination courses for all officers and enlisted men and women. Under the heading of "Current Affairs," of course. Separate facilities for regular and reserve personnel, as approaches would vary considerably.

It could be done. None of the uniformed services wanted to slide back to the days before Genessee Industries was such a large part of its line of supply.

And when the order came to release the name, Xeroxes and printing presses and mimeograph machines in all parts of the earth where the American serviceman was stationed or at sea would be activated around the clock. From Fort Dix, New Jersey, to Bangkok, Thailand; from Newport News to Gibraltar.

The military could deliver over four million votes.

Lester Cooper wondered if it would come to that. Would it really be Andrew Trevayne?

And why?

It would have been comforting to call Robert Webster and find out what he knew; that wasn't possible now. The man from Aaron Green had made it clear.

Webster was frozen out.

Of course, no one was to be told anything yet. But Bobby Webster wasn't even to be *talked* to. About *anything*. Cooper wasn't to initiate or accept any communications whatsoever from Webster.

He wondered what Webster had done.

It didn't matter. He wasn't even curious any longer, if the truth were known. He just wanted his part over with so he could come back to Rutland and spend the days at peace.

No more subtleties.

He just didn't care; he'd do the job for Green—he owed him that. Owed it to Genessee Industries and all his memories, his ambitions.

He even owed it to Paul Bonner, the poor son-of-a-bitch. Bonner was a sacrifice, a necessary casualty, as he understood it.

His only hope was, of all things, executive clemency. From President Trevayne.

Wasn't that ironic?

The goddamn subtleties. . . .

41

"Mr. Trevayne?"

"Yes."

"Bob Webster here. How are you?"

"Fine. And you?"

"A little shook up, I'm afraid. I think I led you into a rotten situation, a very bad scene."

"What's the matter?"

"Before we go into it, I've got to make one thing clear; I mean, I have to *emphasize* it . . . *I'm* the one responsible. Nobody else. Do you understand?"

"I do. . . . I think I do."

"Good. That's damned important."

"Now I'm sure I do. What is it?"

"Your visit to Greenwich. To De Spadante the other day. You were seen."

"Oh? . . . Is that a problem?"

"There's more, but that's primarily it."

"Why's it so serious? We didn't advertise, that's true; on the other hand, we didn't try to hide it."

"You didn't mention it to the papers, though."

"I didn't think it was necessary. The office put out a short statement that violence wasn't the answer to anything. That's what they carried. Sam Vicarson issued it; I approved it. There's still nothing to hide."

"Perhaps I'm not making myself clear. It looks as though you and De Spadante held a secret meeting. . . . There were photographs taken."

"What? Where? I don't remember any photographer. Of course, there were a lot of people in the parking lot. . . ."

"Not in the parking lot. Inside the room."

"Inside the room? What the hell . . . Oh? Oh, good God! Jujubes."

"What was that?"

"Nothing. . . . What about the photographs?"

"They're damaging. I saw a copy. Two copies, actually. You and De Spadante looked like you were engrossed in heavy conversation."

"We were. Where did you see them?"

"Rod Bruce. He's the one who's got them."

"Who from?"

"We don't know. He won't reveal his sources; we've tried before. He's planning to release everything tomorrow. He's threatened to make sure you're linked to De Spadante. And that's bad for Bonner, incidentally."

"Well . . . what do you want me to do? Obviously you've got something in mind."

"As we see it, the only way to deflate the story is for you to speak first. Issue a statement that De Spadante wanted to see you; you saw him two days before he was killed. You wanted the information public for Major Bonner's sake. . . . Make up whatever you like about what was said. We've checked the room; there weren't any bugs."

"I'm not sure I understand. What's Bruce's point? How does Paul fit in?"

"I *told* you. . . . Sorry, it's been a rotten morning over here. . . . Bruce thinks it's another hook into Paul Bonner. If you and De Spadante were still talking to each other . . . it's not very likely he was out to kill you a week ago as Bonner claims."

"I see. . . . All right, I'll issue a statement. And I'll take care of Bruce."

Trevayne held down the button for several seconds, released it, and dialed a number. "Sam Vicarson, please. Mr. Trevayne calling. . . . Sam, it's time for Bruce. No, not you. Me. . . . Find out where he is and call me back. I'm home. . . . No, I won't reconsider. Call me as soon as you can. I want to see him this afternoon."

Trevayne replaced the phone on the bedside table and looked over at his wife, who was in her slip by the dresser, putting the final touches on her makeup. She watched him in the mirror.

"I got the gist of that. Something tells me our day off, antique-wandering, just got postponed."

"Nope. Fifteen or twenty minutes, that's all. You can wait in the car."

Phyllis walked over to the bed and laughed as she pointed her finger at the rumpled blankets and sheets. "I've heard that before. You're a beast, Mr. Trevayne— you dash home from the office, ravish an unsullied maiden, of indeterminate years—plying her with promises; then, the minute your lusts are satisfied and you have a nap, you start telephoning. . . ."

Andrew pulled her down on his lap, feigning a melodramatic grab for her breasts. He touched them, caressed them alternately as she kissed his ear. Their laughter subsided as he gently rolled her off his legs back onto the bed.

"Oh, Andy, we can't."

"We certainly can. It'll take Sam the better part of an hour." He stood and unbuckled his trousers as Phyllis pulled up the sheet, flipping over a side, waiting for him.

"You're incorrigible. And I love it. . . . Who are you going to see?"

"A nasty little man named Roderick Bruce," he answered as he removed his shirt and shorts and got into the bed.

"The newspaperman?"

"He wouldn't approve of us."

*   *   *

Bobby Webster folded his arms in front of him on the desk. He lowered his head and closed his eyes and knew he was very close to tears. He'd locked his office door; no one could barge in on him. Half-consciously he wondered why the tears did not come. The semiconscious answer was so appalling he rejected it. He'd lost the ability to cry . . . to cry out.

Reductio ad manipulatem.

Was there such a phrase? There should be. The years of contrivance; the untold, unremembered, unaccounted for—hundreds, thousands?—plots and counterplots.

Will it work?

That was all that mattered.

The human factor was only an *X* or a *Y*, to be considered or discarded as the case may be. Certainly not taken for more than that, more than part of a formula.

Even himself.

Bobby Webster felt the welling of tears in his eyes. He was going to cry. Uncontrollably.

It was time to go home.

Trevayne walked down the thickly carpeted hallway to the short flight of steps underneath the small sign printed in Old English: "The Penthouse; Roderick Bruce."

He climbed the five steps, approached the door, and pushed the button, causing inordinately loud chimes to be heard beyond the black-enameled entrance with the shiny brass hardware. He could hear muffled voices inside; one was agitated. Roderick Bruce.

The door was opened, and a large black maid in a starched white uniform stood imposingly, forbiddingly in the small foyer. She blocked any view beyond her.

"Yes?" she asked in a lilting dialect formed somewhere in the Caribbean.

"Mr. Bruce, please."

"Is he expecting you?"

"He'll want to see me."

"I'm sorry. Please leave your name; he'll be in touch with you."

"My name is Andrew Trevayne, and I'm not leaving until I see Mr. Bruce."

The maid started to close the door; Trevayne was about to shout when suddenly Roderick Bruce darted into view like a tiny ferret from a hidden nest. He'd been listening from a doorway several yards away.

"It's all right, Julia!" The huge maid gave Trevayne the benefit of a last, unpleasant look, turned, and walked rapidly down the hall out of sight. "She's Haitian, you know. Her six brothers are all Ton Ton Macoute. It's a cruel streak that runs in the family. . . . What do you want, Trevayne?"

"To see you."

"How did you get up here? The doorman didn't ring through."

"He thinks I'm seeing another tenant. Don't bother to trace it down; my office arranged it. The other party doesn't know anything."

"The last time we talked, you threatened me, if I remember correctly. In your office. Now, you come to my office, to me; and you don't look so menacing. Am I to assume you're here to make a trade? Because I'm not sure I'm interested."

"I don't feel menacing; I feel sad. But you're right. I'm here to make a trade. . . . Your kind of trade, Bruce."

"You don't have anything I want; why should I listen?"

Trevayne watched the little man with the small, deep-set eyes and the confident, tiny mouth pursed in satisfaction. Andy felt sick to his stomach as he said the name quietly.

"Alexander Coffey."

Roderick Bruce stood there motionless. His tight jaw slackened, his lips parted, and his face lost all poise of arrogance.

PART 4

42

It seemed preposterous.

It *was* preposterous.

And the most preposterous aspect of it was that no one wanted anything—except his commitment. That had been made totally clear; no one expected him to change one word of the subcommittee report. It was anticipated that he would complete it, present copies to the President, the Congress, and the Defense Allocations Commission and be thanked by a grateful government. Nothing altered, nothing compromised.

Chapter closed.

Another chapter about to begin.

It didn't seem to matter that the report was viciously uncompromising; he hadn't concealed the fact. It had even been suggested that the more severe the judgments, the greater stature it lent his proposed candidacy.

Candidacy.

A candidate for the nomination of President of the United States.

Preposterous.

But it wasn't preposterous at all, they'd insisted. It was the logical decision of an extraordinary man who'd spent five months, when the report was finished, making an independent study of the country's most massively complicated problem. It was time for an extraordinary man unwedded to political harems; the nation cried out for an individual dramatically separated from the intransient positions of doctrinaire politics. It needed a healer; but more than just a healer. It demanded a man who was capable of facing a giant challenge, of assembling the facts and weeding the truth from myriad deceits.

That was his track record, they'd told him.

At first, he thought Mitchell Armbruster was mad, desperately trying to flatter with such excess that his words nullified his intent. But Armbruster had been firm. The senior Senator from California readily admitted that the idea seemed grotesque to him too when first proposed by a nucleus of the National Committee, but the longer he had thought of it, the more plausible it had become—for men of his political inclinations. The President, whom he supported more than he opposed, was not of his party; Armbruster's party had no viable prospects, only pretenders. They were tired men, familiar men, men like himself who'd had their chance at the brass ring and failed to grasp it. Or younger ones who were too brash, too irreverent to appeal to the classic middle. The middle American really didn't want to "rap" or be "right on."

Andrew Trevayne could cross the lines, fill the vacuum. There was nothing preposterous about that; it was eminently practical. It was political—within the craft of the possible that was politics. This was the National Committee's argument. It was sound.

But what of the report? The findings and judgments of the subcommittee weren't compiled in such a way as to win partisan support. And there would be no alterations made for any reasons; he was adamant about that.

So he should be, had been' Armbruster's unexpected reply. The report of the Defense Allocations subcommittee was just that. A report. It was to be filed with the proper committees in the Senate and the House and, of course, the President. Its recommendations would be weighed by both the legislative and the executive; the prosecutable data handed directly to the Justice Department, and where indictments were called for, they would follow.

And Genessee Industries?

The major conclusion of the subcommittee report branded the company as a government unto itself, with powers political and economic that were unacceptable in a democracy. What of this judgment? What of the men responsible? What of men like Ian Hamilton who controlled, and men like Mitchell Armbruster who benefited?

The Senator from California had smiled sadly and restated the assurance of indictments where they were called for. He did not believe he had committed illegal acts. We were still a nation of laws, not insupportable speculations. He would stand on his record.

As for Genessee Industries, neither the Senate, the House, nor the President would settle for less than complete reforms. Obviously, they were mandatory. Genessee Industries was in large measure dependent on government purchases. If the company had abused the resultant privileges to the degree Trevayne believed, it would be severely curtailed until those reforms were instituted.

Andrew should sleep on the idea; say nothing, do nothing. It might all dissolve. Often these conjectures were mere flurries, political desperations. But the Senator, speaking for himself, had come to believe it made great sense.

There would be other conversations. Other meetings. And there were.

The first took place at the Villa d'Este in Georgetown. In a private room on the sixth floor. Seven men had gathered together—all of the same party, with the exception of Senator Alan Knapp. Senator Alton Weeks of the Eastern Shore of Maryland—still wearing the blazer Trevayne remembered from the closed Senate hearing—took command.

"This is merely exploratory, gentlemen; I, for one, will need considerable enlightenment. . . . Senator Knapp, who is with us out of a bipartisan spirit, has asked that he be allowed to speak and then leave. His remarks will be confidential, of course."

Knapp leaned forward on the huge banquetlike table, his palms pressed down on the damask cloth. "Thank you, Senator. . . . Gentlemen, my good friend and colleague from across the aisle, Mitchell Armbruster"—Knapp smiled a short noncommittal smile at Armbruster, who was at his side—"told me of this meeting in response to a query of mine. As I'm sure you realize, the cloakroom has been alive with quiet rumors that a very dramatic announcement might be forthcoming. When I learned further the nature of this announcement, I felt that you should be aware of a little drama going on over in our section. Because, gentlemen, there's been an unexpected turn of events that might have bearing on your discussion this evening. I tell you not only in a bipartisan spirit, but because I share with you the concern with the direction this country takes, especially in these times. . . . The President very likely will not seek a second term."

There was silence around the table. Slowly, without emphasis, but with consciousness, each man looked at Andrew Trevayne.

Shortly thereafter Knapp left the private room, and the process of dissecting Andrew began.

It lasted nearly five hours.

The second meeting was shorter. Barely an hour and a half, but infinitely more extraordinary to Trevayne. In attendance was the junior Senator from Connecticut, an old-middle-aged man from West Hartford whose record was lackluster but whose appetites were reputed to be varied. He'd come to the meeting to announce his retirement; he was going back into private life. His reasons were bluntly financial. He'd been offered the presidency of a large insurance firm, and it wasn't fair to his family to refuse.

The Governor of Connecticut was prepared to offer Trevayne the appointment—provided, of course, that Andrew immediately enroll in the party. "Immediately" meant within the month. Before the fifteenth of January.

By fulfilling the unexpired Senate term Trevayne would be propelled into the national spotlight. His political springboard was assured.

It had happened before; to lesser men, usually. The extraordinary man could capitalize on it brilliantly. The forum was ready-made. Positions could be established swiftly, with strength. Papers would be issued, making irrevocably clear the beliefs of Andrew Trevayne.

For the first time, Andrew faced the concrete reality.

It *was* possible.

Yet what were his beliefs? Did he believe in the checks and balances and independent judgments he so readily espoused? Did he believe—really believe—that the Washington talent was superior talent, needing only to be freed from contemptible influences such as Genessee Industries? And was he capable of leading that superior talent? Was he strong enough? Could he impose the strength of his own convictions on an immensely powerful adversary?

Much had been made at the Villa d'Este meeting of his work for the State Department. The conferences in Czechoslovakia, where he'd brought seemingly implacable opponents together.

But Andy knew that Czechoslovakia was not the test at all.

The test was Genessee Industries.

Could he himself—alone—bring the company to heel? That was the test he wanted, needed.

43

Paul Bonner stood at attention as Brigadier General Cooper came through the door of his small room in Arlington. Cooper waved his hand, half in salute, half in a gesture of weariness, indicating that Bonner should relax, sit down again.

"I can't stay long, Major. I'm due at O.M.B. shortly; there's always a budget crisis, isn't there?"

"As far back as I can remember, sir."

"Yes. . . . Yes. Sit down. If I don't, it's only because I've been sitting all day. And most of this past weekend. I've been up to our place in Rutland. Sometimes it's even more lovely with the snow. You should visit us there sometime."

"I'd like that."

"Yes. . . . Yes. Mrs. Cooper and I would like it, too."

Paul sat down in the chair by his bare steel desk, leaving the single armchair for the General. But the Brigadier would not sit down. Cooper was nervous, agitated, unsure of himself.

"I gather you haven't brought very good news, General."

"I'm sorry, Major." Cooper looked down at Paul, his mouth drawn, his brow wrinkled. "You're a good soldier, and everything will be done for you that can be done. We expect you'll be acquitted of the murder charge. . . ."

"That's nothing to be sorry about." Bonner grinned.

"The newspapers, especially that little prick Bruce, have stopped demanding your neck."

"I'm grateful. What happened?"

"We don't know, and nobody wants to ask. Unfortunately, it will have no bearing."

"On what?"

Cooper walked to the small double window overlooking the BOQ courtyard. "Your acquittal—if it's that—will be in a civil criminal court with military as well as civilian attorneys. . . . You are still subject to an Army court-martial. The decision has been made to proceed with dispatch immediately following your trial."

"*What?*" Bonner got out of his chair slowly. The gauze around his throat was stretched as his neck muscles expanded in anger. "On what basis? You can't try me twice. If I'm acquitted . . . I'm acquitted!"

"Of murder. Not of gross neglect of duty. Not of disregarding orders, thus placing yourself at the scene of the trouble." Cooper continued to look out the window. "You had no right being where you were, Major. You might have jeopardized the safety of Trevayne and his housekeeper. And you involved the United States Army in areas beyond its province, thus impugning our motives."

"That's goddamn double-talk!"

"That's the goddamn truth, soldier!" Cooper whipped around from the window. "Pure and simple. *You* may have been shot at, legally constituting self-defense. I hope to Christ we can prove that. No one else was!"

"They've got the Army car. We *can* prove it."

"The Army car. That's the point! Not Trevayne's car, not Trevayne. . . . Goddamn, Bonner, can't you see? There are too many other considerations. The Army can't afford you any longer."

Paul lowered his voice as he stared at the Brigadier. "Who's going to do the shithouse detail, General? You? . . . I don't think you're up to it, *sir*."

"I won't say that's not called for, Major. From your point of view, I suppose it is. . . . However, it may have struck you that I was under no obligation to come here this afternoon."

Bonner realized the truth of Cooper's statement. It would have been much simpler for everyone except him had the General said nothing. "Why did you, then?"

"Because you've been through enough; you deserve better than you're getting. I want you to know I know that. Whatever the outcome, I'll make sure you'll . . . still be able to come and visit a retired superior officer in Rutland, Vermont."

So the General *was* getting out, thought Paul. The commander wasn't commanding anymore, just making his last deals. "Which means you'll keep me out of the stockade."

"I promise you that. I've been given assurance."

"But I lose the uniform?"

"Yes. . . . I'm sorry. We're approaching a very sensitive situation. . . . We have to go by the book. No deviations. We can't afford the Army's motives to be subject to question. We can't be accused of covering up."

"There's that double-talk again, General. You're not very good at it, if you don't mind my saying so."

"I don't mind, Major. I've tried, you know. I've tried to get better at it during the past seven or eight years. I don't seem to take to it; I just get worse. I like to think it's one of the better traits of us old-line men."

"What you're telling me is the Army wants me conveniently tucked away somewhere. Out of sight."

Brigadier Cooper slumped into the armchair, his legs extended, the repose position of a combat officer in his tent. The way most of them slept after a rotten day at a fire base. "Out of sight, out of mind, out of the picture, Major. . . . If possible, out of the country; which I will propitiously suggest to you, once the court-martial is commuted."

"Jesus! It's all been programmed, hasn't it?"

"There's one possibility, Bonner. It struck me as amusing the other day, around noontime in my backyard . . . with all the snow. Not funny, just ironic."

"What is it?"

"You might get a presidential reprieve. An executive reversal, I think it's called nowadays. Isn't that ironic?"

"How would that be possible?"

Brigadier General Cooper got out of the armchair and walked slowly back to the window overlooking the courtyard.

"Andrew Trevayne," he said quietly.

Robert Webster didn't say good-bye to anyone for the simple reason that no one other than the President and the head of the White House staff knew he was leaving.

The sooner the better.

The press release would read that Robert Webster of Akron, Ohio, for nearly three years a special assistant to the President, was relinquishing his post for reasons of health. The White House reluctantly accepted his resignation, wishing him well.

His audience with the President took exactly eight minutes, and as he was leaving the Lincoln Room he could feel the intense stare of the Man's eyes on his back.

The Man hadn't believed a word, thought Webster. Why should he have? Even the truth had sounded hollow. The words had tumbled forth, expressing, if nothing else, an exhaustion that was real; but the reality was obscured by his trying to explain it. That was hollow, false.

"Maybe you're temporarily burnt out, Bobby," the President had suggested. "Why not take a leave of absence, see how you feel in a few weeks? The pressure gets rough; I know that."

"No, thank you, sir," he'd replied. "I've made my decision. With your permission, I'd like to make the break final. My wife isn't happy here. I'm not either, really. We want to start raising a family. But not in Washington. . . . I think I strayed too far from the barn, sir."

"I see. . . . So you really want to go back to the hinterlands, raise kids, and be able to walk the streets at night. Is that it?"

"I know it sounds corny, but I guess it is."

"Not corny. The American dream, Bobby. Your talents have helped make it possible for millions of others. No reason why you shouldn't have your share of the dream."

"That's very generous of you, sir."

"No, you've sacrificed. You must be damned forty now . . ."

"Forty-one."

"Forty-one and still no children . . ."

"There just wasn't the time."

"No, of course, there wasn't. You've been very dedicated. And your lovely wife."

Webster knew then that the Man was toying with him; he didn't know why. The President didn't like his wife.

"She's been very helpful." Webster felt he owed his wife that, selfish bitch or no.

"Good luck, Bobby. I don't think you'll need luck, though. You're very resourceful."

"Working here has opened a lot of doors, Mr. President. I have you to thank for that."

"That pleases me. . . . And reminds me, there's a revolving door in the lobby, isn't there?"

"What, sir?"

"Nothing. Nothing at all. It's unimportant . . . Goodbye, Bobby."

Robert Webster carried the last of his checked-out effects to his car in the west parking lot. The President's cryptic remark bothered him, but there was relief in knowing that it wasn't necessary to dwell on it. He didn't have to; he didn't care. No longer would he have to analyze and reanalyze a hundred cryptic remarks every time he or the office faced a problem. It was more than relief; he felt a sense of exhilaration. He was out of it.

Oh, Christ, what a magnificent feeling!

He pulled his car up to the sentry box by the gate and waved at the guard. It would be the last time. Tomorrow morning the gate would get the word. Robert Webster was no longer a fixture at the White House, his plastic pass with the sharp photograph and the brief description of his identifying marks no longer valid. Even the guards would ask questions. He was always polite and cheerful with the White House detachment. He never knew when it might be necessary to stretch a time-out check at either end. Cop a little extra time for himself; no big deal, just a few minutes—ten or fifteen, perhaps—so he could "belt down an extra martini" or "avoid some son-of-a-bitch." The gate was always cooperative. They couldn't understand why someone like Bobby Webster ever worried about check-outs, but they accepted his bitchy comments about ducking this or that meeting. What the hell, they had their lousy inspections; Webster had his lousy meetings. Besides, he got them autographs.

How many slightly altered check-outs had there been? How many times had he managed those invaluable extra minutes in which startling information would come over the Teletype—information he'd use but be perfectly capable of proving he could not have received.

The Operator.

Everything slightly altered. For Genessee Industries.

No more. The Operator was out of business.

He sped off down Pennsylvania Avenue, oblivious to the car, a gray Pontiac, that took up the position behind him.

Inside the gray Pontiac, the driver turned to his companion.

"He's going too fast. He's liable to get a ticket."

"Don't lose him."

"Why not? It doesn't make any difference."

"Because Gallabretto *said* so! That makes the difference. Every minute we know where he is, who he meets."

"It's all a lot of shit. There's no contract till he gets to Ohio. To Akron, Ohio. Pick him up easy there."

"If Willie Gallabretto says we stay on, we stay on. I used to work for Gallabretto's uncle. Look what happened to him."

Ambassador William Hill paused in front of a framed, autographed cartoon on the wall of his study. It depicted a spindly-legged "Big Billy" as a puppeteer holding strings tied to small recognizable models of past presidents and secretaries of state. The puppeteer was smiling, pleased that the puppets were dancing to the tune of his choice, the written notes of which were ballooned above his head.

"Did you know, Mr. President, that it was a full year

after this abomination appeared that I learned the music was 'Ring-Around-the-Rosy'?"

The President laughed from across the room, seated in the heavy leather armchair that was his usual spot when visiting the Ambassador. "Your artist friend wasn't very kind to the rest of us. He added injury to insult. If I remember correctly, the last line of that ditty is 'all fall down.' "

"It was years ago. You weren't even in the Senate then. He wouldn't have dared to include you anyway." Hill walked over to the chair opposite the President and sat down. "If *I* remember correctly, this is where Trevayne was seated when last here. Perhaps I'll have some psychic flashes."

"Are you sure it wasn't in this chair? I wasn't with you then."

"No, I recall. As most people who've been here with the two of us, he avoided that chair. Afraid of being presumptuous, I think."

"He may be overcoming his shyness . . ." The telephone rang on Hill's table-desk, cutting the President's words short.

"Very well, Mr. Smythe. I'll tell him. Thank you."

"Jack Smythe?" asked the President.

"Yes. Robert Webster and his wife left on the Cleveland flight. Everything's fine. That was the message."

"Good."

"May I ask what it means?"

"Certainly. Surveillance showed that Bobby's been followed since leaving the White House gate two nights ago. I was worried about him. And curious, of course."

"So was somebody else."

"Probably for the same reason. Intelligence identified one of the men as a small-time leg-man, a 'shadow,' I think we called it in comic-book jargon. . . . He didn't have any more to report than our people did. Webster didn't meet with anyone, see anyone, but the movers."

"Telephone?"

"Airline reservations and a brother in Cleveland who'll drive Bobby and his wife down to Akron. . . . Oh, and a Chinese restaurant. Not a very good one."

"Probably filled with Chinamen." Hill laughed softly as he returned to the chair. "He knows nothing about the Trevayne situation?"

"I don't know. All I know is, he's running. Maybe he told the truth. He said he strayed too far from the barnyard, that it all became too much."

"I don't believe it." Hill leaned his gaunt frame forward on the chair. "What about Trevayne? Would you like me to bring him in for a chat?"

"Oh, Billy! You and your goddamn puppet strings. I come over for a quiet chat, a restful drink, and you keep bringing up business."

"I think *this* business is extremely important, Mr. President. Even vital. Shall I call him in?"

"No. Not yet. I want to see how far he'll go, how bad the fever's got him."

44

"When did they approach you?" asked Phyllis Trevayne, absently poking one of the huge logs in the High Barnegat fireplace.

"A little over three weeks ago," replied Andy, sitting on the couch. He could see the wince of hurt around her eyes. "I should have told you, but I didn't want you concerned. Armbruster said it might only be a . . . political desperation."

"You took them seriously?"

"Not at first; of course not. I practically threw Armbruster out of my office, accused him of all kinds of things. He said he was speaking for a caucus in the National Committee; that he was initially opposed to the idea and still not convinced . . . but coming around."

Phyllis hung the poker on the fireplace brick and turned to Trevayne. "I think it's crazy. It's a blatant device having something to do with the subcommittee, and I'm surprised you went this far."

"The only reason I went this far is that no one yet has

hinted that I alter the report. . . . That's what intrigued me. I suppose I couldn't believe it. I've been waiting for someone, anyone, to bring up the slightest suggestion . . . and I was going to burn them. But no one has."

"Did *you* bring it up?"

"Continuously. I told Senator Weeks that he was liable to be embarrassed. He looked down his patrician nose and said he was perfectly capable"—here Andy mimicked the Eastern Shore politician—"of answering any questions the subcommittee might raise, but that was another matter. No part of the issue at hand."

"Brave fellow. . . . But even so, why you? Why you at this particular time?"

"It's not very flattering, but there doesn't seem to be anyone else. At least that's what their polls tell them. 'No viable contenders on the political horizon' was the way they put it. The heavyweights are worn out, and the young ones are lightweights. Or they wear their pants too tight or they're Jewish or Latin or black or some goddamn thing that makes them unacceptable to our democratized election process. . . . As Paul Bonner would say, 'Horseshit!' "

Phyllis walked-wandered back to the couch, stopping along the way to take a cigarette from a box on the coffee table. Andy lit it for her.

"That's unfortunately perceptive." She sat down next to her husband.

"What?"

"They're right. I was trying to think who they had."

"I didn't know you were an authority."

"Don't kid yourself, Mr. . . . What did that dreadful man call you? . . . Mr. Arrogance. . . . I haven't missed an election in years."

Trevayne laughed. "The seer of High Barnegat. We'll rent you to Nick the Greek."

"No, really. I have a system. It works. Take the name of a candidate and put the word 'President' in front. It either sounds real, you know, *all right;* or it doesn't. The only time I had trouble was in sixty-eight. It didn't sound right with either one."

"A general consensus . . ."

"Of course, it's a little more difficult when there's an incumbent; then you have to split hairs. Which brings to mind, the man in there now sounds pretty okay. . . . I thought you liked him."

"He's not going to run again."

Phyllis' controlled expression changed. She looked at Andy and spoke quietly, urgently. "You didn't tell me that."

"There are several things I haven't—"

"You should have told me that first."

Trevayne understood. The game was no longer a game. "I'm sorry. I was taking things in order of sequence."

"Try in order of importance."

"All right."

"You're not a politician; you're a businessman."

"I'm neither, really. My business interests are secure but peripheral. For the past five years I've worked for the State Department and one of the largest foundations in the world. If you want to categorize me, I'd go under the label of . . . 'public service,' I suppose."

"No! You're rationalizing."

"Hey, Phyl. . . . We're talking, not fighting."

"Talking? No. Andy, *you've* been talking. For weeks; with other people, not with me."

"I told you. It was too loose, too speculative to raise hopes. Or doubts."

"And now it isn't?"

"I'm not sure. I just know it's time we talked about it. . . . I gather I've lost your vote."

"You certainly have."

"Make a hell of a story. Probably the first time in history."

"Andy, be serious. You're not . . . not . . ." Phyllis stammered, unsure of the words but certain of her feelings.

"Not presidential timber," added Trevayne gently.

"I didn't say that; I don't mean that. You're not a . . . political animal."

"I'm told that's a plus for our side. I'm still not sure what it means."

"You're not that kind of extrovert. You're not the sort

of man who goes through crowds shaking hands, or makes a dozen speeches a day, or calls governors and congressmen by their first names when you don't know them. You're not comfortable doing those things, and that's what candidates do!"

"I've thought about . . . those things, and you're right, I don't like them. But maybe they're necessary; perhaps by doing them you prove something quite apart from position papers and executive decisions. It's a form of stamina. Truman said that."

"My God," said Phyllis softly, making no attempt to hide her fear. "You *are* serious."

"That's what I'm trying to tell you. . . . I'll know more on Monday. On Monday I'm meeting with Green and Hamilton. On Monday it could all blow up."

"You need their support? Do you want it?" The questions were asked with distaste.

"They wouldn't support me in a race with Mao Tsetung. . . . No, Phyl, I'm going to find out how good I really am."

"I'll pass that. . . . Let's stick to why Andy Trevayne suddenly thinks he's in the race for such a position."

"Can't you say the word, Phyl? It's called the presidency."

"No, I won't say it. It scares me."

"You don't want me to go any further then."

"I don't understand. Why would you want to? . . . You don't have those kind of demons, Andy; that kind of vanity. You have money, and money attracts flattery, but you're too realistic, too aware. I just can't believe it."

"Neither could I when I first realized I was paying attention." Trevayne laughed, more to himself than for his wife's benefit, and put his feet on the coffee table. "I listened to Armbruster, went to the meetings, because I thought all the conversation was leading up to one thing—the report. And I was angry, angry as hell. Then I understood that wasn't the case. These were professionals, not frightened men caught with their fingers in the till. They're the talent hunters; I can't object to that. When the companies were growing, I spent months scouting corporations here and abroad luring away the best brain power I could buy. I still keep it in mind. Whenever I meet someone I think might be an asset, I make a mental note to call your brother. . . . These men are doing the same thing I was . . . am still doing. Only on a larger scale, with far greater complications. And if in the first few weeks or months I fall on my face, they'll pull the rug out so fast I'll have mat burns. But I'm beginning to think it's important to give those first few months a try."

"You haven't explained why."

Trevayne withdrew his feet from the small table and stood up. He thrust his hands in his trousers pockets and walked on the patterns of the living-room rug, absently placing his feet at specific intervals as a small boy on a sidewalk playing step-on-a-crack. "You really want the nitty-gritty, don't you?"

"Shouldn't I? I love you. I love the life we have, the lives our children have; I think everything is being threatened, and I'm scared to death."

Andy looked down at his wife, his expression kind but his eyes remote, seeing her, yet not focusing sharply. "I am, too, I think. . . . Why? . . . All right, the 'why.' Because the truth might be that I can. I'm not kidding myself; I'm no genius. At least, I don't feel like one—whatever way a genius is supposed to feel. But I don't think the presidency requires genius. I think it does require the ability to absorb quickly, act decisively—not always impartially—and accept extraordinary pressure. Perhaps, above all, to listen. To distinguish between the legitimate cries for help and the hypocrisy. I think I can handle almost everything but the pressure—I don't know about that; not to the degree that's required. . . . But if I can prove to myself that I can jump that hurdle—and one other—I think I want to get into the fight. Because any country that allows a Genessee Industries needs all the help it can get. Frank Baldwin quoted something I made a joke of when he first approached me. He said no man can avoid what he's supposed to do when the time comes for him to do it. I think that's pretentious as hell, and not necessarily accurate. But if through a series of accidents the political cupboard is damned near empty and a good man is going to make it bare by leaving—and the king-makers think, for their own reasons, that I can cut it—I'm not sure I've got a choice. I'm not sure *we've* got a choice, Phyl."

Phyllis Trevayne watched her husband carefully; coldly, perhaps. "Why have you chosen . . . no, that's not right; why have you let this party choose you, and not the other? If the President isn't going to run for a second term—"

"For practical reasons," interrupted Andy. "I don't think it makes a whit of difference which banner a man runs under anymore. Both parties are splintered. It's the man that counts, not the bromides of Republican or Democratic philosophy—they're meaningless now. . . . The President will wait until the last possible minute before announcing his withdrawal; he's got too many bills in Congress. I'll need that time. If only to find out I'm not wanted."

Phyllis remained staring at her husband, without discernible reaction. "You're willing to expose yourself—and us—to that kind of agony, knowing that it might be a complete waste?"

Trevayne was by the side brick wall of the outsized fireplace. He leaned his back against it and returned his wife's look. "I'd like your permission to. . . . For the first time in my life, I'm aware of a threat to everything I think I believe in. It's got nothing to do with parades and flags and enemies—no easy heroes and villains. It's a gradual but certain erosion of choice. Bonner uses the word a lot, 'programmed.' Though I don't think he really knows what it means, what its implications are. . . . But it's happening, Phyl. The men behind Genessee Industries want to run the country because they're convinced they know better than the voter on Main Street, and they have the power to convey their ideas into the system. And there are hundreds like them in corporate board rooms everywhere. Sooner or later they'll get together, and instead of being a legitimate part of the system, they'll *be* the system. . . . I don't agree with that. I'm not sure yet what I *do* agree with, but I don't agree with that. We're ten steps away from our own particular police state, and I want people to know it."

Trevayne pushed himself off the brick wall and walked

back to the couch. He smiled at Phyllis, a little embarrassed, and slumped down beside her.

"That's quite a speech," she said softly.

"Sorry. . . . I didn't mean it to be."

She reached over and took his hand. "An awful thing just happened."

"What?"

"I just put that frightening title before your name, and it didn't sound at all unreal."

"If I were you, I wouldn't start redecorating the East Room. . . . I may freeze in my first *Senate* speech, and it's back to the coupons."

Phyllis released his hand, astonished. "Good God, you've been busy! Do tell. In case I should order new Christmas cards or something. What Senate?"

45

James Goddard backed his car out of the sloping driveway and started off down the road. It was a clear Sunday morning, the air cold, the winds swirling out of the Palo Alto hills, chilling everything in front of them. It was a day meant for decisions; Goddard had made his.

He would finalize it, organize its implementation within an hour or two.

Actually, the decision had been made for him. They were going to let him hang, and James Goddard had promised himself that he wasn't for hanging. No matter the promises, regardless of the guarantees that he knew would be offered. He wasn't going to allow it. He wasn't going to let them solve their problems by having the accusing arrow settle in his direction; accepting the responsibility in exchange for the transfer of money into a coded Swiss bank account. That would be too easy.

He had nearly made that mistake himself—without any settlement. His preoccupation with past history—Genessee history—had blinded him to the fact that he was using his own figures, his own intricate manipulations. There was another way, a better way.

Someone else's figures. Financial projections that couldn't possibly be his.

It was December 15. In forty-six days it would be January 31, the end of the fiscal year. All plants, divisions, departments, and assembly control offices of Genessee Industries had to have their year-end reports in by that date. Submitted in final form to his office.

They were simple P-and-L statements with lengthy addenda of required purchases and payroll adjustments. The thousands upon thousands of figures were fed into computer banks where necessary alterations and imbalances were spotted and taped out for correction.

They were balanced against the master tape of the previous year's budgets.

Simple arithmetic that leaped into the economic stratosphere of billions.

The master tape.

The master plan.

Every year the master tape was sent to the comptroller's office in San Francisco and kept in the Genessee vaults. It arrived sometime during the second week in December, on a private plane from Chicago. Always accompanied by a president of one division or another, and armed guards.

Every complex industry had to include budgeting projections for all contractual obligations. But Genessee's master tape differed from the control data tapes of other corporations in a profound way.

For the commitments of others were generally public knowledge, while Genessee Industries' master tape included thousands of unannounced commitments. And each December brought new surprises seen by less than a dozen pairs of eyes. They spelled out a major portion of the military armaments program of the United States for the next five years. Pentagon commitments that neither the Congress nor the President knew existed. But they existed as surely as the steel and the politicians could be tempered.

Since the master tape was processed on the basis of five-year data—each December brought a fresh fifth year and constantly swelling information for the years preceding. Nothing was ever deleted, only added.

It was Goddard's function as the financial keystone of Genessee Industries to absorb and coordinate the massive influx of listed and unlisted—old and new—material with respect to changing market conditions; to allocate financing to the divisions as necessary; and to distribute contractual workloads among the plants—always operating on the assumption that 120 percent of capacity was the median. Sufficient for optimum local employment statistics, yet not excessive to the point of affording unions undue strength. Seventy percent of that capacity was convertible without profit concern; to be given or taken away as the children behaved.

And James Goddard knew that it was his ability, not the computers', that reduced the incredible mass into workable figures. He separated, isolated, appropriated; his eyes scanned the sheets and with the surefootedness of a large but supple cat he made his swift notations and shifted millions as though he were testing branches, prepared for the unexpected fall but always ready for that last step, that final inch that meant he could leap for the profit-kill.

There was no one like him. He was an artist with figures. Numbers were his friends; they didn't betray him, and he could make them do his bidding.

People betrayed him.

MEMORANDUM: Mr. James Goddard, Pres., San Francisco Division

There is a problem that I believe imperatively warrants your attention.

                                                      L.R

L.R. Louis Riggs. The Vietnam veteran Genessee had hired a year ago. A bright young man, unusually quick and decisive. He was quiet, but not without emotions, not without loyalty; that had been proven to Goddard.

Riggs had been wounded in the service. He was a

hero and a fine young American; not an obscene ass or an indolent, drug-taking hippie the way most of the youth were today.

Lou Riggs had told him that something was going on he should be aware of. Riggs had been approached by one of Trevayne's assistants and offered a bribe to confirm information damaging to Genessee—especially to him as president of the San Francisco Division. Naturally, Riggs refused. Then, several days later, a man who identified himself as an Army officer attached to the Department of Defense threatened him—actually *threatened* him—to disclose private company records that bore specifically on Mr. Goddard's reputation. He also refused, and if Mr. Goddard recalled, Lou Riggs had sent a previous memo requesting a meeting—Mr. Goddard didn't recall; there were so damned many memos. However, when Lou Riggs read in the newspaper that this same Army officer was the one involved with that killing in Connecticut, on Andrew Trevayne's property, he knew he had to see Mr. Goddard immediately.

Goddard wasn't sure what was going on, but the outlines of a conspiracy were there. A conspiracy against him. Possibly being made between Trevayne and the Pentagon. Why else would D.O.D. send an interrogation officer to back up one of Trevayne's assistants? And why had that same officer killed De Spadante's brother?

Why had Mario de Spadante been killed?

It seemed logical that De Spadante was trying to get off his own hook.

Some might be hanged so that others—higher up— would not have to hang.

De Spadante had said that. But perhaps De Spadante wasn't as "high up" as he thought he was. Perhaps the Pentagon considered him too much a liability—God knew he was an undesirable fellow.

Whatever. James Goddard, the "bookkeeper," had made up his mind. It was the moment to act, not reflect any longer. He needed only the most damaging of all information.

There would be approximately eleven thousand cards measuring three by seven inches. Cards with strange square perforations; cards that weren't to be folded, spindled, or mutilated. He had measured several thousand identically shaped cards, and found that eleven thousand would require four briefcases. He had them in the trunk of his car.

The computer itself was another matter. It was huge and required two men to operate. For security purposes the men had to be across the room from each other and punch simultaneously separate codes on the keys for it to function. The codes of each man were changed daily, and the two codes were kept in separate offices. The division president's and the comptroller's.

It hadn't been difficult for Goddard to get the second code for the twenty-four-hour period beginning Sunday morning. He'd simply walked into the comptroller's office and said innocently that he thought they'd been given identical code schedules by mistake. Equally innocently the comptroller withdrew his from the safe, and they matched figures. Instantly it was obvious that Goddard had been wrong; the codes were different. But within that instant James Goddard's eyes riveted on the Sunday figures. He committed them to memory.

Numbers were his only friends.

Still there was the physical aspect of the machine itself. He needed one other person who would be willing to spend nearly six hours in the basement computer room; someone whom he could trust, who realized that his actions were for the benefit of Genessee Industries, perhaps for the nation itself.

He'd been astonished when the man he'd selected had made a financial demand, but then, as he pointed out, it could be considered a promotion, an overdue promotion. Before he realized it, Goddard had hired a special assistant at an increase of ten thousand dollars a year.

It didn't matter. What mattered was this day's business, this day's decision.

He approached the gate and slowed down his car. The guard, recognizing first the automobile and then the driver, snapped a firm two fingers to his cap.

"Good morning, Mr. Goddard. No Sunday off for the front office, eh, sir?"

Goddard didn't like the man's informality. It was out of place. However, there was no time for reprimands.

"No, I have work to do. And, guard, I've asked Mr. Riggs to come in this morning. There's no need to check him out with security. Tell him to report directly to my office."

"Mr. Riggs, sir?"

"You *should* know him. He was wounded fighting for our country, protecting us, mister!"

"Yes, sir. Riggs, sir." The guard wrote the name on his clipboard rapidly.

"He drives a small sports car," added Goddard as an afterthought. "Just wave him through. His initials are on the door panel. L.R."

46

Sam Vicarson sank into the down-filled cushion of the velvet sofa and found his knees disconcertingly parallel with his shoulders. Andrew Trevayne sat at the room-service table and sipped coffee from a Limoges cup imprinted with the words "Waldorf Towers, New York." He was reading from a very thick red leather notebook.

"Jesus!" said Vicarson.

"What?"

"No wonder so many uptight conferences take place in these rooms. Once you sit down, you can't get up; you might as well talk."

Trevayne smiled and went back to his reading. Sam stretched his legs, only to find the position less comfortable. With considerable effort he got up and wandered about the room looking at the various prints on the velour-covered walls and finally out the windows, thirty-five stories above Park Avenue and Fiftieth Street. Trevayne made a notation on a piece of paper, closed the red leather notebook, and looked at his watch.

"They're five minutes late. I wonder if that's a good sign in politics," said Andrew.

"I'd be just as happy if they never showed up," replied Sam, without answering the question. "I feel outclassed. Christ. Ian *Hamilton*. He wrote the book."

"Not any book I'd run out to buy."

"You don't have to; you don't sell legal services, Mr. Trevayne. This guy does. He walks with kings, and he threw away the common touch a long time ago. I don't think he had much use for it anyway."

"Very accurate. You read the report."

"I didn't have to. What did his kid say? That his old man does his thing because he figures no one else can do it as well. Anywheres near as well."

The chimes could be heard in the hotel suite's foyer. Vicarson involuntarily patted down his perpetually rumpled hair and buttoned his jacket. "I'll get the door. Maybe they'll think I'm the butler; that'd be fine."

The first ten minutes were like an eighteenth-century pavane, thought Trevayne. Slow, graceful, assured; essentially chartered, fundamentally ancient. Sam Vicarson was doing very well, Andy considered, watching the youthful attorney parry Aaron Green's thrusts of solicitousness, which barely concealed his annoyance. Green was angry that Vicarson was present; Hamilton barely acknowledged Sam's presence. For Hamilton, thought Trevayne, it was a time for giants; a subordinate was relegated to his properly unimportant status.

"I think you should realize, Trevayne, when your friends on the National Committee made their choice known to us, we were bitterly disappointed," said Ian Hamilton.

" 'Shocked' is more accurate," added Green in his deep, resonant voice.

"Yes," said Andy flatly. "I'd like to discuss your reaction. It's one of the things I'm interested in. Except they're not my friends. . . . I was wondering if they were yours, frankly."

Hamilton smiled. The anglicized attorney crossed his legs and folded his arms, sinking back into the soft cushions of the velvet sofa—the picture of elegance. Aaron Green had a hard-backed armchair next to Trevayne. Sam Vicarson sat slightly outside the triangle, at Andy's right but not in line with Trevayne's view of Hamilton. Even the seating arrangements seemed orchestrated to Andy. And then he realized that Sam had accomplished it; Sam Vicarson had indicated the places for each of them to sit. Sam was better than he thought he was, mused Trevayne.

"If you're considering the possibility that you are our choice," said Hamilton, still smiling benignly, "I think I can disabuse you."

"How?"

"Quite simply, we favor the President. A perusal of our . . . combined contributions, both financial and otherwise, will substantiate that fact."

"Then I wouldn't have your support under any conditions."

"I should think not, speaking candidly," replied Hamilton.

Suddenly Andrew got out of his chair and returned Hamilton's noningratiating smile. "Then, gentlemen, I've made a mistake, and I apologize. I'm wasting your time."

The abruptness of Trevayne's move startled the others, including Sam Vicarson. Hamilton was the first to recover.

"Come, Mr. Trevayne, let's not play those games, which, if I remember correctly, you detest so. . . . Circumstances dictate that we meet with you. Please sit down."

Andrew did so. "What are those circumstances?"

Aaron Green spoke. "The President does not intend to seek a second term."

"He might change his mind," said Trevayne.

"He can't," said Hamilton. "He wouldn't live it out. I tell you this in the strictest confidence."

Andrew was stunned. "I didn't know that. I thought it was a personal choice."

"What's more personal?" asked Green.

"You know what I mean. . . . That's terrible."

"So . . . we meet." Green ended the topic of the President's health. "Circumstances dictate."

Trevayne was still thinking of the ill man in the White House while Hamilton continued.

"As I say, we were disappointed. Not that the idea of your candidacy is without merit; it's not. But, frankly, all things considered, we favor the President's party."

"That's a non sequitur. Why should my candidacy concern you at all, then? The opposition has good men."

"It has the *President's* men," interrupted Green.

"I don't understand."

"The President"—Hamilton paused, choosing his words carefully—"as any man who has completed half a job that will be judged by history, is vitally concerned that his programs be continued. He will dictate the choice of his successor. He'll pick one of two men because they *will* consent to his dictates. The Vice President or the Governor of New York. In conscience, we cannot support either. Neither has the strength of his own convictions; only the President's. They can't win, and they shouldn't."

"A lesson. A lesson was learned," said Green, sitting forward, his hands poised pontifically. "In sixty-eight, Hubert didn't lose to Nixon because he was the lesser man, or because of money, or the issues. He lost the election with four words whined into the television after his nomination. 'Thank you, Mr. President.' He never washed away those four words."

Trevayne reached into his pocket for a cigarette, lighting it while no one spoke. "So you've concluded that the President will ensure the defeat of his own party."

"Precisely," replied Hamilton. "That is our dilemma. One man's vanity. The opposition has only to mount an attractive candidate, accentuate his strength of character—his independence, if you will—and the nationwide gossip will take care of the rest. The electorate has a visceral instinct about puppets."

"Then you think I have a legitimate chance?"

"Reluctantly," answered Green. "You haven't much competition. Who else is there? In the Senate, the party has old men who tremble as I do, or loud-mouthed brats who soil their bell-bottom trousers. Only Knapp has possibilities, but he's so obnoxious he'd be buried. The House is filled with nonentities. A few big governors might give

you a run, but they carry the urban messes on their backs
. . . . Yes, Mr. Andrew Trevayne; Mr. Undersecretary in
State Department, Mr. Millionaire, Mr. Foundation President, Mr. Subcommittee Chairman. You've got a lot of
marbles. . . . You could fall down on the issue of elective
office, but you would get picked right up again on comparisons. The National Committee boys knew what they
were doing when they pulled your name out. They don't
like losers."

"And neither do we," concluded Ian Hamilton. "So
whether we like it or not, you're a political reality."

Trevayne once again got up, breaking the triangle.
He walked to the room-service table, picked up the thick
red leather notebook, and returned, standing several feet
behind his chair. "I'm not sure your assessment is accurate, gentlemen, but it's as good a springboard as any I
can think of for what I have to say. . . . This is the subcommittee report. It will be delivered to the Defense Commission, the President, and the designated congressional
committees in five days. The report itself has been boiled
down to six hundred and fifty pages, with four volumes of
subsequent documentations. Of the report, over three hundred pages are devoted to Genessee Industries. And two
volumes of documentation. . . . Now, I understand your
'bitter disappointment' at the prospect of my candidacy. I
don't like you; I don't approve of what you've done, and I
intend to see you put out of business. Simple? *Capisce?*
As one of your departed colleagues might have said."

"He was no part of us!" interrupted Aaron Green
angrily.

"You *allowed* him; it's the same thing."

"What's your point? I believe I smell a compromise,"
said Hamilton.

"You do. But not your kind of compromise; you don't
come out with anything. Except, perhaps, the comfort of
knowing you can spend the rest of your lives outside the
courts—*and* outside the country."

"What?" Hamilton's complacency was replaced with
his first hint of anger.

"You are a ridiculous man, Mr. Subcommittee!" added
Green.

"Not really. But the word 'ridiculous' is well chosen, if not correctly applied." Trevayne walked back to the linen-covered table and threw the notebook carelessly on top.

Hamilton spoke firmly. "Let's talk sense, Trevayne. Your report is damaging; we won't bother to deny it. However, it is—or certainly must be—riddled with speculations, inconclusive conjectures. Do you think for one minute we're not prepared for that?"

"No. I'm sure you are."

"You realize, of course, that the worst you portend for us are accusations, vehemently denied. Months, years, perhaps a decade in the courts?"

"That's entirely possible."

"Then why should we even consider you a threat? Are you prepared for our counterattack? Are you willing to spend years of your life defending yourself in the libel courts?"

"No, I'm not."

"Then we are at an impasse. We might as well accommodate each other. After all, our objectives are identical. The good of the United States."

"Our definitions differ."

"That's impossible," said Green.

"That's why we differ. You conceive of no other absolutes but your own."

Hamilton shrugged elegantly and raised both his hands in a gesture of compromise. "We are prepared to discuss these definitions—"

"I'm not," replied Andrew standing. "I'm weary of your definitions, your ersatz elitist logic; those tiring conclusions that give you the right to implement only your own objectives. You don't have that right; you're stealing it. And I'm crying 'thieves!'—loud and repeatedly."

"Who will listen?" shouted Green. "Who will listen to a man propelled by a vengeance twenty years old?"

"What did you say?"

"Twenty years ago Genessee Industries turned you down!" Green shook his finger at Andrew. "For twenty years you're whining! We have proof—"

"You *disgust* me!" roared Trevayne. "You're no better than the man you claim is no part of you. But you're kidding yourselves; you and the De Spadantes of this world are cut from the same cloth. 'We have proof!' Good God, do you extort protection money from blind newsdealers, too?"

"The analogy is unfair, Trevayne," said Hamilton, taking a disapproving eye off Green. "Aaron is prone to get upset easily."

"It's not unfair," answered Trevayne quietly, his hands gripping the back of his chair. "You're scheming, out-of-date old men playing an insane game of Monopoly. Buying up this, buying up that—using a hundred different subsidiaries—promising, bribing, blackmailing. Compiling thousands of individual dossiers and poring over them like demented gnomes. One stating that *his* ideas are greater monuments—what was it?—temples, cathedrals! My God, what pomposity. . . . The other. Oh, yes. There shouldn't be any blanket franchises. Only those entitled to vote should have a voice. That's not only out of date, it's out of sight!"

"I deny! I deny I ever said that!" Hamilton leaped to his feet, suddenly, profoundly frightened.

"Deny all you like. But you'd better know this. On Saturday, I was in Hartford; I signed the papers, Hamilton. I had reasons—out of focus but clear enough—to use another attorney. Mr. Vicarson here has assured me everything is in order. On January fifteenth an irrevocable announcement is made by the Governor of Connecticut. I am right now, for all intents and purposes, a United States senator."

"What?" Aaron Green looked as though he'd been slapped harshly.

"That's right, Mr. Green. And I intend to use the immunity of that seat and the stature of that office to hammer away at you. I'm going to let the country know—over and over and over again. Every day, every quorum, every session; I won't stop. If need be—and I've considered it deeply—I'll have my own personal marathon, my own filibuster. I'll start at the beginning and read that entire report. Every word. All six hundred pages. You won't survive that. Genessee Industries won't survive."

Aaron Green was breathing heavily, his eyes leveled at Trevayne, his voice deep with personal hatred. "From Auschwitz to Babi-Yar. Pigs like you make trouble when there is trouble enough."

"And the solutions are not your solutions. Your solutions lead right back to the camps. To the executions. Can't you *see* that?"

"I see only *strength!* Strength is the deterrent!"

"For God's sake, Green, make it a collective strength. A responsible strength. One that's shared, open. Not furtively manipulated by a select few. That doesn't belong here."

"You are a schoolboy again! What is this 'shared,' this 'open'? They're words, sterile words. They lead to chaos, to weakness. Look at the record."

"I've looked at it. Hard and long. It's flawed, imperfect, frustrating. But, goddamn it, it's a better alternative than the one you're suggesting. Look at that track record! . . . And if we're walking into a time when the system doesn't work, we'd better know that, too. Then we'll change it. But openly. By choice. Not by edict; and certainly not by your edict."

"Very well, Mr. Trevayne," said Ian Hamilton, suddenly walking away from the others, his back to them. "You've built a strong case. What are you suggesting we do?"

"Cut bait. Get out. I don't care where; Switzerland, the Mediterranean, the Scottish Highlands, or the British Lowlands. It doesn't make any difference. Just get out of this country. And stay out."

"We have financial responsibilities," protested Hamilton quietly.

"Delegate them. But sever all connections with Genessee Industries."

"Impossible! Preposterous!" Aaron Green looked at Hamilton now.

"Easy, old friend. . . . If we do as you suggest, what is our guarantee?"

Trevayne crossed to the room-service table and pointed

at the red leather notebook. "This is the report as it stands—"

"You've made us aware of that," interrupted Hamilton.

"We have also prepared an alternate report. One that considerably reduces the attention now given to Genessee Industries—"

"*So?*" Aaron Green's sudden interruption was stated emphatically, distastefully. "The schoolboy's not so pure. He wasn't going to change a word. A single word."

Trevayne paused before replying. "I still mightn't. If I do, you have an Army major named Bonner to thank for it. And your own willingness to comply, of course. . . . Major Bonner made an observation once that stuck with me. Perhaps it dovetailed with other opinions, but, nevertheless, he gave the idea focus. He said I was destructive; that I was tearing down, not offering any alternatives. Just a total wipeout, the good and the bad down the drain together. . . . All right, let's try to salvage some of the good."

"We want specifics," said Hamilton.

"All right. . . . You get out and you stay out, and I turn over the alternate report, and the quiet process of cleaning up Genessee Industries begins. No cries of conspiracy—which it is; no demands for your necks—which should be demanded; no total wipeout. I'm sure a task force can be mounted to go after the existing financial fiefdoms. We won't bother with the root causes, because they'll be eliminated. You'll be eliminated."

"That's excessively harsh."

"You came here to make a deal, Hamilton. There it is. You're a political realist; I'm a political reality—your judgment, I believe. Take it. You won't get a better offer."

"You're no match for us, *schoolboy*," said Aaron Green, his emotion denying the confidence of his statement.

"Not by myself; of course not. I'm only an instrument. But through me two hundred million people will learn what you are. As opposed to you, I honestly believe they're capable of making decisions."

The pavane was over. The music finished. The stately

ancients took their leave of the newly established court with as much dignity as was possible.

"Would it have worked?" asked Sam Vicarson.

"I don't know," answered Trevayne. "But they couldn't take the chance."

"Do you think they'll really get out?"

"We'll see."

47

"I'm sorry. I think my letter makes clear the Army's position in the matter. I'm sure Major Bonner appreciates your retaining attorneys for him. From what I gather, there's every reason to anticipate a civilian acquittal."

"But you're still going ahead with your own charges, General Cooper; you want him out of the Army."

"We have no choice, Mr. Trevayne. Bonner's stepped out of line once too often. He knows it. There's no defense against dereliction, disregarding the chain of command. Without that chain we have no military organization, sir."

"I'll insist on seeing him defended in the court-martial proceedings, of course. Again, with my attorneys present."

"You're wasting your money. The adjutant charge isn't murder or assault or even criminal intent. It's simply one of lying to an A.F. officer; misrepresenting his orders so as to gain access to government property. In this case, a jet aircraft. Furthermore, he refused to inform his superiors of his intentions. We simply can't tolerate that kind of behavior. And Bonner is inclined to repeat this type of offense. There's no sound military justification."

"Thank you, General. We'll see."

Andrew hung up the phone and got out of his chair. He walked over to his office door, which he'd shut prior to his call to General Cooper. He opened it and spoke to his secretary.

"I saw the light on two; anything I should take care of, Marge?"

"The Government Printing Office, Mr. Trevayne. I didn't know what to say. They wanted to know when you'd be sending over the subcommittee report. They're getting backlogged with congressional stuff and didn't want to disappoint you. I started to tell them it was completed and sent out late this morning, but I thought perhaps there was some kind of protocol we didn't know about."

Trevayne laughed. "I'll bet they didn't want to disappoint us! Lord! The eyes are everywhere, aren't they? . . . Call them back and tell them we weren't aware they expected our business. We saved the taxpayers' money and did it ourselves. All five copies. But first get me a cab. I'm going over to Arlington. To Bonner."

During the ride from the Potomac Towers to the Army BOQ, Arlington, Andy tried to understand Brigadier General Lester Cooper and his legion of righteous indignants. Cooper's letter—the reply to his inquiry about Bonner—had been couched in Army jargon. *Section* this, *Article* that; Army regulations pertinent to the disposition of authority under the conditions of limited responsibility.

"Horseshit," as Paul Bonner said—far too often for his own good.

The threat of the court-martial charge wasn't the Army's abhorrence of Bonner's behavior; it was its abhorrence of Bonner himself. If it was explicitly the behavior in *principle*, far more serious charges would have been filed against him, charges that could be argued back and forth. As it was, the Army chose the lesser indictment. Dereliction. Misprision, or concealment of intentions. Charges from which there would be no hard-won vindication. Not a slap-on-the-wrist; more a strap-on-the-back. It left the defendant no choice but to resign; there was no career left for him in the military.

He simply couldn't win the fight, because there was no fight. Just a pronouncement.

But *why*, for God's sake? If ever there was a man made for the Army, it was Paul Bonner. If ever there was an army that needed such a man, it was the demoralized Army of the United States. Instead of prosecuting him, Cooper and the rest of his "Brasswares" should be out beating the bushes for Bonner's support.

Beating the bushes. What had Aaron Green said about "beating bushes?" Beating bushes was an undesirable tactic, because the quarry could turn on the hunter without warning.

Was that what the Army was afraid of?

That by supporting Paul Bonner, acknowledging his participation, his commitment to the military, the Army was exposing its own vulnerability?

Were Lester Cooper and his uniformed tribunals afraid of a surprise attack?

From whom? A curious public? That was understandable. Paul Bonner was a knowledgeable accessory.

Or were they afraid of the accessory? Afraid of Paul Bonner? And by discrediting him, they conveniently pushed him out of the picture, out of any frame of reference.

A nonperson.

Banished.

The taxi came to a stop at the gates of the BOQ. Trevayne paid the driver and started walking toward the huge entrance with the gold eagle over the double doors and the inscription: "Through These Portals Pass the Best Damned Men in the Field."

Andrew noticed that to the right, underneath the inscription, was the date of the building's construction: "April, 1944."

History. Another era. A lifetime ago. A time when such inscriptions were perfectly natural, properly heroic.

The days of the disdainful cavaliers.

They were no more. They seemed a little silly now.

That, too, was unfair, thought Trevayne.

The guard outside Paul Bonner's room acknowledged Trevayne's presence, his standing access to the officer under barracks arrest, and opened the door. Bonner was seated at the small steel desk writing on a sheet of Army stationery. He turned in the chair and glanced up at Trevayne. He did not stand or offer his hand.

"I'll just finish this paragraph and be right with you." He returned to the paper. "I think I'm considered a spit-and-polish moron. Those two lawyers you hired are making me put everything I can remember down in writing. Said one thought leads to another if you see it in front of you, or something like that."

"It makes sense. The sequence of thoughts, I mean. Go ahead; no hurry." Trevayne sat down in the single armchair and kept silent until Bonner put down his pencil and shifted his position, throwing his shoulder over the back of the chair as he looked at the "civilian."

And he was looking at a "civilian"; there was no mistaking the insult.

"I'll pay you back for the legal fees. I insist on that."

"Not necessary. It's the least I can do."

"I don't want you to do it. I asked them to bill me directly, but they said that wasn't possible. So, I'll pay you. . . . Frankly, I'm perfectly satisfied with my Army counsel. But I suppose you have your reasons."

"Just added insurance."

"For whom?" Bonner stared at Trevayne.

"For you, Paul."

"Of course. I shouldn't have asked. . . . What do you want?"

"Maybe I'd better go out and come in again," said Andrew with a questioning harshness. "What's the matter with you? We're on the same side, remember?"

"Are we, Mr. President?"

The sound of the words was like the crack of a lash across Trevayne's face. He returned Bonner's stare, and for several moments neither man spoke.

"I think you'd better explain that."

So Major Paul Bonner did.

And Trevayne listened in astonished silence as the Army officer recounted his brief but extraordinary conversation with the soon-to-retire Brigadier General Lester Cooper.

"So nobody has to tell any elaborate stories anymore. All those complicated explanations aren't necessary."

Trevayne got out of the chair and walked to the small window without speaking. There was a contingent—a platoon, perhaps—of young second lieutenants being lectured to by a wrinkle-faced full colonel in the courtyard. Some of the young men moved their feet, several cupped their hands to their lips, warding off the December chill in

Arlington. The Colonel, open-shirted, laconic, seemed oblivious to the climate.

"What about the truth? Would you be interested in that, Major?"

"Give me some credit, *politician*. It's pretty god-damned obvious."

"What's your version?" Trevayne turned from the window.

"Cooper said the Army couldn't afford me. The truth is that *you* can't. . . . I'm the lodestone around your presidential neck."

"That's ridiculous."

"Come off it! You ensure the trial, I'm acquitted—which I should be—and you're clean. Nobody can say you ran out on the soldier boy who was shot at. But that trial is controlled. No extraneous issues; just the pertinent facts, ma'am. Even the Army lawyer made that clear. Just Saturday night in Connecticut. No San Francisco, no Houston, no Seattle. No Genessee Industries! . . . Then I'm quietly drummed out by kangaroos, the world goes on, and no one has to be embarrassed any longer. What pisses me off is that none of you can come out and say it!"

"I can't, because it's not true."

"The hell it isn't! It's all wrapped up in a neat package. Man, when you sell out, you sell out *high*. I'll give you credit, you don't take second best."

"You're way off, Paul."

"Horseshit! Are you telling me you're not in the sweepstakes? I even hear you're going to get a seat in the Senate! Goddamn convenient, isn't it?"

"I swear to you I don't know where Cooper got that information."

"Is it true?"

Trevayne turned his back on Bonner, looking once again out the window at the platoon of second lieutenants. "It's . . . all under consideration."

"Oh, that's beautiful. 'Under consideration.' What do you do next? Run it up a flagpole and see if it gets off at Westport? Look, Andy, I'll tell you the same thing I told Cooper. I don't like this big new wrinkle—this sudden first-team switch—any more than I like a lot of the things

I've found out during the past several months. Let's say I'm square enough to disapprove of the *M.O.*'s. The methods of operation. I think they smell. . . . On the other hand, I'd be a first-class hypocrite if I started getting moralistic at this late date. I've spent my career believing that military goals were their own justifications. Let the elected civilians worry about the morals; that's always been a distant area to me. . . . Well, this is the *big game plan,* isn't it? I don't play in that ball park. Good luck!"

The platoon of second lieutenants was dispersing in the courtyard below; the open-shirted Colonel was lighting a cigarette. The lecture was over.

And Trevayne felt suddenly exhausted, weary. Nothing was as it seemed. He turned to face Bonner, who still remained insultingly casual in the desk chair.

"What do you mean, 'game plan'?"

"You're getting funnier by the minute. You're going to make me blow any chance I may have for executive intervention."

"Cut the clowning! Spell it out, Major."

"You bet your ass, Mr. President! They've got you, they don't need anyone else! The independent, incorruptible, Mr. Clean. They couldn't have done any better if they called down John the Baptist, backed up with young Tom Paine. The Pentagon's worries are over."

"Had it occurred to you that they may have just begun?"

Bonner lifted his shoulder off the back of the chair and laughed quietly—with maddening sincerity. "You're the funniest nigger on the plantation, massa. But you don't have to tell those jokes; I won't interfere. I don't belong up there."

"I asked you a question. I expect an answer. You're implying that I've been bought; I deny it. Why do you think so?"

"Because I know those boys in 'Brasswares.' They're going to ensure your investiture. They wouldn't do that unless they had ironbound guarantees."

48

Trevayne ordered the taxi to let him out nearly a mile from the Potomac Towers. It was a time to walk, to think, to analyze. To try to find logic within the illogical.

His thoughts were interrupted by the sound of automobile horns, blowing angrily at a brown sedan that seemed lost, unsure of its direction. The irritating cacophony fit his own sense of frustration.

Had he really been so naïve, so much the innocent, to have been used so completely? Had his confrontation with Ian Hamilton and Aaron Green been no more than an indulgence—on their part? A sham.

No, that wasn't so. It couldn't be.

Hamilton and Green were frightened men. Hamilton and Green called the shots for Genessee Industries and Genessee ran the Pentagon.

A equals B equals C.

A equals C.

If he, as President could control Ian Hamilton and Aaron Green—make them bend to his demands—then it was only logical that he could control the Pentagon. The means of that control would be in the dismembering of Genessee Industries, cutting the monolith down to size.

He had stated that clearly as his prime objective.

Yet, if Paul Bonner was to be believed—and why not? He couldn't have invented the scenario—Lester Cooper and his colleagues were throwing the full weight of the Pentagon behind his proposed candidacy.

And since their military opinion was formed in the conglomerate thought process of Genessee Industries, their support had to be directed—at least endorsed—by Ian Hamilton and Aaron Green.

A equals B.

Why, then? Why would Brigadier General Lester Cooper and his legion of brass willingly oversee the burial of their own strength? Why would they be *ordered* to?

A equals *C*.

It was one thing for Hamilton and Green to fade out—they had no choice—it was something else altogether for them to turn and instruct the Pentagon to support the candidate who was admittedly destroying them.

Yet apparently they had done just that.

Unless that support was ordered *before* the Waldorf confrontation.

Ordered and put into action before his threats ended the stately pavane high up in the Waldorf Towers.

In which case, Andrew realized that he was not what he thought he was. He wasn't the strong alternative, the man good political men had turned to; he wasn't the considered choice of seasoned professionals who looked into their smoke-filled crystal balls and determined him fit.

He was the candidate of Genessee Industries, personally selected by Ian Hamilton and Aaron Green. And all their talk of bitter disappointment was just that, talk.

Christ, the irony of it! The subtlety!

And the conclusion to be drawn; that was the most frightening part of the whole charade.

It mattered not one whit who held the office of the presidency. It mattered only that no one made waves through which the good ship Genessee could not navigate.

He had provided just that.

He had *delivered* just that.

Four hours ago he had delivered an extraordinary report, made more extraordinary by the fact that vital, incriminating evidence had been withheld.

Oh, Christ! What the hell had he done?

He saw the outlines of the twin steel-and-brick structure of the Potomac Towers in the distance. Perhaps a half-mile away. He began walking faster, then faster still. He looked up and down the avenue for a taxi, but there were none. He wanted to get to his office quickly now. He wanted to find out the truth; he *had* to find out.

There was only one way to do it.

Brigadier General Lester Cooper.

*   *   *

Sam Vicarson was pacing up and down outside the subcommittee's offices when Andrew emerged from the elevator into the corridor.

"Good God, am I glad to see you! I called Arlington and left messages at half a dozen places."

"What's the matter?"

"We better go inside so you can sit down."

"Oh, Jesus! Phyllis—"

"No, sir, I'm sorry . . . I mean, I'm sorry if I made you . . . it's not Mrs. Trevayne."

"Let's go inside."

Vicarson closed the door of Trevayne's office and waited until Andy took off his overcoat and threw it on the couch. He began slowly, as if trying to recall the exact words he should repeat.

"The chief of the White House staff telephoned about forty-five minutes ago. Something happened this morning —it hasn't been released to the press yet, at least it hadn't been a half-hour ago—that caused the President to make a decision you should be aware of. . . . He temporarily exercised executive privilege and had the copies of the subcommittee's report impounded."

"*What?*"

"He had them intercepted at all four destinations— the Defense Commission, the Attorney General's office, and the offices of the chairmen of the Senate and House committees; that's Appropriations and Armed Services. . . . He's talked to the four principals personally, and they've accepted his explanation."

"What is it?"

"Robert Webster—you remember, the White House—"

"I remember."

"He was killed this morning. I mean, he was murdered. Shot in his Akron hotel room. . . . A maid who was in the hallway gave the police a description of two men she saw running out of the room, and someone at the hotel had the presence of mind to call the White House. I mean, Webster was a hometown boy who made good and all that. . . . The White House went to work. Got the papers and the wire services to keep it quiet for a few hours. . . ."

"Why?"

"The description of the killers. It fit two men the White House had under surveillance. . . . That's not right. They had Webster under surveillance, and spotted them following Webster."

"I don't understand you, Sam."

"The two men were from Mario De Spadante's organization. . . . As I said, White House security went to work. Did you know that every conversation on every 1600 telephone, including the kitchen, is automatically put on a microtape and housed in the communications room; checked out, discarded, or kept every six months?"

"It doesn't surprise me."

"I think it would have surprised Webster. 1600 said it isn't common knowledge. But they had to tell us."

"What's your point? Why was the report impounded?"

"Bobby Webster was up to his ass with De Spadante. He was a paid informer. He's the one who removed the men in Darien. According to one conversation, you asked Webster for material on De Spadante."

"Yes. When we were in San Francisco; Webster never delivered."

"Regardless, the President thinks Webster was killed because De Spadante's men believe he was working with you. That he chickened and gave you the information that got De Spadante killed. . . . The assumption is that they cornered Bobby in the hotel room, forced him to tell them what was in the report, and when he couldn't, or didn't, they shot him."

"And if the report involves De Spadante, his loyalists will go after me next?"

"Yes, sir. The President was concerned that if any details of the report were leaked, you might become a target. No one wanted to alarm you, but a security detail picked you up in Arlington. Or they were supposed to."

Trevayne thought of the automobile behind his taxi; the brown sedan that had held up traffic. His brow creased in doubt; he looked at Sam. "Just how long is this solicitous concern for me supposed to last?"

"Apparently until they catch the men who killed Webster. De Spadante's loyalists."

Trevayne sat down behind his desk and reached into his pocket for a cigarette. He had the feeling that he was careening around a steep downhill curve, struggling to hold a wheel nearly out of control.

Was it possible? Was it possible, when he let the sunlight come into the dark corridors of his mind, that he was right, after all?

"As Paul Bonner would say," said Trevayne softly, " 'horseshit.' "

"Why? The concerns seem legitimate to me, sir."

"I hope you're right. I *pray* you're right. Because if you're wrong, Sam, a dying man is trying to protect his place in history."

Vicarson understood; and the look on his face showed that his understanding was the most serious comprehension he'd ever experienced. "Do you think the President is . . . Genessee Industries?"

"Get General Cooper on the phone."

49

Brigadier General Lester Cooper sat in front of Andrew Trevayne's desk. He was exhausted—with the fatigue of a man who'd reached the limits of his ability to cope.

"Everything I've done, I consider it a privilege to have been in my province to accomplish, Mr. Chairman."

"There's no necessity for that title, General. The name's 'Andy,' or 'Andrew,' or 'Mr. Trevayne,' if you insist. I respect you enormously; I'd consider it a privilege if you'd be less formal."

"That's kind of you; I'd prefer the formality. You've manifestly accused me of dereliction, conspiracy, and disregard of my oath. . . ."

"Goddamn it, *no*, General. I did not use those words. I *wouldn't* use them. . . . I think you've operated in an impossible position. You have a hostile electorate that begrudges you every dollar of your budget. You have an Army that demands attention. You have to reconcile those two extremes in an area I know very well. Supply! . . . I'm only asking you if you made the very same compromises I would have made! That's neither dereliction nor conspiracy, General. That's goddamn common sense! If you didn't make them, that would be a violation of your oath."

It was working, thought Trevayne with sad feelings of misgiving. The General was being primed. He stared at Trevayne, his look one of supplication.

"Yes. . . . There's really nowhere to turn, you know. You know, of course. I mean, after all, you of all people . . ."

"Why me?"

"Well, if you are what they say you are . . ."

"What is that?"

"You *understand*. . . . You wouldn't be where you are if you didn't. We're all aware of that. . . . I mean, you'll have our complete, enthusiastic endorsement. It's far-reaching, but, of course, you know that. . . ."

"Endorsement for what?"

"Please, Mr. Trevayne. . . . Are you testing me? Why is that necessary?"

"Perhaps it is. Maybe you're not good enough!"

"That's not right! You shouldn't say that! I've done *everything*—"

"For whom? For *me*?"

"I've done everything I was told to do. The logistics have gone out."

"Where?"

"Everywhere! In every port, on every base. Every airfield. We've covered every spot on earth! . . . Only the *name*. Only the name has to be supplied."

"And what is that name?"

"*Yours* . . . yours, for God's sake! What do you *want* from me?"

"Who gave you those orders?"

"What do you mean—"

"Who gave you the orders to put out my name?" Trevayne slapped the flat of his hand on his desk, flesh against hard wood, the sound sharp and distracting.

"I'm . . . I'm . . ."

"I asked you *who*?"

"The man from . . . the man from . . ."

"*Who?*"

"Green."

"Who's Green?"

"You *know!* . . . Genessee. Genessee Industries." Brigadier General Cooper slumped in his seat, breathing hard.

But Trevayne hadn't finished. He leaned across the desk. "*How long ago?* Were you in *time*, General? Were you on *schedule?* How long ago?"

"Oh, my God! . . . What *are* you?"

"*How long ago?*"

"A week, ten days. . . . What *are* you?"

"Your best friend! The man that gets you what you want! Would you like to believe that?"

"I don't know what to believe. . . . You people . . . you people drain me."

"None of that, General. . . . I asked you if you were on schedule."

"Oh, Jesus!"

"What were the *other* schedules, General? Were you on schedule with everyone else?"

"Stop it! *Stop it!*"

"Answer me."

"How do I know? *Ask them!*"

"Who?"

"I don't know!"

"Green?"

"Yes. Ask him!"

"Hamilton?"

"Yes, of course."

"What can they guarantee?"

"Everything! You *know* that!"

"Spell it out, you *latrine private!*"

"You can't *say* that. You have no *right!*"

"*Spell it out.*"

"It will be what you need. The unions. Management. . . . All the psychological profiles in every section of the country . . . we've got them in Army computers. . . . We'll act in *concert.*"

"Oh, my God. . . . Does the President know?"

"Certainly not from us."

"And nobody's countermanded those orders within the last five days?"

"Of course not!"

Trevayne suddenly lowered his voice as he sat back in his chair. "Are you sure, General?"

"Yes!"

Trevayne brought both his hands to his face and breathed into his palms. He had the feeling that he'd spun wildly off that long, steep downhill curve and was plunging uncontrollably into the turbulent waters below.

Why should there always be the sea?

"Thank you, General Cooper," said Trevayne gently. "I think we've finished."

"I beg your pardon?"

"I meant what I said. I respect you. I don't know that I would have if it hadn't been for Paul Bonner. . . . You've heard of Major Bonner, General? I believe we've discussed him. . . . Now, I'm going to offer you some unsolicited advice. Get out, Cooper. Get out quickly."

Brigadier General Lester Cooper, his eyes bloodshot, looked at the civilian who covered his face with his hands. "I don't understand."

"It's come to my attention that you anticipate retiring soon. . . . May I respectfully suggest that you formally write that letter of resignation first thing tomorrow morning?"

Cooper started to speak and then stopped. Andrew Trevayne took his hands away from his face and looked into the General's tired eyes. The officer made a last West Point gasp at control, but it couldn't work.

"You're not . . . you haven't . . . Am I free?"

"Yes. . . . Christ knows you deserve it."

"I hope so. Thank you, Mr. Chairman."

Sam Vicarson watched the General walk out of Trevayne's office. It was nearly six-thirty. Andrew had timed the meeting with Cooper to begin after five; no one but the three of them would be in the subcommittee's office, and Sam could bar any late visitors or staff members who might unexpectedly show up.

The Brigadier General looked at Vicarson, but there

was no recognition in his eyes, no sense of contact. Cooper stood motionless for several moments, his vacant, absently hostile expression concentrated on the young attorney. And then he did a strange—for Sam, a strangely terrible—thing. He stood erect and brought his right hand up to his visor and held it in a salute. He held his right hand in place until Sam Vicarson acknowledged by nodding his head silently. Only then did the General lower his hand, turn, and go out the door.

Sam walked quickly into Trevayne's office. The chairman of the subcommittee for the Defense Allocations Commission looked as exhausted as the decorated legend he had just confronted. Andrew was slumped back in his swivel chair, his chin resting in the palm of his right hand, his elbow on the arm of the chair. His eyes were closed.

"That must have been something," said Sam quietly. "I thought for a few minutes I should call for an ambulance. You should have seen Cooper outside. He looked as though he'd run head-on into a tank."

"Don't sound so satisfied," replied Trevayne, his eyes still shut. "There's nothing to gloat over. . . . I think we owe a lot to Cooper, to all the Coopers. We ask them to accomplish the impossible; give them no training—training, hell, we don't even warn them—on how to handle the political messiahs we force them to deal with. Finally we hold them up to ridicule when they try to cope." Trevayne opened his eyes and looked up at Sam. "Doesn't that strike you as unfair?"

"I'm afraid it doesn't, sir," answered Vicarson, only slightly mitigating his refusal to agree. "Men like Cooper —men who get that high—can find plenty of soap boxes, a lot of free time on television and radio on which to complain. At least, they can try that before going with Genessee Industries."

"Sam, Sam . . ." said Trevayne wearily. "You wouldn't 'yes' me if my sanity depended on it. I suppose that's an asset."

"Sure, I would. I may need a job someday."

"I doubt it." Trevayne got out of his chair, walked in front of his desk, and leaned back on the edge. "Do you realize what they've done, Sam? They've structured my so-called candidacy in such a way that to win means I win. as *their* candidate. Cooper was the proof of that."

"So what? You didn't ask for it."

"But I would have accepted it. Knowingly, consciously, I tacitly became an intrinsic part of the corruption I've claimed to be against. . . . To smite Lucifer is to smite myself."

"What?"

"Nothing. A little excess employed by Armbruster. . . . Do you see, now? Caesar's wife, Sam. The Calpurnia complex. If elected—or even halfway into the campaign—I couldn't turn on Genessee Industries because I'm as guilty as it is. If I try before the election, I guarantee my loss; if after, I erode the public's confidence in me. They have the ammunition to cripple me: the amended report; they waded me out. It was extraordinary strategy. . . . Thanks to Paul Bonner and a confused, overextended brigadier general, I found out before it was too late."

"Why did they do it? Why did they pick you?"

"For the simplest of all reasons, Sam. The twentieth-century motif. They had no choice. No alternative. . . . I was out to destroy Genessee Industries. And I could do it."

Vicarson stared down at the floor. "Oh, Jesus," he said softly. "I didn't understand. . . . What are you going to do?"

Trevayne pushed himself off the edge of the desk. "What I should have kept my mind on in the first place. Rip out Genessee. . . . Root by goddamn root!"

"That blows your candidacy."

"It certainly does."

"I'm sorry about that."

Andy stopped on his way back to the chair. He turned and looked in Sam's direction, but not at Sam. He looked beyond him to the windows, to the descending darkness that soon would be night in Washington, D.C. "Isn't it remarkable? I'm sorry, too. Genuinely sorry. How easily we convince ourselves. . . . How much easier still are we mistaken."

He continued back to the chair and sat down. He tore off the top page of a memorandum pad and picked up his Mark Cross pencil.

The telephone rang.

"I'll get it," said Sam, getting up from the couch and crossing to the desk. "Mr. Trevayne's office. . . . Yes, sir? Oh? Yes. I understand. Just one minute, please." Vicarson pushed the "hold" button and looked at Trevayne. "It's James Goddard. . . . He's in Washington."

50

James Goddard, president, San Francisco Division, Genessee Industries, sat across the room while Trevayne and Vicarson studied the voluminous papers and computer cards spread out over the long conference table. The room was large, an executive suite at the Shoreham Hotel.

Goddard had been brief nearly four hours ago when Trevayne and his aide first walked through the door. There was no reason, he felt, for extraneous conversation. The figures, the reports, the printed results of the Genessee master tape were all that was necessary.

Let the numbers do the talking.

He had watched the two men; they'd approached the carefully sorted-out display apprehensively. At first they were guarded, suspicious. Then gradually the magnitude of the indictment shook their sense of reality. As their disbelief turned into reluctant acceptance, Trevayne started hammering questions at him; questions he answered—when he wanted to answer them—in the simplest of terms.

Let the numbers do the talking.

The subcommittee chairman then ordered Vicarson to return to their offices and bring back a small multipurpose desk computer. The sort of machine that added, subtracted, divided, multiplied, and held figures in six-column accruals until needed. Without it, Trevayne had said, they'd be there a week trying to reach their own conclusions. With it, and with luck, they might accomplish the job by morning.

James Goddard could have completed the job in two hours, three at the outside.

It was four hours now, and still they hadn't finished. Amateurs.

Occasionally, then with growing rapidity, Trevayne turned to him and asked a question, expecting an immediate reply. Goddard laughed to himself as he "thoughtfully" found that the answer was not within his grasp. Trevayne was reaching the end; he wanted the specific names now, the master planners of the master tape. Goddard could easily supply them—Hamilton and Hamilton's faceless legion of "vice presidents" in Chicago: men who stayed in deep cover, out of sight, manipulating the huge national and international commitments.

They never let him reach that level. They never gave him a chance to show he had the qualifications to set entire courses, to create—with even more accuracy—the fiscal projections spanning the five-year interregnums. How often had he found it necessary to make major alterations within his own sphere because the master tape had carried errors that would have led to financial crises within isolated sectors of Genessee's production? How many times had he sent irrefutable proof back to Chicago that he was not only the public figurehead of Genessee's finances but, in fact, the one man capable of overseeing the work of the master tape?

The replies from Chicago—never written, always a faceless voice over a telephone—were invariably the same. They thanked him, acknowledged his contribution, and restated the premise that his value as president of the all-important San Francisco Division was without parallel. All to say he'd reached the end of his line.

In the final analysis, he was expendable. The public figurehead ready at the crack of a whip for a public hanging. And once that hanging was set, what could he possibly do about it?

Nothing. Absolutely nothing. For his "contributions" were there for all to see. And without the master tape, his "contributions" stopped at his office door.

But there was a way out, his only way.

To move swiftly to the top—his top—of the one conglomerate larger than Genessee Industries.

The United States government.

The kind of deal that was made every day under a dozen guises: "Consultant," "Expert," "Administrative Adviser."

It meant giving up the house in Palo Alto; and the beautiful hills that calmed him so with their majesty. On the other hand, it meant also giving up his wife—she'd never, never consent—and that was a plus.

But the biggest gain of all was his own sense of well-being. For from now on his "contributions" would not only be extraordinary—and acknowledged as such—but also indispensable. The history of Genessee Industries' ascent to its present position covered nearly twenty years. To untangle that extraordinary financial interweaving would take, perhaps, a decade.

And he, James Goddard, "Expert," was the economic legend who could do it. It would have to be done, for it was, after all, an intrinsic part of the history of twentieth-century America. He would record for the millennia that history. Scholars for a thousand years would research his words, study his figures, hold his knowledge in reverence.

The government itself, right up to the highest reaches of decision making, would consider him the indispensable man.

No one could do what he could do now.

To have that acknowledged was all that he wanted. Couldn't Ian Hamilton and the faceless voices in Chicago understand? It wasn't money; it wasn't power.

It was respect. A respect that took him out of the realm of being primed for hanging.

It was nearly five hours now. Trevayne and his voluble, obnoxious assistant had gone through two pots of coffee. The chain-smoking chairman had stopped asking questions; the aide kept shoving cards and papers in front of Trevayne—they'd finally understood the pattern of financial sequence as he'd arranged it. They hadn't acknowledged it, of course, but they fell into a rhythm on the desk computer that silently betrayed the fact.

Soon it would come. The question.

Then the deal.

It would all be spelled out. Nothing left to speculation.

It was really quite simple when one analyzed it. He was merely changing sides, altering his allegiances.

He watched Andrew Trevayne get up from the table and rip the wide paper tape from the machine. The subcommittee chairman looked at it, placed it in front of his assistant, and began rubbing his eyes.

"Finished?"

"Finished?" answered Trevayne with the same question. "I think you know better than that. It's just begun, I'm sorry to say."

"Yes. Yes, of course. Precisely. . . . It *has* just begun. There are years, volumes to be completed. I'm well aware of it. . . . We must talk now."

"Talk? Us? . . . No, Mr. Goddard. It may not be finished, but I am. You talk to others. . . . If you can find them."

"What does that mean?"

"I won't pretend to understand your motives, Goddard. You're either the bravest man I've ever met . . . or so consumed with guilt you've lost all sense of perspective. Either way, I'll try to help. You deserve that. . . . But I don't think anyone's going to want to touch you. Not the people who should. . . . They won't know where your leprosy ends. Or whether they've got a latent case, and standing next to you might make their skin fall off."

51

The President of the United States rose from behind his desk in the Oval Office as Andrew Trevayne entered. The first thing that struck Trevayne was the presence of William Hill. Hill was standing across the room in front of the French doors, reading some papers in the harsh light of the early sun off the terrace. The President, seeing Andy's obvious reaction to a third party, spoke rapidly.

"Good morning, Mr. Trevayne. The Ambassador is here at my request; my insistence, if you like."

Trevayne approached the desk and shook the hand

extended to him. "Good morning, Mr. President." He turned and took several steps toward Hill, who met him halfway between the desk and the French doors. "Mr. Ambassador."

"Mr. Chairman."

Trevayne felt the ice in Hill's voice, the title spoken in an emphasized monotone that skirted the edge of insult. The Ambassador was an angry man. That was fine, thought Andrew. Strange, but fine. He was angry himself. He returned his attention to the President, who indicated a chair—one of four forming a semicircle in front of the desk.

"Thank you." Trevayne sat down.

"What is that quote?" asked the President with slim humor. " 'We three do meet again. . . .' Is that it?"

"I believe," said Hill slowly, still standing, "that the correct words are '*When* shall we three meet again?' The three in question had forecast the fall of a government; they weren't sure even they could survive."

The President watched Hill; his eyes bore deeply into the old man's, his look a cross between compassion and irritation. "I think that's highly interpretive, Bill. A bias I'm not sure would hold up academically."

"Fortunately, Mr. President, the academicians do not concern me."

"They should, Mr. Ambassador," said the President curtly, turning to Trevayne. "I can only assume, Mr. Trevayne, that you requested this meeting as a result of my exercising executive privilege. I intercepted the subcommittee report on grounds you find suspect, and you'd like an explanation. You're entirely justified; the grounds I employed were fallacious."

Andrew was surprised. He hadn't questioned the grounds at all. They were for his protection. "I wasn't aware of that, Mr. President. I accepted your explanation up front."

"Really? I'm amazed. The device seemed so transparent to me. At least, I thought you'd think so. . . . Robert Webster's death was a private war, in no way connected with you. You don't know those people, you couldn't identify them. Webster did and could, and therefore had to be silenced. You're the last person on earth they'd want to touch."

Trevayne flushed, partly in anger, more so because of his own ineptness. Of course, he was the "last person on earth they'd want to touch." Killing him would create a furor, bring about a relentless investigation, an intense hunt for the killers. Not so Robert Webster. No intense pursuit for his killers; Bobby Webster was an embarrassment to everyone. Including the man who sat behind the desk in the Oval Office.

"I see. Thanks for the lesson in practicality."

"That's what this job's all about."

"Then I would like an explanation, sir."

"You shall have it, Mr. Chairman," said William Hill as he crossed to the chair farthest away from Trevayne and sat down.

The President spoke quickly, attempting to vitiate Hill's invective. "Of course, you will; you must. But, if you'll forgive me, I'd like to exercise another privilege. Let's not call it executive; let's just say the prerogative of an older man. Then we can get on. . . . I'm curious. Why did you consider this meeting so vital? If I've been accurately informed, you damn near told the appointments desk that you'd camp in the hallways until I saw you. . . . A tight morning schedule was rearranged. . . . The report's complete. The formalities of leave-taking aren't exactly priority functions."

"I wasn't sure when you'd release the report."

"And that concerns you?"

"Yes, Mr. President."

"*Why?*" interrupted William Hill harshly. "Do you think the President intends suppressing it?"

"No. . . . It's not complete."

There was silence for several seconds as the President and the Ambassador exchanged looks. The President leaned back in his chair. "I stayed up most of the night reading it, Mr. Trevayne. It seemed complete to me."

"It's not."

"What's missing?" asked Hill. "Or should I ask, what's been removed?"

"Both are accurate, Mr. Hill. Omitted and removed. . . .

For what I believed at the time were reasoned judgments, I eliminated detailed—and indictable—information about the Genessee Industries Corporation."

The President sat up and stared at Trevayne. "Why did you do that?"

"Because I thought I was capable of controlling the situation in a less inflammatory manner. I was mistaken. It must be exposed. Completely."

The President looked away from Andrew, his elbow on the arm of the chair, his fingers tapping a slow rhythm on his chin. "Often first—reasoned—judgments are quite valid. Especially when they emanate from such reasonable men as yourself."

"In the case of Genessee Industries, my judgment was in error. I was persuaded by an argument that proved groundless."

"Would you please clarify?" asked Hill.

"Of course. I was led to believe—no, that's not right, I convinced myself—that I could bring about a solution by forcing the removal of those responsible. By eliminating them, the root motives could be altered. The corporation —or companies, hundreds of them—could then be subject to restructuring. Reshaped administratively and brought into line with compatible business practices."

"I see," said the President. "Root out the corrupters, the corruption will follow, and chaos is averted. Is that it?"

"Yes, sir."

"But the corrupters, in the final analysis, would not be rooted," added Hill, avoiding Trevayne's eyes.

"That's my conclusion."

"You're aware that your . . . solution is infinitely preferable to the chaos that would result from ripping Genessee Industries apart. Genessee is the major producer for the country's defense program. To lose confidence in such an institution would have extraordinary effects throughout the nation." The President once more leaned back in his chair.

"That was my initial thinking."

"I think it's sound."

"It's no longer feasible, Mr. President. As Mr. Hill just said . . . the corrupters can't be rooted."

"But can they be used?" The President's tone was steady, not questioning.

"Ultimately, no. The longer they're entrenched, the more secure their control. They're building a base that will be passed on as they see fit; to whom they consider fit. And they deal in their own absolutes. A council of elite that will be inherited by their own kind—protected by unimaginable economic resources. Exposure's the only solution. Immediate exposure."

"Aren't you now dealing in your own absolutes, Mr. *Chairman?*"

Trevayne was annoyed once again by Hill's use of the title. "I'm telling you the truth."

"Whose truth?" asked the Ambassador.

"*The* truth, Mr. Hill."

"It wasn't the truth when you submitted your report. The truth changed. The judgment was altered."

"Yes. Because the facts weren't known."

William Hill lowered his voice and spoke with no apparent feeling. "What facts? Or was it a *single* fact? The fact that you'd compromised your subcommittee for what you discovered was a hollow offer. The presidency of the United States."

The muscles of Andrew Trevayne's stomach tensed. He looked at the President.

"You knew."

"Did you really think I wouldn't?"

"Strangely enough, I hadn't given it much thought. I suppose that's asinine."

"Why? It's not a betrayal of me. I asked you to do a job; I didn't demand political fidelity; or adherence."

"But you did demand integrity, Mr. President," said Hill with conviction.

"Whose description of integrity, Mr. Ambassador?" shot back the chief executive. "Must I remind you of your own admonitions regarding truths and absolutes? . . . Oh, no, Mr. Trevayne, I'm not being kind. Or solicitous. I'm only convinced that you conducted yourself in good conscience—*as you understood it.* . . . Which makes my job easier. For the reason I intercepted the subcommittee report—my sole purpose in exercising privilege—was to stop you from tearing this country apart. . . . From using Genessee Industries as the means to destroy a large section of the economy unnecessarily. Depriving livelihoods, ruining reputations indiscriminately. You can imagine my astonishment when I read what you'd written."

Andrew Trevayne returned the President's stare. "I find that an extraordinary statement."

"No more extraordinary than I found your report. And the fact that you refused to announce—at least to any of the proposed recipients—the exact date when you'd deliver the report. You made no arrangements with the Government Printing Office; you did not, as is customary, avail yourself of Justice Department attorneys prior to the final assembling—"

"I was not aware of those customs; and if I had been, I doubt I'd have complied."

"Courtesy, expediency, and simple protection might have made you aware of them," interjected Hill. "As I gather, your mind was on other, more vital matters."

"Mr. Ambassador, you've been pressing me against the wall since I walked in. I don't like it! Now, with all due respect, I ask you to stop it."

"With very little respect returned, Mr. Trevayne, I shall be guided by my chosen vocabulary until the President asks otherwise."

"Then I do ask it, Bill. . . . Mr. Hill has worked closely with this office, with a number of my predecessors, Trevayne. He looks upon your action more severely than I do." The President smiled gently. "The Ambassador is not, nor will he ever be, a politician. He believes, quite simply, that you're trying to rob me of my second term. I wish you luck; I don't think you can. Or 'could have,' I assume, is more proper."

Trevayne took a silent breath before speaking. "If I had believed for one minute that you were going to run for re-election, none of this would have happened. I'm sorry. Sorrier than I can ever express to you."

The President's smile diminished and was no more. Hill began to speak but was stopped by the President's hand, held up firmly, commanding silence. "I think you'd better explain that, Mr. Trevayne."

"I was told you would not seek a second term . . . the decision was irrevocable."

"And you accepted that."

"It was the basis of my discussions. Finally the only basis."

"Were you told why?"

"Yes. . . . I'm sorry."

The President searched Trevayne's face, and Andrew felt sick. He didn't want to look at this good, fine man, but he knew he could not waver.

"My health?" asked the President simply.

"Yes."

"Cancer?"

"I inferred that. . . . I'm sorry."

"Don't be. It's a lie."

"Yes, Mr. President."

"I said it's a lie."

"Very well, sir."

"You're not reading me, Mr. Trevayne. It *is* a lie. The simplest, crudest lie that can be used in the political arena."

Trevayne's jaw fell slack as he looked at the maturely lined, strong features of the man behind the desk. The President's eyes were steady, conveying the truth of his statement.

"Then I'm a damn fool."

"I'd rather that than face the diminishing returns of cobalt. . . . I have every intention of assuming the standard of my party, campaigning, and being returned to office. Is that clear?"

"Yes."

"Mr. Trevayne." William Hill spoke softly. "Please accept my apologies. You're not the only damn fool in this room." The old man attempted a tight-lipped smile. "We're neck-and-neck on a slow track for last place. . . . We're both a little ludicrous."

"Who specifically read you my premature obituary?"

"It was read twice. The first time was at the Villa d'Este in Georgetown. I went there a skeptic—to see who would try to buy off the subcommittee report. To my astonishment, no one did; quite the opposite, as a matter of fact. I emerged a three-quarters candidate."

"You still haven't—"

"Sorry. Senator Alan Knapp. In what I think was called 'true bipartisan spirit,' he made the announcement that you were leaving at the end of your present term. And the good of the country came first."

The President, turning his head only slightly in Hill's direction, spoke. "You'll follow this up, Bill?"

"The energetic Senator will retire before the end of the month. Consider it a Christmas present, Mr. President."

"Go on, please."

"The second instance was in New York. At the Waldorf. I held what I believed was a showdown with Aaron Green and Ian Hamilton. . . . I thought I'd won; therefore, the report as you read it. Hamilton said you wouldn't live out a second term; you were putting up either the Vice President or the Governor of New York. They couldn't accept either one."

"Scylla and Charybdis strike again, eh, Bill?"

"They've gone too far!"

"They always do. Don't touch them."

"I understand."

Trevayne watched the short interplay between the two older men. "Mr. President, *I* don't understand. How can you *say* that? Those men should—"

"We'll get to that, Mr. Trevayne," interrupted the President. "One last question. When did you learn that you'd been manipulated? Manipulated brilliantly, I might add, now that I see the pattern."

"Paul Bonner."

"Who?"

"Major Paul Bonner—"

"From the Pentagon," said the President as a statement of fact. "The one who killed that man up at your house in Connecticut?"

"Yes, sir. He saved my life; he'll be acquitted of the murder charge. He then faces court-martial; he's being drummed out."

"You don't think that's justified?"

"I do not. I don't agree very often with the Major, but—"

"I'll review it," cut in the chief executive as he hastily scribbled a note on his desk. "What did this Bonner tell you?"

Andrew paused briefly; he wanted to be precise, completely accurate. He owed that to Bonner. "That a brigadier general named Cooper, in a state of depression, anxiety, told him I was the Pentagon's candidate; that the irony of the Major's situation was that in the final analysis . . ." Trevayne paused again, embarrassed by his own words. "Bonner's court-martial might be rescinded by executive intervention. . . . My intervention."

"Good Lord," uttered Hill almost inaudibly.

"And?"

"It didn't make sense. I looked upon my meeting with Hamilton and Green as a success, a capitulation on their part. I was sure of two things. The first was that I was not their candidate; the second, that they accepted my terms. They were getting out. . . . Bonner's information contradicted everything I believed."

"So you called in Cooper," said the President.

"I did. And I learned not only that I was the Pentagon's—Genessee Industries'—candidate, but I had been from the beginning. Every resource of the military—Army intelligence data banks, industrial collusion, even interservice voting indoctrinations—they'd all be used to ensure my election. Management, labor, the service ballot; voting blocs guaranteed by Genessee. There was no capitulation in New York; they weren't getting out. They were *wading me* out. If I got the nomination—God forbid the office—I'd be hanged. To be independent, to expose them at that point, would be to expose myself."

"At which juncture—junctures—you'd destroy your candidacy or—God forbid—the national and international confidence of your administration," completed the President.

"They took considerable risks," said William Hill. "It's not like them."

"What alternative did they have, Bill? He couldn't be bought. Or persuaded. If our young friend hadn't gone to them, they would have come to him. Same solution, on the surface. Orderly retreat as opposed to economic chaos. I would have subscribed; so would you."

"You talk as if you know all about . . . *them*."

"A great deal, yes. Hardly 'all.' I'm sure there are areas you've covered that we're not aware of. We'd appreciate a full briefing. Classified, of course."

"Classified? This material can't be classified, Mr. President. It's got to be made public."

"You didn't think so twenty-four hours ago."

"The conditions weren't the same."

"I've read the report; it's entirely satisfactory."

"It's *not* satisfactory. I spent five hours last night with a man named Goddard—"

"Genessee. President, San Francisco Division," said William Hill quietly, in response to the glance from the man behind the desk.

"He walked out of San Francisco with four briefcases filled with Genessee commitments—extending for years. A good percentage of which have never been *heard* of before."

"I'm sure you'll cover that in your briefing. The report stands as submitted."

"No. It can't! I won't accept that!"

"You *will* accept it!" The President's voice suddenly matched Trevayne's. "You'll accept it because it is the decision of this office."

"You can't enforce that decision! You have no control over me!"

"Don't be so sure of that. You submitted—*officially* submitted—your report to this office. The document is over your signature. Incidentally, we have in our possession four copies with the seals unbroken. To speculate that this single report is not authentic; that it must be recalled because it's been tampered with, shaped by the political ambitions of the subcommittee's chairman, would raise the gravest issues. To allow you to recall it—for whatever the stated reasons—would also make my administration suspect. Our adversaries would claim we demanded changes. I can't permit that. This office deals daily with both domestic and foreign complexities; you will not compromise our effectiveness in these areas because *your* ambitions have been thwarted. In this instance, we must remain above suspicion."

Trevayne's voice conveyed his astonishment. He could hardly be heard. "That's what they would have said."

"I have no compunctions stealing someone's strategy if it has merit."

"And if I stand up and say it's not authentic, not complete?"

"Outside of the personal anguish—and ridicule—to which you subject yourself and your family," said William Hill quietly, staring at Trevayne, "who would believe you? . . . You sold your credibility when you sent out that report yesterday morning. Now you wish to substitute a second? Perhaps there'll be a third—if a group of politicians recommend you for the governorship. Even a fourth—there are other offices, other appointments. Where does the flexible chairman stop? Just how many reports are there?"

"I don't care about other people's opinions. I've said it from the beginning—over and over again. I've nothing to gain or lose."

"Except your effectiveness as a functioning, contributive individual," said the President. "You couldn't live without that, Mr. Trevayne. No one with your abilities could. And it would be taken from you; you'd be isolated from the community of your peers. You'd never be trusted again. I don't think you could live that existence. We all need something; none of us is totally self-sufficient."

Andrew, his eyes locked with the President's, understood the essential truth of the man's words. "You'd do that? You'd have it come out that way?"

"I most certainly would."

"*Why?*"

"Because I must deal in priorities. Quite simply, I need Genessee Industries."

"No! . . . No. You can't mean that. You know what it *is!*"

"I know it serves a function; I know it can be controlled. That's all I have to know."

"Today. Perhaps tomorrow. Not in a few years. It's out to destroy."

"It won't succeed."

"You can't guarantee that."

The President suddenly slapped his hand on the arm of his chair and stood up. "No one can guarantee anything. There are risks every time I walk into this room; dangers every time I walk out. . . . You listen to me, Trevayne. I believe deeply in the capacity of this country to serve the decent instincts of her own people—and of mankind. But I'm practical enough to realize that in the service of this decency there must often be indecent manipulations. . . . Does that surprise you? It shouldn't. For surely you know not all the weapons will be turned into plowshares; Cain will murder Abel; the locusts will plague the land; and the oppressed will get goddamn sick and tired of looking forward to inheriting the creature comforts of an afterlife! They want something down here! And whether *you* like it or not—whether *I* like it or not—Genessee Industries is doing something about these things! . . . It's my considered judgment that it is not a threat. It can and will be contained. *Used,* Mr. Trevayne. *Used.*"

"With every turn," said Hill with compassion, seeing the look of shock on Trevayne's face, "there's the constant seeking of solutions. Do you remember my telling you that? That *search* is the solution. It is continuously applied to such entities as Genessee Industries. The President is right."

"He's not right," replied Andrew quietly, painfully, looking at the man who stood behind the desk. "It's no solution; it's a surrender."

"An employable strategy." The President sat down. "Eminently suited to our system."

"Then the system's wrong."

"Perhaps," said the President, reaching for some papers. "I haven't the time to indulge in such speculations."

"Don't you think you should?"

"No," answered the man, looking up from a page, dismissing Trevayne's plea. "I have to run the country."

"Oh, my God . . ."

"Take your moral outrage somewhere else, Mr. Trevayne. Time. Time is what I must deal with. Your report stands."

As if it were an afterthought, the President shifted the paper and extended his right hand over the desk as Andrew stood up.

Trevayne looked at the hand, held steady, as the man's eyes were steady.

He did not accept it.

52

Paul Bonner looked around the courtroom for Trevayne. It was difficult to find him, for the crowds were milling, the voices pitched high, reporters demanding statements, and the incessant silent pops of flashbulbs were coming from all directions. Andrew had been there for the morning summations, and Paul thought it strange that he didn't remain—at least for a while—to see if the jury would return an early verdict.

It did.

In one hour and five minutes.

Acquittal.

Bonner hadn't worried. As the trial progressed he'd been confident that his own Army counsel could have handled the job without Trevayne's elegant, hard-as-nails attorneys from New York. But there was no denying the value of their collective image. They were the essence of respectability; whenever they referred to the De Spadantes or their associates, there was implied revulsion. So successful were they that several members of the jury nodded affirmatively when the comparison was made between the professional soldier who, for years, had risked his life in the murderous jungles defending the nation's institutions, and the brother-brokers who sought to bleed these same institutions of money and honor.

Trevayne was nowhere to be found.

Paul Bonner made his way through the crowd toward the courtroom door. He tried to maintain a grateful smile as he was jostled and yelled at. He promised to have a "statement later," and mouthed the appropriate clichés about his abiding faith in the judicial system.

The empty, hollow phrases that contradicted the terrible knowledge inside him. In less than a month he'd know the wrath of military intransigence. He wouldn't win that fight. The battle had been decided.

On the courthouse steps he looked for his uniformed escort, for the brown sedan that would take him back to Arlington, to his barracks arrest. It wasn't in sight; it wasn't parked where he'd been told it would be.

Instead, a master sergeant, tunic and trousers creased into steel, shoes gleaming, approached Bonner.

"If you'll follow me, please, Major."

The automobile at the curb was a tan-metallic limousine, two flags mounted in the front, one on each side of the hood above the wide grille. They rustled hesitantly in the December breeze. Enough to reveal four gold stars on each laterally across a red background.

The sergeant opened the right-rear door for Bonner as newsmen and photographers crowded around him firing questions and snapping pictures. Paul didn't need to speculate on the identity of the General in the back seat. The reporters had established it in loud, excited voices.

The Chairman of the Joint Chiefs of Staff of the United States.

The General offered no greeting as Bonner entered and sat beside him. He stared straight ahead at the glass partition separating the driver from his Very Important Passengers.

Outside, the sergeant shouldered his way around the vehicle and got behind the wheel. The car drove off; at first slowly, the driver coldly impatient with the crowd, pressing the horn continuously in an effort to clear his path.

"That little scene was ordered, Major. I hope you appreciate it." The General spoke curtly, without looking at Bonner.

"You sound as though you didn't approve, sir."

The senior officer looked abruptly at Bonner, and then, just as rapidly, turned away. He reached over to the left door panel, to the elasticized pocket, and withdrew a manila envelope. "The second order I received was to deliver this to you personally. It is equally distasteful to me."

He handed the envelope to Bonner, who, bewildered, responded with an inaudible thank-you. The printing on the upper-left-hand corner told him that the contents were from the Department of the Army, not the Joint Chiefs of Staff. He ripped the flap open and extracted a single page. It was a copy of a letter from the White House, addressed to the Secretary of the Army and signed by the President of the United States.

The language was terse, to the point, and left no room for interpretation—other than the degree of anger, perhaps hostility, felt by the author.

The President directed the Secretary of the Army to terminate forthwith all contemplated charges against Major Paul Bonner. Said Major Bonner was to be elevated immediately to the permanent rank of full colonel and entered within the month to the War College for highest-level strategic training. Upon completion of the War College curriculum—an estimated six months—Colonel Bonner was to be assigned as a liaison officer to the Joint Chiefs of Staff.

Paul Bonner put the letter carefully back into the envelope and sat silently beside the General. He closed his eyes and thought about the irony of it all.

But he'd been right all along. That was the important thing.

It was back to work.

What did the beavers know?

Yet he was strangely troubled; he wasn't sure why. Perhaps it was the escalation in rank. Not one jump, but two. It was disconcertingly parallel to a promise made on an icy Connecticut slope, words that ended with ripped flesh and finally death.

But he wouldn't dwell on it. He was a professional.

It was a time for professionals.

Ian Hamilton patted the wet fur of his Chesapeake retriever. The large dog kept running ahead on the snow-covered path to pick up a stray branch or a loose rock, bringing it back to its master for approval.

It was a particularly gratifying Sunday morning, thought Hamilton. Ten days ago he wasn't sure he'd be taking any more Sunday walks; at least not on the shores of Lake Michigan.

All that was changed now. The fear was gone, and his normal sense of elation, the quiet elation that came with great accomplishment, returned. And the irony of it! The one man he had feared, the only one who had the real capacity to destroy them, had removed himself from the chessboard.

Or had been removed.

Either way, it proved that the course of action he'd insisted upon was the correct action. Aaron Green had nearly fallen apart; Armbruster spoke in panic of early retirement; Cooper—poor, beleaguered, unimaginative Cooper—had run to the Vermont hills, his uniform stained with the sweat of hysteria.

But he, Ian Hamilton, who could trace his family back to the origins of the infant colossus, whose forebears were the lairds of Cambusquith, he'd held firm.

Practically speaking—*pragmatically* speaking—he'd felt secure. Far more so than the others. For he knew all they had to do was wait until Andrew Trevayne's "abridged" version was released from the Potomac Towers. Once that happened, who would make, *could* make, the decision to allow him to submit the report in its original form? The rope would be on fire at both ends; Trevayne trapped by his own compromise, and the government's need for equilibrium.

William Hill as much as admitted it.

Big Billy. Hamilton wondered if Hill would ever realize how great a part—unknowingly, of course—he'd played in the development of Genessee Industries. He'd no doubt take his own life if he did. But it was true; Ambassador William Hill had been largely responsible. For over the Washington years Hamilton had watched Big Billy closely. They both were "friends to," advisers to presidents; Hill much older, of course. He'd seen Big Billy's words stricken from the record more than once. He'd sympathized as

Hill's advice to Eisenhower over the U-2 crisis in Paris had gone unheeded—the summit meeting aborted; he'd felt for the old man when McNamara persuaded Kennedy that Hill's judgment on Berlin was in error—the Wall was the result; he'd winced openly when those maniacs at the Pentagon convinced a perplexed, malleable Nixon that the "incursion" into Cambodia was necessary—over the loud, intensely felt objections of William Hill.

Kent State, Jackson. An all but destroyed Joint Chiefs of Staff.

And Ian Hamilton realized that he'd been observing a man whose shoes he might jump into; a version of himself in a few years to come.

Unacceptable.

The alternative was the power and influence of Genessee Industries.

He'd concentrated on that. For everyone's good.

The Chesapeake retriever was now trying to separate a twig from a fallen limb. The twig held firm; Hamilton bent down and twisted it off.

It took considerable strength, he considered, but he wasn't even breathing hard.

Big Billy.

Big Billy had flown out to Chicago—an emissary from the President of the United States. They'd met in private in a suite at the Palmer House.

There were areas of mutual concern to be discussed. Mutual concern. The President wanted to see him, meet with him in Washington.

Accommodation would be reached.

The Chesapeake retriever had found another stick. But this one was different from the others; there were several sharp points where the bark had been stripped from the white wood. The dog whimpered, and Ian Hamilton could see that there was blood trickling down from the mouth over the wet fur.

Sam Vicarson sat on top of the packed, sealed carton and looked around at the empty room. Empty except for the couch which had been there when the subcommittee had taken over the office. The movers were about fin-

ished. The chairs, the desks, the file cabinets had all disappeared, taken back to wherever chairs and desks and
file cabinets went when there was no more use for them.

The cartons were his only concern. Trevayne had told
him to oversee their crating and removal into the truck.
The truck that would take them to Trevayne's house in
Connecticut.

Why in God's name would he want them?

Who *would* want them?

Blackmailers, perhaps.

But these weren't the important files. The Genessee
files.

Those had long since been removed from the Tawning
Spring basement; sealed in wooden crates, with locks and
guards and—as he understood it—driven directly to the
underground vaults in the White House.

Cop-out.

Trevayne had copped out; they'd all copped out.

Trevayne tried to tell him that he hadn't; that the decisions made were for—what were the fatuous words?—
the "greater good." Trevayne had forgotten that he, himself, had termed such words "the twentieth-century
syndrome."

Cop-out.

He wouldn't have believed it a month ago. He wouldn't
have considered it possible.

And, goddamn it, a man—a young man—had to look
out for himself.

He had the options; Christ, did he have options! Trevayne had secured him offers from half a dozen top corporate firms in New York—including Walter Madison's.
And Aaron Green—pretending to have been impressed
with him at the Waldorf—had said he would go to work
next week as the head of his agency's legal department.

But the best of all was right here in Washington. A
man named Smythe, chief of the White House staff.

There was an opening.

What could look better on a résumé than the White
House?

*   *   *

James Goddard sat on the thin, hard bed in the dingy rented room. He could hear the breathy wail of a wood-wind—a primitive recorder, perhaps—and the intermittent, discordant twang of a Far East string instrument—a sitar, he thought. The players were on drugs, he knew that much.

Goddard wasn't a drinker, but he'd gotten drunk. Very drunk. In a filthy bar that opened early in the morning for the filthy, glassy-eyed drunks who had to have that drink before they went to their filthy jobs—if they had jobs.

He'd stayed in a back booth with his four briefcases—his precious briefcases—and had one drink after another.

He was so much better than anyone else in the bar—everyone could see that. And because he was better, the filthy bartender made it a point to be solicitous—which, God knew, he should have been. Then several of the filthy bar's filthy clientele had wandered over and been respectful—solicitous—also. He'd bought a number of drinks for the filthy people. Actually, he'd had no choice; the bartender said he couldn't change a hundred-dollar bill, so the natural solution was to purchase merchandise.

He'd mentioned to the filthy bartender that he wouldn't be averse to having a woman. No, not a woman, a young girl. A young girl with large breasts and firm thin legs. Not a woman with sagging breasts and fat legs, who spoke with a nasal twang and complained. It was important that the young girl with the large breasts and firm thin legs speak pleasantly—if she spoke at all.

The filthy bartender in the filthy apron found him several young girls. He'd brought them back to the booth for Goddard to make his selection. He chose the one who unbuttoned her blouse and showed him her large, pointed breasts. She actually unbuttoned her blouse and pushed her breasts above her brassiere and smiled at him!

And when she spoke, her voice was soft, almost melodious.

She needed money in a hurry; he didn't ask why. She said if she had money she'd calm down and give him a work-out he'd never forget.

If he gave her money, she'd take him to a wonderful

old house in a quiet, old section of Washington where he could stay as long as he liked and no one would find him. And there were other girls there; young girls with large breasts . . . and other wonderful things.

She'd sat down beside him in the booth and reached between his legs and held his organ.

His wife had never, never done that. And the girl's voice was soft; there wasn't the harsh hostility he'd put up with for nearly twenty-five years; there was no inherent complaint, only supplication.

He agreed, and showed her the money. He didn't give it to her, he only showed it.

He wasn't Genessee Industries' "keystone" for nothing.

But he had one last purchase to make from the filthy bartender before he left with the young, large-breasted girl.

The filthy bartender at first hesitated, but his hesitation disappeared when James Goddard produced another hundred-dollar bill.

The old Victorian house was everything the girl said it would be. He was given a room; he carried the briefcases himself; he wouldn't let anyone touch them.

And she did calm down; and she did come to his room. And when he'd finished, when he'd exploded in an explosion he hadn't experienced in twenty-five years, she quietly left, and he rested.

He was finished resting now. He sat on the bed—a bed of such memory—and looked at the four briefcases piled on a filthy table. He got up, naked except for his knee-length socks, and walked to the table. He remembered precisely which briefcase held the final purchase he'd made from the filthy bartender.

It was the second from the top.

He lifted the first briefcase off the stack and placed it on the floor. He opened the next.

Lying on top of the cards and the papers was a gun.

53

It had begun.

This doomed land, this 'Armageddon of the planet, this island of the power-damned where the greeds had fed upon themselves until the greatest good became the greatest evil. For the land belonged to the power-damned.

And the insanity was abruptly, shockingly made clear with a single act of horror.

Andrew Trevayne sat at the dining-room table in front of the large picture window overlooking the water, and his whole body trembled. The morning sun, careening shafts of blinding light off the surface of the ocean, did not herald the glory of morning, but offered, instead, a terrible foreboding. As if flashes of lightning kept crashing across the horizon through the bright sunlight.

An unending daytime of hell.

Trevayne forced his eyes back to the newspaper. The headlines stretched across The New York *Times*, roaring the impersonality of objective terror:

PRESIDENT ASSASSINATED:
SLAIN IN WHITE HOUSE DRIVEWAY
BY BUSINESS EXECUTIVE

Pronounced Dead at 5:31 p.m.

Assassin Takes Own Life; James Goddard, Pres., San Francisco Div. of Genessee Industries, Identified as Killer.
Vice President Sworn into Office at 7:00 p.m.
Calls Cabinet Meeting. Congress Reconvened.

The act was ludicrously simple. The President of the United States was showing newsmen the progress of the Christmas decorations on the White House lawn when in a holiday spirit he greeted the last contingent of tourists leaving the grounds. James Goddard had been among them; as recalled by the guides, Goddard had made numerous tours of the White House during the past several days.

Merry Christmas, Mr. President.

The inside pages were filled with biographical material about Goddard and speculative conjectures about the atrocity. Interviews hastily written, hysterically responded to, were given un-thought-out importance.

And in the lower-right-hand corner of the front page was a report, the obscenity of which caused Trevayne to stare in disbelief.

REACTION AT GENESSEE

San Francisco, Dec. 18—Private aircraft flew in from all over the country throughout the night bringing top Genessee management to the city. The executive personnel have been closeted in meetings, attempting to unravel the mystery behind the tragic events of yesterday in Washington. One significant result of these conferences is the emergence of Louis Riggs as the apparent spokesman for Genessee Industries' San Francisco Division, considered the company's headquarters. Riggs, a combat veteran of Vietnam, is the young economist who was Goddard's chief aide and top accountant. Insiders say that Riggs had for weeks been concerned over his superior's erratic behavior; that the young aide had privately sent a number of confidential memoranda to other top-level management personnel stating his concerns. It was also revealed that Riggs will fly to Washington for a meeting with the newly sworn-in President.

It had begun.

And Andrew Trevayne knew he could not let it continue. He could not bear witness to the cataclysm without raising an anguished voice, without letting the country know.

But the country was in panic; the world was in panic. He could not compound that hysteria with his anguish.

That much he knew.

He knew also that he could not react as his wife had reacted, as his children had.

His daughter. His son.

The lost, bewildered guardians of tomorrow.

The girl had been the first to bring the news. Both children were home for the holidays, and both had been out separately: Pam involved with Christmas shopping, Steve with other young men his age, regreeting one another, exaggerating their first semesters. Andy and Phyllis had been in the downstairs study quietly making plans for getting away in January.

Phyllis insisted on the Caribbean; a hot country where Andy could spend hours on his beloved ocean, sailing around the islands, letting the warm winds ease the hurt and the anger. They'd take a house in St. Martin; they'd use some of their well-advertised money to help heal the wounds.

The door of the study was open, the only sound the hum of the wall vacuum being used by Lillian somewhere upstairs.

They'd both heard the crash of the front door, the hysterical sobs through the cries for help.

Cries for a mother and father. For somebody.

They'd raced out of the study, up the stairs, and seen their daughter standing in the hallway, tears streaming down her face, her eyes afraid.

"Pam! For heaven's sake, what's the matter?"

"Oh, God! *God!* You don't *know?*"

"Know?"

"Turn on the radio. Call somebody. He was killed!"

"Who?"

"The President was killed! He was killed!"

"Oh, my God." Phyllis spoke inaudibly as she turned to her husband and searched his face; Andrew instinctively reached for her. The unspoken statements—questions—were too clear, too intimate, too filled with agony and personal fear to surface the words.

"*Why? Why?*" Pamela Trevayne was screaming.

Andrew released his wife and silently, gently commanded

her to go to their daughter. He walked rapidly into the living room, to the telephone.

There was nothing anyone could tell him but the terrible facts, the unbelievable narrative. Nearly every private line he knew in Washington was busy. The few that weren't had no time for him; the government of the United States had to function, had to secure its continuity at all costs.

The television and radio stations suspended all broadcasts and commercial breaks as harried announcers began their fugues of repetition. Several news analysts wept openly, others betrayed angers that came close to outright condemnation of their vast, silent audiences. A number of the self-hustlers—second rate politicians, third-rate journalists, a few pompous, pontificating articulators of academia—were by chance "in the studios" or "on the other end of the line," ready to make their bids for immediate recognition, spreading their tasteless perceptions and admonitions on a numbed public only too willing to be taught in its moment of confusion.

Trevayne left a single network station—the least irresponsible, he thought—on several sets throughout the house. He went to Pam's room, thinking Phyllis would be there. She wasn't. Pam was talking quietly with Lillian; the maid had been weeping, and the girl was comforting the older woman, conversely regaining her own control as she did so.

Andrew closed his daughter's bedroom door and walked down the hall to his and Phyllis' room. His wife sat by the window, the light of early night filtering through the woods, reflected up from the water.

Darkness was coming.

He went to her and knelt beside the chair. She stared at him, and he knew then that she knew what he was going to do before he did.

And she was terrified.

Steven Trevayne stood by the fireplace, his hands black with ash, the poker beside him, resting on the brick below the mantel. No one had thought to light a fire, and the fact seemed to annoy him. He had mixed new kindling with nearly burnt logs and held the Cape Cod lighter underneath the grate, oblivious to the heat and the dirt of the fireplace.

He was alone and looked over at the television set, its volume low, on only to impart whatever new information there might be.

The Vice President of the United States had just taken his hand off a Bible; he was now the world's most powerful man. He was President.

An old man.

They were all old men. No matter the years, their dates of birth. Old men, tired men, deceitful men.

"That's a good idea. The fire," said Andrew quietly, walking into the living room.

"Yeah," answered the boy without looking up, turning his head back toward the expanding flames. Then, just as abruptly, he stepped away from the fireplace and started for the hallway.

"Where are you going?"

"Out. Do you mind?"

"Of course not. It's a time to do nothing. Except, perhaps, think."

"Please cut the bromides, Dad."

"I will if you'll stop being childish. And sullen. I didn't pull the trigger, even symbolically."

The boy stopped and looked at his father. "I know you didn't. Maybe it would have been better if you had. . . ."

"I find that a contemptible statement."

". . . 'even symbolically.' . . . For Christ's sake, then you would have done *something!*"

"That's off-base. You don't know what you're saying."

" 'Off-base'? What's *on*-base? You were there! You've been there for months. What did you *do*, Dad? Were you on-base? On target? . . . Goddamn it. *Some*body thought. Somebody did a terrible, lousy, rotten, fucking thing, and everybody's going to pay for it!"

"Are you endorsing the act?" Trevayne shouted, confused; he was as close to striking his son as he could ever recall.

"Jesus, no! Do *you?*"

Trevayne gripped his hands in front of him, the muscles in his arms and shoulders taut. He wanted the boy to leave. To run. Quickly.

"If that hurts, it's because that killing took place in your ball park."

"He was insane, a maniac. It's isolated. You're being unfair."

"Nobody thought so until yesterday. Nobody had any big files on *him; he* wasn't on anybody's list. No one detained him anywhere; they just gave him millions and millions to keep on building the goddamn *machine.*"

"That's asinine. You're trying to create a label out of one warped clump of insanity. Use your head, Steve. You're better than that."

The boy paused; his silence was the stillness of grief and bewilderment. "Maybe labels are the only things that make sense right now. . . . And you lose, Dad. I'm sorry."

"Why? Why do I lose?"

"Because I can't help thinking that you—or someone like you—could have stopped it."

"That's not so."

"Then maybe there's nothing left. If you're right." Steven Trevayne looked down at his ash-black hands and rubbed them on his dungarees. "I've got to wash my hands. . . . I'm sorry, Dad; I mean, I'm really sorry. I'm scared."

The boy ran into the hallway; Trevayne could hear him descend the stairs toward the study and the terrace.

. . . maybe there's nothing left.

No.

No, he couldn't react like that. He couldn't allow himself the indulgence others gave vent to. Even among his family; within his family.

Not now.

Now he had to make himself felt, where it counted. Before the continuity was irrevocably established.

He had to jolt them, all of them. Make them realize he was serious. They could not be allowed to forget he held—held firmly—the weapons to depose them all.

And he would use those weapons, for they did not
deserve to run the country. The nation demanded more.

". . . maybe there's nothing left."

But there *was* something. He would provide it.

Even if it meant using Genessee Industries. Using
Genessee properly.

Properly.

Use it or destroy it once and for all.

He picked up the phone. He would stay on it until he
reached Senator Mitchell Armbruster.

PART 5

54

The smoothly tarred surface of the road abruptly stopped and became dirt. At this point on the small peninsula the township's responsibility ended and the private property began. Only now it was under the jurisdiction of the federal government as well; watched, guarded, isolated, as it had been for eighteen months now.

High Barnegat.

The Connecticut White House.

The row of five automobiles sped through the gates of the Greenwich toll station without stopping. The guards on duty saluted as the motorcade went by; a patrolman inside the first booth received a signal from a man standing outside and picked up a telephone. The normal flow of traffic could continue now. The President's column had turned off onto the Shore Road exit, where the local police had cleared the area into the peninsula. The patrolman gave the release order to the Westchester station, waved to the man outside, who waved back, then climbed into a waiting automobile.

The 1600 Security men had dispersed throughout the property in teams of two. The Secret Service agent named Callahan had checked the beach area with his partner, and both men were walking up the steps to the terrace, their eyes professionally scanning the sloping woods as they did so.

Callahan had protected four presidents. Nearly twenty years of service; he was forty-six now. Still one of the best men 1600 had, and he knew it. No one could hold him responsible for the Darien business three years ago—that phone call from 1600 pulling him off duty at the hospital. Jesus! That'd been such a top-level fuck-up, he never did learn how it happened. How someone else had gotten the codes. He didn't ask, either; not after he'd been taken off

the hook. And he was nowhere near the White House
when the assassination took place. Everyone on that detail
was relieved. Strange: he'd been reassigned to Trevayne
and wrote in his surveillance report that his subject had
met with James Goddard a week before the killing of the
President. No one paid much attention, and he never
brought it up afterward. Weird that nobody else did,
though.

People—acquaintances, the small circle of friends he
and his wife had—kept asking him what he thought of
whoever was President at the time. He always gave the
same reply: sober approval bordering on reserved enthusiasm. Totally apolitical. It was the best way.

The only way; you never could tell.

But if the truth were told, Callahan didn't like any of
them very much. He had devised a kind of scale for
himself in judging a president. It was the balance between
the public man and the private man as he saw him. There
would always be differences, he understood that, but Jesus, some of them had gone too far.

To the point where *everything* was an act; the scales
really tipped out. Meaningless smiles at public nothings,
followed by torrents of private anger; furious attempts to
be something that wasn't a person at all. An image.

Not trusting.

Worst of all, making a joke about it.

Perhaps that's why Andrew Trevayne got the best
marks; he kept the scale nearer in balance. Not that he
didn't have moments when his temper exploded over some
goddamn thing or other that seemed inconsequential, but
by and large the private man didn't deny the public man
as often as the other presidents had. He seemed . . .
maybe more sure of himself; more sure he was right, and
so he didn't have to yell about it or keep convincing
people.

Callahan liked the man better for that, but he still
didn't *like* him. Nobody who'd worked in the White House
environment for any length of time could like a man who
mounted such an assault for the Oval Office. A campaign
that literally began within weeks after the assassination,
within days after Trevayne had assumed the abandoned

Senate seat from Connecticut. The sudden position papers, the cross-country tours that resulted in scores of
dramatic press conferences and one television appearance
after another. The man had a hunger, a driving, cold
ambition that he mixed with a shyly ingratiating intelligence. A man with the answers, because he was a man of
today. His supporters even coined a phrase, and it was
used over and over again: "The Mark of Excellence." A
minion at 1600 couldn't *like* a man like that. It was too
obvious he wanted to move in.

Trevayne's preconvention maneuvers had stunned the
White House staff, still under the awesome weight of
adjusting to the most terrible of power transfers, the unexpected, unwanted, unwarranted. No one was prepared, no
one seemed to know how to stop the headstrong, authori-
tative, even charismatic Senator from Connecticut.

And at one point it occurred to Agent Callahan of
1600 Security, no one basically wanted to.

The motorcade streamed into the wide drive in front
of the house; the doors of the first and third vehicles
whipped open before the cars stopped, and men stood
effortlessly half out of the automobiles, their arms gripping
the interior frames, their feet ready to touch the pavement
at the first reasonable instant.

Sam Vicarson leaned against the railing on the front
steps. Sam wanted to be in evidence when Trevayne
stepped out of the limousine. The President had come to
expect that; expected him to be among the first of those
who waited for him at any given destination. He told Sam
that it gave him a sense of relief to know that there would
be one person meeting him who'd give him the information he needed, not necessarily wanted.

Vicarson understood. It was one of the aspects of
working in the White House that he found deplorable. No
one wanted to displease the Man. If that meant burying
unpleasant facts, or disguising them to fit a presidential
judgment, that's what generally happened. It wasn't
necessarily fear that provoked aides to behave this way.
Often it was simply the knowledge that the Man had so

damn many pressures on him that if a few could be lessened, why not?

But most of the time it was fear.

Even Sam had fallen into the trap. Both traps: the sympathy and the fear. He had shaped the précis of a trade report in such a way that upheld the President's thinking when actually there was room for disagreement.

"If you ever do that again, Sam, you're out!"

Vicarson often wondered if it would have been the same with Trevayne's predecessor.

Goddamn, he was a good president! A really *fine* president, thought Vicarson as he watched Andrew get out of the car and hold the door for Phyllis, simultaneously talking with the Secret Service men at his side. People had confidence in him; people everywhere. If comparisons were to be made with those in the recent past, a columnist for the New York *Times* had said it best: ". . . the calming nature of Eisenhower, the grace and fire of Kennedy, the drive of Johnson."

Sam felt sorry for the opposition party, parties. After only eighteen months in office, Trevayne had set a tone, an outlook. He'd established an *attitude*. For the first time in years the country had a collective pride in its leadership. The Man before Trevayne had almost reached that level, but the sharpshooting snipers on the right and left had prevented him. Trevayne, because of either a general desire for tranquillity or the force of his own personality —and his ability to listen—had defused the extremists. It was probably a combination of both, thought Vicarson.

Trevayne was the right man for the right time. Another man might not be capable of sustaining the calm, sometimes more difficult than weathering a storm. Not that there was any lack of excitement. The Trevayne administration had made bold innovations in dozens of areas, but they were dramatic more in concept than in execution. And their announcements were subdued; they were called desirable shifts of priorities, not hailed as landmarks, which a number were. Housing, medicine, education, employment; long-range national strategies were implemented.

Sam Vicarson was enormously, realistically proud of President Andrew Trevayne.

So was the country, he felt.

Sam was surprised to see an old man getting out of the other side of the presidential limousine. It was Franklyn Baldwin, Trevayne's ancient banker friend from New York. Baldwin looked like hell, thought Vicarson. It was understandable; Baldwin had just buried William Hill, the friend he'd known since childhood. Big Billy Hill was gone; Baldwin had to be aware that his own time wasn't far off.

It was a mark of the President's sense of obligation that he had attended Hill's funeral; a mark of his swift grace that he'd insisted on saying a few words before the formal eulogy. A mark of his kindness that he'd brought old Frank Baldwin back with him to High Barnegat.

A "Mark of Excellence." That had been the very appropriate phrase used during the campaign.

Phyllis watched her husband helping Frank Baldwin up the short steps to the front door. Sam Vicarson offered assistance, but Andrew shook his head imperceptibly; enough so the young lawyer understood. The President alone would attend to Mr. Baldwin.

Phyllis felt a surge of quiet pride when Andy did such things, gave meaning to gestures. *The prince doth render concern and the court doth follow, bettered by its better*. A description Froissart gave to the court of Chatillon in his First Chronicle. . . . Prince, young king—and not so young, thought Phyllis. There was much of Froissart, or what the Arthurian chronicler always wanted to find, in Andrew's White House. She knew her husband would laugh at such a suggestion. He'd tell her not to romanticize courtesy, not to find symbols where none were intended. That, too, was part of the aura that Andy exuded; the office magnified his quiet goodness, his confident modesty. Even his humor was laced with self-effacing irony.

She'd always loved her husband: he was a man to be loved. Now she found herself almost revering him, and she wasn't sure that was good or even healthy, but she couldn't help it. She realized that the awesomeness of the office lent itself to reverence, but Andy refused the mantle of heavy-lies-the-head. He gave out no stern reminders that the ultimate loneliness was his, no plaintive cries that decisions were never easy. No hollow dramatics of justification were to be found in his explanations.

But hc had explained.

"A nation that is capable of reaching the planets can tend to its own land. A people who have taken so much from the earth can render a just portion back into it. A citizenry that has supported—fairly and unfairly—the expenditures of millions beyond its borders, can certainly build within. . . ."

And he had proceeded to expedite these deceptively simple inaugural beliefs.

Phyllis followed her husband and Frank Baldwin into the house, where a military aide took their coats. They walked into the large living room, where some considerate soul—probably Sam, thought Phyllis—had lighted a fire. She'd been worried about old Baldwin. The funeral service for William Hill had been one of those long High Anglican chores, and the church drafty, the stone floor cold.

"Here, Frank," said Trevayne, holding the back of an armchair, turning it slightly toward thc fireplace. "Relax. Let me get you a drink. All of us; we could use it."

"Thank you, Mr. President," answered Baldwin, sitting down. Phyllis crossed to the long couch and saw that Sam Vicarson had moved a second armchair opposite Baldwin. Sam was so good at that sort of thing.

"Scotch, isn't that right, Frank? Rocks?"

"You always remember what a man drinks. I think that's how you became President." Baldwin laughed, winking his old eye at Phyllis.

"Much easier, believe me. Sam, would you do the honors for me? Scotch on the rocks for Mr. Baldwin; Phyl and I will have the usual."

"Certainly, sir," replied Vicarson, turning toward the hall.

Trevayne sat down in the chair facing Baldwin, Phyllis next to him at the end of the couch. He reached over and held her hand briefly, releasing it when the old man smiled at the sight.

"Don't stop. It's nice to know a man can be President and still hold his wife's hand without a camera around."

"Good Lord, Frank, I've been known to kiss her."

"Now you *may* stop," added Baldwin with a soft laugh. "I keep forgetting how young you are. . . . It was most kind of you to invite me here, Mr. President. It's much appreciated."

"Nonsense. I wanted your company; I was afraid I was imposing."

"That's a gracious thing to say; but then, I read so often in the newspapers that you possess such qualities. I always knew you did."

"Thank you."

"It's all been remarkable, hasn't it? Do you remember, my dear?" asked Baldwin of Phyllis. "I remember, because I'd never been up here. I always picture in my mind an office, or a home, a club—whatever—when I telephone someone. Especially if I don't know the surroundings. In your case it was a window looking out on the water. I recall distinctly your saying that Andrew . . . the President, was out in a sailboat. A cat."

"I remember." Phyllis smiled gently. "I was on the terrace."

"So do I," said Trevayne. "The first thing she asked me when I got in was why hadn't I returned your calls. I was honest; I told her I was trying to avoid you."

"Yes, I remember your saying that at the bank. At lunch. . . . I beg you to forgive me for interrupting your life so completely." The old man's tired eyes showed that he was, indeed, asking forgiveness.

"Aurelius, Frank."

"Who?"

"Marcus Aurelius. You quoted him. 'No man can avoid . . .' "

"Oh, yes. 'What he's meant to do. At the moment . . .' You called him a mutual fund."

"A what?" asked Phyllis.

"An inept joke, Phyl. As I came to learn."

Sam Vicarson returned with a silver tray on which there were three glasses. He offered the tray first to Phyllis, and as she nodded, he caught Trevayne's glance.

Although it was customary to serve the President after the
First Lady, he would approach Baldwin next.

"Thank you, young man."

"You're a regular maître d', Sam," said Phyllis.

"It's all those parties on Embassy Row." Trevayne
laughed, taking a glass. "Will you join us, Sam?"

"Thank you, sir, but I'd better stay with communications."

"He's got a girl in the kitchen," mocked Phyllis in a
stage whisper.

"From the French embassy," added Andrew.

The three of them laughed while Baldwin looked on
with amusement. Sam bowed slightly to the old man.

"Nice to see you again, Mr. Baldwin." He left as
Baldwin inclined his head.

"I see what they mean. Or I think I do," said the
banker.

"What's that?" asked Phyllis.

"About the atmosphere around the White House these
days. The easy relationships; even when things aren't easy.
The pundits give you a lot of credit for that, Mr. President."

"Oh, Sam? He became my right arm, and sometimes
my left as well, three years ago. He came with the
subcommittee."

Phyllis couldn't help herself. She wouldn't let Andy
continuously sidestep the compliments he deserved. "I
agree with you and the pundits, Mr. Baldwin. Andrew's
made considerable progress in deformalizing the privy
chambers. If the word's still in use."

"My wife, the doctor," interrupted Trevayne with a
chuckle. "Which word?"

" 'Deformalizing.' It's rarely used, but it should be. I
haven't heard it recently."

"I thought you meant 'privy chamber.' Whenever I
come across the term in history books, I think of a
bathroom."

"That's historically sacrilegious, isn't it, Mr. Baldwin?"

"I'm not sure, my dear. . . ."

"Just don't tell the pundits I'm turning the White
House rest rooms into playgrounds."

The small laughter that followed warmed Phyllis. Old

Baldwin was being amused, taking his mind off the sadness of the day. His sadness.

And then she realized the humorous byplay was only a momentary deflection. Baldwin's memories wouldn't be lightened. He spoke.

"Billy Hill and I honestly believed that the subcommittee was our well-conceived gift to the country. We never dreamed that our gift, in reality, would be the next President of the United States. When we finally understood that, it frightened us."

"I would have given anything in the world to have had it otherwise."

"Of course you would. A man has to possess extraordinary drives to want to be president, in the ordinary process. He has to be out of his mind to want the office under the conditions . . ." Baldwin stopped, aware of his indiscretion.

"Go on, Frank. It's all right."

"I apologize, Mr. President. That was unwarranted and not meant . . ."

"You don't have to explain. I think I was as surprised as you. And the Ambassador. Certainly as frightened."

"Then may I presume to ask you why?"

Phyllis watched her husband closely. For in spite of the fact that the question had been raised a thousand times publicly, ten times that privately, the answer—answers—had never really satisfied her. She wasn't sure there *was* an answer beyond the best instincts of a brilliant, anguished man who measured his own abilities against that which he had seen, observed closely, and was horrified by. If such a man could hold the seat of power and deliver—as Andy had said to her in very private moments—even his second best, it had to be better than what he'd witnessed. If there were any answers beyond this simple truth, her husband wasn't capable of verbalizing them.

Not to her satisfaction.

"In all honesty, what I provided was unlimited funds for both campaigns. The preconvention and the election; beyond whatever the party could raise. Under a dozen different labels, of course. I'm not proud of it, but that's what I did."

"That's the 'how,' Mr. President. Not the 'why.' As I understand you."

Phyllis now watched the old banker. Baldwin wanted his answer; his eyes pleaded.

And Baldwin was right, of course. The how was relatively inconsequential. But God, it has been insane, thought Phyllis. Limousines arriving at all hours of the day and night, extra phones installed, endless conferences—Barnegat, Boston, Washington, San Francisco, Houston; Andrew had plunged into the eye of a hurricane. Eating, sleeping, resting: they were forgotten.

She forgotten. The children forgotten.

"You've read all that, Frank." Her husband was smiling his shy smile, which Phyllis had come to suspect. "I meant what I said in all those speeches. I felt I was qualified to weld together a great many conflicting voices; that's not a good metaphor. I guess one doesn't weld voices. Perhaps 'orchestrate' is better; reduce the dissonance. If the level of shouting was lowered, we could get at the root causes. Get to work."

"I can't fault that, Mr. President. You've succeeded. You're a popular man. Undoubtedly the most popular man the White House has had in years."

"I'm grateful for that, but more important, I think it's all working."

"Why were you and Ambassador Hill frightened?" Phyllis found herself asking the question without thinking. Andy looked at her, and she knew he would have preferred her not to pursue the subject.

"I'm not sure, my dear. I find that the older I get, the less sure I am about anything. Billy and I agreed on that less than a week ago. And you must remember, we've always been so positive. . . . Oh, why were we frightened." A statement. "I imagine it was the responsibility. We proposed a subcommittee chairman and found we'd unearthed a viable candidate for president. Quite a jump."

"But viable," said Phyllis, now concerned by the sound of old Baldwin's voice.

"Yes." The banker looked at Andrew. "What frightened us was the sudden, inexplicable determination you displayed . . . Mr. President. If you think back, perhaps you'll understand."

"It wasn't my question, Frank. It was Phyl's."

"Oh, yes, of course. It's been a difficult day; Billy and I won't have our lengthy debates anymore. No one ever won, you understand. He often told me, Andrew, that you thought as I did." Baldwin's glass, at his lips, was nearly empty, and he looked at the rim; he had used the President's first name and obviously was sorry that he had.

"That's a superb compliment, Frank."

"Only history will confirm that, Mr. President. If it's true."

"Regardless, I'm flattered."

"But you *do* understand?"

"What?"

"Our concerns. According to Billy's reports, Bobby Kennedy's machine was a Boy Scout troop compared to yours. His words, incidentally."

"I can bear them," said Andrew with a half-smile on his lips. "You were offended?"

"We couldn't understand."

"There was a political vacuum."

"You weren't a politician . . ."

"I'd seen enough politicians. The vacuum had to be filled quickly. I understood that. Either I was going to fill it or someone else was. I looked around and decided I was better equipped. If anyone else had come along to alter that judgment, I would have bowed out."

"Was anyone else given the chance, Mr. President?"

"They—he—never appeared."

"I think," said Phyllis Trevayne somewhat defensively, "my husband would've been very happy to have gone scot-free. As you say, he's not basically a politician."

"You're wrong, my dear. He's the *new* politics, in all its pristine glory. The remarkable thing is that it works! Utterly and completely. It is a far greater reformation than any revolutionist could conceive of—right, left, or up the middle. But he knew he could do it. What Billy and I could never understand was *why* he knew he could."

There was silence, and Phyllis realized, once again, that only her husband could reply. She looked at him and saw that he would not respond. His thoughts were not for display, even for his old friend, this wonderful old man who had given him so much. Perhaps not even for her.

"Mr. President." Sam Vicarson walked rapidly into the room, his expression denying any emergency, and by so doing, giving the message that an emergency existed.

"Yes, Sam?"

"The confirmation on the media exchange came through. From Chicago. I thought you'd want to know."

"Can you locate the principals?" Trevayne's words shot out quietly, sharply; on the edge of abrasiveness.

"In the process, sir."

"Get them."

"Three lines are working on it. The call will be put through downstairs."

"You'll pardon me, Frank. I haven't taught Sam the corporate procedure of procrastination." Trevayne rose from the chair and started out of the room.

"May I fix you another, Mr. Baldwin?"

"Thank you, young man. Only if Mrs. Trevayne . . ."

"Thank you, Sam," said Phyllis, holding out her glass. She was tempted to ask the presidential aide to disregard the "usual" and pour her some whiskey, but she didn't. It was still afternoon; even after all the years, she knew she couldn't drink whiskey in the afternoon. She'd watched her husband as he listened to Sam Vicarson. His jaw had tightened, his eyes momentarily had squinted, his whole body stiffened, if only for an instant.

People never understood that it was these moments, handled with such ease and apparent confidence, that sapped the energies of the man. Moments of fear; incessant, unending.

As with everything he ever engaged in, her husband drove himself beyond the endurance of ordinary men. And he had finally found the job in which there was no surcease. There were times when Phyllis thought it was slowly killing him.

"I mourn an old friend whose time had come, my dear," said Baldwin, observing Phyllis closely. "Yet the look on your face makes me somewhat ashamed."

"I'm sorry." Phyllis had been absently staring at the

hallway. She turned to the banker. "I'm not sure I know what you mean."

"I've lost my friend. To the perfectly natural finality of his long life. In some ways, you've lost your husband. To a concept. And your lives are so far from being over. . . . I think your sacrifice is greater than mine."

"I think I agree with you." Phyllis tried to smile, tried to make the pronouncement lighter, but she could not.

"He's a great man, you know."

"I'd like to believe that."

"He's done what no one else could do; what some of us thought was beyond doing. He's put the pieces back together again, let us see ourselves more as we *can* be, not as we were. There's still a long way to go, but he's provided the essentials. The desire to be better than we are; and to face the truth."

"That's a lovely thing to say, Mr. Baldwin."

Andrew looked at Sam Vicarson, who'd just shut the study door. They were alone. "How far has it gone?"

"Apparently all the way, sir. Our information is that the papers were signed several hours ago."

"What does Justice say?"

"No change. They're still researching, but there's not much hope. They restate their original thesis. The purchase—or absorption—simply can't be traced to Genessee Industries."

"We traced it, Sam. We know we're right."

"You traced it, Mr. President."

Trevayne walked to the study window and looked out. To the terrace and the water below. "Because it was one thing they didn't have. One thing we kept from them."

"May I say something, sir?"

"Two years ago, I doubt you would have asked. What is it?"

"Isn't it possible that you're overreacting? Genessee has acted responsibly; you've controlled . . . them. They support you."

"They don't *support* me, Sam," said Trevayne softly, harshly, without looking at Vicarson, his eyes still on the water. "We have a nonaggression pact. I signed a nonaggression pact with the twentieth-century syndrome. The no-alternative holy ghost."

"It's worked, Mr. President."

"You may have to keep that judgment in the past tense." Andrew turned and stared at the lawyer. "The pact is broken, Sam. It's no longer tenable. It's smashed."

"What are you going to do?"

"I'm not sure. I won't allow Genessee to control a large segment of the American press. And a chain of newspapers is exactly that. It can't be tolerated." Trevayne walked to his desk. "Newspapers . . . then will come magazines, radio, television. The networks. That they will not have."

"Justice doesn't know how to stop them, Mr. President."

"We'll find a way; we have to."

The telephone hummed; it did not ring. Vicarson swiftly crossed to the desk beside Andrew and picked it up.

"President Trevayne's office." Sam listened for several seconds. "Tell him to stay where he is. The Man's in conference, but we'll get back to him. Tell him it's priority." Vicarson hung up. "Let him stew until you're ready, sir."

Sam walked away as Andrew nodded his appreciation. Vicarson knew instinctively by now when the President wanted to be alone. This was one of those moments. He spoke as Trevayne sat down at his desk.

"I'll head back to communications."

"No, Sam. If you don't mind, go up and keep Phyl and old Baldwin company. I don't imagine it's easy for either of them."

"Yes, sir." For two or three seconds the young aide just watched the President of the United States. Then he abruptly left the room, closing the door behind him.

Andrew picked up a pencil and wrote out a sentence in clear, precise letters. "The only solution is in the constant search for one."

Big Billy Hill.

And then he wrote one word: "Horseshit."

Paul Bonner.

And then he added: "?"

He picked up the telephone and spoke firmly.

"Chicago, please."

Fifteen hundred miles away, Ian Hamilton answered.

"Mr. President?"

"I want you out of that merger."

"Perhaps it's academic, but you have no viable proof that we're involved. The little men from your Justice Department have been nuisances."

"You know. I know. Get out."

"I think you're beginning to show the strain, Mr. President."

"I'm not interested in what you think. Just make sure you understand me."

There was a pause. "Does it matter?"

"Don't press me, Hamilton."

"Nor you us."

Trevayne stared out the window, at the ever-moving waters of the sound. "There'll come a day when you're expendable. You should realize that. All of you."

"Quite possibly, Mr. President. However, not in our time."

ABOUT THE AUTHOR

ROBERT LUDLUM is the author of sixteen novels published in nineteen languages and twenty-three countries with worldwide sales in excess of one hundred sixty million copies. His works include *The Scarlatti Inheritance*, *The Osterman Weekend*, *The Matlock Paper*, *The Rhinemann Exchange*, *The Gemini Contenders*, *The Chancellor Manuscript*, *The Road to Gandolfo*, *The Holcroft Covenant*, *The Matarese Circle*, *The Bourne Identity*, *The Parsifal Mosaic*, *The Aquitaine Progression*, *The Bourne Supremacy*, *The Icarus Agenda*, *Trevayne* and *The Bourne Ultimatum*. He lives with his wife, Mary, in Florida.